LUCY HUGHES-HALLETT is the author of *The Pike: Gabriele d'Annunzio*, which won the Samuel Johnson Prize, the Duff Cooper Prize, the Costa Biography Award and the Political Book Awards Political Biography of the Year. Her previous books are the acclaimed cultural histories *Cleopatra* (1990) and *Heroes* (2004). *Cleopatra* won the Fawcett Prize and Emily Toth Award. She lives in London.

Praise for *Peculiar Ground*:

'So clever and beautifully written, it gripped me from start to end. I abandoned work and family to finish it'   RODDY DOYLE

'Unlike anything I've read. With its broad scope and its intimacy and exactness, it cuts through the apparatus of life to the vivid moment'   TESSA HADLEY

'Ambitious and accomplished ... a polyphonic narrative ... rich with detail ... leaves you hoping that this late conversion to fiction will prove only the beginning'   *Observer*

'Hughes-Hallett's ambitious first novel dances between past and present, history and modernity ... magically and movingly evoked, it remains in the imagination long after the reader passes beyond its gates'   *New Statesman*

'It's a teeming, heaving whirligig of a novel that opens in Restoration England just after the Civil War, before accelerating forward to various points in the twentieth century. The sheer abundance of character and incident here would break most writers, but Hughes-Hallett retains terrific control of her subject matter in a novel ⬛⬛⬛⬛⬛⬛⬛⬛⬛⬛⬛⬛ patterns of personal ⬛⬛⬛⬛⬛⬛⬛⬛⬛⬛⬛⬛ *Daily Mail*

'A rich layering of history and fiction ... Erudite, elegant but easy-going'
The Times

'Extraordinarily accomplished ... absolutely involving, thanks to beautiful description and a very fine understanding of human emotion ... Tolstoyan in its sly wit and descriptive brilliance'
Guardian

'Hughes-Hallett deftly loops together the accounts of the sprawling cast of utterly believable characters to create a sensual meditation on the nature of paradise'
Mail on Sunday

'That rare thing: a fresh classic. Ambitious, satisfying and mature, *Peculiar Ground* is spellbinding'
Country Life

'Elegant, inventive, mystical'
Daily Telegraph

'Stunning for both its historical sweep and its elegant prose'
Kirkus

'Richly evocative'
Tatler

'Characters to get involved with, stories to follow – perfect to get lost in'
Woman & Home

'An evocative debut novel'
Vogue

'Full of interesting things, with the sweep of human life built into its fabric'
Literary Review

Cleopatra: Histories, Dreams and Distortions
Heroes: Saviours, Traitors and Supermen
The Pike: Gabriele D'Annunzio

LUCY HUGHES-HALLETT

PECULIAR
GROUND

4th ESTATE • London

4th Estate
An imprint of HarperCollins*Publishers*
1 London Bridge Street
London SE1 9GF

www.4thEstate.co.uk

First published in Great Britain in 2017 by 4th Estate
This 4th Estate paperback edition published in 2018

1

Map drawn by John Gilkes

Printed and bound in Great Britain by
CPI Group (UK) Ltd, Croydon, CR0 YY

For my brothers,
James and Thomas,
with love

We are a garden walled around,
Chosen and made peculiar ground;
A little spot enclosed by grace
Out of the world's wide wilderness.

ISAAC WATTS

Dramatis Personae

1663–1665
John Norris – landscape-maker
Arthur Fortescue, the Earl of Woldingham
The Countess of Woldingham, his wife
Their children – Charles Fortescue, Arthur Fortescue and a
    little girl
Sir Humphrey de Boinville, brother to Lady Woldingham
Lady Harriet Rivers, Lord Woldingham's sister
Cecily Rivers, her daughter
Edward
Pastor Rivers – brother to Lady Harriet's late husband
Another pastor
Robert Rose – architect and comptroller
Meg Leafield
George Goodyear – head forester
Armstrong – ranger
Green – head gardener
Slatter – farm overseer
Underhill – major-domo
Lane – steward
Richardson – apothecary
Lupin, a pug-dog

1961–1989

Living at Wood Manor

Hugo Lane – land agent
Chloe Lane – his wife
Nell – their daughter, aged eight in 1961
Dickie – their son, aged five in 1961
Heather – nanny
Mrs Ferry – cook
Wully, a yellow Labrador, and later his great-nephew, another
    Wully

Living at Wychwood

Christopher Rossiter – proprietor
Lil Rossiter – his wife
Fergus – their son
Flossie/Flora – Christopher's niece, aged eighteen in 1961
Underhill – butler
Mrs Duggary – cook
Lupin, a pug-dog, and later another Lupin, also a pug-dog
Grampus, a black Labrador

Visitors

Antony Briggs – art-dealer
Nicholas Fletcher – journalist
Benjie Rose – restaurateur, interior designer, entrepreneur
Helen Rose – his wife, art-historian
Guy – Benjie's nephew, aged thirteen in 1961

On the estate

John Armstrong – head keeper
Jack Armstrong – his son, aged seventeen in 1961
Doris, Dorabella, Dorian and Dorothy – all spaniels
Green – head gardener
Young Green, his son

Brian Goodyear – head forester
Rob Goodyear, his son
Slatter – farm manager
Meg Slatter – his wife
Bill Slatter – their son
Holly Slatter – Bill's daughter
Hutchinson – estate clerk

In the village
Mark Brown – cabinet-maker

Nell's fellow students at Oxford in 1973
Francesca, Spiv Jenkins, Manny, Jamie McAteer, Selim Malik

In London
Roger Bates – wartime military policeman, subsequently in
    Special Branch

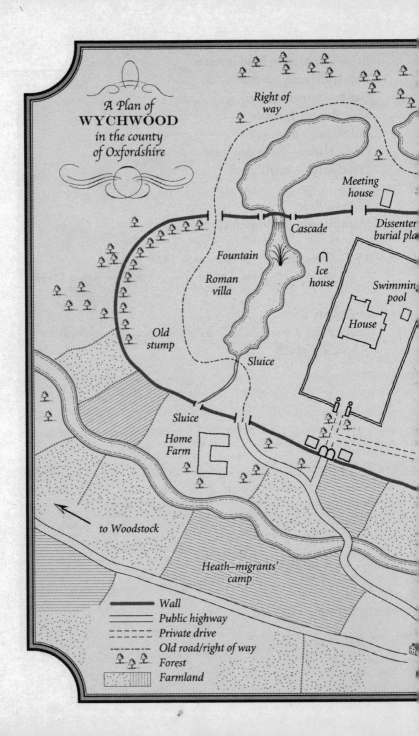

A Plan of **WYCHWOOD** in the county of Oxfordshire

Right of way

Meeting house

Cascade

Dissenter burial pla

Fountain

Roman villa

Ice house

Swimming pool

House

Old stump

Sluice

Sluice

Home Farm

to Woodstock

Heath–migrants' camp

	Wall
	Public highway
	Private drive
	Old road/right of way
🜨 🜨 🜨	Forest
	Farmland

Quarry

Lakes

Leafield church

Sawmill

Cider well

Tennis court

Goodyear's cottage

Beech Avenue 'Grand Vista'

Secret garden

Kitchen garden

Beech Avenue 'Tower Light'

Lime avenue

Right of way

Public road

Wood Manor

Armstrong's cottage

River Evenlode

The village

PECULIAR GROUND

1663

It has been a grave disappointment to me to discover that his Lordship has no interest – really none whatsoever – in dendrology. I arrived here simultaneously with a pair of peafowl and a bucket full of goldfish. It is galling that my employer takes more pleasure in the creatures than he does in my designs for his grounds.

He is impatient. Perhaps it is only human to be so. He wishes to beautify his domain but he frets at slowness. When we talked in London, and I was able to fill his mind's eye with majestic vistas, then he was satisfied. But when he sees the saplings reaching barely higher than the crown of his hat he laughs at me. 'Avenues, Mr Norris?' he said yesterday evening. 'These are sticks set for a bending race.'

The idea having once occurred to him, he set himself to realising it. This morning he and another gentleman took horse and, like two shuttles drawing invisible thread, wove themselves at great speed back and forth through the lines of young beeches that now traverse the park from side to side. There was much laughter and shouting, especially as they passed the ladies assembled at the point where the avenues (I persist in so naming them) intersect, the trees forming a great cross which will be visible only to birds and to angels. I confess the gentlemen were very skilful,

3

keeping pace like dancers until, nearing the point where the trees arrive at the perimeter, where the wall will shortly rise, they spurred on into a desperate gallop in the attempt to outdistance each other, and so raced on into a field full of turnips, to the great distress of Mr Slatter.

They are my Lord's trees, his fields and his turnips. Like Slatter and his muddy-handed cohort, I must acknowledge the licence his proprietorship gives him, but it grieved me inordinately to find that eleven of my charges, my eight hundred carefully matched young beeches, have been damaged, five of them having the lead shoot snapped off. I attended him after dinner and informed him of the need for replacements. 'Mr Norris, Mr Norris,' he said. 'It is hard for you to serve such a careless oaf, is it not?'

He authorised me to send for substitutes. He is not an oaf. Though it pained me, I took delight in the performance of this morning. He incorporated my avenue, vegetable and ponderous, into a spectacle of darting grace. But it is true that I find him careless. To him a tree is a thing, which can be replaced by another thing like it. Is it lunacy in me to feel that this is not so?

We who trade in landskips see the world not as it is but as it will be. When I walk in the park, which is not yet a park but an expanse of ground hitherto not enhanced but degraded by my work in it, I take little note of the ugly wounds where the earth has been heaved about to make banks and declivities to match those in my plan. I see only that the outline has been soundly drawn for the great picture I have designed. It is for Time to fill it with colour and to add bulk to those spare lines – Time aided by Light and Weather. I suppose I should say as well, aided by God's will, but it seems to me that to speak of the Almighty in these days is to invoke misfortune. It is more certain and less contentious to note that Water also is essential.

*

Of the people who manage this estate my most useful ally has been Mr Armstrong, chief among my Lord's rangers. For him, I believe, the return of the family is welcome. He is an elderly man, with the hooked nose and abundant beard of a patriarch. He remembers this house when the present owner's father had it, and he rejoices at the thought that all might now be as it was before the first King Charles was brought down. I think he has not reflected sufficiently on how this country has changed in his lifetime, not only superficially, in that different regiments have succeeded each other, but fundamentally. It is true that there is once more a Charles Stuart enthroned in Whitehall, but the people who saw his father killed, and who lived for a score of years under the rule of his executioners, cannot forget how flimsy a king's authority has proved.

Armstrong and Lord Woldingham talk much of pheasants – showy birds that were abundant here before the changes. Armstrong would like to see them strut again about the park. He has sent to Norfolk for a pair, and will breed from them. For him, I think, I am as the scenery painter is to the playwright. He is careful of me because I will make the stage on which his silly feathered actors can preen.

For Mr Goodyear, though, I am suspect. He is the curator of all of Wychwood's mighty stock of timber. The trees are his precious charges. Some of them are of very great antiquity. He talks to them as familiars, and slaps their trunks affectionately when he and I stand conversing by them. I do not consider him foolish or superstitious: I do not expect to meet a dryad on my rambles, but I too love trees more than I care for most men. Goodyear is loyal to his employer, but it seems to me he thinks of those trees as belonging not to Lord Woldingham but in part to himself, his care for them having earned him a father's rights, and in part to God. (I do not know to which sect he is devoted, but his conversation is well-larded with allusions to the deity.) He is ruddy-faced and hale and has a kind of bustling energy that is felt even when he is still. I will not enquire of him, as I do not enquire of any man, which party he favoured in the late upheavals, but I think him to have been a parliamentarian.

Today I walked with him down the old road that leads through the forest to the spring called the Cider Well. The road is still in use, but very boggy. 'His Lordship would like to close it,' said Goodyear. 'I suppose he may do so if he wishes,' I said. Goodyear made no reply. I have heard him allude to me as 'that long lad'. I think he has judged me too young to be competent, and too pompous to be companionable.

Passing the spring, we dropped down into a valley, its mossy sides bright with primroses. The rabbits had already been at work on the new grass beneath our feet, so that the track was pleasant to walk upon.

A woman I had seen before – old but quick of step – was walking ahead of us. Goodyear called to her. She looked back over her shoulder, nodded to him, and then darted aside, taking one of the narrow paths that slant upwards, and vanished among the trees.

'You know that person?' I asked.

'I'd be a poor forester if there were any soul in these woods without my knowledge.'

I ignored his pettish tone. 'Does she live out here, then?'

'She does.'

'I encountered her in the park on Sunday. She made as though she wished to speak to me, but thought better of it.'

'It's best so. Don't let her bother you, sir.'

I let the matter rest and began to talk to him of the plans I have discussed with Mr Rose, the architect. Rose is one of the many Englishmen of our age who, following their prince into exile, have grown to maturity among foreigners. There are constraints between such men and those of us who stayed at home and picked our way through the obstacles our times have thrown up. Rose and I deal warily with each other, but our work goes on harmoniously. In Holland Mr Rose interested himself in the Dutchmen's ceaseless labours to preserve their country from the ocean to which it rightfully belongs. My Lord calls him his Wizard of Water.

We would build a dam where this pretty valley debouches into a morass, and thereafter a series of further dams. Thus contained and rendered docile, the errant stream will broaden into a chain of lakes. The three upper lakes will lie without the wall, as it were lost in the woods. The last watery expanse will be within the park and visible from the house, a glass to cast back the sun's light and duplicate the images of the trees clumped about it.

It was as though Goodyear could see at once the prospect I sketched with my words, and soon we were in pleasant conversation. Willows, judiciously positioned, he rightly said, would bind the dams with their roots, and red alders might give shade. The 'tremble-tree', he suggested (I understood him to mean the aspen, a species of which I too am fond), ranged along the watery margins, would give a lightness to the picture, and his tremendous oaks, looming on the heights above, will take off the brashness of novelty, so that my lakes will glitter with dignity, like gaudy new-cut stones in antique settings.

How gratifying it would be to me, if I could enjoy such an exchange of ideas with his Lordship!

*

I could wish nutriment were not necessary to the human constitution, but alas, whatever else we be (and my mind swerves, like a wise horse away from a bog-hole, to avoid any thought that smacks of theology), we are indisputably animals, and animals must eat. My situation here is agreeable enough when I am in my chamber. In the drawing room – where Lord Woldingham expects me to appear from time to time – I am less easy. In the great hall where we dine I am wretched.

It is not the food that discommodes me, nor, to be just to the company, the mannerliness with which I am received. I am my own enemy. My self, of which I am pleasantly forgetful at most times, becomes an obstacle to my happiness. I do not know how to present it, or how to efface it. See how I name it 'it', as though my self were not myself. My Lord and his friends talk to me amiably enough. But the contrast between the laborious politeness with which they treat me, and the quickness of their wit in bantering with each other is painfully evident.

As I write this, I feel myself to be quite a master of language, so why is it that, in conversation, words fall from my lips as ponderously as dung from a cow's posterior? I will be the happier when the guests depart, and so, I fancy, may they be. Although the old portion of the house has not yet been invaded by the joiners and masons, the shouting emanating all day long from the wing under construction is an annoyance. And now that the work on the wall has begun, the park is encumbered with wagons hauling stone to every point on its periphery. The quarrymen set to at first light. We wake to the crack of stone falling away from the little cliff, and our days' employment has as its accompaniment the clangour of iron pick on rock.

One congenial companion I have found. She is a young lady, not staying in the house, but frequently invited to enjoy whatever entertainment is in hand. She came to me boldly outdoors today.

I had been conferring with Mr Green, who is the chief executor of my wishes for the garden. He is, I consider, as worthy of the name of artist as any of the carvers and limners at work on the house – but because he is tongue-tied, those precious gentlemen are apt to treat him as a mere digger and delver. His own men show him the utmost respect.

Those goldfish that so put me out of countenance on my arrival have proved the seeds from which a delightful scheme has sprouted. The stony paving of the terrace is to be bisected by a canal, within whose inky water the darting slivers of pearl and orange and carnation will show as brilliant as the striped petals, set off by a lustrous black background, in the flower-paintings my Lord has brought home with him from Holland.

'I hear, Mr Norris, you are rationalising Wychwood's enchanted spring,' said the lady.

'You hear correctly, madam. Some small portion of its waters will trickle beneath the very ground on which you now stand. More will feed a fountain in the valley there, if Mr Rose and I can manage it.'

'But have you appeased the *genius loci*, Mr Norris? You cannot afford to make enemies in fairyland.'

I was taken aback. I could not but wonder whether she teased. Were she any other young lady I would have been sure of it. But she is as simple in her manner as she is in her dress. Her name is Cecily Rivers.

*

'I am glad you and my cousin are friends,' Lord Woldingham said to me this morning as I spread out my plans for him. He is my elder by a decade, and inclined to mock me as though I were a callow boy. We were in the fantastically decorated chamber he calls his office. Looking-glasses, artfully placed, reflect each other there. When I raised my eyes I could not but see the image of the two of us, framed by their gilded fronds and curlicues, repeated to a wearisome infinitude. I, Norris the landskip-maker, in a dun-coloured coat. He, who will flutter in the scene I make for him, in velvet as subtly painted as a butterfly's wing seen under a magnifying glass.

I do not much like to contemplate my own appearance. To see it multiplied put me out of humour. My Lord's remark was trying, too. Often when it comes to time for inspecting the plans he finds some conversational diversion. I did not know whom he meant.

'Your cousin, sir?'

'My cousin, sir. You can scarcely pretend not to know her. Pacing the lawn with her half the afternoon. I have my eye on you, Norris.'

He made me uneasy. He loves to throw a man off his stride. In the tennis court, which abuts the stables, I have seen the way he will tattle on – this painter is new come to court and he must have him paint a portrait of his spaniel; this philosopher has a curious theory about the magnetism of planetary bodies – until his opponent lets his racket droop and then, oh then, my Lord is suddenly all swiftness and attention and shouting out *Tenez garde* while his ball whizzes from wall to wall like a furious hornet and his competitor scampers stupidly after it.

I had no reason to fumble my words but yet I did so. 'Mistress Rivers. Your cousin. I did not know of the relationship.'

'Why no. Why would you, unless she chose to speak of it?'

'She lives hereby?'

'Hereby. For most of her life she lived here.'

'Here?'

'Yes. In this house. Cecily's mother was not of the King's party. She stayed and prospered under the Commonwealth while her brother, my father, wandered in exile.'

'And now . . .'

'And now the world has righted itself, and I am returned the heir, and my aunt is mad, and her husband is dead, and my cousin Cecily is delightful and though I do not think she can ever quite be friends with me, her usurper, she has made a playmate of you.'

'Your aunt is . . .'

'The quickness your mind shows when you are designing hanging gardens to rival Babylon's, Mr Norris, is not matched by its functioning when applied to ordinary gossip. Yes. My aunt. Is mad. And lives at Wood Manor. Hereby, as you say. And Cecily, her sweet, sober daughter, comes back to the house where she grew up, in order to taste a little pleasure, and to divert her thoughts from the sadness of her mother's plight.'

I must have looked aghast.

'Oh, my dear Aunt Harriet is not wild-mad, not frenzied, not the kind of gibbering lunatic from whom a dutiful daughter needs protection. My aunt smiles, and babbles of green fields and is as grateful for a cup of chocolate as one of the papists, of whom she used so strictly to disapprove, might be for a dousing of holy water. I am her dear nevvie. She dotes on me. She forgets that I am her dispossessor.'

It is true that yesterday afternoon Miss Cecily and I walked and talked a considerable while on the lawns before the house. Had I known my Lord was watching us I might not have felt so much at ease.

*

It is Lord Woldingham's fancy to enclose his park in a great ring of stone. Other potentates are content to impose their will on nature only in the immediate purlieus of their palaces. They make gardens where they may saunter, enjoying the air without fouling their shoes. But once one steps outside the garden fence one is, on most of England's great estates, in territory where travellers may pass and animals are harassed by huntsmen, certainly, and slain for meat, but where they are free to range where they will.

Not so here at Wychwood. My task is to create an Eden encompassing the house, so that the garden will be only the innermost chamber of an enclosure so spacious that, for one living within it, the outside world, with its shocks and annoyances, will be but a memory. Other great gentlemen may have their flocks of sheep, their herds of deer, but, should they wish to control those creatures' movements, a thorny hedge or palisade of wattle suffices. Lord Woldingham's creatures will live confined within an impassable barricade. As for human visitors, they will come and go only through the four gates, over which the lodge-keepers will keep vigil.

Mr Rose took me today to view the first stretch of wall to have been constructed. He is justly proud of it. It rises higher than deer can leap, and is all made of new-quarried stone. When completed, it will extend for upward of five miles.

I said, 'I wonder, are we making a second Paradise here, or a prison?'

'Or a fortress,' said Mr Rose. 'Our King has had more cause than most monarchs to fear assassins. Lord Woldingham is courageous, but you will see how carefully he looks about him when he enters a room.'

'His safety could be better preserved in a less extensive domain,' I said.

'He craves extension. He has spent years dangling around households in which he was a barely tolerated guest. There were times when he, with his great title and his claim on all these lands, had no door he could close against the unkindly curious, nor even a chair of his own to doze upon. He has been out, as a vagabond is out. Now, it seems, he chooses to be walled in.'

The wall is a prodigy. It will be monstrously expensive, but I am gratified to see what a handsome border it makes for the pastoral I am conjuring up.

*

This has been a happy day. It is never easy to foresee what will engage Lord Woldingham's interest. I was as agreeably surprised by his sudden predilection for hydraulics as I had been saddened by his indifference to arboriculture. Having discovered it, I confess to having fostered his watery passion somewhat deviously, by playing upon his propensity for turning all endeavour into competitive games.

We were talking of the as-yet-imaginary lakes. I mentioned that the fall of the land just within the girdle of the projected wall was steep and long enough to allow the shaping of a fine cascade. At once he gave his crosspatch of a pug-dog a shove and dragged his chair up to the table. I swear he has never hitherto looked so carefully at my plans.

'What are these pencilled undulations?' he asked. I explained to him the significance of the contour lines.

'So where they lie close together – that is where the ground is most sharply inclined?' He was all enthusiasm. 'So here it is a veritable cliff. Come, Norris. This you must show me.'

Half an hour later our horses were snorting and shuffling at the edge of the quagmire where the stream, having saturated the earthen escarpment in descending it, soaks into the low ground. My Lord and I, less careful of our boots than the dainty beasts were of their silken-tasselled fetlocks, were hopping from tussock to tussock. Goodyear and two of his men looked on grimly. If Lord Woldingham stumbled, it would be they who would be called upon to hoick him from the mud.

The hillside, I was explaining, would be transformed into a staircase for giants, each tremendous step lipped with stone so that the water fell clear, a descending sequence of silvery aquatic curtains.

'And it will strike each step with great force, will it not?'

'That will depend upon how tightly we constrain it. The narrower its passage, the more fiercely it will elbow its way through. This is a considerable height, my Lord. When the current finally thunders into the lake below it will send up a tremendous spray. Has your Lordship seen the fountain at Stancombe?'

Here is my cunning displayed. I knew perfectly well what would follow.

'A fountain, Mr Norris! Beyond question, we must have a fountain. Not a tame dribbling thing spouting in a knot garden but a mighty column of quicksilver, dropping diamonds. I have not seen Stancombe, Norris. You forget how long I have been out. But if Huntingford has a magician capable of making water leap into the air – well then, I have you, my dear Norris, and Mr Rose, and I trust you to make it leap further.'

The Earl of Huntingford is another recently returned King's man. Whatever he has – be it emerald, fig tree or fountain – my Lord, on hearing of it, wants one the same but bigger.

So now, of a sudden, I am his 'dear' Norris.

This fountain will, I foresee, cause me all manner of technical troubles, but the prospect of it may persuade my master to set apart sufficient funds to translate my sketches into living beauties. It is marvellous how little understanding the rich have of the cost of things.

'My master,' I wrote. How quickly, now the great levelling has been undone, we slip back into the habits of subservience.

*

This morning I walked out towards Wood Manor. I set my course as it were on a whim, but my excursion proved an illuminating one.

The road curves northward from the great house. I passed through a gateway that so far lacks its gate. Mr Rose has employed a team of smiths to realise his designs for it in wrought iron tipped with gold.

The parkland left behind, the road is flanked by paddocks where my Lord's horses graze in good weather. It is pleasantly shaded here by a double row of limes. Their scent is as heady as the incense in a Roman church. The ground is sticky with their honeydew. The land falls away to one side, so that between the tree-trunks I could see sheep munching, and carts passing along the road wavering over the opposite hillside, and smoke rising from the village. It was the first time for several days, sequestered as I have been, that I had glimpsed such tokens of everyday life. I had not missed them, but I welcomed them like friends.

I became aware that I was followed by an old woman, the same I had now seen twice already. My neck prickled and I was hard put to it not to keep glancing around. I was glad when she overtook me and went hurriedly on down the road.

I had not intended to make this a morning for social calls, but it would have seemed strange, surely, to pass by Miss Cecily's dwelling without paying my respects. I had told Lord Woldingham, before setting out, that I needed to acquaint myself thoroughly with the water-sources upon his estate. He seemed surprised that I might think he cared how I occupied myself. He was with his tailor, demanding a coat made of silk dyed exactly to match the depth and brilliance of the colour of a peacock's neck. The poor man looked pinched around the mouth.

The house Lord Woldingham is creating will extend itself complacently upon the earth, its pillars serenely upright, its longer lines horizontal as the limbs of a man reclining upon a bed of flowers. Wood Manor, by contrast, is all peaks and sharp angles, as though striving for heaven. The house must be as old as the two venerable yew trees that frame its entranceway. As I passed between them I saw the sunlight flash. A curious egg-shaped window in the highest gable was swiftly closed. By the time I had arrived at the porch a serving-woman had the door ajar ready for me.

'Is Miss Cecily at home?' I asked.

'You will find her out of doors, sir,' she said, and led the way across a flagged hall too small for its immense fireplace. An arched doorway led directly onto the terrace. Cecily was there with an elder lady. Looking at the two of them, no one could have been in any doubt that this lady was her mother. The same grey eye. The same long teeth that give Cecily the look (I fear it is ungallant of me to entertain such a thought, but there it is) of an intelligent rodent. The same unusually small hands. Both pairs of which were engaged, as I stepped out to interrupt them, in the embroidery of a linen tablecloth or coverlet large enough to spread companionably across both pairs of knees, so it was as though mother and daughter sat upright together in a double bed. The mother, I noticed, was a gifted needlewoman. The flowers beneath her fingers were worked with extraordinary fineness. Cecily appeared to have been entrusted only with simpler tasks. Where her mother had already created garlands of buds and blown roses, she came along behind to colour in the leaves with silks in bronze and green.

I addressed my conversation to the matron.

'Madam, I hope you will forgive the liberty I take in calling upon you uninvited. I am John Norris. I have had the pleasure of meeting Miss Cecily at Wychwood. I was walking this way and hoped it would not be inconvenient for you if I were to make myself known.'

She replied in equally formal vein. So I must be acquainted with her nephew. Any connection of his was welcome in her house. She hoped I enjoyed the improved weather. No questions asked. No information divulged. The maid brought us glasses of cordial while we played the conversational game as mildly and conventionally as a pair of elderly dogs, in whom lust was but a distant memory, sniffing absent-mindedly at each other's hinder parts. But then she demonstrated that she could read my mind.

'I suppose young Arthur has told you that I am deranged? You will be puzzled to find me so lucid.'

Cecily murmured something, but the older lady persevered. 'He tells everyone so. He has reasons for the assertion. One is that there is some truth in it. My mind's eye sees the world's affairs in a manner as blurred and uncertain as that with which my corporeal eyes see that tree. Fine needlework, as you observe, I am good for, but for keeping a lookout I am useless. And although in cheerful sunlight like this I can be as bright as the day, in dark hours I grow dull.'

'I am sorry to hear it,' I began awkwardly. She didn't pause.

'So you see, judging that to lie unnecessarily is to lay oneself open to exposure when one could be safely armoured in truth, he broadcasts an opinion that is not quite a falsehood, and under this cover he hides his other purposes.' Her voice trailed away.

Cecily laid down her needle and took her mother's hand.

'Mr Norris cannot be as concerned with our affairs as we are, Mother,' she said. 'He is an artist. A maker of landscapes.'

'A painter?'

I explained that, no, the kind of picture I make is not the representation of a scene, but the scene itself. That while God makes countryside, man refines it into landscape (an audacious joke, but one I thought I could allow myself in this secluded place). That nature and the unnatural make happy partners, and flourish when coupled. I said that those painters who depict what they call pastoral scenes seldom or never show brambles or stinging nettles or the mud churned up on a riverbank by herds of beasts. Their pastorals are all artifice, their pastures in fact gardens.

I was becoming excessively wordy. It is mortifying to know, as I do all too well, that when I talk with greatest satisfaction, expatiating on a subject that truly engages me, then I am most tedious. Becoming self-conscious, I fell quiet.

'Mother,' said Cecily, 'you are tired. Mr Norris would like to see our orchard, I dare say.'

The lady appeared sprightly still, but she acquiesced. 'Lead him to it then, and show him.'

I would truly have welcomed the opportunity to inspect the orchard, which was admirably well set out. I was struck by the fireplaces inserted into a wall, which I fancied must have been of double thickness, with a cavity which could thus be filled with heated air. So peaches and apricocks could lean against warm brick, even when the untrustworthy English sun had failed to shine upon them. This ingenious arrangement was a novelty to me. I would have liked to give it my full attention, but as soon as we were within the enclosure, Cecily turned.

'I wonder how much Lord Woldingham has spoken to you of me.'

'Very little, but to say that Wychwood was your home while he was abroad.'

'Our home yes, but always his house. My parents were not his usurpers. They were his stewards while, for his safety, he could not be with us.'

My eyes, which I believed to be shaded by the brim of my hat, dwelt with pleasure on a blossoming tree. Damson, *Damascenum*, if I was not mistaken. This family's divisions formed a familiar tale. Barely a household in the land has not been so cut up. I wondered why she was so eager to take me into her confidence.

'But he spoke of my mother?'

'He did, and forgive me for repeating what may distress you, but she is correct in supposing that he told me that her wits had failed.'

'She is also correct in saying that his motives for so speaking of her are several. That there is a smidgeon of truth in the allegation, she openly accepts, as you have heard. Many people of her age are forgetful. She is no longer so ready as she once was to apprehend new ideas. At night she is sometimes seized by unreasonable fears, and her distress then is painful . . .'

A tiny hesitation. I thought she had meant to say 'painful to witness', but had silenced herself for fear of seeming to complain.

I said, 'She seems as gracious a lady now as she ever must have been.' I was greatly pleased to see that someone had thought to underplant the apple trees with anemones, so that the blush of the blossom's fat petals was counterpoised by the blue fringe of the little ground-flowers' raggedy show.

'Lord Woldingham is not quite the person he pretends to be. He is considerate.'

I bowed my head slightly. It was not for me to discuss my employer's qualities with a connection of his.

'I think that when he asked my mother to remove herself and her daughter from Wychwood, he pacified his own conscience and the opinion of those around him with a pretence that she was incapable. She needed absolute tranquillity, he said, and he could grant her this old manor as a refuge. His wife did not want another mistress in the great house.'

I have so far encountered Lady Woldingham only fleetingly, in London. I would gladly have asked for Cecily's impressions of her, but we were not under-servants to gossip about those set above us.

'Now he sustains the myth of her incapacity for another reason. It is a shield for us.'

She had my attention. I would like to have understood her. But we were interrupted. The old woman who had seemed to follow me came through the wicket that led from the orchard out onto a paddock and thence to the woods. A boy, delicate-featured, accompanied her, carrying a basket. Cecily went to her and took her hand.

'Meg, this is Mr Norris,' she said. 'It is he of whom I spoke. He who would make lakes with the well-water.'

The other spoke no word, but regarded me intently.

Soon thereafter Miss Rivers indicated that my visit should be concluded. As I walked away I saw her and Meg pacing, heads together, beneath the fruit trees. The boy was swinging by his hands from an apple bough. It pained me to observe that Cecily walked quite needlessly over a patch of grass where I had noticed the glistening spears of coming crocuses. How many purple-striped beauties must have been crushed prematurely by the wooden sole of her clog!

*

This morning I found myself, unintentionally, spectator to an affecting scene.

The room that serves me as an office overlooks the yard. In times to come, carriages will set visitors down before the new portico. That they will enter the house through an antechamber shaped like a Grecian temple is not, to my mind, Mr Rose's happiest notion. For the present, though, they come clattering in the old way, by the stables, so that the horses' convenience is better served, perhaps, than that of the persons they transport.

A din of wheels on cobblestones and the shouting of grooms. I went to the window. A great number of chests and bundles were being lowered from the carriage's roof. Only the luggage, then, I thought, and made to return to my writing desk, when a man ran across the yard below in a state of undress that shocked me. A footman run amuck. But no, the shirt flapping out of his breeches was fine, its billowing sleeves trimmed four inches deep with lace. The stockings in which he darted so noiselessly over the paving were silken; the breeches, scarce buttoned, were of a lavender hue with which I was familiar, but not from seeing them on a servant's shanks. That shaven head, that I had never before seen unwigged, bore on its front a face I knew. By the time I had identified him, Lord Woldingham was down on his knees on the cobbles and three small children were climbing him as though he was a rigged ship, and they the midshipmen. He was laughing and snatching at them and in a trice the whole party had tumbled over in a heap. Various bystanders – whom I took to include nurse and nursemaids, governor and tutors – remonstrated and smiled by turns. And all the while the grooms kept on with their work, seeing to the horses and unloading the carriage with an almighty bustle.

The children and their sire had only just righted themselves, and begun to shake off the straw tangling in their hair, when half a dozen riders trotted into the yard. Lord Woldingham turned from his little human monkeys and stood a-tiptoe, until his wife was lifted down from the back of a dappled grey. My Lady is scarce taller than the eldest boy, very pale and small-featured. He could have picked her up and swung her in the air, as he had done to the children, but he was now all decorum. He bowed so gracefully that one hardly noticed the absence of plumed hat from hand, or buckled shoe from foot. I could not see the lady's face clear, but it seemed to me she made no reference, by smile or frown, to his scandalous appearance, but simply held out a hand, with sweet gravity, for him to kiss.

*

I walked out after breakfast with Mr Rose, at his request, to prospect for a suitable site for an ice-house. In Italy, he tells me, the nobility build such houses, in shape like a columbarium, for the preservation of food.

A broad round hole is made in the ground. It is lined with brick and mortared to make it watertight, and a dome built over it with but a narrow entranceway, so that it looks to a passerby like a stone bubble exhaled by some subterranean ogre. The chamber is filled to ground-level with blocks of ice brought from the mountains in covered carts insulated with straw. Even in the fiery Italian summers, says Rose, the ice is preserved from melting by its own coldness. So the exquisites of Tuscany can enjoy chilled syrups all summer long. Better still, shelves and niches are made all around the interior walls of the dome, and there food can be kept as fresh as in the frostiest winter.

I was inclined to scoff at the notion. We are not Italian. We have neither mountain ranges roofed with snow, nor summers so sultry that a north-facing larder will not suffice to keep our food wholesome. Mr Rose took no offence, saying jovially, 'Come, Norris. The air is sweet and my poor lungs crave a respite from plaster-dust. You will wish to ensure my stone beehive is not so placed as to ruin one of your fine views.'

21

He plays me adroitly. At the mention of a *vista* I was all attention. My mind running away with me, as it has a propensity to do, in pursuit of a curious likeness, I was picturing his half-moon of a building, rising pleasantly from amidst shrubs as a baby's crown emerges from the flesh of its dam. Or I would perhaps surround it with cypresses, I thought, if they could be persuaded to thrive so far north. Then this humble food-store could make a show as pleasing as the ancient tombs surviving amidst greenery upon the Roman *campagna*.

(I let that last sentence stand, but note here, in my own reproof, that I have not seen the *campagna*, or any of Italy. I must guard myself from the folly of those who seek to appear cosmopolitan by alluding to sights of which they have but second-hand knowledge. The Roman *campagna* is to me an engraving, seen once only, and a fine painting in the drawing room here, whose representation of the landscape is doubtless as questionable as its account of its inhabitants. If the picture were to be believed, these go naked, and many of them are hoofed like goats.)

Mr Armstrong found the two of us around midday. He rapidly grasped the little building's usefulness for the storage of meat and, accustomed as he is to lording it over his underlings, began to give Mr Rose orders as to where he should place hooks for the suspension of deer carcasses or pairs of rabbits. 'Once you've made us that round house, Mr Rose,' he said, with the solemnity of a monarch conferring a knighthood, 'we'll eat hearty all year.'

He kept rubbing his hands together. It is his peculiar way of expressing pleasure. I have seen him do it when the two fowl – the Adam and Eve of his race of pheasants – arrived safely in their hamper after traversing the country on mule-back. Already his inner ear hears the rattling of wing-feathers and the crack of musket shot. He fought for the King. The scar that traces a line from near his cheekbone, over jaw and down into his neck, tells how he suffered for it. It is curious how those who have been soldiers seek out the smell of gunpowder in time of peace. Most of the keenest sportsmen I know have experience of battle.

'Have you anything in your pocket worth the showing?' asked Rose. The question seemed impertinent, but Armstrong gave an equine grin. His back teeth are all gone, but those in front, growing long and yellow, make his smile dramatic. He reached into the pouch, from which he had already drawn a pocket-knife and a yard-cord for measuring, and, opening his palm flat, showed three small black coins. It came to me that it was for the sake of this moment that he had sought out our company. Rose took one up daintily, holding it by its edges as though it were a drawing he feared to smudge. 'Trajan,' he said, 'Traianus,' and he sounded as happy as I might be on finding a rare orchid in the wood. 'Silver.' He and Armstrong beamed at each other, then both at once remembered their manners and turned to me.

'Mr Norris,' it was Armstrong who spoke first. 'If you can give us more of your time, we'll show you what lies beyond those lakes of yours.'

'Yes, come,' said Rose. 'We have been much at fault in not letting you sooner into our secret. Mr Armstrong and I are by way of being antiquaries.'

The two of them led me at a spanking pace down to the marshy low ground where the last of the lakes will spread and uphill again through bushes until we were on the slope opposing the house, and standing on a curiously humped plateau raised up above the mire.

It was as though I had been given new eyes. I had been in this spot before, but had seen nothing. This mass of ivy was not the clothing of a dead tree, but of an archway, still partially erect. Those heaps of stone were not scattered by some natural upheaval. They are the remains of a kind of cloister, or courtyard. This smoothness was not created by the seeping of water. Armstrong and Rose together took hold of a mass of moss and rolled it back, as though it were a feather-bed, and there beneath was Bacchus, his leopard-skin slipping off plump effeminate shoulders, a bunch of blockish grapes grasped in hand, all done in chips of coloured stone.

We were on our hands and knees, examining the ancient marvel, when we were interrupted.

'Oh Mr Rose, shame on you for forestalling our pleasure! I have been anticipating the moment of revelation this fortnight.' Lord Woldingham was there, and others were riding up behind him. Servants walked alongside a cart. There were baskets, and flagons, and, perched alongside them, three boys and a little moppet of a girl – Lord Woldingham's offspring and the boy I had seen at Wood Manor.

'Here are ladies come to see our antiquities. And here are scholars to enlighten us as to their history.' Lord Woldingham was darting amongst the horses. As soon as the groom had lifted one of the ladies down, he would be there to bow and flutter and lead her to the expanse of grass where I was standing, the best vantage point for viewing the mosaic. I would have withdrawn, but Cecily Rivers detained me. It is as gratifying as it is bewildering to me to note that she seeks out my company. I am accustomed to being treated here as one scarcely visible, but her eyes fly to my face.

'So Mr Norris,' she said, 'you have discovered our heathen idol? I told you this valley had supernatural protection.'

'You spoke of fairies, not of Olympians.'

'Do you not think they might be one and the same? Our one, true and self-avowedly jealous God obliges all the other little godlings to consort together. Puck and Pan are mightily similar. And this gentleman, with his vines and his teasel, is he not an ancient rendering of Jack in the Green?'

'The *thyrsus*,' I said, 'resembles a teasel in appearance, but the ancients tell us it was in fact made up of a stalk of fennel and a pine cone.'

She laughed. Of course she did. I was afraid of the freedom with which her mind ranged, and took refuge in pedantry. A dark-haired gentleman in a russet-coloured velvet coat came up. She turned, and I lost her to him. I believe he is my Lady's brother.

Rose beckoned me away. 'We'll leave them to their fête,' he said. Armstrong remained and I could see, glancing backwards, that he was displaying the Roman pavement as proudly as though he had made it himself.

*

This morning my Lord's eldest son was drowned. The boy and his brother were playing around the quagmire where lately the father and I had wallowed in mud. He slipped in water barely deep enough to reach his ankle-bone, if upright. He toppled face forward, wriggled round to rise, and in so doing thrust his sky-blue-coated shoulder so deep into the slime it would not release him. He died silently, while the other child whooped and shouted. How great a change can be effected in a paltry minute. The littler boy had made a slide at the base of what will be the cataract. Governor and tutors, seeing how he might so precipitate himself into the ooze, rushed to forestall him. And so the cadet was saved, at mortal cost to the heir. He fell unwatched.

A forester, perilously perched halfway up one of the distant ring of elms, ready to hack off a branch shattered by last winter's storms, saw him lie, and shouted down to his mate, who began to race down the slope, his arms flailing as he leapt over clumps of broom and young bracken. He was wailing like the banshee; words, in his horror, forsaking him. Desperate to save, he increased the danger. Those near enough to where the poor boy lay to have helped him, looked not towards him, but at the man hurling himself so crazily downhill. So seconds were lost, and so the mud seeped into the little fellow's mouth and nostrils and stoppered up his breath.

When I saw them clambering over their sire two days ago I thought I was looking at happiness.

Lady Woldingham sits by her dead boy as still and quiet as though the calamity had rendered every possible action otiose. The other children are brought to her from time to time, when their nurses despair of stilling their howls. She looks at them as though glimpsing them dimly, across an immense dark moor. To what purpose speech, in the face of such grief?

I cannot bear to come anywhere near my Lord.

*

The guests have all gone. They will return for young Charles Fortescue's funeral, but yesterday they started up and fluttered away with a unanimity to match that of a murmuration of starlings. I would that I could do the same.

Ten years ago it was a common thing to see how, when a man's brother or father was accused, that person's friends would seem not to notice him when he passed by in the street. One would fuss with the fastening of a glove rather than catch his eye when it came to choosing where to seat oneself in the coffeehouse. Then I thought that we were all cowards, but prudent with it. When a country has been at war with itself every citizen has a multitude of reasons to fear exposure – exposure of miscreancy, but exposure also of those actions which might at the time of their performance have seemed most honourable. Now I think that the shrinking from those marked by misfortune was not the ephemeral outcome of civil war. It was not only that we feared spies and informers. There is something appalling about misfortune itself.

The tribulations of others are our trials. By our response to them we shall be judged, and I fear that, awkward as I am, it is a trial I am bound to fail.

It is less than a week since I wrote in these pages that Lord Woldingham was careless. I thought him boisterous and gay. I made of him a benevolent despot who would fill this house with colour and bustle. I mocked him, just a little, and so timidly that even I could not hear myself do it. I was like a child who thinks his parents omnipotent, and so licenses himself to jeer at them, and then is terrified to see them cry.

There was crying aplenty yesterday, but not from him.

He had not sent for me. But I knew that, however irksome he found my attendance, to stay away from him longer would prove me inhuman.

I found black clothes. Not difficult for me – my wardrobe is sober. When I judged that Lord Woldingham would have break-fasted, and might be walking out in the garden, with his dog Lupin waddling behind, I prepared to encounter him there.

As I stepped out of my room I all but knocked down a maid whose hand was already lifted to beat upon the door. It wasn't until I looked at the note she handed me that I knew where I had seen her before – at Wood Manor. Cecily apologised for making so peremptory a request but asked me to come at once, and discreetly. My uncertain resolution to offer my condolences to my employer was laid aside in an instant.

There is a horse provided for my use. I told the groom I might be out a considerable while. I am not a confident horseman, but I asked the cob to hurry, and, heavily built as she is, she obliged with a pace that quite alarmed me. She made her way to Wood Manor almost without my guidance. Cecily was waiting in the entrance hall, and led me at once to a small room where the woman Meg sprawled on the rushes in a corner, bundled in a cloak, her head thrown back against the distempered wall, her eyes closed.

'She has been set upon,' said Cecily. 'They chased her with dogs.'

'Is she hurt?'

'I think only very much afraid. She is prone to fits. Perhaps she has had one. Our man found her and saw off her assailants and brought her here across his saddle.'

'I am no physician.'

'Mr Richardson will be here shortly. But it is not only medicine we need. My cousin's men harass her and her companions, but I do not think he knows it.'

We stood in the centre of the room, speaking urgently and low.

'If he is informed, he will surely discipline them.'

'Today is not . . .'

She was right. I too shrank from the idea of pestering him in his grief. But there was a worse reason for Cecily's hesitation.

'They say she killed the boy.'

I began to protest at such idiocy, and then recalled that I myself have been afraid of Meg.

'But he died surrounded by his attendants. The woodcutters, the other children. So many people were present. Not a one has said that she was there.'

'They say she can kill with a wish.'

The woman moaned, and a little blood ran from the corner of her mouth. The room smelt of last year's apples. The sole window was veiled with cobwebs, and kept tight shut. We were as though imprisoned.

'My mother too. They call the two of them weird sisters.'

I am a man of reason. I live in a nation that has been riven by doctrinal disputes for more than a century. I have listened to temperate, kindly disposed people swear that they will never again feel any affection for a brother, or a friend, because that other holds an opinion they cannot share as to what precisely takes place when the priest mumbles over the wafer of a Sunday morning. I am not an atheist. I marvel, as any natural philosopher must, at the intricate and ingenious thing the world is. But I am sure that, whatever the Creator may be, no human conception of him can be incontrovertibly right. Bigotry is abhorrent to me.

But worse even than the intolerance of churches (and chapels, and conventicles) is the frenzy of the weak when fear drives them to blame their fellow beings for the catastrophes which lie in wait for us all.

'I had thought that that madness was passed by.'

Cecily seemed to be holding herself upright with a great effort. 'Meg's teacher was called a witch, and ducked, and died of it.'

'Before the wars, surely.'

'There are many who remember it.'

'But your mother. No one would presume. Lady Harriet is not the kind to be suspected of witchcraft.'

Cecily gestured irritably, a mere twitch of her hand. 'Witchcraft is a meaningless word. A mere pretext. This is because my mother and Meg both worship in the forest.'

I had no idea what she meant. She didn't deign to help me.

'We cannot wait. Go to my cousin and tell him what is being said. Say that my mother is in danger. Here is Mr Richardson. Go quickly.'

In her nature playful gentleness and a tendency to be dictatorial are most oddly combined. I bowed myself out quite sulkily, as the apothecary was ushered quickly into the little room from which I had just been summarily expelled.

My Lord received me calmly, albeit his face looked blurred, as though he had been roughly handled in the night. I delivered my condolences, to which he made only perfunctory answer, and my message, which he seemed to understand more clearly than I did. There ensued much galloping about. A carriage was sent. Lady Harriet, complaining feebly, was brought back with her daughter and ensconced in one of the recently vacated guest-chambers. Her maid came after on a cart. Meg was carried in, still as in a dead faint, with Mr Richardson attending, and laid among cushions on a settle in my Lord's study.

Lord Woldingham gave orders that all the estate workers should be called together on the grass patch before the house.

Once a sizeable crowd had gathered, he took his hat and went out to them, I following along with the people of the household. All in black, he looked oddly reduced.

'You know that I have suffered a great loss. I speak now to all of you, to those who knew me when I was an infant in this place, and to those who have shared my exile. I have been away a long time. But do not suppose that Wychwood was ever left behind me.

'We have all observed, from conversing with our grandparents and other elders, that the very first impressions are the most deeply inscribed. Even one who can scarce remember whether it be time to rise or to go to bed will marvel at a butterfly seen half a century ago. Another asks fondly after a dog who died before our King's father came to the throne, even if he cannot recollect the latter end of that unhappy monarch.

'I am not yet in my decline, but I assure you that many of the dreary days of exile have been erased from my mind, while pictures from my first three years, passed in this very house, have comforted me in my absence. Yesterday morning my boys were playing with a wooden ark they found in their nursery. I have gone so far, and my homeward course has meandered so unconscionably, it seemed a miracle to see the little dents in the rump of the wooden elephant. It is a marvel that the mind can sling a bridge across so sad a gulf of time, and yet I tell you all that as I handled the toy I could feel again the pleasure with which, as a child, I bit down on that piece of painted wood.

'The milk-teeth that made those little wounds are shed, but the jaw in which those teeth grew is here' (at this he tossed back the curled tresses of his long wig as though presenting his throat to be cut). 'You have yet to know me, but I am one of you. One of the men of Wychwood.'

This was not at all what the assembled listeners had come to hear. A man loses his child, and then alludes to the boy only in passing, as an unnamed player in a scene with an inanimate toy. It seemed as though my Lord had no heart. What did they care about the vagaries of memory? They had expected him to display his mourning to them. The women, especially, appeared downright offended.

This opening, though, was but the overture. Having tuned his instrument, Lord Woldingham launched abruptly into a lament as ardent as the divine Orpheus's. 'I have lost a child. Not for the first time. My firstborn left this life, when he himself had barely glimpsed it, before I could ever see him, ever touch him. I was so far away. But my Charles who died yesterday was near to me. My wife brought him to me in Holland, and from thenceforward it was as though I, who had been homeless, had a home. Father and mother can build a house, but it is no more than a shelter from bad weather until a child runs through it. I used to walk by a pond near to my lodging at The Hague, and I thought it dreary. Then this boy came, and chuckled to see the geese come splashing down on the muddy water, and the unlovely mere became delightful. I am thankful that I have two babes yet. But just as a parent's love is big enough to embrace every child that comes, so it will never shrink to cover over the wound left where one of those precious ones is missing.'

People were glancing up at the windows of my Lady's apartments on the first floor, but there was nothing to see there.

'I have been a child in this place, and so have many of you. I have lost a child here. Many of you will have had private cause to grieve over the clashes of our country's unhappy recent history. You will know, as I do, how it is to mourn. Some of you have already offered me your sympathy. I thank you. Others have held back discreetly. I thank you too.'

He was speaking very smoothly and soberly. I noticed Mr Goodyear looking at him with an appraising air, but not unkindly. I have heard that Goodyear is a bard, whose storytelling has made him a known man in this region.

My Lord proceeded. 'Some among you have said most generously that they would do anything possible to alleviate the sadness of this time. There is something I would ask of you.

'A woman has been brought to this house today grievously ill. She has been so frightened and harassed that her mind has become a blank. I do not know whether she will ever revive from this strange vacancy. She is Meg Leafield. She has been a faithful servant of this family, and I would have had her treated with respect as one of my own. Some of you may have imagined you were performing my secret wish in troubling her. I declare most roundly that that belief was mistaken.

'I am no sectarian. It is my wish, as it is His Majesty the King's – and he is wise in this – that we should put aside our quarrels and strive to make this a peaceful nation, whose people are united in their desire to see their country prosper.'

The peacock was crossing the elevated lawn behind the assembled listeners. Its attention caught by the gathering beneath it, it interrupted its gawky pavane and turned in our direction. Very slowly, with a loud dry rattling of quill upon quill, it elevated its showy panoply of tail-feathers – green, bronze, purple, black and tawny, all metallic and glinting, a sumptuous medley setting off the blue of the creature's throat as an immense brocaded skirt shows off the jewel-coloured satin of a stomacher.

Lord Woldingham has longed to see this. I have observed him with Mr Armstrong, one whole afternoon, following the bird around, attempting to interest it in its mate, or in some tidbit or other, in a vain attempt to persuade it to perform the trick for which it had been purchased. Now, as it turned itself this way and that, as though set upon compelling admiration, I wondered whether it would cheer him, or throw him from his intent.

He ignored it. He was saying, 'I do not enquire into the niceties of your relationships with our Maker. Worship in church or chapel, with vicar or presbyter, or with a wayside preacher whose pulpit is the hedge. It is all one to me, so long as you treat each

other with civility. Those of you who have been long abroad, as
I have, may have a quarrel with some of our fellows who have
flourished here. I say put those quarrels aside. We want no venge-
ance, no hunting down, no settling of scores. I have heard it said
that to make peace with an opponent is shameful and unmanly. I
say it is an honourable thing, a wise and benevolent thing, a thing
on which God, however you may imagine him, will smile.'

'I applaud our employer's breadth of mind,' murmured a voice
in my ear. 'Surely, though, to speak of "imagining" the divinity is
over-bold.' It was Mr Rose. I was surprised at his addressing me
in such an insinuating tone. I dislike whisperers. I nodded, but
didn't turn my head.

Now Lord Woldingham's rumblings gave way to a thunder-
clap. He strode through the crowd, and mounted the plinth I
have had prepared ready for the ancient marble figure of Flora,
which is making its way towards us by painfully slow degrees.
My Lord's agent in Rome purchased it there. Now it is creeping
along the canals of France, drawn by huge shaggy-heeled horses.
Some time this summer, it will make the dangerous crossing to
these shores before being heaved aboard another barge to float
upstream to us here. The stone nymph will be twice the height of
Lord Woldingham, whose quickness of movement and forceful-
ness can lead one to forget that he is, in person, just a wisp of a
man. But on the plinth, his funereal satins lustrous in the sun, he
seemed as darkly substantial as the improbably gigantic bronze
mastiffs recently set up as guardians of Wychwood's new front
door. The assembled people had stepped nervously aside to let
him pass; now they swivelled to see him again. The sun was in
their eyes; he a silhouette against a background of white sky. For
the first time he raised his voice.

'A harmless, helpless woman has been ill-treated here. Shame
on you. A member of my own family, to whom you all owe
deference, has been slandered. More shame upon you. There has
been nonsensical babble of witchcraft. We are not savages, to give

credence to such piffle. My son is dead and you foul the pure grief of his family with superstitious blatherings. Let me hear no more of this. Those of you who have frightened Meg Leafield will come to me and explain yourselves. Lady Harriet is my aunt, and my honoured guest. When she pleases to return to Wood Manor, she goes under my protection. Any man or woman who breathes a word against her makes an enemy of me.'

He stood silent for upwards of a minute. No one fidgeted or uttered a word. When he stepped down he did so deliberately, and walked back into the house with the demeanour of one following a coffin, but that his eyes were turned, not to the earth, but upwards as though defying the gloomy clouds to rain upon him.

I went to my office and occupied myself with new sketches for the parterre. Seeing my Lord so elevated had brought home to me how the proportions of the terrace will appear altered once Flora queens it over the space. The eye must be led to her, and the flowerbeds must seem to flow out from her, the bringer of flowers.

*

I am as much a fool as that ridiculous peacock. The fowl, disdaining its proper mate, has become enamoured of one of the garden boys. The display it made for us all yesterday was an attempt to catch the youth's attention. It follows him around with pathetic constancy.

He was at work in the rose garden as I set off for my walk this afternoon. As he spread horse-dung on the beds (not all of a gardener's tasks are fragrant), the amorous bird was on the pavement alongside him, its cumbersome fan extended, turning very slowly, first to one side and then to another, as though imploring him to notice how the vari-coloured filaments in its plumage flared and changed in the shifting light.

The boy, who is very young, is being plagued by the others' teasing. I think he hardly understands the game of love yet.

I walked out towards Wood Manor and had a happy encounter. I have had much to think about these past hours – sad matters for the most part. Yet, as I write these words, I find myself absurdly gay.

*

I will allow yesterday's entry to stand. At least it is evidence that I am sensible of my folly. There is no dishonour in loving an admirable woman, so long as I refrain from pestering her with my suit.

What seems to me now most reprehensible is that my pre-occupation with things private to myself makes me negligent of my employer's grief. Lovers, it is rightly said, are solipsistic imbeciles.

Wychwood sitting nearly on the summit of a low hill, the land falls away from it on three sides. To the west, a set of ancient stone steps leads down to a sunken lawn, cupped by steep banks and floored with violets. This was a pond once, made by Romans perhaps, or by the monks who had a dwelling here after the Romans had gone. Mr Green tells me that when his men were levelling the ground they found a rubble of petrified sods within which time and decay had drawn the skeletons of ancient fishes. The tiny bones had dematerialised to leave an effigy of themselves made of nothingness, a vacuity which might, had the gardeners' spades not chopped them up, have survived, insubstantial and indestructible as the soul is to a true believer, for ever and ever, amen.

I walked there this afternoon. Lupin the pug snuffled about me. When he saw me take my hat and open the door to the garden he came scuttling bowlegged down the corridor to join me, his claws clicking on the flagstones.

The world being full of graceful creatures, it puzzles me why the ugly should be so prized. After I had paced with Lupin half an hour, though, I found myself touched by the fortitude with which he bears the deficiencies of his bodily design. His walk is an ungainly waddle. His skin was made for a being twice his size and bunches around his neck like an ill-fixed ruff. He snorts and grunts, half suffocated. As he struggles for breath, liquid trickles from his nose, and he laps it up with a busy and repulsive action of his tongue, the only neat thing about him.

I was meditating on the capriciousness of Providence, which kills a likely boy too young, and allows the survival of another being so evidently unfit, when I was struck hard at the back of my right knee.

The blow felled me. Half recumbent on the grass, I looked around and could see no sign of my assailant. Kneeling beside me, clucking and fidgeting with my waistcoat buttons, was old Meg. I am ashamed to admit I pushed her back roughly. The pain in my knee was sharp, but I was more shaken by the force of my fall. My previous reverie continued *ad absurdum*. How much more stable our posture would be, I thought groggily, had we four legs. In this respect Lupin was my superior. Balancing precariously on only two vertical supports, my body – when one of those supports was knocked out from under me – had lapsed to the horizontal with a most unpleasant thump.

Two people shot out of the thicket on the far side of the lawn. One was the boy I had previously seen with Meg. The other was Mr Rose, hatless, and demonstrating that a round belly is no diminisher of agility.

Rose shouted, 'Are you hurt, Mr Norris?'

He caught the boy and hugged him from behind. The two swayed like wrestlers, the boy's feet kicking. Meg went to them, met Rose's eye deliberately and spat on his shoe. He let his arms fall limp. The boy sat sullen where he had dropped.

'He threw that stone,' Rose said to me.

He was looking past Meg as though she were of no account. She slapped his face. I was astonished to see him flinch like a chastened scholar. When last I had heard of her, she was lying insensible. Now she was articulate.

'One boy dead, and you bullying another,' she said. She tied her shawl crosswise over her chest and returned to my side. She lifted from the ground, not a stone, but a sphere of solid wood, finely turned, about the bigness of an apple and painted blue.

'The gentlemen give him farthings to find their balls for them, and fling them back,' she said, addressing me as though we were old acquaintances. 'That a child should have to pick up toys for grown men!' There were iron hoops set here and there about the lawn, and mallets propped against a bench.

I sat, then stood. I said to the boy, 'Men are not rabbits, to be shied at.' He looked up at me through his hair and I had a shock. His face was that of Lord Woldingham's deceased son.

Mr Rose approached, stroking the round hat he had retrieved from a bramble. He shook his head at Meg and came to inspect my injury. The damage to my stockings was greater than that to my person. 'You'll do,' he said. He bent and murmured to Meg, and passed on up towards the house.

I turned to the old woman and addressed her formally. 'Mistress Leafield,' I said, 'I have wondered about you. This mishap has at least had the advantage of making us known to each other.'

We hobbled together, I leaning on her shoulder, to a stone bench. There, with Lupin and the boy growling at each other on the ground beneath us, she explained herself, and other things beside.

She was playmate to Lady Harriet, and to my Lord's father, when they were all infants, because she was their wet-nurse's child. She stayed with Lady Harriet, studying alongside her. 'My Lady is an artist,' she said. 'You have seen it. The rich don't honour silk-workers as they do paint-workers, but artists know their own. Mr Rose has the greatest respect for her. He brings the woodcarvers and plasterers to Wood Manor, and urges them to emulate her designs. I, though, was the better scholar.'

I had thought her ignorant and mute. How often in these past few days have I had to repent of a hasty judgement.

'I learnt mathematics indoors,' she said, 'of my Lady's governor. I learnt physic in the wood, taught by fairies.' She looked carefully at me with small lashless eyes. I betrayed no scepticism, nor any inclination to burn her alive. 'You are phlegmatic, Mr Norris,' she said.

'I am readier to learn than to condemn.'

The fairies, she explained, came to her not as weird visions, but speaking across aeons of time through the stories preserved and cherished by the people of the locality. From them, and from her own experiments, she had found out ways of using plants as remedies and preservatives. She had discovered that she had the gift of calming the frantic with incantations. She knew how to alleviate pain with simples. 'There are some agonies which are too piercing for anyone to suffer them and live,' she said. 'I can help the sufferer to escape the pain by *trauncing*, by passing over temporarily into the place of death. There are some who do not return, and I have been blamed for that, but I do not doubt they were grateful to me.'

A silence fell. Perhaps she expected remonstrance. I waited for her to continue.

'Lady Woldingham is in a grievous state,' she said. 'I can help her. Or rather this boy can.'

'He is your grandson?' I asked.

She looked taken aback, as though I had displayed extraordinary ignorance. 'No,' she said. 'No, not mine.'

Mr Rose came back down the steps.

Meg called the boy to her. They went hurriedly away through the little bushes.

'You are shaken up,' said Rose. 'Here, take my arm.' I was glad to do so. It is true that I felt atremble. My face in the looking-glass was like porridge, lumpen and grey. I went to my room and slept an hour or two, as babies do when they have been dropped.

My habits are regular and somewhat ascetic. I rise early, and go punctually to my rest. It is unusual for me to be abed in daylight. Perhaps that is why I had such visions in my sleep. I seemed to be lapped around in a mist in which all colours were present, glimmeringly pale. I was swirled as in mother-of-pearl liquefied. I had no weight. Nothing grated upon me or pinched me. 'Comfort' is a state we do not prize enough. It is not so sharp as joy, or so exalted as rapture. But in my sleeping state I felt how delicious it is to be warm, to be wrapped in softness, to feel clean and smooth as milk, to be caressed by things silken and delicate. I rolled as in a heavenly cloud, freed of the dizziness one might feel if truly suspended in air, freed of the downward pressure that makes our flesh a burden to us. I was as jocund as the cherubs on my Lord's painted ceilings.

The delight, intensifying, awoke me. My knee was aching. The pearly flood in which I had revelled had dwindled to a patch of slime on my sheet. My celestial tumblings had had an all-too-earthly outcome. I am glad that I had not seen Cecily as I dreamt.

I went downstairs to find a lugubrious silence. It is late. I asked for some supper to be brought to my room. I sit now to write in a state curiously suspended between contentment and anxiety.

I think about that boy. I wonder how Meg means to use him for the consolation of the bereaved mother.

*

Walking in the park, I met Cecily Rivers. I showed her the secret garden I am making in the woods for Lady Woldingham. We passed a remarkable few hours. I think it has not, to ordinary observers, been a bright day, but as I view it now, in retrospect, it dazzles me.

The mother of Ishmael told the angel that her name for the divinity was Thou-God-Seest-Me. To be seen, is that not what we crave? An infant reared by loving parents is cosseted by the vigilance of mother or nurse. Fond eyes dote upon its tiny fingernails, the gossamer wisps of its hair. Once grown, though, we fade from sight. We merge with the crowd of our fellows, all jostling for notice, all straining to catch fortune's eye. To believe, as many do, that God has us perpetually under surveillance must be a very great consolation for our fellow-men's neglect.

It is years, now, since I have felt myself held in the beam of a kindly gaze. Today, though, Cecily looked at me. She spoke to me. She touched my sleeve and laughed at me. She carried herself towards me not as though I was Norris the fee'd calculator of areas and angles; not as though I was the desiccated fellow politely withdrawing when the company dissolves into its pleasures; not as though I were a kind of gelding, neutered by misfortune and hard work. Thou-Cecily-Seest-Me. She sees me industrious, and full of energy. She sees me bashful, and considers it a grace. She sees that my eyes and hair are brown and my fingers long. She sees that I am a young man, and proud. She sees me not as a paving to be stepped on uncaring, but as a path to be followed joyfully. How do I know all this? Not by words.

I have been startled by her seeing. I have felt the carapace, in which I have lived like a tortoise in its shell, crack and fall away from me.

She did not have to reveal herself to me. She was already admirable in my sight.

What passed between us today is not as yet for writing down. Unshelled, I shudder with happiness, and I am afraid.

*

What I call the 'secret' garden is no such thing. How could it be, given that it has been dug and planted not by elves, but by men? It is, however, well secluded.

It was my Lord's fancy to make his wife a place where she could walk unregarded. He promised it to her while they were still in London. 'I will refrain,' he told her, 'even from looking at the plans. This will be as private to you as your closet. I hereby swear – with Carisbrooke and Mr Norris as my witnesses – that, except in some extraordinary emergency, I will never set foot within its bounds.' Carisbrooke is a grey and red parrot whom my Lord's father kept in the castle of that name, when he was there with the late King. It is much given to screeching.

Lady Woldingham, who does not share his mania for privacy, made a pretty speech as to how her husband would always be welcome, wheresoever she might be. He waved it aside. We were in the drawing room of their great house on the Strand. Through the windows we could see the sluggish river-water, the woods on the south bank and, near to, the garden through which servants were carrying barrels up from the landing stage towards the low-arched kitchen entrance.

'See there,' said my Lord. 'This garden is a thoroughfare. How can you muse on the beauties of creation, when you are likely to be knocked aside by some stout fellow lugging a tub of molasses?'

He had then been only a few weeks back in his family's home and he was full of fidgets. For many of those returned with the King, London felt full of hostile eyes. I think one of the reasons he summoned me so frequently was that it comforted him to think that as soon as his presence at court could be dispensed with he would remove to Oxfordshire; to the Eden I was to create for him there. London is too historied. The park at Wychwood seemed, in his imagination, as unsullied by humanity as the first settlers imagined the Americas to be.

The secret garden became my pet project, my hobby-horse. When the complexities of the great park bewildered me, when I could struggle no more with the awkward geometry of its slopes and hollows, with the inconvenient patches of infertile ground, whether boggy or parched, which threatened to interrupt my lines of planting, then I would pull out the portfolio in which the secret garden's plans were stored. I have heard of an architect, who when at work on a palace, built himself a flimsy house of cards for his recreation. So I, worn out by the consideration of trenches and drains, would play at designing this sylvan enclave, barely the size of a tennis court. Surrounded by woodland trees, it would show like a fairy's bower. There would be a pond, fed by a stream, and paved walks on which my Lady could tread with ease. The plants would be chosen for their fragrance, and for the daintiness of their blooms. My Lady is small. I had sometimes to remind myself that she is nonetheless a grown woman, as I found myself designing a garden in miniature, a plot as pretty as a Persian rug on which a child could play among tiny tufted flowers.

There I was today with Cecily. There my life swung around, as a shutter upon a hinge.

*

The boy's funeral took place this morning. Afterwards, I was abroad until late. When I returned to the great house, I found it a peopled darkness. My Lord and Lady kept to their rooms. The paucity of candles signified mourning, but the sumptuously dressed people still thronging the state rooms talked with an animation that shocked me. I am not censorious of elegancies of appearance – such frivolities are too slight to merit moralising upon them. But there is something brazen about the contrast between the blackness of mourning garb and the vanity of adorning the dreary cloth with black lace and glinting jet, or of wearing an inky bodice cut low as that of a courtesan out to snaffle herself a king.

The funeral feast was still upon the table, and a cabal of ancient gentlemen sat over it, exchanging lugubrious reminiscences as the wine went round. I profited by the strange disruptedness of the household, to dine informally, setting myself alongside this chorus of old vultures, and accepting a dish of venison brought to me by a footman who seemed quite done in by weeping. His bleary eyes and puffed face hauled my mind back to the scenes of the morning. The children gazing at their brother's catafalque, their faces grey as though they saw it seethe with worms. The rector, his surplice probably unworn since the late Lord Woldingham went out, fumbling with a ring that had snarled itself in the redundant flurry of lace about his wrists. My Lady swaying like an ill-propped effigy. Choirboys with censers sending up fumes of music and incense together. An awful ache in the throat, as though to draw breath in that gilded chapel were to risk suffocation.

*

I have reached the sanctuary of my room at last, much torn about and bewildered. I will not write more tonight. I have been detained by events that have so puzzled me I am not yet ready to set them down. I have been abominably ill-treated. I am half-minded to depart this place tomorrow.

*

This morning a maid brought me a letter from Cecily. She has asked me to destroy it, but first I will make a digest of it in this journal, which I believe is secure. No one in this household has any wish to delve into the secret thoughts of Norris the landskip man.

I have been culpably ignorant of the community in which I temporarily dwell.

We have all become accustomed to suppressing our curiosity. Just as among felons in a gaol it is held to be discourteous to enquire for what heinous deed one's companion is condemned, so we citizens of this unhappy country have learnt to close our eyes and ears to the vexed histories of our fellows.

We do so at peril to our humanity. To be inquisitive may be dangerous, but to be wilfully blind is cruel. I had no inkling, before, of the consequences to humankind of the grand schemes my Lord and I have been elaborating.

Cecily's prologue can be rendered in brief. She makes no allusion to what transpired between us in the secret garden. Instead she apologises for having involved me in matters that may prove troublesome. She regrets her failure to confide in me earlier. She explains that our fortuitous meeting yesterday, and its sequel, have taken me so far into a tangle of secrets that she feels it is her duty to help me understand them. Here I stand back. Let her continue in her own words.

'My mother and I are of the dissenting party. There. You already deduced as much. For all that I know, you may be of our mind. Or perhaps you find us stiff-necked and perverse. I think, though, that you would not do us unnecessary harm.

'When we encountered you yesterday we were carrying beribboned baskets, as though stepping out for our pleasure, in quest of spring flowers. We often do so. My cousin's men are accustomed to seeing us bearing home primrose plants nestled in damp moss.

'You, though, may have wondered what might have induced my mother to venture so far abroad. At the same hour on the previous day she had returned to Wood Manor, exhausted by the effort of sustaining her part in the funeral. Nonetheless she insisted on sallying out.

'I had not intended to invite you to accompany us to the meeting-house, but my mother's sudden weakness rendered your assistance most welcome.

'I believe that you were amazed when you saw such a numerous congregation, and began to learn how such a gathering has come to be a regular occurrence in these woods.'

Here I resume the thread. Cecily is right. I was amazed.

When I awoke yesterday I had not slept easy. My night-time musings were delicious, but not restful.

The morning at my desk was unproductive. The house was sombre. Black cloth draped the looking-glasses, and hung in ugly festoons over the long windows. I continued, because I had not been ordered to desist, to plan for happier times. I was puzzling over the design for a stage *al fresco*.

My Lord, until fate smote him so cruelly, had been amusing himself with plans for masques and ballets to be performed on summer evenings in the fan-shaped hollow, so like an ancient amphitheatre, which closes the vista across the great lawn. He has asked me to consider it, and I took delight in the task. Narrow terraces, sustained by stone walls, will be planted in spring with rare tulips. In high summer the bulbs will be digged up, and mats laid down, with cushions upon them. My Lord's friends, gorgeously dressed, will be ranged along the terraces like Chinese porcelain displayed upon ledges.

I was planning the pergola that will back the stage. My sketches are attractive, but I was vexed by some technical matters. More seriously, I felt uncertain for whom I laboured. Who now in this house thinks of plays and players? I asked a servant to bring me a bite to eat and, fortified with ale and cold mutton, I was glad to go forth into the park.

There I met the two ladies of Wood Manor. I cannot pretend that I had been unaware that I might intercept their walk, nor that that consideration had not been chief among my motives for walking out. (See how a lover's bashfulness contorts my syntax.)

As I came upon them it was evident that Lady Harriet was fatigued. I took her basket from her and gave her my arm as far as a fallen oak that made an adequate, if scarcely luxurious, seat. I offered to return to the house to ask for conveyance home for them. But Lady Harriet insisted that she would soon be rested and would not disappoint 'the brethren'.

To give the ladies time to recover themselves I explained what I have planned for the western end of the park, over which, from our makeshift seat, we enjoyed a fine prospect. I talked of groves of the balsamic poplar, whose myrrh will fill the park with celestial odours, and of the fallow deer (some dozen of whom were grazing in our eye-line) whom I would have banished for the protection of my stripling beeches, but on the retention of which Lord Woldingham has set his heart. He has even sent abroad for a pair of albinos in the hope of breeding a race of white harts. Animal, vegetable, mineral. He favours the first; I the second; Mr Rose the third. Despite his name, the architect thinks only of stone and of water.

The course of the wall (our triumvirate's joint venture) in this quarter is now partially cleared. Where soon there will be a sturdy barrier there is now a vacancy, a strip of no-grass, no-brambles, no-bracken, no-trees. In my mind's eye the wall is already handsomely there, its stone the colour of a breadcrust, its solidity giving definition to the park as a fine frame does to a picture. To the others, I suppose, the band of raw and rutted earth must have looked as shocking as a wound.

After some half an hour had gone by, Lady Harriet appeared restored. I offered to accompany them on their way. Cecily accepted. Despite what had passed between us, she treated me as formally as ever. When I pressed her hand, in assisting her, she turned away.

We crossed the wall's foundations, traversed a part of the wooded periphery which the workmen have yet to reach and made our way downwards through dense, low-growing holly trees whose blackish foliage left the forest floor bare but for the skeletons of leaves, crisp and lacy as carvings done by midgets. We went silently, our feet sinking softly into mould. I had never come this way before. Of a sudden we stepped from our dim passage into brilliant light.

Across the glade rose a barn-like structure. Its roof was of thatch, its walls of wattle panels fixed to stout stone piers. Gathered before it was a company of about a hundred souls. Some I recognised. Before I could take in more of the scene my arms were grabbed and pulled behind me, and my wrists tied. I was hustled across the grass towards the great door of the building. My two companions watched this outrage serenely. I called out as I struggled, but they seemed absorbed in converse with those about them. It was as though they had led me deliberately into a trap.

My captors were middle-aged men, decently dressed. They spoke not a word to me. A boy, running backwards before me the better to jeer in my face, was as voluble as they were taciturn. The little lordling's landskip limner. Porky pig the pug-dog. Verminous village vandal. Mr Long-nose. Mr Long-wall. Mr Long-wind. Windy wabbler.

It is true my nose is long, but not monstrously so. The allusions to pig and pug had more to do with the lad's taste for alliteration than with my appearance.

The interior of the building was fitted up like a parliament, with benches facing each other to either side. I was led to the very centre and invited to sit on a low chest. My bindings were loosened, though not removed. I waited quietly – really I did not know how else to comport myself – while all those who had been standing about on the grass filed in. The majority of them looked like working people, some like desperate vagrants, but there were gentry as well. They seated themselves in orderly fashion, the men to one side, the women to the other. Cecily entered with Lady Harriet, and found seats on the front-most bench, so that, had I felt it fitting, I could have reached out and touched her hand. She looked steadily at me, and made a tiny shrug, as though seeing a reproach in my eye that I did indeed most heartily intend.

A gentleman passed between us, brushing awkwardly through the cramped passageway to assume a commanding position by a lectern directly in front of me. He asked me to rise, so that we two were posed like play-actors, visible to all eyes. There ensued this exchange.

He – You may be surprised, Mr Norris, to hear me say that we welcome you to our assembly. Your treatment at our hands has so far been rough. We pray you to forgive us. We have reasons to be suspicious of strangers.

I – I await your explanation, sir.

He – I must ask you first if you are one of the chosen.

I – If you mean by that, sir, am I one of those who believe God has singled them out for grace in this life and glory in the next, and who maintain – on no grounds other than their own conviction – that all others are to be damned to perpetual torment, then I must answer in the negative. I am not of that sect.

I think now it was pompous of me, and unmannerly, to reply so downrightly, but I was ruffled up by the man-handling to which I had been subjected.

He (laughing) – I thank you, sir, for your candour.

I – I am a Christian. I bear ever in mind Christ's teaching regarding the love we owe to our neighbours. He was not particular as to the manner in which that neighbour might worship, or the minutiae of that neighbour's conception of the Almighty. Nor am I. I have my own ideas, which I will keep private. I do my work. I make my living. I hope to be useful.

He – And virtuous, Mr Norris?

I – By my own lights. With whom do I speak?

He – We do not reveal our names here. It is a matter of courtesy as much as of security. We are under the King's protection, as all his subjects are. Nonetheless, there are those who believe they are acting for the monarchy when they chase and torment us. Just as there are people in Lord Woldingham's following who thought to please him by bullying one of our sisters.

I thought, Meg?

The man was suave. I supposed him to be some kind of a preacher, but nothing in his dress distinguished him as such.

He – You see that we have established a settlement here in the forest. Since the coming back of the King we have thought it prudent to remain here in seclusion. We are not hide-aways. Our presence is common knowledge in all the villages around. By keeping ourselves apart, though, we avoid provoking rancour. This hall, rough as it is, is our temple. Nature provides us with the materials for our dwellings, and with most of our food.

I – Why do you tell me all this?

He – Because you endanger our peaceable and harmless existence. I will explain. But first please join us in our worship.

My bonds were removed. I was led to a place opposite Cecily and her mother. The people rose to their feet as one. The small sounds of the forest, the rustlings and chirpings, the twitterings and flappings, came clearly to us through the open door. And then those sounds were progressively erased, rather as the goings-on of the world become muffled for one who is overcome by faintness. Something had taken over my auditory faculties. Time passed before I understood that that something was itself a sound.

A droning – wavering but insistent – not unlike that which emanates from a beehive in midsummer. Not melodious, not expressive; a kind of energy, the musical equivalent of the air that can be seen to pulse and shimmer above heated iron. I glanced to right and left. The rows of men stood intent, their lips loosely set. The sound surged and ebbed, surged and ebbed. I saw that a stocky man at the farthest end from the door was gesticulating discreetly, as though regulating its flow. I do not know exactly when I understood that the sound was human, that all the men around me were emitting sound as simply and powerfully as all day long we emit breath.

The hum became a rumble and then, as though borne on its powerful wave, an answering call, articulate this time, arose from the benches opposite as all the women lifted up their voices.

> We are a garden walled around,
> Chosen and made peculiar ground;
> A little spot enclosed by grace
> Out of the world's wide wilderness.

Cecily and Lady Harriet were singing with the rest, though I could not distinguish their voices amidst the consort.

> Like trees of myrrh and spice we stand,
> Planted by God the Father's hand;
> And all His springs in Zion flow,
> To make the young plantation grow.

I bowed my head. The Woldingham boy's funeral did not touch me as I felt it ought, for all the beauty of Wychwood's chapel with its curiously twisted ebony columns, and for all the skill of the musicians and the purity of the castrato's voice. This woodland ceremony, though, moved me. The tears that had failed to fall before pricked at my eyelids. It was as though I grieved, not for a boy with whom I was barely acquainted, but for all that have been lost. So many, many dead in a lifetime of wars. My brother. The children that he might have begotten. The children whom I have not had.

> Our Lord into His garden comes,
> Well pleased to smell our poor perfumes,
> And calls us to a feast divine,
> Sweeter than honey, milk, or wine.

Prayers followed, which seemed to me unconscionably long, and impertinent with it. Surely the Almighty does not wish to be pestered with requests for mild weather; and to thank him for the flourishing of cress and early lettuces in the garden-plots of these particular people was to make the presumption that he thus puts himself out, not for all mankind, (and rabbit-kind for that matter), but solely for the benefit of the congregation of this chapel-in-the-woods. Perhaps I was unduly irritable, but I detected a smug suggestion that God's great munificence could be brought forward as proof that the present company might look down in unamiable condescension on those beneath them – to wit, the rest of the human race.

There was to be no sermon. Rather, anyone who chose was invited to step forward and give an account of their spiritual progress. These recitations were tedious. Petty sins; trite regrets. I had to struggle not to fidget. When a great commotion without brought the ceremony to a sudden end I welcomed it at first as a relief.

Men with staves and swords barged into the meeting place. The preacher rose up to remonstrate, but the newcomers pushed rudely by him and began to drag out certain persons. Those who had been hearkening quietly, with bowed heads, to their brethren a moment before, now set up a great hullaballoo. Men and women alike rose from their seats to obstruct the arrest of their fellows. In the mêlée I felt myself grasped firmly by the elbows and hustled down an open pathway between the benches and out by a side door.

We were in a narrow space between the building's side and a thicket of hawthorn. A cleft in the tight-growing bushes, like the opening of a cave, showed a passageway into the forest. The man on my left was one of those who had laid hold of me before. He said, 'Go now with all speed. Run. Follow that path. It leads to the sawmill. Thence you can return to the great house without it seeming that you have been here.'

I was flustered and angry. 'I cannot abandon the two ladies,' I said.

'It is better for them, too, that you are clear of this. Run.'

Before I could argue, he and his companion had slipped back into the 'temple' and closed the door. Alone, I heard the shouting grow more vehement, and the ugly clatter of falling furniture. A cat flew past me, its ears back, and vanished into the wood. I went after it.

So much for what I saw and underwent. Let Cecily's letter explain. It is not, though I was momentarily fool enough to imagine it might be, a missive of love.

You are aware that my parents were of the Parliamentary party. My father was not one of those who signed the order for the killing of the late King Charles, but he accepted his share in responsibility for that solemn and awful deed. He himself died soon afterwards.

My Uncle Woldingham, on going abroad for his safety, wisely decided to make of the division of opinion between himself and his sister, not a crack which would ever widen until our family was riven in two, but a strength. He wrote to my mother, asking her to become the steward and, for a while, the mistress of Wychwood. And so it fell out that while my cousin – heir to a great estate – grew up as a wanderer and a mendicant, I lived like a princess, roaming through Wychwood as though it were my own domain.

I was a princess in plain worsted, though, and one who sewed and scrubbed alongside her courtiers. My mother had not estranged herself from her noble family lightly, only in order to return home to live like a lady, careless of lesser folk. She filled Wychwood with those who had been my father's fellow-revolutionaries, and sharers in his tribulations before their party prevailed.

We were like those who first heard Christ's calling – or so we pretended. All was shared. Food, clothing, shelter. The women cared for each other's children. The men laboured side by side. But there were those who cried out loudly against the depravity of the wealthy and the sin of covetousness, who would yet secretly take precious volumes from the library. There were others whose indignation against the ungodly led them to the brutish destruction of things, not theirs, which had been made for God's glory. Paintings were burnt. Tapestries were hauled down to be used as blankets, and allowed to fray and tatter.

My mother began to fear the people whom she had invited to share her home. I want you to understand, Mr Norris, lest you judge us too harshly, that this was a community founded in love. Its members were sincere. But there was too much envy and too much rancour and there were those who took an obnoxious pleasure in the chastising of the ungodly.

Two women tried to leave the community – they were dragged back and beaten and forced to beg forgiveness on their knees before us all in only their smocks. Now people like us are called dissenters, but our brethren would not tolerate dissent. My mother and I slept in the long gallery, along with all the other women, some of whom were such that my mother in her earlier life would never have sat at table with them, let alone lain down alongside them. This in the name of Christian humility, but the pastor who ordered it took the great chamber for himself. In the night he would call upon such women as he said were in need of a shriving. His chosen penitent would be ushered into his room and we would hear them from behind the two sets of oaken doors – he thundering, she crying out to him and to God for mercy – and the fearsome swishing of his staff.

My mother wrote to my father's brother, Pastor Rivers. You met him today. He came with his friends and assumed command of the community. The other pastor left early one morning, striding down the gallery over our poor bedding, his cheeks puce above his tight white kerchief, bellowing like a bullock going to the slaughterhouse. I do not know how he was prevailed upon to go. My mother and Uncle Rivers, wishing to remove their flock from the great house which had so corrupted them, established the settlement in the woods, and there our meeting-house was built.

Cecily's letter goes on to describe a parallel world, one which permeates the one I have inhabited so blindly, as a tincture of juniper dissolves into clear water, transforming its nature unseen. To his Lordship, surveying his domain from his new-fangled sash windows, his park seems a paradise frequented only by those who toil for his pleasure. But it is populous. People cross it on paths that thread through stands of hazel and slip behind dense-growing young ash trees. People tread sunken ways of such ancient use that they traverse the park like trenches, their banks so overgrown with flowering plants that any pedestrian's head passing there-along would show like a bladder bobbing on a foamy green stream.

These comings and goings, furtive as those of fox or stoat, are the means by which a society maintains itself. Trade routes, the paths along which babies are carried to the grandparents who will tend them while their mothers work, the tracks down which the workers plod outward at dawn, and homeward at evening. All these scarcely visible, unsanctioned thoroughfares cross the park. All will become impassable once the wall rises, with its iron gates, its lodges like guard-houses, its rigid distinction between the privileged space within it, and the inferior world without.

I have spoken to my cousin [writes Cecily], but his misfortunes have marred him. He longs for privacy, for a place in which he can confine himself, and where he can play unrebuked. You will have noticed how childlike he is.

With his grand projects, he has thoughtlessly exposed us to the jealousy of the intolerant. Among the labourers who have come to carry out the works there are those who hate and fear people of our persuasion.

Meg was ill-treated by some of the ignorant who, having no authority, have only fists and violent words as weapons. My cousin can quell them. But those who broke in upon us, as you saw, carried the King's warrant. Some of our friends have been carted away – to Oxford, we believe. I fear for them.

She sent me no tender glance yesterday. Nor does her letter contain any word that might not have been addressed to a formal acquaintance.

*

Mr Goodyear fell into step beside me as I walked in the park this morning. It is not only his troop of foresters who acknowledge his authority. I have noticed how the generality of my Lord's people defer to him. I believe that he and Meg Leafield are nearly related. A great estate is like an island, a closed community whose denizens must perforce marry each other, so that it is not uncommon for all to be connected by ties of blood, but these two – an old woman, spry of intellect but creaking of body, and a thriving man who, were he but a gentleman, would be admired as a modern Hercules – have some especial bond.

'You'd think, wouldn't you, sir, that being as proud as he is of that coloured pavement, Lord Woldingham would wish it preserved.' Goodyear had been an onlooker at my Lord's fête at the house of Bacchus.

'Most certainly.'

'So why is he allowing you to drown it?'

I explained that no such thing was intended. The lake-waters, if my calculations prove true, will rise to approximately two feet beneath the level of the Roman villa's floor. 'It will be preserved most carefully. It will make a charming picture, when the undergrowth is cleared away from the ruins and the ancient archway is reflected in the water.'

Goodyear nodded. 'There is another one, you know,' he said.

'Another picture in mosaic?'

'Beneath the chapel.'

'Chapel?' Lord Woldingham laughs at me for being as tedious a parrot as Carisbrooke. But one can gain time, in conversation, by repetition.

'You were there yesterday.'

At Wychwood, there are eyes in every tree.

'Be so kind as to tell me about it.'

'When Miss Cecily's uncle was choosing a spot for his meeting-house, as he called it, he asked me for my opinion.'

Nearly all those who now serve their returned Lord have passed years living here without him. Only gradually will he discover what they know about his land.

'I took him to that place because the ground is level and easily worked. There's water. And there's the pebble-picture. I said to him, "The two lads will bring you luck."'

He waited. I took my cue, parrot-fashion. 'The two lads?'

'That's the picture, you see. Two boys. Little ones. Lying as it were, head to tail, to make a ring. There's a story about them.'

I had only to nod for him to proceed.

'There was once a king's son, and in the same city there was a wise woman, and the wise woman had a son too. And there came a great rain, and the waters rose until there was no more difference between the land and the sea. And all the animals crowded onto hilltops that stood up out of the water like islands. And the people gathered there too.'

Goodyear had adopted an incantatory style of speech, as storytellers do, but he lapsed back into his normal pitch to deliver a piece of commentary. 'It's much like the story of the great flood in Noah's time, you'll be thinking, sir?' I nodded again. He went on.

'The King saw that there were no fields to till, and no green stuff for the cattle to eat. And he called the wise woman. And he said to her, "How am I to save my people?" She said, "You must take the thing you love most in the world and set it in a boat and send it out onto the water, and the rains will cease." So the King set his crown on a damask cushion, and placed it in an ivory casket, and put it in a boat, and caused that boat to be launched out onto the current. He stood on the shore, weeping and wringing his hands as the boat went swiftly towards the horizon, and he saw that it was seized by a whirlpool, and sucked down into the belly of the flood. He waited then for the rain to cease, but instead the wind grew wilder, and where the rain had fallen before like water gushing from a drainpipe, it began now to fall like cascades from heaven.

'The King called for the wise woman and told her what he had done, and she said, "What a man feels for a circle of gold is covetousness. What a man feels for a crown is a lust for power. I spoke of love."

'The King had a horse. He had bought the creature from a merchant who came each year from the East with a ship laden with wonderful things. The horse was faster than any other in the country and its coat shone like quicksilver. It knew its master so well, and was so obedient to him, that when the King rode upon it it was as though he had become like the centaur, in which man and beast are as one. That horse, too, the King sent out onto the waters. That horse, too, was swallowed down by the flood. And instead of ceasing, the rain fell so thick it was as though the ocean had mounted up in one great watery mass, to fall again on earth.

'The King called for the wise woman again. He said, "I have given the crown, which is the token of my magnificence and my power. I have given the horse, that performed my will as readily as my hand does, and that could outrun the wind, and that would take sugar from my palm with lips that were as soft as velvet and as feeling as a musician's fingertips." She said, "What kind of a father are you?" And he understood her, and he fell to his knees on the ground, and his gorgeous robes were sodden with the wetness that was all around, and he said, "No. Not for my kingdom. Not for all my people. Not my son." And the wise woman said, "You must." He said, "What you ask of me is cruel. You too have a son. Would you do so?" and she said, "I would and I will."

'So the young prince came out of the palace and the wise woman's son was waiting for him by the shore. The two boys had been born on the same day, and they were as like as your left foot is to your right foot. They were both dressed in smocks of sky-blue, and they sat side by side in the boat, and none knew any more which was the prince and which was the cunning woman's child. And the boat was launched upon the flood.

'The whirlpool seized it, as it had seized the others, and then the two boys held out their arms to each other, and they tilted their heads back as dancers do when they dance in a ring. The boat went from under their feet and was lost to them in the depths of the ocean. The spinning water whirled them about, but, as it turned them, so they turned within it, and their circled arms were as a wheel laid flat upon the water, and that wheel turned faster and ever faster, till those whirling boys rose into the air, and the speed of their spinning was such that it carried them on upwards until all that could be seen of them was a circlet of blueness against the terrible black of the storm clouds. And the rain stopped absolutely, and the clouds were driven from the sky. The King and the wise woman stood together watching, with tears clouding their sight, but had they been as sharp-eyed as killer birds they would have seen their children no more.'

Goodyear had adopted the pose I have seen storytellers assume on fairgrounds, legs braced apart for stability, hands on hips, his face upturned as though he sought words in the air. I was greatly impressed by his tale. I was curious to know its origin. The boys on the Roman pavement, I felt certain, must be the Gemini of the zodiac, for these Roman fragments often treat astrological themes. I feared, though, to offend my companion if I made a parade of my scholarship.

He passed both hands over his head and scratched it. 'That's the story I have heard,' he said.

'I am much obliged to you for it. Is it . . .' I hesitated. 'Is it one you heard from your parents?'

My instinct had been correct. He acted as though enquiry was improper. 'It is from this place,' he said, and looked at me teasingly.

We were in the far part of the park, above the ruined villa. Beneath us we could see Lord Woldingham and his wife strolling with their attendants along the valley floor. He offered her his arm and they walked together, their companions falling back, to the boggy place where their child had died. There they stood, apparently without speaking, for a considerable time.

*

When I'd finished writing in my journal last night I fell asleep as though dropping through a trap.

A commotion awoke me before it was light. I shoved aside a pillow so that it covered over my papers. Mr Rose, who is lodged near me, was already in the open doorway. 'Come, Norris,' he said.

I followed him along the corridor that leads into the oldest part of the house. He ushered me into a room holding a narrow bed and a wooden bucket. A bunch of dusty lavender, curiously bound with faded blue ribbon, was suspended from a hook in the window embrasure. The sheets were smoothed.

'This is where Meg Leafield was quartered,' he said.

Seeing me still baffled, he went on.

'She is gone. I heard a scuffling past my door but when I looked out there was no one there. I think, Mr Norris, that we should follow her.'

A mouthful of water, boots, coat, muffler. I was ready. A resentful lad brought out our horses. Rose set off at a canter. At the entrance to the holly grove we dismounted and left the animals to graze. In the midst of the wood we left the path and trod softly to a little hummock. Lying flat on its apex, we could peer through the topmost branches of the trees before us, and see the clearing and the meeting-house spread beneath. The sun rising behind us set a blush in the sky and flooded the scene with long shadows and caressing light.

A great concourse of women. At its centre stood Meg Leafield. And so, the only male in sight, did the boy who threw a ball at me. Meg seemed to be pulling at his clothes.

'You've been here,' said Rose.

'I have.'

'You recognise that boy.'

'You know that I have seen him before. He knocked me down.'

'But do you understand who he is?'

I stared, mute.

'He's Cecily's boy,' said Rose. 'Edward.'

The boy Edward's shirt was off. The women were handing garments to Meg. He stood quiescent in his breeches. Meg helped him gently into new clothes far finer than those he had shed.

A lawn shirt. Stockings and high boots. An embroidered waist-coat and a sky-blue coat. I saw what was being done. My hands were shaking.

'His cousin, then,' I said. 'They seem to be of an age.'

'We must stop this,' said Rose.

He scrambled to his feet and ran aslant down the slope, as

clumsy as a charging boar, trampling small branches and sending stones clattering. I followed.

The other women looked round startled but Meg was unperturbed. Rose leapt the last few feet, and landed amongst them, impelled forward like a falling rock by the speed of his own going. He is a stocky man, broad-beamed and short-legged. I was almost as nonplussed by his urgency now as the women were. I slipped and scrambled after him with dread shadowing my mind and chilling my limbs.

My circuitous return from this spot two days previously had allowed me to calculate its position in relation to the great house, and to the course of the stream. Not far from where we stood is a pond, much obscured by bulrushes, but nevertheless tolerably deep. This pond is the embryo from which one of my lakes will grow. From the height where we had lain in hiding I had seen it glint.

Rose had Meg by the shoulders and was shaking her. I would have restrained him, but the women were quicker. They haled him off her and wrapped themselves around him, disabling him as a great sea-monster might disable a ship by embracing it with its tentacles. I hung back. Meg stepped up to me and to my astonishment took me gently by the hand.

'Your friend misunderstands us. We intend no harm to this boy, as we have done no harm to the other.'

'I am at a loss,' I said. 'I am as puzzled by your proceedings as I am ignorant of what interpretation Mr Rose would put upon them.'

'He thinks we are witches,' she said, the last word uttered with derision.

Rose, still under restraint, was shaking his head vigorously.

'I sincerely doubt it,' I said. 'Mr Rose is a scientist. He loves lucidity, and measures the world with set-square and rule. He is not one to babble of sorcery.'

'Perhaps not, but he thinks that we are.'

Someone stepped out of the gaggle of onlookers and took my other arm. It was Cecily. 'I will subdue him,' she said to Meg.

And so she did. With her hand in the crook of my elbow I quieted. A man in love is as spiritless as a lapdog. She took me to a heap of logs, and sat upon it beside me. We watched in silence as Meg finished dressing the boy.

'Say what you will,' I said to Cecily *sotto voce*, 'this is a kind of conjuring.'

The boy, Edward, was now the living copy of his dead cousin. He gazed steadily at Cecily, who inclined her head as though in approbation.

'Who is his father?' I asked. It was unmannerly. All this mystification made me tart.

'In the community in which I was raised all children were loved by all. All the men were their fathers.' Her voice was low and even.

'That is not an answer.'

'I agree with you.'

'Then who?'

'What is your motive for enquiring?'

'I aspire to be your husband. I would know who you are.'

Her gaze was still fixed upon the boy.

'Lest I shame you?'

I made no reply, but waited.

'Mr Norris, I will not be questioned.' Cecily stood and took young Edward by the hand. They went together in the direction of the pond. Meg led the other women after, Rose captive among them. I stayed, ignored.

A gang of masons was coming along the track from the quarry. Great blocks of stone, granular like gigantic sugar lumps, rocked on makeshift carts – tree-trunks laid over the axles of solid wooden wheels. Men stood on or by them, watching the ropes, ready to holler out if one of these man-made boulders showed a tendency to shift. The six horses were as heavy-built as bulldogs and twelve times as tall and long. The strength and sweat being expended on giving Lord Woldingham his privacy would serve to construct a sizeable town.

Saplings of hazel and elder screened the one group from the other. Only from my standpoint was it possible to see men and women both. A man rocking atop a boulder, like a seaman balancing on a spar, gave a shout. The women startled and froze, only Cecily and young Edward walking on oblivious.

The men moved into action with awful slowness. The horses were halted; wooden chocks were wedged behind the wheels to stop the cart and its load rolling backwards. The men, whose legs and arms were already sheathed in leather (quarrying is dangerous work), shrugged their jerkins on, despite the warmth of the day. Deliberately, they picked up clubs or knotted ropes. Cecily and the boy had crossed the track now, and were silhouetted against the green water.

The men barged through the undergrowth. The group of women tightened. I saw Rose shake himself free and step forward, a silly little tub of a man. These men were his team. He raised both arms, as though surrendering to them, or inviting an embrace. They divided, and passed him by, as stream-water passes by a saturated log. As they approached the women they were wagging the tongues in their mouths in a song that was no song. Dig a dig a dig a dig a dig a dig. Guttural. The human voice used not to communicate, but to terrorise.

I knew that to intervene would be useless, but I ran forward yelling with all the breath in me and waving my arms as though to fight off a swarm of wasps. I had not breakfasted. Tiny coloured sparks seemed to obscure my vision. As the clubs began to pound and the ropes to whack, I saw Cecily and Edward, his coat as brilliant as speedwells in the grass, step from the verge into the pond. They neither paused nor looked back. The water was still. Clear of the shadowy wood, their figures were brightly illuminated. I could see them plain, from the paired chestnut heads to the wooden heels of their sturdy shoes. Beneath, their reflections hung from them, suspended upside down, foot-sole from foot-sole. They stepped on the surface of the water as easily as though it were clear green glass.

1961

Friday

All the smells in the changing hut were peculiar. Indoor smells were warm – floor-wax, ironed sheets, toast. Outdoor ones were fresh and wet. These fell into neither category. There was the urinous whiff from the rush matting. The tang of creosote. Rubbery smells from bathing caps and the thick soles of sandals. The dusty breath of the high yew hedges, the aura of the overhanging pine trees, which smelt nothing like her father's pine shaving soap and whose needles covered the ground behind the hut with a carpet which was at once prickly, if an upturned needle spiked your foot, and as silky as vegetable fur.

Nell and her brother came almost every morning. It had to be mornings because by the time they'd digested their lunch the tall trees' shade had made the unheated pool a rectangle of green-black chill. The pool wasn't designed for children. There was a coir-sleeved diving board, springy as a catapult, but there was no shallow end. They had to climb in down the metal ladder, goose-bumps rising as the water reached the ruching of Nell's bathing dress, or Dickie's matted wool trunks. A clumsy turn and a plop backwards into the inner tubes of car tyres that served them as coracles. Her mother swam up-down, up-down, up-down, but Nell and Dickie just drifted, jack-knifed as though in hammocks, their lips gradually turning blue as their noses burnt pink.

It was quite different when other grown-ups came. Her mother was no distraction. You only noticed your mother when she went away. But when Mrs Rossiter came and sat down beside Mummy on another of the wicker chairs, and got Mr Underhill to bring a tray, and started being amusing (all the grown-ups agreed Mrs Rossiter was amusing), the drift of Nell's thoughts between the blank sky and the shivering water was obstructed. It was Mrs Rossiter's pool. It was so kind of her to let them use it. But Nell was beginning to understand, from the way her mother's voice changed, and from the shoulders-back propriety with which she sat to drink her lemon barley water, that people being kind could make you feel worse rather than better.

Nell was interested in Mrs Rossiter, in the leopard-spotted chiffon scarf she wore round her neck, and the way her voice came grating, not flowing, from her mouth. She had no children. Her pug-dog was called Lupin. She knew how to drive an aeroplane.

That Friday it was not Mrs Rossiter, but her husband's niece, who came through the arch in the yew hedge that led onto the winding path through shrubberies, down to the croquet lawn, and beyond that to the stony terrace with the huge magnolia tree where they sometimes had tea. She was as tall as a grown-up but she wasn't one quite. She pulled her dress over her head and there was her bathing dress already on and she held her nose with one hand and stuck the other straight up in the air as though to make a pole she could slide down and jumped straight in.

The waves made Nell's tyre rock and slurped over the sides of the pool. The girl came up and with her hair wet she looked like a child (ladies wore bathing caps). She bounced a little in the water and said, 'I'm a dolphin,' and began circling the tyres doing funny little dives which made her bottom stick up into the air each time her head disappeared. Dickie giggled. Nell was too frightened to begin with, but then she began to laugh too and the girl seemed to like that and she dived more and more and sometimes she'd shoot up so that she was standing up into the air as far as her waist and she blew out water like a whale. Nell laughed so much a warm gurgling feeling filled her up and her throat ached. Everything seemed very bright and noisy. All that flying water catching the sun like mirrored ribbons. All that splashing and laughter in that hedged-in space in which her mother was always anxious that they shouldn't shriek. It was as though the girl didn't know and wouldn't care how polite they always had to be when they came up to Wychwood.

Nell didn't entirely like it. It was as though the pool garden, an enclosure so rich in significance she would dream of it for the rest of her life, was just water, the topiary just bushes. But the girl, who was called Flossie, seemed to her wonderful.

Antony

There was always something a mite humiliating about the way Lil Rossiter used to whistle me up for a weekend. It wasn't the last-minute invitations I minded. I've never really understood why it should be considered a slight to be treated as a reliable substitute for a defaulting guest. What rankled, however often I was subjected to it, was the lack of a greeting.

Of course I was always expected. The car waiting to meet me at the station, and the suavity with which Underhill dispatched me to my room, testified each time to the fact that I was at Wychwood because my hostess had wished that I should be. But you would never have known it from her vague 'Ah, Antony . . .' as she saw me coming into the marble hall at drinks time.

It wasn't only me. I saw her being equally offhand with others. But for them there would be a compensating moment later, when she turned on them with a quick smile and did that startling thing of leaning over and talking right into the other's ear as though what she was saying – usually quite banal in fact – was so intimate and risqué it must be treated as entirely confidential.

With me she tended to remain, right through until Monday morning, as nonchalant as she was with the servants or the boring wives.

I suppose it sounds as though I didn't really like Lil, and perhaps that was true then, but I always welcomed her call. We were connected in a tenuous way – step-relatives rather than blood ones. She was three years older, and she'd made a fuss of me at family weddings and so on when I was a child. Grown up, she still took me for granted as one might a sibling (neither of us had any real ones). I was more than presentable (I'm still pretty good-looking for my age). I was a useful companion for her outings. We gossiped. She'd insist I go with her (usually at very short notice and with no consideration for the fact I had a job to do) to give an opinion on any picture she was buying. On slow mornings in the gallery I would ring her, getting a brusque brush-off one time in three, but on other occasions long, satirical accounts of her last night's doings at Quaglino's. In company she virtually ignored me. I was like one of Racine's confidantes, a person of negligible interest *per se*, who was party to some conversations that were very interesting indeed.

I don't think she ever for a moment realised back then that – begrudgingly enthralled by her as I was – it was someone else whose presence gave those weekends, for me, their marvellous bouquet.

For the last few years I have been subjected to repeated questioning. I have been asked to recreate in meticulous detail encounters that were furtive and disappointing at the time and look shabby in retrospect. That sounds sexual, but I'm talking here not about my incompetent attempts to gratify desires I'd scarcely acknowledged to myself then, but about my even less successful go at making the world a better place. The sessions are frightening, but also – to my surprise – almost unbearably tedious. There is, though, an unlooked-for benefit. Sullenly obedient, hauling up memories, I find, trapped in the net with all the slimy stuff, pearls and bright fish. My interrogators (absurdly overdramatic word for these human clipboards) get banal information. But I find lost time, transformed into treasure trove.

They're making their record of me. This – fragmentary and self-indulgent – is mine. I'm not particularly keen on examining my life. Sorry Socrates: but surely we should all be licensed to consign our past silliness to oblivion. Sorry Freud: repression seems to me a jolly useful thing. But I like taking out little bits of my life, and looking at them. I kept a sketchy kind of diary (some of it encrypted of course) and now I'm patching the gaps with memories I've netted. People have photograph albums, don't they? Same kind of thing.

The weekend I'm remembering was the last of the summer, not because summer was over but because the grouse season had begun and the Rossiters would be going north. They both shot. I don't think Christopher did so with much enthusiasm away from home. Presiding over days when his estate was laid out in all its mellow loveliness for guests come to kill his pheasants was gratifying, but he was really more of a fishing man. He was self-contained, dreamy even. But he could strike a salmon with a swiftness that was matched by the unexpectedly sharp humour with which he responded to any misguided smart-alec's attempt to underestimate him. Lil, on the other hand, loved everything about shooting. It was very unusual in those days for a woman to join the guns and she knew what a piquant figure she cut – dainty and lethal in pleated skirts and tight-waisted tweed jackets. She was a genuinely good shot, and it amused her to see how that affronted some men.

So that August weekend at Wychwood had the kind of languor to it of a siesta before a taxing evening. Soon there would be sleeper-cars and sport and then – for some of the house-party – the brisk back-to-work of September. But we were still in the season of moving like somnolent dogs from one patch of shade to another. Iced coffee under the cedar tree. Picnic tea down by the upper lake in the hideous pagoda of which Christopher's father had been so proud. Long afternoon hours when it seemed as though everyone had vanished, when the only living beings announcing their presence were the peacocks with their yearning cries.

*

The estate office. A long room by the stables. Plentiful windows, but set high in the walls, so that although the low, late sunlight comes in, the men indoors can't see into the yard. Whitewashed walls. Shiny oilcloth maps. A brick floor worn down in the middle like an aged bed.

At a green-baize-covered table, Wychwood's cabinet is in session.

Christopher Rossiter (head of state, or rather, proprietor) is at the centre of one side of the table. Hugo Lane (Nell's father and Rossiter's prime minister, or land agent) is on his left. Across the table, with the sun in their eyes, sit Mr Armstrong (minister for pheasants) and Mr Goodyear (minister for trees).

Armstrong is tall and gaunt, with the curt manner of a military leader. On shooting days, when he is marshalling his small army of under-keepers and beaters, he asserts his authority with the cock of a tufted silver eyebrow or, to a beater who strays out of line, a guttural roar. Mr Goodyear is a generation younger and physically his opposite – stout of body, florid of face. Both grew up within a mile of where they are sitting. Both spend hours and hours of every day alone in the woods. Both are greatly respected by their men, but Goodyear, who drinks in the Plough and is celebrated county-wide as a storyteller, is the more loved. They have first names of course, but neither Christopher nor Hugo would dream of using them. None of those present have ever wondered whether this formality is courteous or insulting. Hugo calls Christopher 'Christopher' when they're alone together. Christopher sometimes responds in kind, and sometimes calls him 'Lane'. This use of the surname is socially neutral: it means only that they have reverted for a while to the manners of their school-days. In referring to each other in the presence of the other men, they use the Mr.

Mr Hutchinson, clerk to the assembly (and to the estate), sits at the end of the table to keep the minutes, holding the fat blue-marbled fountain pen his wife gave him for their wedding anniversary. The matching propelling pencil is still, and will for years remain, nestling unused in its white-satin-lined presentation box. Christopher, just back, with huge relief, from London, is in a grey suit. Hugo is in jodhpurs. All the men wear ties.

Hugo – This won't take long. You'll be busy getting Doris ready for her triumph next week, Armstrong.

Armstrong's nervy little spaniel always wins the canine beauty contest at the village fête. Now he turns aside the implied compliment gracefully.

Armstrong – I gather Mr Green's going to give us quite a surprise.

Goodyear – Giant figs, is it?

Christopher – Any figs at all are a miracle in Oxfordshire. I hope he gets the Cup. But now, Mr Lane thought . . . (*tails off*).

Hugo – Yes, let's rough out the drives for the first three shooting days. If we know what needs doing before Mr Rossiter goes to Scotland, we can get cracking on it while he's away. Armstrong, how's Church Break looking?

Armstrong – Crawling. Crawling with them it is. You better get your eye in, Mr Lane. Time to get the clay pigeons out, I reckon.

Mr Hutchinson sniggers. Hugo Lane is an outstandingly good shot, and proud of it. Armstrong is teasing him.

Goodyear – You're going to have to be careful not to shoot these ramblers, though.

The others are taken aback.

Christopher – Ramblers?

Goodyear – There's a fellow down in the pub pretty well every night now banging on about rights of way. He's got this idea there's an old, old road went along Leafield Ride to the Cider Well, and all the way on alongside the lakes, through the park and home farm to meet the Oxford road. He's going to walk it, he says, and no one can stop him, he says, because it's a public highway. And I've heard he's going to do it on Saturdays.

Christopher (*to Hugo*) – Do you know about this?

Hugo – No. Who is this chap?

Goodyear – He makes furniture. Bashes the chairs around to make them look old and sells them to those mugginses in Burford. Good-looking boy. Just moved into the village a month or two back, but he's nephew to the groom at Lea Place. The thing is, he's got other people worked up about it. Says there'll be a hundred of them soon, and they'll just walk wherever there's an old green road, and if you try to stop them they'll take you to court.

Christopher – Can they do that?

Hugo – Not if I have anything to do with it.

Christopher – But really. Legally?

Goodyear – He says you can't keep people out. Not if there's a right of way.

Hugo and Armstrong exchange glances.

Hugo (*to Christopher*) – Bunny had some of these chaps marching through the home farm at Swinbrooke, day after day, and the police wouldn't lift a finger.

Armstrong – If these jokers are running around on a shooting day . . .

He doesn't need to finish the sentence. All five men present can imagine the consequences. Pheasants disturbed before the drive, or flying back during it. Dogs all confused. One of these rambler-types stepping out in front of the guns, playing silly buggers. And then, oh Christ, if one of them got shot.

Goodyear – They're going to ruin the countryside, that's what they're going to do. Someone lit a fire by the Cider Well three weeks back, left a patch of black earth as big as a bicycle wheel.

Hugo – Actually, that would have been me. Dickie's birthday. We were cooking sausages.

Christopher winks at Goodyear, who grins. The way Hugo indulges his children is a running joke. Armstrong remains stony-faced. He once found Nell and Dickie digging a tunnel under the fence around one of his breeding pens. They wanted to help the baby pheasants escape.

Hugo (*bracing himself*) – I'll go and see this fellow. What's his name, Goodyear?

Goodyear – Mark Brown.

Christopher (*who has stayed calm through this exchange*) – What about the hellebore?

The forest is home to a rare strain of hellebore. It's an unlovely plant with black antennae sprouting from the centre of its greeny-yellow bracts, of interest only to botanists, but to them a treasure. It grows nowhere else in the British Isles. Hugo looks at Christopher, as he frequently does, with the startled expression of one hearing excellent good sense spoken by a cat. Christopher is so gentle and so disinclined to project his own personality that it is easy to forget, not only that he is lord of this domain, but also that he is very acute.

Hugo – Yes! We can get those Nature Conservancy bores back.

Everyone is cheered. The Nature Conservancy people tried, two years ago, to declare Wychwood a precious relic of England's primaeval forest, to be protected in all ways possible from change and development. They made quite a to-do about the hellebore. Then Christopher and Hugo between them managed, by polite unhelpfulness, to make what they saw as this unwarrantable bit of bossiness go away. Now their old adversaries are possible allies.

Goodyear also gets the point. If he's not going to be allowed to scythe the hellebores, controlling the undergrowth the way he and his father before him have been doing for over forty years, well, perhaps that's a small price to pay for having his woods declared out of bounds for towny interlopers. To Goodyear, whose house is three-quarters of a mile from the nearest tarmacked road, even the villagers are townies.

Hugo – I'll go and have a word with this fellow Brown – see where that gets us. Okey-doke. So. Armstrong. We start with Church Break, and then?

And so the rambler question is put out of mind. Half an hour later, their heads full of autumnal images, the men disperse, Armstrong to put his pretty bitch through her paces yet again, Goodyear to walk the track which leads through the forest to his cottage, Christopher to play the host, Hugo to retrieve his horse from the stables, submit silently to the groom's loquacious judgement on her unfitness and ride her home, cantering down the avenue muffled with dark late-summer leaves, Wully scampering along behind.

*

Nicholas was sleek, talkative and busy. Seeing him at Paddington, Antony had a momentary desire to dodge behind a pillar. This impulse overcame Antony on any chance meeting, a shaming residual trace of the gauche boy he had almost succeeded in over-painting with his adult persona: Antony the effortless conversationalist, Antony who was so adroit in embarrassing situations, Antony who could charm clients into believing that a meeting resulting in a transaction immensely profitable to himself was an engagement he had set up purely so that they could delight in each other's company. It was that Antony who took over now (he really liked Nicholas), and waved and strode forward, throttling, without fuss, regret for the novel he could otherwise have been reading on the train.

'I suppose we're going to the same place?'

'Ant. Good. Good. I want you to tell me everything there is to know about Germany.'

'I can only tell you what I know, which is mostly about Altdorfer. I take it that's not what you want.'

'It'll do to start with. Are you going First? Do you think we could get teacakes?'

Antony, who had a second-class ticket, didn't answer the former question. They climbed into the dining-car, and settled in. Dull-metal pots of tea and hot water. White damask tablecloths and napkins. Heavy knives. Seats upholstered in dense stuff like brutally shaved carpeting, prickly as burrs. Tiny dishes of raspberry jam.

'I've got to do something on Berlin.' Nicholas wrote for a newspaper. He liked to present himself as an amateur whose accurate summations of complex political situations were all the more wonderful for the fact that he brought so little prior knowledge to them. He did not expect anyone to believe in this act: he would have been affronted if they did. It made for good conversation, though. Even off-duty, at Lil's house-party, he would be drawing everyone out, and giving pleasure as he did so. There is nothing so flattering as being treated as though you might have something useful to say.

Nicholas himself was not to be drawn. His bonhomie was a blackout blind. Gratified by his questioning, acquaintances forgot to question him in turn.

'I won't be much help to you. It was over five years ago now, and I was in Munich.'

'Ah yes. Art and naked gymnasts in the Englischer Garten.' Each of these men – both bachelors in their thirties – had wondered, without pressing curiosity, about the other's sexual orientation.

'Yes, and Bavaria isn't very German – it's full of ochre Italianate palaces. Actually, I don't know really where Germany is.'

'That's been the trouble, hasn't it? Trying to cobble together a fatherland out of a lot of squabbling siblings. Attempting the impossible puts people into a bad temper. And then they lash out.'

'We do it too, of course. Inventing our nation.'

'Yes.'

Both at once looked out of the window. The Thames Valley cradled the railway line as it skirted water meadows in which black and white cows plodded. Willows marked out the curves of the invisible river. Hanging beechwoods curtained the horizon. Low sun on a square church tower. They both laughed, catching each other's thought.

'Perhaps we really are living in the place you see on tourist-board posters,' said Antony.

'Yes, and look,' rapping a pot-lid, 'there's honey still for tea. But I'm not letting you off. How much did your Bavarian friends care about their Prussian brothers? What would they sacrifice to hang on to Berlin?'

'I never had that sort of conversation. I was there to see the Alte Pinakothek, which our side had smashed to smithereens.'

'Twelve years before.'

'Nicholas, twelve years is nothing. The place was wrecked. The house I stayed in was the only one in the street left standing. The family had lost two sons. I was sleeping in the younger one's room, and for all they knew he could have been killed by an elder brother of mine. I was very polite and so were they. We didn't talk about the war. We didn't talk about the occupation, or about bombing, or about my hostess's nervous tic. We talked a little bit about politics, but only as if it was an entirely theoretical subject on which none of us could possibly hold a personal opinion. We certainly certainly certainly weren't going to talk about German nationhood.'

Nicholas looked quizzical. 'Conversation must have been a little bloodless.'

Antony laughed. 'It's unbelievable, isn't it. Already we're so bored of peace that "bloodless" is a pejorative term. Of course it was bloodless. That was the point.'

'But seriously, you're such a flâneur. Whatever you did or didn't talk about over the dumplings at home, you went out. I know you. You must have met people.'

'No. Sorry. Up early for a walk. The Pinakothek every morning. Library every afternoon. No dumplings, but an awful lot of pork and mushrooms. Then evenings writing my paper on Altdorfer. To which I owe the job that allows me, as you say, to gad about now.'

A pause. Nicholas, thwarted, casting around for a more promising approach. Antony – smooth, obliging, emollient Antony – opaque.

Ticket collector. Antony's second-class ticket. Embarrassment masked by jollity. And, soon, the car awaiting them at Finstock Halt.

*

Nell and her father went up to the big house after tea. Daddy drove the Land Rover, with Wully's chin resting on his left shoulder. Nell was on the bonnet, sitting in the spare wheel, her small hands scrabbling for a purchase on the rubber, her hair tangling in front of her eyes. Her mother didn't know she did this. Nell, constantly aware of how she might be jolted out and tumble under the front wheels and be squashed, was terrified, but she never said so. Fear was the price she gladly paid for the privilege of being her father's fellow-conspirator.

Summer after tea was the best time. As the sun descended the flowers turned luminous. And the grown-ups grew brighter and strange too, changing into their evening clothes. Mr Rossiter met them on the steps, already dressed in a silk smoking jacket patterned with twisty petal shapes. Paisley – a new word for Nell.

They looked to see, as they always did, whether the giant brown dog-statues flanking the door had a present for Wully. There was a sugar lump between the left-hand one's front paws. Then they went through the house, and out onto the terrace that overlooked the part of the park where the land swept down to the lake and up again to the double row of conker trees screening the village nearly a mile away. This was the Rossiters' special bit of park, where ancient oaks stood isolated in deer-nibbled grass and where any rider was exposed to the stare of all the house's high sash windows. It was grander and plainer than the expanse behind, where Nell's family picnicked between the avenues and played kick-the-can around stands of bracken, or where she could ride her pony through the copses alongside her father, hidden from anyone who might laugh at her still needing the leading-rein.

'They need feeding, Nell,' said Mr Rossiter. Down the middle of the terrace ran a canal, where giant goldfish lurked. They were immeasurably old, their shell-like pallor uncanny. Nell suspected them of cannibalism – why else would the little red and orange fish flashing above them never get a chance to become as gross and slow as they? She had a recurring dream, from which she would wake screaming, in which someone she couldn't see would say, in a gentle, insinuating voice, something she could never afterwards remember. These bloated fish, glimmering in murky water, were ominous in the same kind of whispering way.

She went to the little building at the end of the canal, where the fish food, smelling of cowpats, was kept in an enamel bin. With its frilly arched windows and stone pinnacles, this pavilion was Nell's architectural ideal. Wychwood itself, its garden front a pilastered cliff of grey-tawny stone, was too grand for her to comprehend it. In all her daydreams the princess with waist-length golden hair and the ever-sympathetic identical twin sister lived in a palace that was the fish-food house built large.

'Who've we got so far?' her father was saying. He knew, and so did Nell, that house-parties were Mrs Rossiter's treat, and that Mr Rossiter was apt to slip away from them after dinner to go fishing. Nell's father was Mr Rossiter's agent but also his ally in wife-teasing, guest-dodging and – up to a carefully judged point – making fun of the people Mrs R asked down from London.

'You've met Flossie.' That was the girl who had swum with them that morning. 'Jolly girl. There's two more just come off the train. Antony.' He was another regular visitor. Nell liked him because he always spoke to her but she could never understand his jokes. 'Nicholas. And there's a couple Lil took to in Scotland last year. Helen and Benjie. Lovely woman. Husband runs a restaurant and wears suede shoes.'

Nell's attention was on the fish. The faded monsters lay still while the brilliant tiddlers snapped at the smelly flakes. The insects, called water boatmen although the whole point of them was that they didn't need boats, skated over the meniscus, as confident as Jesus. So that story might be ordinary-true as well as deep-down-true. (Nell's mother had explained the difference, but only the Bible was allowed the latter. If Nell said anything that wasn't ordinary-true, then it was a lie.) Perhaps Jesus had the same kind of special feet. She stared as hard as she could at the insects, but even when she opened her eyes so wide they felt they might pop out she couldn't see their feet at all. Looked at under a microscope, might they be like tiny canoes?

'We won't use the pool after this weekend,' said Mr Rossiter. 'Get them to empty it on Monday, will you, Hugo, and refill it ready for when we get back? It's turning into weed soup, isn't it, Nell?'

Her father was nodding, but Nell couldn't say a word. It was true that the walls of the pool were coated with green slime, and the pine needles floating on it clustered into fairy log-jams, but wouldn't it be rude to admit it? And anyway she was dismayed. She knew that refilling the pool took two whole days, and afterwards the water was much, much colder. 'Oh can we swim tomorrow, then?' she said.

'No, Nell,' said her father, quick-sharp. They never came up to the pool when there were weekend guests. But 'Yes,' said Mr Rossiter, and when her father looked awkward he went on, 'just this time. Flossie said she had fun with the children this morning.'

Helen

When people first meet us they think, what can Helen see in that buffoon. And then after a while, not long at all usually, they think, how can he stand her. She's so dull. Next they're inviting us to stay. And then they're never going to invite us to stay again because Benj has made a pass. At the hostess, or the host. Or the dog, for goodness sake. When he became besotted with that absurd white fluffy thing of Cressida's. Wouldn't leave it alone all weekend. But more likely the teenage daughter, or the au pair. And then they begin to think, she's so dignified. And clever. And you don't notice it at once, but isn't she beautiful. What can she see in that clown.

Lil understands, I think. She and Christopher aren't an obvious pair either. I like coming here. I'm glad she took me up, as one might take up *petit point*, or the clarinet, or a pretty orphan. Relationships based on caprice suit me. I take what comes my way. Benj floated in and scooped me up as though I was a small hairy dog. No one had ever treated me with such disrespect, and I found it restful. I don't suppose we'll be together for ever, even though he depends on me more than he knows. In bed, we are harmonious.

He drove down today, with Guy in the front, so they could talk, he said. He likes being the raffish uncle. He offers the boy cigarettes, which he refuses, and takes him out to Muriel's or the French Club. Showing off. Benj isn't really a bohemian. He likes to lunch at the Ritz. But he knows the young are impressed by that kind of thing. Guy is nothing like as snubbing as most teenagers but this afternoon he barely spoke – he gets car-sick. Benj rambled on. His ridiculous car is another thing I like about my husband. I made a nest on the backseat, with the fur rug full of zipped-up pockets for your Thermos or your knitting. Of course Benj doesn't knit but he likes ingenious contraptions. That thing like a fire extinguisher which supposedly creates soda water.

I read through my bit on mazes. If I can have a draft ready this week the typist at the Institute will make sense of it before term begins. Another thing that others might resent, but I find a relief, is that nobody ever asks about my work. Nicholas did as soon as he met me, because he's inquisitive, but that's different from being interested. I think it helped him bring me into focus (serious, unworldly, perhaps a bit of a crank) but he didn't actually want to know about it. I've liked all the journalists I've met, but they don't have much range.

After we dropped Guy with his friend – that drowning look he gave, the ordeal of a whole weekend's politeness – I got in the front and Benj fiddled with the radio and we sang along together. Everything about Frank Sinatra is abhorrent to me: the cockiness, the smug voice, the assumed sophistication. All polish, no patina. But, for better or worse, I sing along.

We've been given the tapestry room. North-facing. That must be a lucky coincidence; no one here would give a toss about the way sunlight fades vegetable dyes. But our window, mullioned and small-paned, is in the centre of Wychwood's axis. Sitting here at the tiny writing table (the bigger one, as usual, is cluttered with useless stuff – three-panelled mirror and silver brushes and crystal caskets full of cotton-wool balls), I'm looking straight, or nearly straight, down the beech avenue to a church tower. So arrogant. So grand. Before the other wing was built, in the days when this must have been the best bedroom, people were being killed for entertaining the wrong kind of religious faith. Here, though, a church tower is a gazebo, just something to close the view.

I'll wear my grey dress with tight sleeves tonight, and amethyst beads. No point trying to out-sparkle Lil. I'm the serious one. A bit fierce. What can she see in that buffoon?

*

At drinks time Benjie was not wearing suede shoes, but a smoking jacket of patchwork silk in purple and pink, and he and Lil were both so animated that between them they created an uproar. At Wood Manor, though, it was so still you could feel the night falling as stealthily as dropping eyelids. Nell, bathed and in her nightie, looked out of her bedroom window, the one shaped like an egg, and saw her mother walking between the herbaceous borders towards the summerhouse where her father was clattering the ice in the martini jug. He wore a smoking jacket like Mr Rossiter's and his velvet slippers with gold letters on the toes. Her mother was in Nell's favourite dress. Blue and silver stripes, the stripes turning the long skirt into a ribbed bell, and arranged diagonally around the top to make a lovely symmetrical puzzle of her chest and arms. Pale dress and pale tobacco plants glimmered in the warm dark. It was a lonely thing to see her mother so unaware of her. When Nell got into bed her parents' voices came up to her still, until they went indoors and all she knew of them were the rectangles of light the dining-room windows threw on the lawn, the brilliant negatives of shadows cast by adulthood into the dreamy cave of childhood and sleep.

Antony

Not Lil's most brilliant assembly, but I was lucky to be seated next to Christopher's niece Flossie. Barely eighteen, and not the least bit awed by the set-up. Her father is in Persia, something to do with oil. With her parents abroad, Wychwood is her weekend home. She was funny about her London life: the publisher's typing-pool full of women looking forward all morning to unpacking their fussy little greaseproof-paper parcels full of lunch; the debs' hostel in Belgravia; the landlady who sits all day in her room off the hall ready to pounce on anyone breaking the rules and receiving a male visitor. 'We all loll about in our pink quilted dressing gowns eating Rice Krispies for breakfast and pretending not to be competitive about where we've been the night before.' She made the vision of these frowsy human rose-buds at once erotically suggestive and ridiculous. She's a racy, ebullient girl. I can see why Lil makes a pet of her.

On the other side Helen, who's doing something at the Warburg, so we could talk shop. She invited me to come and see some Mughal miniatures. Claims that one shows a knot garden identical with the one at Montacute. Sounds improbable to me, but I'll go along politely. Benjie's always been a shameless show-off and he's adopted a new persona since I knew him in Berlin. Now he's a fat Flash Harry – ye gods, that smoking jacket!

We didn't linger long after the women had gone out. Cole Porter impersonations round the piano afterwards. I don't blame Christopher for slinking away.

*

Christopher walks down Tower Light. No forebear of his planted this avenue. Its beeches are older by several human generations than his traceable family tree, as old as the house his grandfather bought largely for the pleasure of possessing them. He is digesting his dinner and planning to smoke a cigarette. To any observer it would appear that he was alone, but alongside him, stealthy as the small creatures coming out now for their night's hunting, walks his ghostly son. Christopher cannot see his child, but he has a sense of him, like the flicker of a dim light just out of his line of vision.

He doesn't know whether the boy – he was called Fergus – ever comes in the same way to Lil. He's never asked her. Nor does he know whether the visitation is a consolation or an aggravation of grief, but he deliberately makes times, like this one, in which it can occur.

The boy whom he sees but doesn't see is not as tall as he would have been now. All the details of his appearance are those of the child he was when he died. The knob of his ankle-bone rubbed red by the upper rim of his sturdy buckled sandals. The delicacy of the tendons at the back of his neck. The sharp wings of his shoulder blades beneath his Aertex shirt. His solemnity, which hasn't yet been varied in these séances – as it was in life – by wild giggles.

Down and up again. The avenue runs for four miles, rising and falling as it traverses the forest between the two villages which abut Christopher's estate, running from church tower to church tower, cutting a passage from one public building to another through a great expanse of woodland sequestered and private.

Christopher arrives at the wall and passes through the iron gates. Twice as tall as he is, they are awkward to manoeuvre. Inside the wall the park stretches palely away between the massive trunks. Beyond the wall the beeches are backed by dense woodland. Turn off down a smaller ride, then onto a rutted track to the sawmill, always going down now, into gloom, and there, at the lowest point, abruptly the trees retreat, and the mauve sky reveals itself, reflected in water. Across the dam to the spot where the bank curves outwards to make a platform and the trees lean obligingly aslant as though to avoid the backward flick of his line.

The smell of water-mint enfolds Christopher. This muddle of trampled grass has been crushed by his own feet. This is where he likes to come, night after summer night, making a hide for himself – a confined vantage point from which, instead of moving lordly though the land he owns, he can retreat and watch it being itself, unmastered.

For the next two days, he will be on parade. He likes house-parties more than most of his guests probably imagine. Lil plans them and invites the guests, and shepherds them from room to room, from game to picnic to tête-à-tête. Christopher remains aloof, but – as Lil is consciously aware and as he perhaps intuits – he is an essential part of the entertainment. Tall, gentle Christopher, with his scrupulous courtesy that fails to mask his indifference to most of his visitors, is of a piece with his setting. He completes the picture. And they in turn complete, for him, the thing he has constructed here, and which needs their eyes.

*

The paper's Berlin stringer was filing down the line.

Today quote *Hero of the Soviet Union* close quote *Marshal Konev arrived in Berlin as commander of all Soviet forces in Germany* period

In May comma *1945* comma *Konev led the Red Army in the Battle of Berlin* period

It has been reported that his Cossack troops butchered an entire defeated German division comma *using their sabres to cut off arms raised in surrender* period

Konev's appointment signals a hardening of the Soviet line on German affairs period

At a factory in East Berlin yesterday comma *East German Chancellor Ulbricht was heckled by a worker calling for free elections* period

Ulbricht responded by saying free elections had brought the Nazis to power period

Quote *Whoever supports free elections supports Hitler's generals* exclamation mark close quote

New paragraph

West Berlin continues to be inundated with refugees from the East period

The twenty-nine camps set up to receive them are all now full period *Twenty-one aeroplanes* comma *chartered for the purpose* comma *took off from Berlin today loaded with refugees en route to cities in the West* period

An official said today quote *if it goes on like this* comma *East Berlin will be a ghost town* close quote period

The copy-taker said to his neighbour on the desk, 'I was in Berlin in '49 – national service – what a dog's dinner!' and passed the typed-up report with its four carbons to the runner, who carried it to the night editor on the foreign desk, who took it to the editor, who said, 'Has Nick seen this?'

'I'll be reading it to him.'

'This Konev. What do we know?'

'A very big potato. Just setting him out on the board is aggressive.'

The editor was known to love chess. It irritated him the way his subordinates played up to him by using board-game terminology.

'So the Soviets are huffing and puffing.'

'Mmm. Shall I call Nick back in?'

'Where the hell is he?'

'Some fancy-pants weekend in the country.'

'Leave him there for now. As long as you've got the number.'

That evening, a few miles east of Berlin, domestic staff at the House of the Birches, which had once been Hermann Goering's hunting lodge, were preparing to entertain. East German premier

Walter Ulbricht had invited most of his senior officials and their wives to visit him there at four o'clock the following afternoon. It was hot. A lovely weekend for a garden party.

*

When Christopher sloped off, Nicholas put in an appearance in the drawing room, drank coffee and bustled about flirting so no one could say he wasn't doing his bit socially. Then he slipped away too and set up camp in what passed in that house for a cosy study. Linen-fold panelling, a ceiling dripping plaster stalactites. The room had been deprived of one of its walls around the time of the Glorious Revolution, and now formed an L with the pilastered drawing room where Christopher and Lil hung the paintings of which they were properly proud.

He accepted a whisky and soda when Underhill appeared like a well-disciplined genie, drew the curtain across the joint of the L, and settled down in a tapestried chair beneath an upside-down pendent obelisk to try to make sense of the reports that had come in that day. Ted had rung about the Konev story. He'd heard Reuters' man in Berlin had a hunch that the East Germans were going to do something very soon, but what it was he couldn't guess. Not exactly what you'd call hard news.

Nicholas began to scribble out a think-piece on the limits of totalitarianism. Khrushchev being as much at the mercy of his party as Kennedy was at the mercy of the American electorate, both of them having to act tough for their respective constituencies, both of them probably clever enough to know it was a charade, the perils into which that play-acting might drag all Europe, de da de da de da de da.

Voices. Antony was showing young Flossie the pictures. The obstreperous Benjie had tagged along.

Flossie – 'Gosh! Is it a Cimabue?'

'Yes it is.'

Privately, as Nicholas knew, Antony had his doubts, but he was a loyal friend and a discreet dealer. So yes it unequivocally was.

'Looks lonely. Is that a bit of his friend on the right?' Benjie getting in on the conversation.

'Yes, it appears to be a fragment from the right wing of an altarpiece. See how it is hinged here. There would have been another two or three angels, a heavenly chamber group.'

'The hands are so . . .'

The hands, indeed, were ineffable.

'Girly? Or perhaps he is a girl. Or a fag. Look how he's leaning into the other's shoulder.'

Was Benjie an ass, thought Nicholas, or was he just pretending to be one? Nicholas had met Helen when she came into the office with her copy – she reviewed for the arts pages occasionally. And they'd talked, and one day they'd had lunch together, and another day they'd walked along the river east from Fleet Street past the Tower and he'd shown her one of his favourite places in London, Wapping Pierhead, where the tall Georgian houses run down to the river's edge and even the pavements still seem to reek of the cloves and nutmegs that made their first owners rich, and he thought she was beautiful in a steely-cool Celtic kind of way. Her eyes were as pale as gooseberries. There followed some very, very private afternoons in his flat. This was the first opportunity he'd had to observe her husband.

He stepped out from behind his arras. He wasn't going to get any more work done with them prattling on the other side.

Antony was saying, 'Either or neither. Angels, being insubstantial, are spared the indignities of sex.'

Benjie poured himself whisky and drifted about the room. He was looking at Flossie as much as at the paintings. Polite girl that she was, she kept making little nods and mmms. There's nothing harder to sustain than an appearance of interest, even when it's genuine. She was beginning to look a bit strained when Benjie called her over to see Christopher's chess-set. Booty of the Raj. Ivory and ebony, laid out on a great scagliola table.

'Do you play? I'll give you a game.'

A murmur that was like a verbal blush. Was this rude to Antony? How to reconcile the demands of all these different grown-ups? She had put on a dramatic dress for dinner, low cut, and made of bands of stiff papery silk in clashing bright colours, but for all that, and despite her lacquered hair, she was still a child. 'All right. You'll easily beat me.'

'So I hope.'

Simple words, but uttered as though they had a salacious double meaning. If Benjie wasn't an ass, he was certainly a bit of a lecher.

The others left them to it, and went out onto the terrace where Lil and Helen were sitting. Nicholas and Lil dropped into the banter that had become their normal mode of conversation. Silly stuff, he thought, but as bracing, she's so quick, as tennis is for those who are good at it. Christopher loomed up on the rim of the ha-ha, his rod on his shoulder like the Good Shepherd's crook, and crossed the lawn and joined them and for a while Nicholas felt easier than he had for weeks. The distant events that would occupy him through the night gave way to the immediate. The scents of stocks and jasmine. Pale roses glimmering. The dog collapsing heavily onto the flagstones and sighing like the grampus for whom he was named. He and Helen tended to ignore each other in company, but her being there, near him in the darkness, was a plus.

There was a scraping and a clatter indoors. Flossie came out. She didn't say anything, just sat herself down in the corner between the great magnolia and Lil, who had to shuffle along the stone bench to make room for her. She looked like a cat mutely complaining about a rainstorm. Murmuring from indoors: Underhill saying, 'I'll clear it up, sir.' Helen made no move. It was pretty clear to everyone what had happened – what sort of thing anyway. Nicholas and Lil kept up their tennis game, giving the girl time to collect herself. Why? wondered Nicholas. Surely it was Helen who needed their solicitude. Ignobly, he was pleased.

Pretty soon they all went up. At midnight Nicholas called the copy-desk, and got handed on to Ted, who wanted a background piece for the Sunday paper on Soviet military capacity. At five in the morning he finally got to bed, while in East Berlin the Stasi prepared to demonstrate that the myth of German efficiency had a basis in fact.

Saturday

Nell walked across the cattle grid by Underhill's lodge, her feet in her sandshoes only just making enough of a bridge from one bar to another to stop her slipping through. Hedgehogs got trapped down there sometimes. She'd been frightened once to hear a rustling, and then so amazed she could still conjure up the prickle of it, to see the dished face. Wild animals, even little funny ones, were like glimpses of another world carrying on with its business in secret, not caring at all about people. Perhaps even being enemies. Hedgehogs had fleas.

She was pushing her bicycle, and once safely over she got back on it, using the brick edge of Mrs Underhill's delphinium-bed to help herself up. Wood Manor was separated from the park by paddocks and a belt of trees. It had its own feeling, the feeling of home. The feeling inside the park wall was different; quieter somehow, a bit gloomy, old.

Swoop down the hairpin bend, faster than you'd really want to so that you could get most of the way up the slope beyond. The Land Rover passed her, hooting, the canvas roof off and Dickie in the back, waving wildly with both arms. By the time she reached the estate office her father was already walking up the beech avenue with Mr Green the head gardener, and she had to bump and rattle over the pebbly path down the centre of it, with

Dickie, because he was annoying, and Wully, because he was so pleased to see her after their half-hour separation, barging into her and making her wobble.

'We'll start emptying the pool Sunday, then, once they've all gone indoors to dinner. We've got all the beans to pick next week so Mrs Duggary can get them in the freezer while Mr and Mrs R are away. And the lettuces'll be bolting.'

Nell wanted to protest about the pool, because she'd have liked a last swim on Monday morning, but she could tell her father wasn't really listening. Mr Green liked to keep up a continuous report on his own doings but he didn't seem to mind talking on and on without anyone saying even 'mmm' or 'really?' He was just filling the time with his warm buzz until Daddy was ready to tell him whatever needed to be told, and sure enough, after a bit Daddy came back from wherever his thoughts had been and shouted at Wully and started to tell Mr Green about how they would make a new rose garden with a sundial. Nell went ahead, freewheeling down the sloping path that slanted away from the avenue towards the narrow gate that led into the garden, and passed on through the rhododendrons and on down to the pool.

Flossie was floating on her back with her long hair mermaidy around her. Nell was so pleased to see her there she ran into the changing hut and took off her stiff canvas shorts and left them sitting on the floor as though there was a person still in them, and kicked off her sandals and took off her blouse with its Peter Pan collar (surely Peter Pan didn't look like that) so roughly that a button came off, and ran back out in her best rose-trellised bathing dress with her inner tube and plopped straight in even before Daddy was there.

'Hello little fish,' said Flossie.

'You're the fish. I'm in my boat.'

'So you are. Silly old me with my goggley eyes. I thought for a moment you were a totally round flatfish of a previously unknown species.'

Flossie was not a grown-up not a child but something anomalous and exciting like a centaur or a psammead. She ducked her head under the water and when she came up her mouth was an o and she was blowing a bubble like the goldfish. Daddy came through the arched gap in the hedge, hesitated, and then said hello in an odd voice.

'I can't speak,' said Flossie. 'I'm a fish.'

He laughed then. Mummy would have told Nell off for not waiting but he seemed to think it was all right.

'Watch out that fishing boat doesn't spot you. And Nell, if you feel seasick, ask the fish to help you – I think it's a kind one.'

He went with Dickie into the changing room, the one for boys across the little hallway. On the doors hung girly and boyish things . . . antlers for the boys, a necklace made of nutshells for the girls. Mrs Rossiter had laughed when Green hung them there – 'Does he suppose we can't find our way around a hut?' – but they had stayed, adding to the hut's oddity. It looked, Nell thought, like a house where savages lived, all made of sticks and straw and things you pick up.

Her father dived in while Dickie lay tummy down on his coracle and flapped his hands. For a while they were all fish. Then they were all water boatmen. And then more grown-ups arrived and Flossie said she was cold, and got out and put on sunglasses, which is something no child ever did so it was as though she had swapped sides. She couldn't have been that cold because she didn't go and change but sat down on the low wall between Antony and Nicholas. Daddy got out too and stood in front of them, and Nell had that lonely feeling again because they were all laughing, and Nicholas was teasing Flossie and making Daddy tease her too and it was lovely for them but horrid for her because they had all completely forgotten her and she was left with just Dickie, and the fact that you happened to be in the same family with someone and both of you children absolutely did not mean that that someone was the person you wanted to be left with.

Dickie splashed her on purpose, and she was angry and grabbed his coracle and tipped him into the water, which was rather awful because she knew he couldn't really swim.

'For goodness sake, is no one watching that child?'

Mrs Rossiter arriving with two people Nell didn't know. The man kicked off his shoes and jumped in the water with all his clothes on and got hold of Dickie, who was all right really because he was clinging onto the inner tube, just not inside it any more, and dragged him quite roughly to the side of the pool. Dickie was crying and swimming-pool water was coming out of his mouth and nose so he was much more blubbery than the crying by itself would have made him. Nell stayed still, and everything was happening very slowly in bright light. Quiet like her nightmare. Mrs R and Daddy were staring at each other across the pool. They both looked older than usual and as though they had to cling on tight to something or they might fall.

'So. Lane.'

She never called him Lane. She called him Hugo. Calling people by their surnames meant they were less important. In a way Daddy was less important because he worked for the Rossiters, but usually you couldn't tell that.

'If you can't do your job, you could at least take care of your son. And what on earth are you all doing here in the first place? Get rid of your bloody dog.'

The strange man had climbed out of the pool and Wully was licking his wet ankles. Daddy growled at Wully, and then shouted at Nell, 'Come on out.' Then he walked slowly round the pool and said something very quiet to Mrs R, and took Dickie by the hand and walked with him into the changing hut. Nell got out, and ran behind them, but she could hear Nicholas talking in his joking voice again, and saying, 'Benjie to the rescue! There you were pretending to be a lounge-lizard and all the time we had a hero in our midst.'

She could see the man called Benjie taking off his wet trousers and she could hardly believe it. Underneath he wasn't wearing bum-bags like the ones Daddy wore but tiny knicker-shaped swimming trunks like Dickie's, but they weren't all woolly, they were shiny and slithery like snakeskin, and the most amazing thing was that they were patterned with green and purple scales just like a snake.

*

So what about Nell's mother? Why was she so seldom in evidence? Because she didn't want to be, is why.

Chloe Lane had realised that to be inconspicuous was a precious pass to freedom. Chloe's so sweet, said Lil. Chloe, could you be an angel and . . . Chloe, I cannot think what to do about . . . Why not ask Chloe? She'd do it (open the fête, chair the WVS, judge the school's dressing-up competition) so much better than me . . . Chloe fits in so perfectly! I don't know why I always look like a cockatoo . . . Chloe's so clever with flowers . . . Chloe's so clever . . .

Every single one of Lil's compliments was an order, or a demand, or a subtle derogation. At Wood Manor Chloe was her own and her servants' and children's mistress. At Wychwood she was the agent's wife. She stayed away. Dancing attendance was Hugo's job.

*

The park was blond. Dry grass, exhausted by summer, lay aslant all one way, like the hair on an animal's back. At midday the horse-chestnut trees were dark to blackness, the beeches purple. Bleached, the landscape became mineral – shining in shades of jet and copper and silver-gilt. Even the sun was sombre: light this bright and desiccating carried its antithesis within it. Only in the evening, the hour of Christopher's liberation, would the light soften and waver, as the deer swam silently across the broad rides and the midges trod air above the lakes.

Antony left the noisy group by the pool and walked down, across the terrace, past the canal and on into the severe corridor of the double yew hedge. Halfway along was a trellised arbour with a stone bench and an unsteady wooden table. He sat. Directly opposite him was a gap in the hedge, framing a view of the park. Antony knew what would shortly appear there. He had seen it approaching. And there, sure enough, tightrope walking along the ha-ha's stone lip, came Jack Armstrong.

This wasn't a coincidence. He had seen, as he was seen. Seventeen years old, self-absorbed. Thin, slightly round-shouldered, long neck, vulnerable Adam's apple, copper-coloured hair. He knew Antony was there. He didn't look round, just paced past heel to toe, slow, arms outstretched for balance, back-lit. There's a damp look to very young skin, a clamminess which is faintly repellent to all but those who lust after it, and for them, as marvellous as mother-of-pearl. Antony didn't move. Jack crossed the gap. An interval. Deer fidgeted beneath the horse-chestnut trees in the middle distance. A Land Rover crossed towards the home farm. Antony remained still. Then Jack reappeared, upside down, walking on his hands, almost made it across the gap, arms visibly trembling, tumbled, attempted a somersault, botched it and rolled out of sight with a snort.

Between the cliff of the hedge and the precipice of the ha-ha was a strip of grass, walled with yew on one hand, with nothing but air on the other. Open to the park, concealed from the garden. Antony stood up and walked through the gap: found him.

Helen, walking wet-haired and barefoot along the green corridor, saw Antony go. Inquisitive, she followed onto the grassy ledge. Seeing what had drawn him, she stepped quickly back.

*

After lunch the grown-ups went quiet. Most of them were under the cedar tree, Helen and Antony on rugs, Benjie hogging the swing-seat. In the drawing room Christopher was dozing. Nell came in, silent in her sandshoes, took two pearl-grey damask cushions, and carried them off, as hasty and triumphant as a dog with a stolen cutlet, to the wedge of space between a high-backed sofa and the wall. Stillness. Nell's small shuffling noises as she made her nest. A book sliding out of Christopher's hand and down the slope of his thigh. Voices from the tennis court, as inconsequential and tinny as the chattering of mechanical toys. Nearer at hand the peacocks' screaming, so eerie and yet so familiar to everyone in the household that they heard it not as sound, only as an intensification of atmosphere. In came Nicholas.

'What's going to happen?' asked Christopher, opening his eyes, the rest of him still unmoved.

'I don't believe anyone, the main actors included, could tell you.' Nicholas was leaning against a column, silhouetted against the French window and the deserted lawn. 'Not a single one of them fully comprehends the possible options.'

'Do you?'

'No. But the ones I can think of scare me rigid.'

Like a nanny going off-duty, Nicholas had laid aside his teasing, bustling manner. He talked to Christopher as though continuing a long and searching conversation, even though this was the first time the two of them had spoken to each other directly that weekend.

'But the bomb?'

'It's the tiger at the bottom of the garden and everyone knows the wise course is to leave it be, but everyone is itching to prod it with a stick just to see what happens. And at every point along the way towards whatever kind of climax we're heading for, it's possible to say, well, look, it's all right so far. Until you reach the point where it really isn't all right. But no one will know where that point is until they've passed it.'

'Kennedy will want to prove how good his nerve is.'

'Unfortunately.'

'But what does Khrushchev want?'

'Dear Christopher, if we knew that . . . Berlin is maddening for the Russians. It's maddening for everyone. It's geographical nonsense. For Khrushchev this rush for the exit is a humiliation. It shames him internationally. It weakens him with his own people.'

'But no one, surely, is going to start chucking atom bombs about because a few thousand Germans want to live in a different part of Germany?'

'I don't think the Russians would. Not deliberately. But for most Americans Berlin is just a battlefield in a foreign war they thought they'd won. For them unleashing mayhem there is conceivable precisely because they can't conceive of its reality.'

Nell lay, arms curled around her knees, imagining herself as round as a snail. In this very room, hiding behind this very sofa, she had heard her mother and Mrs Rossiter talk about atom bombs. Everyone, everyone, everyone in the whole world would die. And all the animals. And no one would ever be born again. Or if they were they'd be peculiar shapes and be so ill they'd just die almost at once. The only thing alive would be grasshoppers. She'd seen a grasshopper in Cornwall. Perhaps the whole world would be like a beach, dead sand and big green things that leapt, and had hard bodies, and horrid tickly legs. She couldn't believe it. If it was true then why weren't Mummy and Mrs R crying? She sometimes thought about old people and wondered why they weren't all crying all the time because they must know they were going to die quite soon. But if everyone . . . The thought was too laborious to complete.

And now Mr Rossiter and Nicholas. They were so quiet and serious. Mr R was often like that, but he always smiled when he talked to her which made him not frightening. But Nicholas frightened her now because it was as though he had been in fancy dress and now he was his real self and all the pretending had been to cover up the awful thing. And they were talking so quietly. She knew she wasn't supposed to have heard any of this. It was like when she found her uncle dressed as a pirate in Daddy's dressing room, before her birthday party, and she had spoiled the surprise of the treasure hunt, and he was as embarrassed as she was and she had to go away quickly and pretend she hadn't seen. Now she had to be not there. She fixed her eyes on the dark-haired angel hanging in the patch of the opposite wall that was all she could see past the sofa's arm, and lay snail-still.

Christopher was talking now, his voice gentle, as though he was stalking a thought that would bolt if startled.

'When I was a boy here, my parents used to talk about the invasion. Germans would arrive in the village dressed as nuns, they were saying. Can you imagine how exotic that was? I'd never seen a nun. They were going to drop out of aeroplanes. The Blitz had taught us that anything could fall out of the sky. There was no limit to the ways in which normality could be exploded. I was very much afraid, and at the same time I couldn't take it seriously. We kept knapsacks packed with clean vests and choco-late, so we could take to the hills. What hills? What were we going to do in them? Our nanny had told us over and over again that you couldn't live on chocolate.'

'American schoolchildren are being taught, now, to hide under their desks when the warning comes. Is it kind to suggest there's any chance of survival, or is it just dishonest?'

A pause.

'Macmillan believes Khrushchev can be talked down, and Jack and Mac are close,' said Nicholas.

'Those Kennedys put ambition before the clan. Remember Joe losing at tennis here? Perfect manners, of course. But he cared dreadfully.'

Of course Nicholas didn't remember. He would have been a child when Kennedy *père* was *en poste* in London, but he refrained from saying so. He liked Christopher's benign assumption that each one of his acquaintances was acquainted with all the others.

'Khrushchev is wily. So is Brandt and he thinks he can ride on Kennedy's coat-tails.'

More names of people she didn't know. Snail-Nell became a dog and – as dogs do – she slept.

Antony

It transpired that Christopher had expressly invited the Lanes to swim that morning, and Lil rang up and apologised very graciously, and explained that she had been so shaken by seeing the boy in trouble that she had lost her head. I think she really was mortified. She can be spiteful, but humiliating the man in public like that wasn't her usual style.

By late afternoon everything was affable again. Hugo Lane, with what degree of soreness I couldn't determine, had returned to the house to make up a tennis four. I met his little girl on the terrace trailing after Mr Green (they seemed to be good companions) as he set off to pick vegetables for dinner. I was curious to see a part of the domain I didn't know, so I joined their expedition. Green wore corduroys gartered with raffia below the knee but, for all that he looked like an illustration from an Edwardian children's book, he liked talking motorbikes. I egged him on to expatiate on the rival merits of the Triumph and the BSA (Beezer, he called it) while Nell walked, humming to herself, behind.

The walled garden is a good quarter of a mile from the house. The entrance is all but choked by a fig tree. Green, who likes his peach trees splayed against the walls as though crucified and his strawberry-beds neatly tucked in under veils of tarred netting, is uncharacteristically lax in his treatment of this tree. Figs aren't easily come by in Oxfordshire: he's inordinately proud of, and indulgent towards, his enormous green pet. We had to duck under its lowest branches, Nell grabbing a great stubby-fingered hand of a leaf as we passed. Beyond were rows, racks, bamboo canes tied into tepees, pergolas – all sharply angled contraptions, framed by exactly squared-off box hedges at shin-height – all striving ineffectually to contain the voluptuous lollings of vegetation.

Within the high brick walls it was intensely still and hot. There was no view out except upwards to the white sky. The scents were of stagnant water and dried hay and lightly rotted compost. Nell and I stopped by a sprawl of tomato vines and began to pop tiny red fruit into our mouths, where they felt warm, and lightly furred, and autonomously alive. Green's pain at seeing his babies so devoured was writ large on his face, but so was his awareness that I was privileged and that Nell – at whom he might otherwise have growled – came under the aegis of my guestly protection.

'Does your father let you wander just anywhere?' I asked her. I wasn't looking for information, just filling a pause.

'I'm with Mr Green. I must always make sure there's a grown-up who knows where I am. And I mustn't go swimming on my own. And I mustn't go upstairs unless Mrs Rossiter asks me to.'

'And is it lovely coming over to Wychwood?'

The question didn't seem to mean much. To her, Wood Manor and Wychwood were continuous, the whole domain her home. I wasn't really paying her much attention, when she said something that compelled it.

'Daddy and Mrs Rossiter like to talk about grown-up stuff sometimes so it's good for me to be with Mr Green.'

'And what about Mr Rossiter and your father?'

'Um. Well they talk about things I like.'

Hugo Lane was a very good-looking man. I hustled Nell towards some gooseberry bushes and set her to picking me a handful. Hairy semi-transparent jade-green globes full of viscous fluid and little black pips, the germs of life. The *hortus conclusus* was suffused with carnality now; not pretty fertility symbolism but gross reminders of sex. Was I jealous, and if so, of whom? I didn't like what I was imagining.

*

The ghostly boy did come to Lil too. She saw Fergus flailing in the pool, and although he resolved himself all but instantaneously into Hugo's little Dickie, the glimpse opened an oubliette down which she dropped into the blackness of the night he drowned. Hours later, bored on the tennis court, she was still dazed.

She hated playing doubles with an overactive partner. Benjie, pink-faced and surprisingly adroit in his absurd flowery shirt, was leaping about at the net, intercepting the balls that should have given her a chance to demonstrate the elegance of her long passes. Annoying, but useful in that the game granted her a respite from conversation. Lashing out at Hugo like that had been unforgivable. As Flossie's tennis partner he seemed at ease, gently teasing the girl as she missed one backhand after another, but watchfully helping her out as well. But he was under an obligation to behave, which made it all the worse that Lil had abused her freedom to misbehave with impunity.

Walking back up the avenue, she slowed down to talk to him. Benjie, abandoned mid-anecdote, latched unperturbed onto the only other available audience and went ahead with Flossie.

'You gave me a fright this morning.'

'I know. I could kick myself. I was being a rotten father. And what must have gone through your mind.'

'I saw Fergus. Just for a second. Less than a second.'

'I'm so sorry.'

'No. I'm sorry. That's what I wanted to say. Let's forget it now.'

A hiatus.

'Do you want to show me where the new rose-beds are to go? Green could get started on it next week.' Hugo's voice was light and steady.

'I suppose they can all amuse each other for a minute or two.'

She led him through a green arch, across a round lawn entirely encircled by blackish yew hedge, out beneath another arch, down steps foaming with alchemilla into an alleyway bounded on each side by rows of pleached limes.

'I thought down at the bottom there, you see? This view needs an ending.'

'A sundial's not really big enough for the centrepiece,' said Hugo. 'You'd need an obelisk. Or maybe a flowering tree. A weeping pear.'

'But if it was on a stone plinth? With a threepenny-bit-shaped arrangement of rose-beds around it, and then a wrought-iron gate beyond?'

Hugo laughed. 'Not just a few shrub-roses then. Actually, you know, a fountain would be the thing. We could bring Norris's Triton up from the home lake. It's wasted there. We could pipe the water down from the canal.'

'Boboli-under-Wychwood.'

A smile. A pause.

'Lil.'

'Not now, Hugo.'

Another hiatus.

'I . . .'

'Never when Christopher's here.'

'No. Of course.'

And yet they didn't move.

The alley was open-ended. Where the proposed sundial or fountain might one day stand was now a gap in the garden's perimeter, a hole beyond which the park shimmered, and out of which the magical seclusion of the garden leaked. Across this breach Antony and Nell were seen to walk. She was turned to him, talking earnestly, and beyond him saw, tiny at the other end of the alley, Lil's brilliant-blue blouse, and then her father, and at once span round and ran towards them.

'There are tiny tiny lizards in Mr Green's watering pond.'

Both Hugo and Lil noticed the awkward way Antony checked and dithered, before waving his hat and passing on towards the house.

*

My very dear Nicholas

Lil is a monster, she really is. She makes me laugh but she is just so dangerous. Look at the way she's luring that nice young agent into her web. Christopher sees it all, of course he does, but he's too grown up to flap about it. Lil should be careful, though. He may not be jealous, or not very, but he is fastidious. If he gets disgusted with her he could just drift out of her reach.

She knows about us, I can tell. So that's why we're both here now. You must have told her. I most certainly didn't. You must be mad. She can keep secrets all right if she chooses to, but mostly she doesn't. She'll have told Christopher by now.

But perhaps it doesn't matter because last night it came to me that I don't have to put up with Benjie's fooling around any more. That girl is a child. I know it's harsh. I know he needs me and I could depend on him for ever if I chose. But I know now that I no longer love him. There are no children to worry about. And there is you. So it's your turn now to make a decision. If you don't respond I'll never reproach you. But here I stand.

Helen

*

Rose garden. Water garden. Moorish saucer sunk into the soil of Anglo-Saxon Oxfordshire. Lil and Christopher had travelled down through Spain the first summer after the war's end, through a landscape foul with invisible blood, so absorbed in each other they barely enquired what might have happened there. Stopping the car at midday, they had hidden from the sun, as from an armed enemy, under cork trees, eating ham that wrenched at their teeth and hard bread. In the villages men who looked old, but perhaps were no older than they were, sat on planks balanced on oil drums and stared at them as they drove by. A passing car was an event – not necessarily a welcome one. Women spat in Lil's direction, and crossed to the other side of the street. Not hostile exactly, just avoiding the bad luck a stranger might bring.

Lil had brought pre-war dresses her mother had passed on to her – rayon in abstract geometrical prints, bias-cut Liberty lawn covered with convolvulus, silvery-green pleats like the chitons of Athenian caryatids. The dresses stayed in the suitcase, while she wore the invisibility cloak of a dusty-blue shirt-waister. Christopher drove, though she was better at it, and on mountain roads she shut her eyes so as to stop herself whimpering with fear. In Ronda they rented a room above a cheese shop and stayed there for long, long afternoons. The high hard bed. The bolsters bristling with horse-hair. The shiny pine-green satin cover. The deliquescence of two bodies. Down into the streets at twilight to join the *paseo*, so languid from hours of sweat/sex/sleep their legs felt tremulous as a newborn donkey's. Sherry. Pork-fat thyme-scented. Churches decorated with effigies of tortured saints. Sleeping and waking again hours later to the sound of singers lamenting, lamenting, lamenting. Spain was all grief – its architecture grim – its people grandly dour. There they were happy.

At Wychwood, eight years later, Lil set Hugo, the new agent, to making her a garden to rival Aranjuez, and he mistranslated it into a Cotswold fantasia in pink and green.

*

Nicholas found Helen's letter on his dressing table. Talk about madly indiscreet! He put it in his inside pocket and thought, What am I feeling? And didn't have an answer ready. Exasperation: couldn't she tell he was busy? Joy. A bit of each, obviously. And shame. What a contemptible cold fish he seemed to be. Through his bedroom window he could see her on a rug, propped up on her elbows, Antony cross-legged beside her, making daisy chains while they talked. She didn't look as though she was waiting for a signal that would determine her future. She looked, as she always did, sleek as one of those fancy grey oriental cats. If I am a cold fish, he thought, she is my fair Miss Frigidaire.

They were all having tea on the terrace (iced coffee, actually) when Underhill came and murmured to Nicholas that he was wanted on the telephone again. Helen looked up sharply, but the others were laughing at Benjie. He had launched into a series of anecdotes about louche goings-on in the art world and Antony, who knew most of the people involved, was dodging his questions and getting more and more embarrassed (which was of course the point).

The telephone was in a sort of mahogany sentry box in the marble hall. While he talked, Nicholas was being eyed by the stuffed bear, rampant, from whose outstretched and fearsomely clawed forearms the dinner gong depended. It was the foreign editor. One of the stringers had a source in East Berlin, who had been told by an old schoolfriend that if he was still keen to move his mother to the West he should drive her over *instanter*, that very afternoon. The old schoolfriend was in a position to know whatever was up in the Deutsche Demokratische Republik.

'So you'd better get back here, just in case.'

'Does it stand up? Anyone corroborating?'

'I've got half the desk working on it, but nothing solid yet. The entire Foreign Office knows there's something in the offing, but the Americans aren't sharing information, and there's nothing coming in from the East. Or that's their story. You heard what that senator said in Ohio?'

'About a wall? You think he might have known something? It sounded to me like wish-fulfilment fantasy. Please, somebody, put up a barrier so we don't have to think about these commies any more. You can't enclose a country.'

'Tell that to Hadrian. Tell that to the Chinese emperors.'

'How could they do it?'

'Our man says his driver says someone who drinks in the same bar claims to have seen eighteen lorries loaded with barbed wire parked on the site of a bombed-out factory in the Soviet sector.'

Lorries and wire are solid things. Nicholas felt an eerie shuddering as the membrane dividing speculation from the real was breached.

'They could do it. They just about could. Walls apart, they could close the frontier. And they most certainly would like to.'

'So say goodbye to Lord and Lady Muck and get on down here.'

'For goodness sake, old man, you've got half a dozen writers there already.'

'I want you here talking to your friends in high places. And if something happens tonight we'll be scrambling to keep up.'

Needed or not, Nicholas wanted to be there. Packing took no time. He ran Underhill to ground in the dining room, where he was upbraiding a maid for using lilies in the flower arrangements (it was his rule that flowers for the dining room must be scentless), and asked him for train times, a man to bring his suitcase down, and a car to the station, all before he'd announced his departure to his hosts.

Christopher went white. Lil, apparently incurious as to what kind of crisis it was that was calling him back, acquiesced in his change of plan with an ease which would have been hurtful if she hadn't hung onto his arm and followed him out to the front steps. (No chance of a private word with Helen.) There, beneath the portico, which was that patchwork of a house's only chill and pompous part, she looked him seriously in the eye and said, 'Dear Nicholas, you know, you're a very good friend.' And then there was a jump in time, like a gramophone needle leaping a groove, as they both thought that what was happening was, beneath all the enjoyable bustle, perhaps deathly.

The next train wasn't for three-quarters of an hour. Time for Nicholas to walk to the station, and get a bit of mind-settling peace. Armstrong's son Jack had brought the Bentley round. Ridiculous for such a routine errand, but the boy loved the enormous green car. Nicholas gave him his bag, and said, 'Thanks, but I'm walking. I'll see you on the platform.'

*

Avenues radiated out from the house. Horse-chestnut trees, heavy graduated layers of dense green, darkened the drive which led downhill. Beyond the twin lodges – stocky little Doric temples with incongruous back gardens full of hollyhocks and beanpoles – the drive crossed the river on a stone-parapeted bridge, and, leaving the beautiful artifice of the park, re-entered the world of cowpats and thistles and telegraph poles, rising again towards the village between the fields of the home farm. The car went that way with his luggage, but Nicholas veered off to the left, following a path trodden by deer.

Approaching him aslant came Hugo Lane. Still invisible to each other, the two men were following lines that would intersect near the end of Tower Light. Wully's progress – pale hay-coloured against pale hay, snuffling, chasing what, chasing nothing, chasing anything – was the embroidery looping across the steady weft of the men's progress and the warp of the marching trees. Each was startled by their meeting.

'Going back to the Great Wen?' Already Nicholas had a whiff of the city about him.

'Have to, alas.'

Hugo had gone home for picnic tea under the copper beech with Chloe and the children. Milk and jam doughnuts. Who can eat half a doughnut without once licking the sugar off their lips? Dickie had laughed so hard at Nell's sugar moustache he had snorted into his milk, splattering it all over the tartan rug and getting some of it the wrong way down inside himself as well, leading to gurgling and back-slapping and eventually tears. When Heather appeared to begin bathtime rituals, Hugo whistled up Wully, took a twelve-bore from the gun cupboard, filled his pockets with cartridges and walked back into the park.

Nicholas eyed the gun. 'Pigeons?'

'Yes. Fun for me, and a bit of a help for Slatter.' (Slatter was the farm manager.) 'They're demolishing his peas.'

'Do you eat them?'

'Used to when I was a soldier. My batman skinned them and made them into stew. Not now, though. Chloe doesn't like them. Too fiddly, she says, and she thinks they're dirty. She grew up in London.'

'Ah. And she imagines the lovely plump pigeons that live off the fat of the land hereabouts are as pestiferous as those horrid things in Trafalgar Square.'

'Quite. That's part of it. But then she's fond of them too. Loves the call. "Take two cows, Taffy." She and the children answer it back. One of their favourite games. I'm glad, you know, we've bumped into each other.'

'Yes?'

'You and Lil. You're very old friends.'

'Yes.'

Nicholas watched Hugo's face and saw his trouble. Whatever it was he wanted to say must not, most emphatically must not, be said. Nicholas opened a way out for him.

'Of course you realise her little fury this morning was about Fergus.'

'Yes – I was an ass. I've apologised. And so's she. But it was idiotic of me.'

'The not having more children. I don't know whether that was a decision, or just bad luck.'

'It's a shame,' said Hugo. 'She and Christopher are so kind to our two.' He seemed distracted now. 'But look here, is there something up?'

'That's what I'm off to find out. There are rumours from Berlin.'

'There's nothing we can do, is there, to keep people safe?'

Chloe, Nell, Dickie, Wully, poor old Silver (already doleful enough with his laminitis). Heather even, Lil and Christopher. Actually everyone on the estate. The roll-call of those beings for whom he was responsible sounded in Hugo's head, but his manner was insouciant. Nicholas had seen how, when a horse fell at a point-to-point, the crowd alongside the fence moaned and dithered but Hugo had vaulted one-handed over the rail, and sat on its head until the vet arrived. Even with Armageddon in prospect he acted as though he didn't believe it was anything he couldn't handle.

'Well, not if the worst comes to the worst,' said Nicholas. 'Nobody wants it to. Of course. Not on either side. The difficulty is that the military chaps have to do their job, and their job is to get ready to fight, and go into it unflinching. And they're awfully impressive, most of them. The top men have all fought a war already. The politicians have to have a very strong nerve to stand up to them.'

Nicholas had been making phrases as he walked, drafting a think-piece which would almost certainly be obsolete before he could get it on paper.

Hugo said, 'Scotland will be safer, I suppose.'

'Well, cities will be the main targets. But naval bases. Railways. And if anything happens it's likely to be sudden. Not much chance of putting together an evacuation plan.'

'If you had children . . .'

'I'd keep them with me.'

They looked at each other. Among the things that lay between them, too perilous to discuss in any voice other than the clipped, offhand tone they'd been using, were the extermination of the human race and an improper flirtation. Piquant, thought Nicholas, that it was the latter about which he felt most curious. Limitless, the frivolity of the human mind. Or was he just speaking for himself?

He said, 'I'm catching the six-twenty,' and Hugo called Wully to heel and they walked together down a line of oaks, as ugly and splendid as rhinoceri, to the iron filigree of the gates. Fifteen foot high, and too heavy for the rusted brackets on which they should have swung, this pair were never opened. Hugo showed Nicholas the place, some twenty feet along, where the wall had collapsed. Mending it would be another job to be done before winter, and the installation of a smaller, more serviceable gate, but for now there was only a panel of larch-lap fencing to keep the deer in and trespassers out, with a swing door next to it improvised from a couple of hurdles. Through the ramshackle portal, Nicholas strode out into the world.

Leaving Wychwood gave him, as it did each time, the mingled anxiety and exhilaration of a rebirth. Womb-warm and sequestered, it was at once a sanctuary and a place of internment.

*

The Plough, Saturday night. The first drinkers were quiet. Each man (they were all men) nodded to the landlord as he entered. His usual drink would be poured. He would carry it over to his usual seat. The evening sun shone horizontally through a back window, glaring into the eyes of the men on the bench alongside the door. They didn't mind. They knew almost to the minute how soon it would drop behind the publican's row of currant bushes, and cease to bother them. They drank very slowly, a sip at a time with long, long intervals between.

After a while the beer did its work, and they began to talk, not addressing anyone in particular but speaking in a low rumble out into the room. It was as though they were returning to an exchange which had been going on for years in this place. They were the old men of the village, though most of them still did a bit of work.

The younger ones would be in later, and tonight they would be boisterous. The village eleven had won its match against Shipton. There would be toasts and celebrations and, very likely, singing.

The old men looked forward to it. They liked a bit of jollity. They weren't comfortable exactly. The benches were narrow and hard. The pub's distinctive and ineradicable smell, of ashtrays and stale beer and dirty hair and bodies, was displeasing to men who spent their days out of doors and relished freshness. But they were at rest. Someone made a joke, and chuckled a bit. The joke, which was scurrilous and not new, was picked up and passed around, repeated in half a dozen different voices with minute variations. Appreciation was shown. Not loud laughter, but one man patted a table top as though to mime applause. Another nodded repeatedly. Another lit a pipe, in celebration of the wit.

By the time Goodyear arrived a couple of hours later the place was crowded. The cricketers, some still in their white flannels, stood in a tight phalanx in the centre of the room. The unshaded lightbulb dangling from the ceiling was reflected in sweaty red faces and oiled hair. There were still no women present.

Mark Brown, who was the wicket-keeper, saw Goodyear and waved him over. These two were the Plough's acknowledged entertainers. Outside, they liked each other well enough, but their interests conflicted. Here, they treated each other with scrupulous respect.

'I'd best go first,' said Goodyear. 'These here victorious heroes are going to want to end up with a singsong.'

'I reckon you're right there.'

'Got your guitar with you?'

'I've got better than that. I've got the organist.'

A lean gangly man blushed as Brown pointed a thumb at him. The big hands which hung, so awkward-looking, from his too-short shirtsleeves, were actually wonderfully deft. With them he could knead dough (he was the baker), he could take catches no other man on the village side could have reached, and on Sundays he made the church organ roar its way through hymns ancient and modern. Saturday nights, his instrument was the accordion. Goodyear gave him a nod and went to pick up the pint the landlord had already poured for him.

'Now this is one you'll have already heard,' he said. He'd turned his back to the bar, his elbows propped comfortably on its rim behind him as he spoke. He didn't raise his voice. It was as though he was talking solely to the two or three men nearest to him. There was a general shuffling, though, and a falling silent. The old men by the wall leant forward, contorted hands on smooth corduroy knees. The younger ones planted their legs wide and crossed their arms, ready for a good long one.

'It's about a lord and lady,' said Goodyear, 'and they lived in a great house. They had a hundred rooms crammed with silver folderols and tiger-skin rugs. In winter they had fires blazing in every room. In summer they had a fountain playing in the hall to keep them cool, and gardens full of roses. Every time one of their horses ran, it would win a socking great gold cup, and they'd put that cup on the shelf with all the dozens of others they'd got. Their pheasants were the size of turkeys and their lakes were full of thirty-five-pound trout. That's three times the size of the one Bill over there caught last week.'

A smirk from Bill, a narrow-shouldered man with a livid scar down the left side of his face, who was a labourer on the home farm and spent his summer evenings by the river.

'Their trees were the tallest and stoutest in the county, and their woods were so excellently maintained the nettles and brambles had all dwindled away for shame, and rare orchids grew there and the birds flocked to make their nests there because word had spread across the land, and the sky as well, that their forest was the finest ever seen.'

Whoop-whoop for Goodyear the forester.

'They had it made, those two, but were they happy? No they were not. There's probably some fool in this room who thinks that a pot of money, and all that luck, might solve all his problems.' Noisy assent. 'But that lord and lady were lonely. They'd have hunting parties and dancing parties. In summer there'd be picnics in the park and shows on a stage in the topiary garden with little boys singing like God's angels and young women dancing like temptresses sent by the Devil. But when the guests went home the old sadness would settle on the house. The lord was a good, kind man but he was getting wrinkled and his hair was falling out. She was younger, and when she dressed up smart, with shiny red fingernails and patent-leather shoes, she was still as sleek as a three-year-old on the way down to the paddock, but she had a worried look to her. The trouble was, they had no children.'

Mr Armstrong sat by the chimney. The fire wasn't lit on this August night, but, fire or no fire, the Windsor chair by the hearth was the place of honour, and Armstrong occupied it. On the other side of the chimneybreast sat his uncle and predecessor in the head-keeper's job, another Mr Armstrong, hands shaken by a perpetual tremor, blue eyes faded to a rainy grey. The elder Armstrong's hearing, after a lifetime around guns (in Wychwood as a child, beating and picking up; on the Western Front as a teenaged soldier; Wychwood again for decades of keepering), was shot to pieces. But he liked the conviviality of the pub. He'd had some fifteen years of grouchiness, angry at being old, angry at being deaf, angry at being superseded by the boys he used to thunder at when he caught them stealing pheasants' eggs. Now, though, he'd forgotten his grievances, along with much else besides. Curious and a bit timid, he looked across at his brother's son and thought, without being certain that he knew him, That's a proper-looking man.

The younger Armstrong was not so happy. He didn't like the tenor of this story.

Perhaps Goodyear, too, saw dodgy matter coming up. He swerved off into fantasy. 'The lady went walking in the woods and met a fox in a trap. She pitied it and set it free.' Goodyear met Armstrong's eye here and winked. Armstrong shook his head. Pretty well everyone in the room was aware that Armstrong was widely suspected of trapping foxes. Those who joined his army of beaters thought, Fair enough, he's got a job to do. Those who spent their winter Saturdays following the hunt thought, That'll make the old bugger squirm.

'That fox,' said Goodyear, 'was a fairy. As soon as it was freed it licked its mangled foot and the lady was amazed to see that the wound healed in a trice. And she was even more amazed when the creature sat back on its haunches and spoke to her, and its eyes looked as clever as any human's.'

The lady's disinterested kindness had earned her the fairy's goodwill. Her dearest wish would be granted. She wished, naturally, for a child. In Goodyear's version the longed-for baby was a boy, there was no christening, and there was no spindle.

'The fox had told the lady that the little fellow was to eat no mushrooms. Everyone in those days gathered mushrooms in September. And most of them stuck to the usual ones, with their pink gills, and very good suppers they had. But some clever-clogs know-it-alls said they could eat the yellow-frilled toadstools, and the mauvey-grey ones that looked like umbrellas, and the ruddy-coloured ones that looked like babies' ears. And every year they'd be smacking their lips and saying "Exquisite! Exquisite!" and for every dozen of them there'd be one who made a mistake, and died of it. So when the fox said "No mushrooms", the lady just thought that was wise advice.'

So, no mushrooms anywhere on the lord and lady's land. The sale of fungi declared a punishable offence. Traders searched at the boundaries of the estate, and not only mushrooms confiscated but anything, from dried apricots to vanilla pods to sticks of liquorice, that might be preserved mushrooms in disguise, taken away and burnt and so prevented from coming anywhere near our lord and lady's darling boy.

The cricketers around Mark Brown were muttering to him – requesting their favourite songs. Goodyear knew his audience. He speeded up.

'It was the fox, of course – trust a fox to make the mischief' (a little wave to Armstrong, who vouchsafed a nod) 'who sneaked in with the spore of a mushroom on its paws. And come autumn, that mushroom grew up as plump and pink-and-white and pretty as the boy's prettiest nursemaid. And he was out walking one day with his pug-dog, a little black one with a terrific snore to it, and he saw the mushroom and put it in his mouth.'

With some regret, Goodyear decided to leave the near-death, the weeping and wailing, and the fox-spirit's last-minute intervention, until he resumed the story the following week. For now, he'd climax with the thorny hedge.

'Just as soon as that mushroom settled on the boy's tongue he fell down as though struck by lightning, and that dog of his was quiet for the first time in its life, and all around him the earth began to heave and split.'

This was one of Goodyear's great set pieces. His repertoire was large, but not inexhaustible, and his listeners liked it that stories came round again pretty often. The thorny hedge was a favourite. The first tendrils writhing up through the earth like beseeching fingers. The bramble stems snapping like whips as they sprung from the ground and reached for each other, tangling together to form a barrier barbed with a million thorns, thorns which rapidly hardened into weapon-grade metal.

'Tiger's claws were nothing on these hooks, which grew and grew until they could have ploughed deep ridges into a man's back. The house, the garden, the park were encircled. No one could enter or leave.

'The boy, with his big round eyes and chubby hands, lay there like a dead mouse laid as bait in the middle of a great trap – the kind of steel trap the fox had been caught in.

'The people couldn't go anywhere. They didn't fall into an enchanted sleep. They kept on with their work, but the fox's curse didn't allow them to take any benefit from it. They ploughed and harrowed and planted, but they couldn't carry their crops to market, and eating the food they raised was mere dull chomping, without pleasure because they couldn't go out to buy salt. The fish escaped downriver from the lakes, and no more came. The horses grew fat and lame from lack of exercise. Everyone knew that they would have to wait until the boy grew up before the curse was lifted, so they tended him carefully as he lay unconscious. And as though to mock them the turf of the park was covered now, not only in the proper season, but all year round, with toadstools that stank, and oozed purple. And the thorny hedge grew so high they could no longer see the sky, and the peacocks dragged their tails gloomily around the garden, where it was now always as dark as night, screaming out their sadness, and all night long the people lay awake, listening to the thorns of the hedge clashing against each other with a horrible noise like the gnashing of tremendous teeth.'

Goodyear caught the baker's eye, and raised his right hand and beat time as he said it again. The Gnashing of Tremendous Teeth. And as he did so the accordion let out a crashing chord and everyone that end of the room jumped and the accordion jangled on and the baker and Mark Brown locked eyes and stamped their feet and soon everyone was stamping and hollering, and then

Brown was clambering onto a bench, and his powerful bass voice was mastering the chaotic music and they were all belting out 'Don't Fence Me In', while Goodyear sat down, he who had been playing on them so confidently, and every muscle in his body was leaping and twitching as the adrenalin that had fuelled his invention released itself like poison into his veins.

*

At four o'clock on Saturday the 13th of August, 1961, Walter Ulbricht's guests began to arrive at the House of the Birches. While they strolled by the lake, or settled indoors to watch a comic film, their host was signing an order authorising his lieutenant and Politburo chief, Erich Honecker, to implement the plan code-named Operation Rose. Over two thousand East Germans had crossed into West Berlin since morning, more than had ever previously done so on a single day.

At ten Ulbricht called together his guests, tired and tipsy after six hours of partying, and announced that he was taking action that very night to bring 'the still-open border between socialist and capitalist Europe' under 'proper control'. Having given them this dangerous information, he told them that there was still plenty to eat and drink and that they should set to again, and enjoy themselves as well as they could. Until the operation was successfully concluded they would not be permitted to leave his house.

They were captives, and so were all their compatriots. From that night onward, East Germans would not be permitted to leave their country.

*

What a change a day can work. On Friday night almost everyone in the house had Benjie down for a crass groper. But in any community, a person's perceived character is subject to fluctuations as mysterious in their coherence as the wheeling of a school of fish. In a classroom, an office, a cabinet, a house-party, the grey man can stand forth astonishingly, revealed as the next leader by a barely perceptible alteration of the light. A change of temperature, and the buffoon becomes the wit.

As they were going to bed on Friday Lil told Christopher a bit about Benjie, and in the morning Christopher, meeting Nicholas pacing – uncharacteristically dishevelled – down the Grand Vista before anyone else was up, passed the information on, and when at breakfast Nicholas, by this time shaven and suave again, began questioning Benjie about the operations of the Allied military police it transpired that Antony had known Benjie in Germany and knew more about him than either of them was letting on, and thought he was considerable, and by the time Benjie and Lil were strolling up to the pool, from which Nell's laughter rose bubbling, no one was wondering any more how he had impressed himself on the queenly Helen, and the previous night's episode, which had left a glass broken and Flossie huffy and shaken, had faded to just that – an episode.

All day Saturday Lil had reason to be grateful for the ebullience with which he supported her as she shepherded everyone away from anything conducive to unease. And all day Flossie was being reassured by his delicacy. For a fat man, he was a surprisingly nimble dancer. For a comical-looking fellow, he was a surprisingly subtle flirt.

By nightfall the metamorphosis was complete. He was re-clad in his disguise of jolly uncle. In that persona, softly, softly, he was re-approaching her. She was too young to know, yet, that the physically comic are as racked by desire as the desirable, and that they must be inexhaustibly patient and devious if they are not to be forever left out.

'Dull for you that Lil hasn't laid on any other young things. Not like her to miss an opportunity for filling the place with golden-haired youth.'

They were side by side on the sofa – the one behind which Nell liked to lurk, the one whose sides were damasked walls strapped together at the corners with heavy silk ropes and whose seat was so deep that there was nothing for it but to lie back, comfortable but disabled. Benjie's shirt front was spotted with drips. Impossible to drink from a brandy glass while nearly supine.

'Lil's introducing me to grown-up society. She once told me you had to have at least one pretty girl in every house-party and then the interesting men will come. She likes giving me that sort of advice.'

'Well you're certainly pretty.' A leer, but too perfunctory to be annoying, or to make Flossie feel she should sit up.

'I didn't . . .' She broke off. She'd given him his cue. Pointless to act self-deprecating. Actually Flossie thought herself very pretty indeed. Not that she was vain, or even all that self-confident, but gazing into the mirror sometimes, at night, she so adored her looks it seemed quite incomprehensible that no one (no one who counted) had yet fallen for her. Benjie, of course, didn't count. Nor, she now thought, had he fallen. The pass he'd made over the chessboard was the tribute obligatory from a man who affected to be a bit of a roué to a girl with whom he happened to find himself alone.

'Why are you here?' They were by this time so relaxed her rude question seemed perfectly permissible.

'Because we were invited.'

'No, but I mean are you old friends with Lil or something?'

'Or something.'

Flossie gave up.

'I suppose we should go to bed.'

'Hang on a bit. There's something I want to ask you.'

She turned towards him, and found he was kissing her, and found to her surprise that what she felt was delight.

Lil

Go to sleep. Wrong word. Going is willed. Going is active. But you don't *go* to sleep: sleep comes to you and bashes you around the head. Sleepers are felled. Sprawled. Stunned. They snore and sweat and mutter. All day I'm Lil, smart and taut, juggling with knives, bright and hard and essential as the diamond in a watch's works. They spin around me. They love me for it. Control is my gift to them. But then, come night and sleeping pills, a trapdoor opens and I drop.

Fall asleep is better. Fall, that's closer to what we do. We fall down a rabbithole, down a helter-skelter. Sometimes the shock is extreme enough to wake us, to jerk us back up onto solid ground. But mostly we're gone, feet waving silly in mid-air, hurtling helpless towards whatever our minds, guards dropped, have unleashed.

Wychwood is around me. As I fall it rocks and spins, but only in the worst times does it vanish and leave me unhoused. Unhouseled means unsanctified. House is holiness. I am the *genius loci*, the lady of the lake, lady of the drawing room, lady of the croquet lawn, lady of . . .

In the walled garden the unicorn lays down clumsily, encumbered by its horn, and the apples fall from the blossoming trees. Flossie swims underwater with the goldfish, her long hair streaming the length of the canal, enveloping the lily pads in swirls of golden wire. Gold on black water, lacquer-dark, flecks of light in the resin, layer upon layer, the Japanese screen, the cormorants, the ladies' hair which trails so far beyond their kimonos' hems it tangles through the puffs of gilded cloud and there's a kitten playing and a tiny boy. Tiny boy. Fergus's round face beneath the peat-brown water. Rembrandt's brown varnish lapping Saskia's thighs. Painted water is solid, real varnish is transparent, skin becomes pearly. I am a drowned sailor, I lie on my pillows as flaccid as jelly. I dissolve.

*

Helen – You didn't reply.

Nicholas – This thing that's happening, it's really quite significant.

Helen – It's really quite significant that I'm offering to leave my husband to be with you.

Nicholas – Is it an offer? It feels like a demand.

Helen – So you only wanted me part-time. You said you loved me.

Nicholas – I do love you.

Helen – But what?

(*Male voice, inaudible, apparently interrupting Nicholas.*)

Nicholas – Helen, my dearest, I really can't talk now.

Helen – (*hangs up*)

Dodging the stuffed bear, Helen glanced into the dimly lit drawing room and saw with a rippling series of emotions that her husband and Flossie were still lolling there together. Flossie was definitely a bit drunk. Benjie probably not. Helen passed on, her bare feet silent on the stairs. Helen: so intelligent, so self-possessed, but now all her fine mind could tell her was 'Nobody loves me' – that desolate childish plaint. Back in their room she sat at the dressing table for a long time, staring at herself in the mirror, silently mouthing words. When she heard Benjie coming down the corridor she snapped the light off and slipped into bed. She was still awake when the birds started up their racket.

*

Eight hours after his party had started, Ulbricht's guests were tottering. Those fortunate enough to have found seats to stretch out upon were asleep. Most of the men were drunk: most of the women querulous. In the salon the band still played.

At midnight sirens wakened nearly thirty thousand East German servicemen. Officers opened envelopes marked 'Top Secret' and read out the night's astonishing orders. Many of the listeners immediately concluded that this would be the beginning of a war with the West. They were all, of course, socialist materialists. Nonetheless, some of them prayed.

At one a.m. on the morning of Sunday the 14th of August every streetlight in East Berlin went out. Finding their way by moonlight, units of the army, of the police and of the 'combat groups of the working class', moved into position. They formed a human fence (one man per metre) along the 27-mile-long border that cut through the city. All public transport on the Eastern side came to a halt. Passengers arriving from the West at Friedrichstrasse station were prevented from leaving their trains.

All along the border, construction brigades began work. Honecker had planned the operation meticulously. Hundreds of tons of concrete, barbed wire and timber had been amassed – bought in moderate quantities, in the name of civilian contractors, from numerous different suppliers across Europe. Everything necessary, from protective gloves for handling the wire to special clamps for fixing it to concrete posts, had been similarly acquired, and placed in position. This enormous exercise in clandestine shopping had been accomplished so adroitly that only a handful of people had noticed and wondered at it.

Trucks lugged concrete uprights, manufactured out near the Polish border, from the sites around the city's periphery where they had been stockpiled. By one-thirty a.m. the construction workers were setting them up. Others began to fix barbed wire to hooks. The workers were guarded by regular troops. Once the wire fence was securely fixed, these soldiers set up tripods for their machine guns. Their guns pointed eastwards. They weren't invaders. They were their own people's jailors. Soviet tanks formed a ring around the city.

At four a.m., in a hotel in West Berlin, an American reporter was woken by a telephone call from a photographer with whom he sometimes worked. 'It's happening,' said the photographer. 'You'd better come on over here.' The reporter began to dress, picked up the phone again and asked for coffee. 'Sorry, sir,' said the switchboard operator. 'There's no room service.' 'Come on,' said the reporter. 'Just do me a favour here. I've got to go to work. Just get me a cup of coffee.' 'No room service,' said the telephonist again. 'None of our staff from the East have come to work tonight. No room service.' The reporter finished tying his shoelaces and ran down the stairs, and out onto the street, and kept on running until he reached Potsdamer Platz and saw the wire.

As the sun rose Ulbricht's party guests were allowed, at last, to go home.

Sunday

Sunday was the only day of the week on which the Lane family ate breakfast together. Chloe went fasting to Communion, and by the time she got home, the afterglow of holiness and sweet wine as soothing in her as the balm of Gilead, the house would be smelling of the warm bread rolls they had instead of the daily bacon and egg. Heather, slatternly in her dressing gown, brought the children down, then vanished back to the night nursery for her weekly lie-in. Mrs Ferry carried the rolls out from the slate-shelved larder, ceremoniously covered with the special pink and white embroidered cloth. It was Nell's solemn duty to warm them in the oven, which she was usually forbidden to touch.

They ate them with slices of ham, and then with honey. There was hot milk for the children, tinted purple with Ribena, and real coffee for the grown-ups out of the silver coffee pot that had belonged to the great-aunt who had bequeathed to Chloe a houseful of lacquered knick-knacks and hand-painted porcelain, and who had insisted on giving Nell her name. The morning sun fell quiet on the black and white geometry of the dining-room's paved floor. The grown-ups were allowed to read the papers, which made them inattentive to table manners. Nell licked honey off her fingers, and closed her eyes and wondered at her eyelids, so thin that the sun shone pinkly through them.

This Sunday, though, her mother and father were arguing about someone called George, who was going to be in prison for a long long time. Nell had read bits of *The Count of Monte Cristo*. Prison was a place of perpetual darkness where people's hair and fingernails grew as long as witches'.

Hugo said, 'You can't say "poor fellow" about a traitor.'

'But traitor to what? Blake was being true to his idea of what was right.'

'Oh for goodness sake.' Hugo didn't really enjoy this kind of arguing. Chloe did, but sometimes Nell could see how, though she might seem to be getting all worked up about something in the papers, really it was Daddy she was cross with. Like Dickie getting furious with Nell when she wandered off in the middle of a croquet game because she just didn't care who won. Chloe wanted to talk about George. She wouldn't have minded Hugo disagreeing, but 'for goodness sake' spoiled the game.

'But really. He's actually Dutch, did you know that?'

'And came here to save himself, and settled down very comfortably thank you, and went to Cambridge and had a lovely time punting, and then decides all the people he's been chums with can be killed, for all he cares. Honestly, darling, you can't feel sorry for a chap like that.'

'But why not?' Fresh from the altar, Chloe was full of Christian charity.

'People were killed because of him. People on his own side.'

'No, it wasn't his side. I mean I know he was an enemy, but there can be good traitors. Like there can be good Germans. Think of the aunts.'

This was a bit of a swerve, and Chloe, recollecting herself, had executed it deliberately to restore good humour. The aunts were a pair of ladies whose relationship with the family was genea-logically vague, but warm. They lived together in North Oxford, along with a gentleman called Foxy (his real name was too long to be easily pronounceable), and wore lace-up shoes and heavy tweed skirts over which chiffon scarves incongruously drifted. They had been self-appointed godmothers to Chloe, and were now to Nell and Dickie. They were Austrian actually. Legends of their youth involved crenellated castles overlooking lakes, disappointing young men in white flannels, a poet or two. Though they had fetched up in Oxford well before the war, they had neither of them really mastered English. For Nell – who had been sent to stay with them while the parents were on holiday – to think of the aunts was to feel the slithery fineness of face powder in a gilded round cardboard box, to smell Foxy, who seldom spoke but reeked pleasantly of something vegetable like dried-up moss, to sense the odd peacefulness of their house, where no one had to be decisive or busy, or do anything other than exchange fragmentary quotations from the works of unfashionable poets, and wonder aloud when it would be time, finally, to throw out the dusty arrangements of dried flowers.

'Are the aunts traitors?' asked Nell now. The thought was interesting. Hugo, who was less fond of the elderly threesome than his wife was, perked up too.

'Well maybe they are,' he said. 'Maybe they were secretly working for Hitler, sending secret messages back to Berlin about which cabinet minister cheated at croquet.'

'Would Hitler want to know?' Nell was doubtful.

'Yes, yes. Of course he would. Because then he could blackmail them. Imagine if it got out that a fellow had moved his ball. Just a tiny little nudge when everyone else had turned to see Mrs Ferry coming with the lemonade. He'd be blackballed from his club. He'd be jeered at on the platform at Paddington. He'd be done for. Fate worse than death. So in his despair he'd be a helpless tool of the Nazis, and Aunt Irma would be his handler, and meet him for picnics in Christ Church Meadow, and slip him macaroons with messages written in invisible ink on the rice paper on their underside.'

Nell and Dickie were both giggling now. This was baffling nonsense, but they loved it when their father set out on one of his flights into absurdity.

'But Hitler died ages ago.'

'Yes, and anyway in the dark days of the war the aunts saw the error of their ways and longed to cut their ties to their evil master. And one day they noticed that the new gardener, Boris, had a peculiar accent. Of course he'd told them he was from Somerset, and being foreign they couldn't tell the difference between a proper West Country burr and the terrifying tones of a secret agent from Vladivostok.'

Hugo was acting it all out – the way Boris put his hand to his back (all gardeners had bad backs). The aunts throwing their hands up in dismay. It was as good as charades. Dickie laughed himself into hiccups.

'So one day, among the gooseberry bushes, Boris told Aunt Lottie the truth. He was a Russian spy, and he knew all about their dastardly behaviour in passing secrets to the German enemy. So . . .'

A pause as Hugo worked out the next twist. Chloe had unclenched and was smiling vaguely, leaning back, rocking on her chair's back legs, even though she told the children off so sharply when they did the same.

'So now he was going to blackmail them, because if he revealed their dreadful secret and if they went into Fullers for walnut cake all the nice ladies having tea would stand up and hiss at them. So of course they were putty in his hands.'

'What's putty?'

'Hush. So they became Russian spies for a bit, but then . . . They went to a sherry party in Christ Church with an excellent fellow who has parties on Sunday mornings.'

'Mr White!' said Nell and Dickie in unison. Their parents went frequently to such sherry parties.

'And he took pity on the poor aunts, because he could see they were really good Germans.'

'Good Austrians,' said Chloe.

'Good traitors,' said Nell.

'And he said they could be triple traitors and spy for England as well, and so their good spying cancelled out both kinds of bad spying and they went back to Park Town in time for lunch and they had roast beef and Yorkshire pudding because now they were jolly old English spies.'

'So there are good spies?'

Hugo, suddenly snapping out of it. 'Well I wouldn't want to be one. Or for you to be one.' He wasn't playing any more. 'Imagine lying to everyone around you. Even if it was for a good cause. You couldn't like a person who did that. I don't think I'd like the good Germans who helped us, not really, however useful they were. And I certainly don't like Blake. He ought to be shot. Unwept, unhonoured, and unsung.'

'That's enough. Come on. Hats and gloves and meet you by the front door in ten minutes.' Chloe was pushing the children, arms outstretched around them without touching, like Mr Slatter coaxing a dawdling cow. Heather, dressed now and waiting in the hallway, ushered them on up the stairs.

'You've got them properly confused now,' Chloe said to Hugo, 'and I won't have you telling them you'd shoot people.' But she said it lightly. The argument was over.

An hour later the family sat, in ascending order of age, in the agent's pew behind the Rossiters': sailor suit; yellow linen coat and flowered bonnet; blue dress with a bolero failing to meet over a huge striped bow which matched the hat; dark suit, white shirt and Brigade of Guards tie. After the psalm Hugo walked over to the lectern, and read slowly and impressively from the Old Testament. The story of Samson. His hair was as oiled and gleaming as that of the hero about whom he read, his voice expressionless. He was good at this.

As Nell listened, images swam through her mind. The terrified foxes with flaming tails. The woman weeping and pleading. The warrior who married the daughter of his enemy. The bees swarming around the poor dead lion whose picture was on the Golden Syrup tin. The riddle, its answer treacherously revealed. The hair strewn on the floor (blonde ringlets, she saw in her mind's eye, like brass corkscrews). The hips and thighs smitten by the serrated bone. The ass, shaggy and greasy-smelling like her own sweet donkey but reduced to a horrid weapon. So many creatures to grieve over. Betrayal.

Christopher was the only occupant of the pew in front. 'You've got a houseful of heathens, then?' said Hugo, following him out.

'Wireless-worshippers,' said Christopher. 'You've not heard the news? They're all still around the breakfast table, bowing down to that thing as though it was the burning bush.'

'What's happened? There was nothing much in the papers.'

'No. But Nicholas rang early and told us to switch on. The Reds have closed the border in Berlin. In the middle of the night.'

'How?'

'With miles and miles of barbed wire. Thousands of concrete posts. Men with machine guns in a human wall all across the city.'

'My God. All in one night? It's unbelievable.'

'It is.'

In Chloe's mind a ring of fire sprang up around Brunhilde. When your daughter looks like taking an interest in a new world order, wall her in with flame.

Hugo, who wasn't interested in opera, said, 'German efficiency for you.'

'Let's hope so. If the Russians put them up to it we're all up shit creek without a paddle.'

Mild, courtly Christopher occasionally came out with risqué colloquialisms. Hugo could read, passing serially behind the surface of Chloe's inadvertently expressive face, a tremor of shock, an impulse to signal to the children that it was not all right to use such words, an effort at self-control. Mustn't be rude to the boss; probably the children didn't understand anyway; to fuss about a bit of ripe language in the face of a potentially terrifying international crisis would look preposterously prissy. She really did hate that sort of talk, though. It was to her, like the scritching of chalk on blackboard, or the way rhubarb turned the inside of one's mouth from satin to sandpaper.

Perhaps Christopher could read her face too. Smoothly switching tone he said to Hugo, 'Lil asks if you'll come up for tennis again after lunch.' He caught a flickering, silent exchange between husband and wife. Living on the edge of the deer-park, Hugo could slip home for elevenses and odd times throughout the day – a plus – but he was also (and Christopher was more alive to the annoyances attendant on this than Lil was) all too easily available to his employers, something which Chloe found irksome. Christopher added on his own initiative, 'All four of you. I expect you'll want to swim again before the pool's emptied, won't you, Nell?'

Nell was bewildered. Was something awful happening, or not? If there was going to be a war how could the grown-ups be talking about tennis? It had always puzzled her. When her parents were at school there were bombs dropping out of the sky and people they knew were being killed, and yet all the usual things carried on all the same. Lessons, and eating shepherd's pie, and going to parties, even. That seemed the strangest thing of all. Now she knew, from the way Nicholas and Mr Rossiter had talked yesterday, that this thing that was going on was frightening, but still her mother was trying to edge into the shade of one of the churchyard yew trees because she hated getting sunburnt – as though having pearly pale skin really mattered even now.

Antony

Earlier that year I had had occasion to visit Sunderland. Being an art-dealer takes one into some intriguing milieux. A ship-owner intended to invest some of his money in old masters, and wanted to get our relationship off on a right footing by showing me the stupendous work he did, before humbling himself by requesting my guidance.

We rode around in a car smelling so strongly of new leather and cigar smoke that all my recollections of the day are queasy. He took me to his office, hung with pictures of the ships his family had built and owned, some of them painted in Hong Kong by Chinese artists with an unfamiliar approach to perspective, some simple drawings done by teenaged mid-Victorian second mates, some moody romantic oils of sails silhouetted against scudding clouds. One of these, he told me, confidently but over-optimistically, was by Turner. He offered coffee, cognac and chocolate biscuits, all of which I declined. I was introduced to a succession of men, his managers, who clearly thought, and made me feel, how footling an occupation I had compared with theirs. Then we drove down towards the waterfront.

A street without pavements, on each side an unbroken brick phalanx of several dozen identical two-up-two-downs. He'd told me to sit in front with the chauffeur. He wanted to astonish me, and he so far succeeded that at first I almost missed the marvel. The street came to a dead end bounded by a metal wall so high I could no more take it in than the mouse could comprehend the elephant. A ship. Dry land and appropriate scale ended simultaneously. This enormous thing subverted all expectation. It was so big and solid and heavy, and yet it floated, as those squatting houses and their heavy-booted occupants would never float. It belonged in vast spaces. It would dwindle to tininess amidst boundless empty seas. It was a marvel. I have spent much of my life appraising images designed to induce awe and wonder, but I had never before seen anything so impressive. Here was the product of skills I could barely imagine, and hard, dangerous labour. Lying there, alongside the pygmy homes of the puny little humans who had built it, the ship was as astonishing as an annunciating angel.

That Sunday morning at Wychwood my memory of the ship kept recurring. Berliners had woken to find that the next street lay in another country. This they'd known ever since the war's end, but to know something is a very different thing from seeing it, especially when it is so implausible.

Frontiers are drawn on maps as lines, but in experience they are broad smudges, gradual transitions. The heather and midges begin long before you get to Scotland. By the Italian lakes you are already, or still, in Austria. The people who live along a border – in peacetime anyway – walk over it, plough over it, overlook it. Physically, it doesn't exist. Yet here was a nation throwing up a palpable wall along an impalpable division. It was eerie. The materialisation of the imaginary. A haunting.

'And it's not even a wall,' said Lil. 'We keep calling it that, but Nicholas says it's really just a barbed-wire fence.'

It was lunchtime. The long stone table at which we were eating was shaded by the cedar, gigantic, black and medicinally fragrant. The food at Wychwood was always fabulous. Little round pots of some sort of pink fish mousse, then cold lamb cutlets with new potatoes and a bright-green sauce made of Mr Green's mint and the yoghurt which Lil, perhaps alone in Oxfordshire, demanded from the harassed village shopkeeper. It was imported from Bulgaria, and we all accepted its sourness as being of the nature of the beast (it was, we understood, animate). It was only several years later, once the local equivalent became available, that I realised it had gone off in transit. But how deliciously cosmopolitan it seemed. Posies of nasturtiums brilliant against white damask. Wine in glasses so fine that Benjie, generally popular now but still cack-handed, broke one simply by grasping it too firmly as he arrived at a punchline. And all around us, rendered even more than usually lovely by the hazy light of a dying summer, that grandiose assemblage of stone – carved by humans, embroidered by lichen – ancient trees, bleached parkland beyond the ha-ha, the admirable garden in which the formality of watercourses and topiary set off the great free sweep of the lawns.

'Really, it does seem incongruous to be sitting here and talking about barbed wire. Let's try roses instead. Hugo, is that Madame Alfred Carrière?' Helen's interjection was welcome. I suppose it is for the hostess to decide whether talking politics at mealtimes is permissible, but the truth was I was getting tired of the subject. Not just nervous, as I had reason to be, but bored. It wasn't as though anyone present actually had any new information to impart, and since we'd been harping on Berlin all morning, as we passed, in repeatedly re-forming groups, from terrace to pool to the deckchairs laid out beneath the pergola, the airing of purely speculative views had become tedious.

Hugo began to replan Helen's London garden for her, using the crumbs of Bath Oliver biscuits as rose-bushes, and a twisted napkin to represent a serpentine path. Lunch ended, the two of them crossed to the sunken garden beyond the screen of wisteria so that he could show her his favourite hybrid musks. His doting shadow followed – little Nell. And so, after a pause during which she listened to an exchange of banter between Flossie and Benjie (now fast friends) with that air of oh-so-flatteringly rapt attention that Christopher and I were probably the only people present to know was fake, did Lil.

Lil

Night time is the right time . . . Wrong. So wrong. The right time is this time. After-lunch-time. Siesta sexta hora sixth hour sex hour. Christopher in Seville leaning across the table to stroke my inner elbow with his long olive fingers. The frisson. I had never even known that elbows . . . So smooth, his chest. No hair. Seeing him in the tiny bathtub in that hotel with the shoeshine boys bleating outside our window. The shock of the beauty of a naked man, enormous in that cramped bathroom, like a fox trapped in a hutch. The table he leant across was covered with little dishes. The kidneys oozing blood and the potatoes chequered with red chilli. The white rubber rings of calamari. So fastidious, so neat. His green linen jacket spotless, the sleeve avoiding all that spiced oil, his hand cool touching that place, that part of me I had never paid attention to, which had kept secret, even from me, its astonishing capacity for pleasure. How did he know to do that? His creation perhaps, conjuring up nerve endings just so that he could set them trembling. Looking into his eyes. Now I understand about that. You hold yourself together by looking into a man's eyes, like watching the verge at night to prevent yourself driving into the oncoming car. Oncoming swoon. That was fifteen years ago and he still wears those pale, pale green jackets. His clothes always the same, as though he doesn't care about them, but actually because he does care very much. He's wearing one now.

So why am I here, crossing this lawn, exposed by the sun like a robber exposed by a policeman's torch? Glaring. Jeering. Silly Lily. I'm as much of a fool for Hugo as his dog and his daughter. Five years younger than me. A perfectly nice wife. He walks off and fat yellow Wully heaves himself up and follows. And so does Nell. And, oh Lord how shaming, so do I.

*

Alone together (Heather had walked down to the cottages to spend her afternoon off with her friend Sharon Armstrong, Mrs Ferry had washed up lunch and bicycled home), Chloe and Dickie lay flat on their backs on a tartan rug. They were falling upward into space.

'There's a star, there's a star, oh Mummy hold tight.'

He was gripping Chloe's second and third finger – as much of her hand as he could get into his fist – so hard her ring dug painfully into her bone, but she didn't try to extricate herself. Dickie was certainly not going to let go. Up was down and down was up and he was plummeting front-first into vacancy that went on and on for ever.

'It's very very cold, isn't it? It's so cold we might die. Our noses might drop off. You won't let go, will you? A a a a a . . .' He was dipping his head from side to side.

'What's happening?' asked Chloe, sounding as distant as though they really were drifting apart, connected only by a safety line, in danger of losing each other in a lightless wilderness of something that wasn't even air. She was close to falling asleep. Because Hugo and Nell were up at Wychwood she and her little boy had had their secret best lunch: potted shrimps on toast, then strawberry jelly and custard with Battenberg cake – a composition in pink and yellow, Dickie's favourite colours, with top-of for a treat. Not that he'd ever wear pink, or anything girly. Thank goodness he had male cousins, otherwise everything would have had to be new. Mrs Hollis at the garage made Nell's dresses out of things Mrs Rossiter gave them. They were always too small for Chloe, so *that* embarrassment was spared. At parties Nell was snazzy in swirl-patterned Pucci silk or beige broderie anglaise, Lil's sleek shifts remade with incongruous puffed sleeves and sashes.

'There are *things*,' said Dickie squeakily. His head was slapping from side to side. 'They're going to hit me.' He was trying to curl himself up into a ball.

Chloe pulled herself back to full consciousness. Dickie was exasperatingly good at getting himself into a state. 'Spaceship to spaceman Dickie,' she said in a robotic voice. 'Spaceship to space-man Dickie. We're bringing you back into the ship. Relax. Relax. Relax.' Dickie's head was still now. 'Those things you're worried about, Dickie. We know what they are. We can see some space-marbles whizzing around you now. That's a very rare occurrence. Just look at them, Dickie. Aren't they wonderful colours? Aren't they like bits of rainbow?'

Dickie's eyes opened wide – he loved his collection of marbles too much ever to play with them. They were laid out on a solitaire board on his bedroom floor so he could see them first thing in the morning, just by leaning out of bed. 'Space-marbles aren't hard like earth-marbles. They fly about very fast and furious, but they're more like bubbles really. They can't hurt you. Now go completely limp, spaceman Dickie, and we're going to pull you in through the hatch. And spacedog Mummy will be coming in first to show you how.'

She sat and then stood, and held up her arms, hands with palms together, as though for a dive, to make herself narrow enough to pass easily through a porthole. Dickie did the same, and slipped feet first into the spaceship. 'We're safe. We're safe. We're safe,' he sang, to the tune of 'The Farmer's In His Den' and they took each other's hands and span five times round to celebrate their return from the aching cold and dark of intergalactic space to the familiar setting of sundial and parched lawn.

'Can we go to the secret pond?' said Dickie. Only just back from one adventure, and perhaps aware that he hadn't acquitted himself entirely heroically, he wanted another one immediately.

'Socks and boots on then,' said Chloe. She had once seen a grass snake where they were going next, and although she really did believe it was a grass snake, well, it could have been an adder. She didn't mention snakes to the children at all. Just said that they had to wear boots in the forest because of nettles.

'I like the bottoms of gumboots,' said Dickie as he struggled into them. 'They look like sweets.'

'They do, don't they,' said Chloe, and they each had a fruit gum in honour of their boots – yellow for him, purple for her.

From Wood Manor's upper lawn they could step through a narrow gate into the paddock where Silver and his friend Cinderella stood knee-deep in grass. When Hugo took Nell out for a ride, Cinderella, who was a donkey, ran along behind them like a big bony dog. The idea had been that Dickie would learn to ride on her, but whenever anyone mounted her she bucked. 'I don't think I like riding,' said Dickie, his lips mauve with fear, and Hugo, who found teaching his children less fun than he'd imagined it might be, added 'Pony for Dickie' to his list of things to do one of these days, which might mean never.

The paddock formed a crescent around the garden, and beyond it the forest began. They passed through a tunnel of rhododendrons, then out into one of the broad avenues where nothing much grew under the huge beech trees to either side.

'Heather says the trees are thousands and thousands of years old.'

'Only about a quarter of one thousand,' said Chloe, and then wished she hadn't.

They held hands. Dickie hummed, a monotonous little noise as peaceful as bee-buzz. It was rare for them to be alone together like this. Why, wondered Chloe, do I pay Heather to have these precious times with the children? What on earth do I do all day long?

Ten minutes brought them to the tree whose low-hanging branch made a horse the children could ride. Dickie sat on it and bounced. 'It's all mine today,' he said, and then was quiet. Nell's absence made this afternoon easy, but also just a little dull. Chloe sat in the roots of the tree, absently cleaning her fingernails with a twig. In their own personae they were not sure how to talk to each other. She thought, with anguish, Only two years and he'll have to go away to school. In a clearing beyond the riding-tree a shaft of sunlight was full of insects, a pillar of twitching radiance rising from the bracken. Chloe thought, This is boring, and, This is what makes me happy.

Twelve trees further down the avenue – Dickie picked up a single leaf under each one, which was how he'd learnt to count – they turned onto the narrow path to the ruin of a garden.

One of Wychwood's long-ago owners had had it made as a present for his wife. Outside the park, it must have represented quite an excursion for her, even though the wrought-iron gate was still visible behind them, spanning the ride. She and her friends would come in a pony-trap, with parasols, and a cart following bringing hampers, and her musicians. There was even a miniature ice-house there in the woods, so that wine and apricots could be chilled ready for her repast.

Chloe and Dickie scrambled over the broken-down wall. Inside there were tall dark trees which emitted a scent peculiar to this place, and a little trellised pavilion whose copper-clad dome was bright with verdigris, and in front of it the empty saucer of a dried-up pond.

Dead centre of the dry pond lay a thumb-thick black snake, as neatly coiled as a Catherine wheel. Chloe stopped short. Never show the children you're afraid. Dickie slipped his hand away and threw himself onto the verge and began to roll. The game was to tumble around and around the pond's sloping clay sides until gravity pulled you down into the middle. For Nell's last birthday Hugo had borrowed the roulette wheel that Mr Slatter manned at the village fête, and the children had played for Smarties. '*Faites vos jeux! Faites vos jeux!*' yelled Dickie now, tipping himself over the pond's rim. Chloe dropped to her knees, and lunged down grabbing him roughly by the shoulders. He burst into tears. The snake, quite slowly, unwound itself, took a look at them and then was gone in a flicker.

Dickie saw it. 'I want to go home! I want to go home!' he shouted.

So did Chloe. Carrying him as though he was a baby, she hauled Dickie over the wall, and didn't put him down again until they were back in the beech avenue. There, the afternoon's second shock, there where they had never before seen anyone they didn't know, anyone who didn't work for Wychwood, and therefore in a way for Dickie's father, they saw coming towards them over the sun-spotted beech mast, lots of people, perhaps twenty, with big sticks.

*

Up at Wychwood Helen was paying serious attention, but being sparing of her compliments, which all three of her interlocutors – perhaps most of all Nell, who knew how much her father and Mrs R cared for the rose garden – found hard.

'You see,' said Hugo, 'the springwater is pumped up into the canal, then flows through a hidden ditch to drive this fountain, then runs through a buried pipe to feed the pond in the kitchen garden and trickles on down to the lake. What we really want to do is to have another go at getting the fountain at the head of the home lake to spout. As far as I can make out Norris and his fellows just couldn't get it working, but the original plans are stupendous.'

As Hugo spoke, in Lil's mind's eye there were white founts falling in the courts of the sun. The Moors' marvellous irrigation channels set quicksilver streams gushing across the red hillsides of Andalucia. Poems inscribed on rose petals floated along marble-paved channels from one alabaster-panelled pavilion to another. Lemon groves spread their sharp sweet fragrance. Cithars twanged. Striped silk robes fell back to reveal the flash of damascened scimitars. Burnished flies by the myriad settled on mounds of decapitated Crusader heads.

Helen, to whom the hydraulic arrangements of Wychwood's garden summoned up no such vision, looked vacant. Hugo brought himself back to the local wonders. 'The spring's magic, you know. We have to let the witches in to fill their medicine bottles from it.' Nell knew this was a fact. Mrs Slatter, who bi-cycled up to Wood Manor with cream and butter on Wednesdays, and could cure everyone else's warts but could do nothing about the funny lumps on her own chin, was one of the witches. The other was Mrs Slatter's sister Mrs Leatherset, but she was known to be mad, and to have gone for her husband with a carving knife. She was no longer asked to wash up after dinner parties.

Helen ignored the mention of witches, which she took to be a sop to the credulous (Nell). She really was, to everyone else's vague irritation, interested in roses to the point of pedantry.

Neither Lil nor Hugo, both of whom loved this garden, cared much to know the names of rose varieties. Hugo's own garden was stocked chiefly by cuttings taken (as gifts or thefts) from the gardens of friends. To learn roses' names from a book, and buy them in a sort of shop, were practices of the unfortunate ill-connected, the kind of people who bought their engagement rings, rather than finding them in their mothers' jewel boxes. The Wychwood roses were propagated by cuttings from their ancestors. It pleased both the Rossiters to believe (erroneously) that the blowsy pink flowers arranged in their library were identical with, and directly related to, those that had been enjoyed there by a favourite of the first Queen Elizabeth. Lil tried to suppress the thought, but Helen's questions about whether this was Fritz Nobis or that was Zéphirine Drouhin seemed like the outflow of a dull mind. As soon ask Cimabue what pigments he mixed into his paints: a question Antony would have found fascinating, but for which Lil – who liked to respond to art on a spiritual level, as though it were a kind of materialised ectoplasm – would have had no time.

Sharply she changed the subject. 'So Benjie knew Ant in Germany?' she asked Helen.

'Mmm.'

'In Munich?'

'No before that, in Berlin.'

'Ant? I didn't know he'd been in Berlin.'

'Well while he was with the military police he was there.'

Lil was silenced. It was unpleasant to learn at second hand, and from someone she had just begun to find annoying, that there were things she didn't know about a man she thought of as her protégé and pet. Antony was younger than her, and nothing like as rich, and, being unmarried, somehow not quite adult. It was disturbing to come up against testimony to a life he led away from her, without mentioning it, a life that had been going on for years.

'Was Benjie a policeman? I didn't know.' (Deflecting her ignorance to where it was innocuous. Benjie, being a comparatively new acquaintance, was allowed to have as-yet-unexamined passages in his past.)

'Yes. He doesn't like to talk about it much. The men he was having to round up were just boys who'd gone crazy with fear, and then even crazier with relief once the fighting was over. I think he saw shocking things, and then to come back to find all that simple-minded rejoicing.' Helen's voice tailed off. The simple-minded were everywhere.

'So what were they doing?' asked Lil. Christopher had spent most of his war in Whitehall, but he went to Germany after the surrender, and stayed out there until their wedding. 'Mopping up Jerry,' he called it. The only story he had ever told her was about flighting duck over marshes near the Baltic coast. 'There was a chap told off to be my loader,' he said. 'Polite. Spoke perfect English. I asked him how he learnt it. He said he had an English tutor. Seemed a bit surprising for a keeper. And then it turned out he owned the place. I was shooting his duck on his land, with his gun. And he was loading for me. And I don't suppose he was going to get his land back.' The story always ended 'Wonder what happened to him,' but, as far as Lil knew, Christopher had never tried to find out, and he couldn't remember, perhaps had never known, perhaps wanted not to know, the dispossessed landowner's name. But that was a story about a German. Who were these people Helen was talking about? 'What boys?' she said.

Helen hesitated.

Lil pressed on. 'The boys doing shocking things.'

They were on the shady side of the artificial dell. Lil sat on the marble bench. Helen sat beside her. Hugo propped a foot on the wrought-iron chair with its lily-of-the-valley-patterned back (rust just showing through – needs repairing – remember to mention it to Green).

Nell stretched out on the slimy green stone beneath the bench, the women's legs fencing her in – Lil's smooth, bare and pale, propped on the funny rope-soled shoes she bought in France in lots of different colours (yellow was best), Helen's in stockings with tiny tiny hairs poking through the nylon mesh. There was something horrid about stockings, the way they pretended to be invisible but weren't. Like cut toenails, or pale rags of seaweed. Nell disliked too the little rubber bobbles of suspender belts. She didn't didn't didn't ever want to have to wear such things.

'Well you know,' said Helen. 'They'd been trained to kill Germans, and the older ones had actually been fighting, and probably they'd had brothers or friends or whatever who'd been killed.'

'Don't make excuses,' Hugo had said to Nell. 'If you've done something wrong, just own up and say you're sorry. No one cares about your excuses. They're just boring.' It was when she forgot to feed her budgerigar and Dickie had shrieked and shrieked when he found it lying upside down with its little blue claws clenched. It had died because she didn't love it – she knew that. So all the stuff she sobbed out about how she thought Heather was going to feed it, and anyway you weren't supposed to give them too much to eat, was just nonsense. When you didn't love things you lost them. Like the dress with the stiff frills her mother had had made for her, which was shaming and babyish and always fell off its hanger and lay scrumpled in the bottom of the wardrobe without her having done anything to make it happen, just failed to give the dress the appreciation which would have kept it safely in place. She knew not to make excuses about that too. Helen's excuses sounded like fibs, and she hadn't even said yet what she was making excuses for.

'So, you know, when it was over, and there were so many people dead, and so many empty buildings and so much stuff lying about they went sort of mad. Looting. Benjie talks about men walking down the streets carrying clocks and looking-glasses and lamps. Ridiculous. They couldn't possibly have got the stuff home. Just seeing something up for grabs and wanting to grab it.'

'I was there too,' said Hugo quietly.

'Of course, I'm sorry. What am I doing telling you about it?'

Lil had never heard Hugo talk about his national service. Even this admission of having been in Germany was a rare opening, through which, being Lil, she immediately thrust a question. 'Did you see, well, what did you see?'

'Not much really. I was just a new lieutenant, lowest of the low. But there was a chap. Roger Bates. I'd known him at school. My friend fagged for him. He was a regular officer but he'd got hold of a military police uniform. And the MPs were allowed to go into the locals' houses. We were absolutely forbidden to, of course. He used to put it on, and go round banging on people's doors. They'd give him things to make him go away. Or he'd threaten to send his men round, who'd have smashed the place up, and these wretched people would give him a silver candlestick or what-have-you. Extortion. He was recognised by another chap who knew he was in the wrong uniform. His room was crammed with loot. They couldn't move him at once, so he was being held in this old office we were using as a command post. And I had to sit with him. I had a revolver. If he'd tried to escape I was supposed to shoot him. We just sat and every now and then I'd offer him a cigarette. I just can't tell you how long that night felt.'

There was a pause. Helen said, 'Embarrassing for you.' But she didn't sound sympathetic. Lil was baffled. How, in the wreckage of a defeated nation, could a contretemps between two Old Etonians have seemed so significant? 'What happened to him?' she asked.

'Odd thing is,' said Hugo, 'I've no idea. I never heard anything about a court martial. Someone told me later he'd made a run for it next day when they were changing trains. Absolute fiasco.'

The story fizzled out. Hugo seemed disinclined to make any further attempt to describe conditions in post-war Germany. Helen let him off by throwing in another surprise.

'Benjie used to think that Antony might be another fake. Not looting, or anything like that, but that he might have been passing himself off as military police for his own reasons.'

'What?' Lil bridled. She was liking Helen less and less. 'Are you suggesting . . .?'

Hugo said, 'But Antony wouldn't . . .' Antony who was so jolly with Nell, and never registered by even the most nearly imperceptible nuance of manner (Hugo was alive to all of them) the fact that the agent, whether or not he'd been to school with all the other men around the table, was an employee rather than a guest. Hugo liked him almost as much as Lil did.

'Well I don't know.' Helen recovered from her faux pas with a change of tack. 'But . . . He's so amiable. Perfect undercover agent. It wasn't so hard, back then, to move from one sector to another. His German's excellent, and he speaks Russian too.'

'Antony spying for Russia?' said Lil. 'Really, for goodness sake.' This whole conversation was becoming preposterous, and tiresome.

'He might have been spying *on* Russia, though,' said Hugo.

'You're right,' said Lil. 'We'd never know, would we? Remember when he bought the Titian for Sunny and we spent a whole weekend trying to get him to tell us who his client was?'

'Poor Ant. You were ruthless. Gosh, you even got him down on the floor and tickled him to make him talk.'

'I know. Torture! Ant in his lovely herringbone tweed. He hates to have his dignity undermined.'

Hugo and Lil were laughing into each other's faces. There was something else covert in the rose garden now, but Nell, beneath the bench, didn't sense it. Shrinking back against clammy green stone, she thought: Antony; spy; 'Imagine lying to everyone around you'; 'ought to be shot'.

*

The walkers' sticks were just for walking with. They were all quite friendly. When Hugo met someone on Wychwood land, someone who didn't belong, he would say 'Can I help you?' in a way that was unmistakably menacing, but Chloe, trapped by a lifetime of good manners, could not but be gracious.

The man carrying the map said, 'Good afternoon,' civilly enough.

There was a terrier with them, and a couple of sheepdogs. Dickie stopped crying.

'Um,' said Chloe, 'are you looking for something?'

'No,' said the man, who had very curly hair. 'Just walking.'

He seemed to be waiting for her to pass, but they were going her way. Helplessly, she walked along beside them, Dickie running ahead now with the dogs. What on earth would Hugo say?

'This is Mr Rossiter's land,' she tried. 'Wychwood. You know it's private?'

'It is,' said the curly man. 'But there's a right of way through here.'

'I didn't know that,' said Chloe.

'Work here, do you?'

'Well, my husband does. He's the agent.'

'Oh yes.'

'So are you all on a sort of outing?' The habit of making polite conversation was unsubduable. For goodness sake, she thought to herself, if a burglar came into our bedroom I'd be asking him if he'd had a tiring journey.

'I suppose so,' said the man.

Another woman walking just behind said, 'Yes we are. We're having a lovely time. It's so peaceful here, isn't it, Bill?' the latter question addressed to the man beside her.

Chloe smiled at them. Small talk seemed like the only possible refuge from this excruciating situation.

'Did you all come together?' she asked vaguely.

'Well,' said the woman, 'Mark here had the idea. He's local. And he told Bill. And most of the rest of us, we all come from the same estate.'

'Oh I see,' said Chloe, to whom the word 'estate' was reassuring. 'Is it near here?'

'Banbury,' said the woman. 'A bit of a step. But we fancied a day out. Our friend gave us a lift in his van.'

'So, is that Sandford?' asked Chloe. Sandford belonged to a friend of Christopher's. Hugo was often invited to shoot there, and sometimes Chloe went for lunch. When the Sandford water meadows froze over there was a great skating party on New Year's Day, with baked potatoes cooked in the bonfire, and tin trays for the children to slide around on while the huge pink sun went down behind the ruined priory.

'Banbury,' said the woman again. To her the word 'estate' had different connotations – modern, urban. Chloe left it. Already she was shaping the story as she would tell it to Hugo that evening. He'd say, 'Honestly, Puss, you'd never make a policeman.'

*

Back in the rose garden, Nell popped her head out between the ladies' legs.

Hugo, accompanied always by Wully, was apt to treat his daughter with the same nonchalance as that with which he treated his dog. 'You shouldn't just whistle her up, you know,' said his wife. 'She is human.' 'No, I'm not,' said Nell, 'I'm Daddy's other dog.' 'Super,' said Hugo. 'Spaniel?' Nell, who was a greyhound, gave him a look of silent disdain, but lolloped after him all the same.

Now he took her reappearance as a matter of course, but the two women were startled. Her head nudging their ankles was alarmingly animal. They'd known she was there, but perhaps they wouldn't have talked quite as they did had she been in plain sight. She took charge.

'Have you seen the goldfish?' She was addressing Helen who, aware that the conversation had become frigid, said, 'No but I want to,' and the pair of them set off across the lawn, Helen queenly as ever, Nell her stocky little infanta, or perhaps her petted dwarf, the two of them stepping repeatedly from darkness into light as they crossed the shadows of the yew pillars.

Watching them Hugo said, 'See the stripes. That's the way I planned it when I planted those yews ten years ago. Not bad at all, is it.'

'Really not bad in the least. You're an artist,' Lil said, meaning it, but with a safety-lock of sarcasm on her voice.

Nell took Helen to the canal, in deep shade now as the sun dipped behind the big cedar. The water, darkened, was strangely more transparent. The fish passed slowly, so vast that only portions of their reticulated flanks showed in the gaps between the lily pads.

'Have you ever touched one?'

'I did once. They're not slimy.'

Their faces floated on the surface of the cedar-green water, rippled into fairground horrors.

'I'd be afraid. Aren't you?'

'I don't like it when they gollop their food. But I know they won't hurt me. It's more frightening to think about the tunnel.'

'Tunnel?'

'Like Daddy said. There are all the underground tunnels that the water swishes through in the dark. So if you fell in you might be swept away.'

'I don't think they'd be big enough for you to pass through them.'

Exactly. This was so obtuse that Nell despaired of making her understand that that was just what haunted her. To be sucked into the mouth but not swallowed. Imagine being trapped in the black water, skeins of air-bubbles and waterweed escaping past into the subterranean labyrinth. And the great pale fish bumping and shoving to get by.

'Can you dive?' she asked, which was meant to be a diversion, because for her diving was a quick splashy business, but Helen responded by talking about Greece, and boys diving for sponges so deep down that it was dark at midday, and there were octopuses bigger and paler than the goldfish, twining their tentacles around the remains of wrecked ships hundreds and hundreds of years old, and the green hands of ancient bronze gods gesticulating to no one but the fishes as they reared up through the shifting sand that glittered in the spangles of light that fell, like coins, from the far-distant surface.

'You've been to Greece?' asked Nell. She had a book about gods and goddesses. She was very much afraid of the picture of the Minotaur.

'Yes.'

'I've never been abroad.'

'You will. But where you live would seem to most people as foreign as Greece.'

'Why?' The childish question that Nell had sworn to herself she would stop asking.

'Wychwood is like an island. No one in the outside world lives like this.'

Nell thought about the outside world. She pictured the village, where older girls walked in pairs on summer evenings, their luminous pink and green socks glowing as eerily as those Greek octopuses. And of St Giles's Fair in Oxford, where the gypsy boys pranced so elegantly in and out between the whirling arms of the Waltzer, and where her first ever purse – blue and white flower-patterned plastic – had disappeared from her pocket. And of London, where her mother went on the train every Tuesday, wearing black, and she sometimes went too, with gloves on because London was so dirty, and where her great-great-aunt used to lie in a four-poster bed hung with pink satin, grinding her teeth because she was so terribly terribly old. It might be that, to Helen, Wychwood was an island, like the one in Peter Pan, full of adventures and oddity, but to Nell – who did her lessons at home with Mrs Hopwood – the outside world seemed stranger and more far away.

'You mean people in Berlin?'

Helen looked sharply at her, a look that Nell could read easily. This child is quicker than I realised. I must watch what I say. 'I was thinking just of ordinary people here in England who don't get invited to houses like this.'

'I'm not invited. This is Daddy's work.'

'My work isn't like this at all. It's a little grey room full of filing cabinets.'

Nell was startled. She hadn't imagined Helen had work. None of her parents' women friends did. Nonplussed, she changed the subject.

'Were you in Berlin with Benjie and Antony and Daddy?'

'No. No. Girls didn't go. Well, a few did, but not me.'

'So those things they were talking about – no girl ever saw them.'

'Hardly any English girls. But all the people who lived there.'

'So war is like a boarding school, a place men go away to.'

'Mm. Their island perhaps. And they don't really like talking about it, mostly. I'm glad Benjie's different in that way. He'll talk about anything.'

'Are you quiet because he's so noisy?'

Helen laughed. 'You're a very wise person, Nell. You understand a lot, don't you.'

The exchange of personal appraisals broke their complicity. 'Hugo will be looking for you,' said Helen, and Nell led the way back, through the curving double yew hedge which brought them round to one of the garden's surprises. The hedged walk ended at a ten-foot stone wall with a flattened baroque archway through which a fountain was revealed, theatrically low-lit by the ruddy sun. Lil was in the opening, her head thrown back against the smooth dressed stone. Hugo, facing her, had propped a hand on the wall just above her shoulder. Between their rhymed and curving bodies the water glittered, fluorescent. Helen seemed to stumble, then walked on forward calling their names.

*

That Sunday in Fleet Street was mayhem. When the office went quiet shortly before midnight on Saturday, Nicholas walked home along the river. By the time he got to the flat the telephone was ringing. The editor was hauling him back in. He went straight out again without having even put his briefcase down. All his memories of the day had as part of their atmosphere the fact that his teeth felt so gritty, and he hadn't changed his socks. Doing without sleep, it turns out, is easier than doing without toothpaste.

They'd put three reporters on the first plane to Berlin as soon as the news started coming in over the wires and there wasn't really much that the rest of them could do, but no one wanted to risk missing out. Nicholas's beat was Pall Mall. He'd never been to so many clubs in one day (he had the sense to stick to soda water), or got so little substance from so many hours of talk. Everyone had an opinion. No one had much information. It was hellish hot, and people he'd never seen unbuttoned before were turning up to their offices in Whitehall wearing tennis shoes, as though they'd heard the news on the way out into their gardens and hurtled straight into town.

The Travellers' was seething with handsome craggy types who'd hiked around the Black Forest in the '30s or shot boar in the Thuringian mountains, or got themselves beaten up in Weimar Berlin – none of which, frankly, was any use to Nicholas. In the Reform people were hurrying up and down the mirror-box of a staircase, or hollering to each other from the liver-spotted marble balconies as though they were rehearsing for *Last Year in Marienbad*. In the smoking room he tracked down an old mucker who'd given up Fleet Street three years back and gone into the civil service – Trade and Industry. How banal, his fellow-hacks had thought at the time, how bourgeois. The ministry of travelling salesmen. Now he was the man who knew something.

'The GDR has been buying up every sack of cement going for the past year,' he said. 'We've been wondering about it. They talk a lot about their construction works – motorways, new housing, homes fit for the heroes of the battle for industrial renewal blah di blah. But as far we can make out, they're not actually building that much. There's a chap I could put you on to at the big cement works up in Lincolnshire who can give you chapter and verse.'

Nicholas took the number, but it wasn't British industrialists he needed to talk to. He wanted a line to Honecker. He met his Foreign Office friend in St James's Park. They bought orange ice lollies, took their coats off, bagged some deckchairs and lolled side by side under a plane tree. The other man flicked his MCC tie at a passing duck. 'It may be the end of the world,' he said, 'but it's also Sunday and I'm buggered if I'm going to keep this thing on all day.'

It was like schooldays during exam time, when normal lessons are suspended and everyone was buzzing with a mixture of feelings which looked like elation. But when Nicholas was still in lower school one of the senior boys in his house hanged himself in exam week. Obviously there were a lot of people scared witless the day the wall went up, and that probably included some of the ones he talked to, but you wouldn't have known it from the way they behaved.

His contact told him as much as he knew, but it wasn't much. Soviet troops encircling the city. This number of tanks. That number of planes scrambled. 'One thing I'm pretty sure of,' he said, 'Khrushchev doesn't want this to turn into a shooting match. But that doesn't mean it won't happen.'

'Is Kennedy reliable?' Nicholas asked.

'No one knows. He's not been tested. But when it comes down to it, it'll be some nineteen-year-old Flash Harry who gets scared and pulls a trigger, and then . . . The trouble with ultimata is that they create a chain reaction. You do this. We'll do that. And so on.'

Nicholas saw a girl he knew on the other side of the lake. She was wearing a striking dress – big checks of black, white and electric blue, very low waist like a flapper. Helen used to tell him he was more observant of women's clothes than any other man she knew. He kept an idle eye on the girl while he talked. She had taken her shoes off and she was walking back and forth under the trees in an aimless kind of way. The person she was waiting for appeared. Nicholas knew him too, and also knew his wife. The girl put her bare arms – very thin, very brown – around his neck. They kissed for a long time. It was that kind of a day.

In mid-afternoon someone managed to get some photographs back, and every editor in Fleet Street was scrapping for them. Women standing on their front doorsteps penned in by a tangle of wire, like the servants in Sleeping Beauty's palace gaping at the thorns that had hedged them in overnight. Metal and concrete. Very young soldiers holding up their guns like they'd been turned to stone. Endless interviews with the people who got across just in time, and stories about the ones who had planned to go, and now never would. The War Office weren't saying anything. Nicholas wrote a think-piece for Monday's paper, and left the office almost exactly twenty-four hours after he'd returned to it, and walked home again.

He kept crisscrossing the river, looping from bridge to bridge. He liked seeing that great silent muscular body of water gleaming black beneath his feet. He was too tired to do anything you could properly call thinking. He knew, though, what were some of the things he ought to have been thinking about. Helen. That he ought to make a will. That he ought to ring his mother. Helen.

So he wasn't party to what went on at Wychwood that Sunday, and it all seemed rather trivial to him at the time. All he could gather afterwards was that young Nell strayed out into the garden at night and had some sort of hysterical fit. Upsetting, and of course Lil and Christopher were always edgy about children in any kind of danger. And then, it was after that that they began to go their separate ways. Helen went up to Scotland with them a couple of weeks later, and she told him she never saw them exchange a word. But something happened to Antony too, something indeterminate, but which began to make a bit more sense later on.

Helen

Nicholas and me. Hugo and Lil. It's so trite it's embarrassing. Women yearn, and the men indulge us, but as soon as they have what they think are more important things to do they're off like bloody Odysseus leaving Calypso as fast as his silly misogynist legs could carry him. Ships, not legs.

When the telephone rang we were all out on the terrace. Nell was down on the flagstones patting the stomachs of the two Labradors and they were swooning with pleasure and then as soon as that fusspot of a butler whispered in Hugo's ear, and he went off to take the call, the yellow one shook himself and scurried after him and Nell looked up with such a forlorn face I wanted to say, 'Yes. You're right. Don't I bloody well know it. Love hurts. It's wretched, isn't it, but you're going to have to get used to it. There's only one answer. Find yourself something else to do.' But I can't honestly think of any work I've ever done that I wouldn't have postponed for a day or two if Nicholas had wanted my attention.

Notice I'm identifying Nicholas as my man, not Benjie, but I really don't know why. If you tell a man you're ready to run off with him (in writing, for Christ's sake – what in hell came over me?), and he says he's too busy to talk, you probably need to think about repairing your marriage, don't you? I'd like to put it down to the onset of World War Three, and no doubt Nicholas will, but frankly it's not a sufficient answer. If he had time to say I'm busy, he had time to say Yes.

Pull yourself together, Helen. And remind yourself that before he's forty he'll be completely bald. But oh, the smoothness of him. The way he looks at me sideways when he's brought off a bon mot. The way he gathers up my hair behind and kisses my nape. The worshipful look on his face when he takes off my shoes. The way we seem to read each other's minds. Or did I just imagine all that?

I glanced over at Benjie. In a couple of hours we'd be driving off together. Driving off, anyway. He was looking at Flossie and his face wasn't just lustful, it was yearning. I thought, I'm losing him. Not leaving. Losing. Why should he put up with not being loved? Some men can. They seem to quite like being belittled by women who accept their homage as though it was the kind of shapeless sticky sweet a child might make for you. But I thought, Benjie could be so much happier without me, and as soon as I'd thought it, I knew it was true. Flossie's very young, but she's already a substantial person. She's funny, and I love the fluorescent plastic pyramids dangling from her ears. Oh Helen. Oh Helen, so poised and cool. Came on a Friday with her husband and her lover: left on a Sunday all on her ownsome. Coolness and poise: I'm going to have to cling to them, but they're not comforting companions.

It was Hugo's wife on the phone, the elusive Chloe. She'd met some trespassers in the forest. Hugo and Christopher got into a huddle. Christopher kept moving those beautiful long hands of his from side to side as though he was smoothing out a table-cloth, but Hugo didn't want to be smoothed. He'd got his dander up.

He recruited the cook and her washer-uppers as messengers and sent them zipping around on bicycles (very few of the cottages were on the telephone). 'We should ride, Christopher,' said Hugo. 'I've told everyone to meet us by the Old Stump.'

Christopher nodded. He waved vaguely at his guests, and laid his hand on the top of Lil's head as he passed behind the stone bench. She didn't look round. She was talking to Antony. But she raised an answering hand and touched his. Both gestures were extraordinarily precise and graceful. Those two are *married*, I thought, in a way I've never felt myself to be. Despite everything, I think I was right.

*

No one was thinking about Berlin any more. And no one was thinking about Nell. She sat dismayed on the stones, like a starfish-patterned tin bucket abandoned on the beach with the tide coming in. It wasn't really that bad, because all the ladies were still there, and Antony and fat Benjie. But how could Daddy just have gone off without even saying anything like 'Wait here'? It was as bad as when she'd seen him in the garden with Lil, having obviously forgotten all about his daughter. If you had children you had to look after them. You just had to. It was the grown-ups' idea to have babies, because they wanted to, and that meant they just had to go on and on looking after her, whatever else was happening. She was obscurely aware that it was unfair to blame her mother, but she did so anyway. Had Chloe even asked whether Nell was all right?

Lil saw her looking lost and threw her a brandy snap. 'Catch, Nell.' Nell couldn't catch, and the fragile tube cracked open, smearing creamy stuff all over her shorts, and then she really felt like crying until silly old Lupin waddled over and licked the cream off and she thought she could make a friend of him at least. It was all right Daddy pretending she was a dog, but she didn't like Mrs R tossing food at her like that. She knew perfectly well that Mrs R wasn't interested in her. She'd probably be annoyed that she'd been left behind. So Nell had not only been abandoned by the ones who were supposed to love her, she'd been foisted onto people who didn't even like her particularly. It was like being an orphan.

Nell was working herself up into a state. Home felt immeasurably far away. Time slowed down. She, who was generally so self-contained and busy on her visits here, couldn't think what to do. And so she did nothing except shake her hair forward, and listen to Mrs R and Antony rattling on, and concentrate hard on picking the scabs off her ankle-knobs and knees.

*

The Old Stump was an oak tree whose upper branches had all been stripped off by a storm, or a sequence of storms, and whose massive trunk, still putting out greenery, had been quartered vertically, as by some titanic meteorological axe. Its roots shouldered their way out of the ground around it making a patch, wider than its remaining canopy, full of wooden loops and knots, like the back of a piece of embroidery done by fumble-fingered giants. Here Christopher and Hugo settled down to wait for whatever reinforcements might join them.

Mark Brown was enjoying himself tremendously. He'd been sorry to put the agent's wife into such an awkward position. She seemed like a nice woman. After she'd left them, looking anxiously over her shoulder, he and his train of disciples had strolled easily out of the shadowy woods, where shafts of light dazzled eyes adjusted to dimness, and along a ride which led down into a sunlit valley. They'd stopped to drink from the spring, catching the water in cupped hands, being very careful not to trample the banks unduly. No one picked any of the vivid little purple orchids that poked up from among the fine tassels of the flowering grasses. No one made undue noise. They dropped nothing – not a Kleenex or a lolly-stick would mark their passage. He'd given them all a pretty stern talking-to. He coached the cricket team for the secondary modern. He knew how to give orders without seeming to boss.

'We're the goody-goodies here,' he said. 'We're smug, and we've got to stay that way.' Everybody laughed, because he was known – he liked to be known – as a bit of a rebel.

He wore polo-neck jerseys, and tennis shoes every day. His curly hair was longer than was usual, and at the Street Fair he had got up on the platform and sung some folk songs. People had been a bit embarrassed by it. He seemed to take the singing rather more seriously than it merited and a lot of people found his fake American accent ridiculous. There was a girlfriend who was only around at weekends because she had a job in London. Several of the young women of the village hoped that it might be impossible to sustain the relationship that way. Mark was well aware of this. There were two he had his eye on. He flirted with both of them – why not? But he hadn't made a move yet, because he found it hard to choose between them, and in a village this size running two local girlfriends just wouldn't be on.

The furniture he made was beautiful. He knocked up country-style carvers and pine chests for the Burford shops, but for his private clients he made chaises longues and oval dining tables which were fluid continuous curves with no extraneous decoration, ghostly pale in silvery-grey limed oak. When he was asked why he'd moved back down from London he said it was because the thing he loved most in the world was wood, so it made sense to live where there were trees. People always laughed when he said it, but it wasn't a joke.

His knowledge of wood won him Mr Goodyear's respect. Sometimes he almost regretted having got so involved in this rights-of-way thing, not a real regret, but a twinge or two, because he could imagine an alternative life in which he and Goodyear were partners. He wanted to plant timber, to see it grow, to make it into the chairs and sleigh-beds and rounded cabinets with which he filled his sketchbooks. He'd call the business Nutters. He was pretty sure he could make it a success. But Goodyear would not be involved. Goodyear, after today, was not going to be pleased with him.

Antony

Lil was a bit irritated by Hugo's sudden swing into action, but once Benjie and Helen had driven off in what Benjie called the Toadmobile – preposterous shiny thing, but beautiful actually – she wanted to witness whatever fracas there was going to be. As usual I, dear dependable Ant, was there to be her cavalier.

Flossie had taken pity on Nell. (Disconcerting how a girl of her age could switch so easily between childishness and adulthood; there was certainly a frisson between her and Benjie.) Now the two girls, far closer to each other in age than Flossie was to any of the rest of us, were lying on their tummies absorbed in a game involving dropping bay leaves on the goldfish. Which left me and Lil at liberty to saunter after her two men.

A track descended the slope in a series of S-bends. There was no formal avenue here, but there were trees, and an undergrowth of brush, so that we saw the Old Stump beneath us only intermittently. Hugo and Christopher were sitting side by side on the ground, smoking, their horses cropping the grass behind them. Hugo smoked Senior Service out of the packet. Christopher's Gitanes were transferred every morning for him, by Mr Underhill, into a flat red-gold case with his initials engraved on it in Lil's handwriting. Together, at ease like that, they looked like two boys. For a moment I felt a kind of anguish for Lil. When we joined them we were clearly going to be *de trop*.

By the time we reached the Old Stump Armstrong, the keeper, and the garrulous head forester Mr Goodyear were both there. And along the valley towards them, following the verge of the lake and therefore as close as they could get to the old road that had once passed through this valley, alongside the stream, came the ramblers. There was a good-looking curly-haired chap in front, with a map and a forked stick. Among the couple of dozen or so people behind him, most of them looking like they were on a librarians' day out, I saw a flash of that extraordinary colour, at once orange and purple. Auburn hair. My Jack.

Lil

Tournaments. Men charging each other for pleasure. Iron-clad man on iron-clad horse transformed into a single missile of terrifying force and velocity. Going at each other with all the speed the human race was then capable of, each aiming a lance made from a great tree-trunk at the opponent's weakest point. In play. There really is something pathological about masculinity.

But that's a Helen-thought. I don't really think like that. 'Lil,' she says to me, 'you're a traitor to your sex.' Watching Christopher and Hugo taking their stand now I'm moved by the romance of it, by how debonair they are, how easy and cool. I'd have been one of the women watching the jousting, with their gossamer veils and golden filigree hairnets and floating silken sleeves, light and pretty and fragile and absolutely avid for blood. I'd have tossed a glove to the boldest killer. I'd have clapped my dainty hands when his opponent fell, and never even looked to see whether he rose again, and I'd have hung a golden chain round the champion's neck with my picture, encircled with emeralds, in a locket, and with it the key to my bedchamber. There's something pretty reprehensible about femininity too.

How I do embellish. But how dreary life would be if it was only what it is.

The people walking up from the lake aren't at all like chivalric warriors. There are some of the sort of women who turn up at the church bazaar with great boxes of stuff made out of raffia. Where does raffia come from, I wonder? I believe prisoners and lunatics make things out of it too. And there are some youngish men, wearing enormous serious boots, as though going for an afternoon walk along the lake required special equipment, like climbing Everest. The one in front looks like someone I might know. I wonder how he got into all this. Ant and I hang back, loitering by the Old Stump. I hope our being there somehow makes the whole thing less embarrassing. They're not going to hit each other, or anything awful, with me watching, surely.

Hugo steps forward and begins his 'Can I help you?' routine. The curly-haired one is all ready. He has his map, and his arguments, and he's not going to let himself be intimidated. They talk back and forth. Curly is dogged. Hugo's getting angry. And then at last Christopher, who's been listening, hands in pockets, rocking a bit on his heels, takes his turn, and speaks quite curtly and waves his arm towards the home farm, as though to say, Enough of all this, party's over, off you go. And off they go looking as pleased with themselves as though they'd been defying the Ku Klux Klan.

*

Christopher rode back to Wood Manor with Hugo, to give Basily some exercise, and to talk over the queer, unsettling, little incident. He wasn't used to finding that the law was not on his side. Then he turned homeward down the lime avenue, ambling along the road sticky with fragrant gum.

His horse's skin twitched and rippled as the flies settled on its neck. Its ears flicked. Its tail swished. The patience of horses under the predations of flies moved Christopher. Big unhandy beasts. He wondered about their pleasures. Dogs were capable of happiness, because they loved, so the loved-one's voice, the loved-one's hand patting a belly, the loved-one's shoulder to drool on, were all occasions for bliss. So much was obvious. But horses' minds were impenetrable. One knew when they were afraid or irritable, but happy? Basily would dip his head to have his nose rubbed, but his breath was a breeze from another sphere. His eyes conveyed nothing.

It was gloaming. Beneath the hulking trees it was already so dark that motes of blackness danced before Christopher's eyes. A relief after all the comings and goings of the weekend to be alone for this twilit ride. Coming out into the grand vista he kicked Basily into a canter – big man, big horse, rocking together in clumsy accord.

Flossie would be on the train by now. Antony was staying on for the night: they'd give him a lift up to London tomorrow. Nell would stay too. Did they make too much of a favourite of her? He must see to it that Dickie got some treats when they were back from Scotland. Take the boy fishing. But even as the thought passed through his mind it snagged on something. That other boy. Of course he might not even have liked fishing. Too easy to get sentimental imagining what might have been. Fergus wasn't perfect. Pretty slow really. Perhaps had he lived he would have been an endless worry to them.

Must talk to Armstrong about his Jack. Not his fault the boy was there this afternoon. Just something vague. Never, never say the obvious. Nothing wrong with being a flower-arranger. But the poor old chap was breaking his heart over it, over the not wanting to be a keeper but much more over the other thing. I've seen Antony eyeing him. Funny how they can pick each other out. Would I, Christopher wondered, have handled it as well as Armstrong does if Fergus had been that way inclined?

Back in the house it was the usual cold stuff for Sunday supper, with the chutney Mrs Duggary made every year from Green's abundant surplus tomatoes, actually one of the best meals of the week. Cold consommé in the pink and gold Sèvres pots, and Mrs D had left baked potatoes in the bottom oven. They ate in the kitchen. Probably in all their lives his parents had never done that. The long washing racks still hung above the Aga: as a child he used to hide in the folds of the drying sheets until one day he got lost and tangled himself further as he wriggled for a way out. Was that where his claustrophobia came from? He couldn't stand low ceilings. Aeroplanes were torment. Most restaurants were too pokey for him, and nowadays the very smartest seemed to be the most cramped. He liked the places his father used to go – the Ritz with its silly-sweet rococo, and Simpsons with all the hoo-ha with the trolleys.

Dinner was soon over. They were all tired. Nell begged to stay, so Lil took her up to bed. They listened to the news but seemed to learn nothing from it. The notion of the division of a city hung inert in their minds. Coiled barbed wire, tanks marshalling, politicians making threats. There was the before-thunder feeling of something momentous and awful beginning but something to which it was so far impossible to put a name. Was this a calamity, or did it really hardly matter at all? As soon as the news ended Nicholas rang. He'd been listening too, still in his office. He seemed barely more comprehending than they were. They said 'surreal', 'sneaky', 'aggressive', but the words fell flat.

Afterwards Christopher stalked off into the garden, muttering 'cento passi': his Italian governess had taught him one should always take a stroll between dinner and bed.

'I'll have a midnight swim, I think,' said Antony. 'How about you, Lil?'

'No. Early bed for me. Sleep tight. Underhill will get someone to call you at six, you poor thing. Tea? I'll leave a note.'

'Please.'

And so they parted.

Nell

The dreams I have about that house. Sometimes it grows and ramifies until it spreads in a stony tangle across all of the park, and I wake struggling, pinned down by its multiplying stable yards and greenhouses and endlessly self-duplicating pilastered facades. I've been trapped on ever-diminishing corkscrew staircases in gothic towers, which had no correspondence whatsoever to anything in the stately architecture of Wychwood by daylight. In my dreams I've been old there, and ill there, and sexually enraptured in rooms which never really existed there but which carried Wychwood's atmosphere of grandeur and – in retrospect I can feel it, though then I could not – of beleaguerment and of grief.

It was the house of my childhood – much more so than Wood Manor, the house in which I actually lived, perhaps precisely because I didn't live in it. It was my enormous doll's house, the setting of my daydreams and my adventures. My imaginary friends and imaginary pets (the lion, the nest of dragon-pups, my witchy green-eyed godmother) lived there. It was – is – a majestic house. Of course that was part of it. Young as I was, I could feel the force of prestige acquired over centuries, and of those superb lichened walls. But there was also a magic it wrought especially for me. At home I was an ordinary little girl, part of a family, but at Wychwood I was singular, a kind of mascot, spoken to, singled out, allowed, even, on the night after the wall went up, when I'd insisted on sleeping there because it was the end of things and the Rossiters were going away, to stay up for dinner.

Actually dinner was rather dull. Lil had had a bath and changed into a kind of silk housecoat, and the men had put on smoking jackets, but there were no candles on the table, no flowers, no wine. Christopher was kind, telling me how he and his sisters used to eat their supper at that very table while the cooks bustled about, making their parents' dinner – croquettes and vol-au-vents and soufflés – all those fiddly, labour-intensive foods people used to contrive before simplicity became the thing.

On that Sunday evening, though, we ate the same sort of food we had at home, and the grown-ups were all tired. This listless kitchen supper was not at all what I'd expected my first grown-up dinner to be like. What I'd heard about Antony made me awkward with him. I couldn't look at him, or make the kind of impudent jokes he usually liked.

When Lil said she'd take me up to bed, I was happy to go. She smoothed down the bedspread I loved, the one covered with wild roses. It was made, she said, by an old woman who was mad but kind and who had lived in our house, in Wood Manor. The knots that marked the roses' stamens were so fine I imagined the fingers that stitched them must have been as delicate as the tines of silver forks. She said she'd read me a chapter of *The Princess and the Goblins*, but I was asleep before she'd turned a page.

Then the nightmares. I was in the room I'd had before, with the four-poster bed, and the silk-roped bell pull with its ivory handle that I was to tug if I was afraid, but the fear of being in the wrong if I did so had always been greater than simple night-terrors. So when I woke again, hearing the gruff voice of the wireless, I lay still for a while, counting the peacocks on the damask canopy, trying to stifle the horror of that dream. The image of my father and Lil in the archway wouldn't leave me. Sunlit but dreadful in an uncomprehended way. Words clanged in my mind and half-sleep made me defenceless against them. Atomic. Spy. Unwept. Antony.

The need to be with people became very strong. Out into the corridor. Through the creaking door that led into the gallery around the marble hall. They were in the little sitting room where the wireless was kept, beneath rows of antlers. There were only two comfortable chairs in there. I imagined Antony perched on the fender. Then the hoarse voice stopped. Christopher passed across the hall and I dropped to the top step, and hugged the grey wood of the banister.

Antony and Lil appeared beneath me, then parted. She to bed. He to swim. The pool. I remembered and was aghast. Why not call out? Because it was naughty to get out of bed after bedtime. Not that I'd have expected them to scold me, but I was panicky, so instinct took over, and by instinct I was furtive. Lil went by so close I might have tripped her up, but her eyes must have been dazzled as she passed into the shadowy upper gallery from the bright hall. Antony took the other branch of the double staircase. When he came out of his room again, in a dressing gown and sandshoes, I followed him, barefoot, silent. Antony. Spy. Unwept. Unwarned.

My pyjamas were mauve and flowery – dim. If I'd been in my white nightie he would surely have seen me and spoken to me and I would have had to say. The pool was empty. Mr Green had said he'd empty it. No one else knew. Even my father hadn't been listening. Antony would do a running dive off the springy board. He always did. Deep breath, eyes shut, waiting for the splash and rush and gurgle up his nose and past his ears. But there'd be no freshness. No water. The bottom of the pool in winter was furred with brown pine needles, but when it was first emptied it was green, with a sludge of dead insects and rotted leaves, which Mr Green's boy would shovel up and put on the hydrangea beds. And this time, Antony's brains.

He walked slowly. The tobacco plants alongside the path were ghostly white, their scent voluptuous. I'd never been out so late. I'd never smelt them before. This man had always been kind to me. Men went to war, where they did things they didn't want to talk to girls about. This sort of thing. Killing people. Killing enemies. Killing spies. I didn't wish him any harm but I wanted him not to exist any more because to think of him now was so awkward. He dropped his dressing gown on the paving. He was naked, and that terrified me.

The trees kept off the sky. The yew hedges made a rectangular block of even blacker night that fitted like a lid above where the pool should have been shimmering. I could still have spoken. I was by the hut. I could have called and he would have heard me but I was shaking and I felt sick and my forehead was wet, and anyway how could I speak to a naked man. He stood on his toes and ran onto the board, light as a ballet dancer, and threw his arms up and bounced and flew.

*

Christopher heard the splash and the scream together, threw away his cigarette and ran, Grampus hurtling with him, jostling and impeding him. By the time he reached the pool Antony was crouched, dripping wet, over Nell's small body. And from the other direction came Hugo. Christopher would never ask him or anyone else why he was there, prowling the garden after dark. Hugo reached for his daughter, and when she began to whimper, he said quietly, 'That's the end of that, then. I'll take her home.' And he stalked off, carrying her. It was the first time, Christopher thought, he'd ever seen him without his dog.

1973

June

Jamie McAteer was built like a seal. An unwaisted torso packed with muscle. 'I've got arms and legs,' he said to the woman, a friend's aunt, who pointed out the resemblance on a nippy summer's day by the Moray Firth. 'Seals don't.' He was pleased, though. He was eight years old when the comparison was made, and twelve years later, although he hardly ever recalled it directly, it still affected the way he thought about himself. Someone who swam in his own element, inscrutable, coolly appraising from a distance. Like a seal lifting his head above the water and staring intently at picnickers on the shore. Harmless-looking, comical even, but with power hidden beneath the waterline. It would have surprised most of the people Jamie met at Oxford to know what a very high opinion he had of himself.

Nell Lane knew. Barrel-chested and pink-cheeked, Jamie looked cherubic, but also brutal, like a film-noir gangster with a moniker like Baby-Face or Little Joe. Someone to be afraid of. Nell had never seen a seal.

*

The first time they had sex, the first time Nell had sex at all, was towards the end of the midsummer night's party at Wychwood. They'd arrived together in Selim's car. Selim was slight, but his car was massive. Both were famous for their beauty. The car was a green Bentley on whose hashish-scented leather backseat Selim had often slept when he hadn't enough petrol for the drive out to the unheated farmhouse where he lived with five others, way off towards Blenheim. Its engine was a masterpiece of early-twentieth-century engineering: its starting mechanism was a mess. Anyone getting a lift with Selim had to be ready to jump out and push the temperamental juggernaut while he delicately toyed with its choke.

The two boys and Nell knew each other because they all attended a weekly seminar in New College, and because they had all, by diverse routes, come to know Antony Briggs. Jamie had interviewed Antony for *Cherwell* when the latter – home after nearly a decade in Berlin and elsewhere – arrived in Oxford as the new curator of the Ashmolean's Renaissance collection. Selim had been given an introduction to him by an England-returned uncle who – for reasons none of the family back in Lahore chose to investigate – knew people all over the place. When Flora Rose asked Antony to invite any bright young things he thought would be an adornment to her party he had judged each of them interesting enough to qualify. So now – like Nell – they were on their way to Wychwood.

Nell found Selim unnervingly attractive. She was glumly certain that the feeling was not mutual. Not the slightest tremor of erotic interest reached her from him, despite the way he had of lightly laying hold of her wrist when speaking to her. An irrational dread possessed her that he could somehow read her mind. (Not that he'd have been interested in doing so, probably.) Just as she was always anxious whether people at the telephone exchange were listening in to her conversations, so she would have liked some definitive reassurance as to the absolute privacy of unvoiced thought. In Selim's presence tiny muscles in her upper lip convulsed, making her embarrassingly conscious that she had a mouth. A mouth could kiss, should anyone care to take advantage of the fact.

*

Flora Rose stood plumb in the centre of Wychwood's marble hall murmuring to a maharajah whom she kept beside her because his gold brocade coat so nicely set off the deep red of her own dress. Hostess and potentate each wore a quantity of diamonds on their heads – he, in a brooch fronting his turban; she, on two fern-shaped clips holding back her hair.

There was a Mr Rose. He was older, genial, a nifty dancer and much shrewder than he seemed. What people asked each other, though, on the nights on which the couple gave a party at Wychwood, was 'Are you going to Flora's this time?'

'Flora darling, you look like the scarlet whore of Babylon, just not quite so frightening.' Her husband's nephew Guy drawling down at her from his great height. Actually, in his coat of many colours, bought in Tangier, he was the one looking biblical. Flora smiled but reached past him for Nell, whose ideal of an elder sister she had been for years, and who hugged her now saying, as no one else any longer did, 'Flossie!'

*

When Flora found herself, at the age of thirty, de facto chatelaine of Wychwood, a number of rather shaming questions occurred to her. Had Benjie foreseen this? Not likely. When he made his pounce, in this very house, Lil and Christopher were still very much together, still securely ensconced. And if he had, did that make him hateful, or was he just worldly-wise? And wasn't she being a tad disingenuous? Hadn't she too, often daydreamed that

Christopher might hand the house over to her? (Not that she was his natural-born heir – there were some equally eligible cousins who were probably furious.) When he and Lil withdrew from each other – he to Scotland, Lil to London – had not she, Flora, come here month after month with their permission, camping out in the smallest spare room at first, but little by little making the whole place her playground, until Christopher finally acknowledged the fait accompli, made over enough money for the house's maintenance and asked her to treat it as her own?

She removed the white panelling masking the gilded Cordoba leather on the smoking-room walls (Lil liked rooms pale and clean). She got rid of the savage antlers Christopher's father had been so proud of. Underhill packed them in sawdust and dispatched them back up to the glen from whence they had come. Flora doubted they were ever unpacked. Christopher didn't shoot any more, didn't even eat meat.

She saw herself as patron and muse. She would make the marvellous old house the setting for better things than quarrelsome charades and shooting weekends. She would create a court. She would gather together artists and performers: she would give phantasmagorical parties that would be talked about for a lifetime, for centuries perhaps.

She invited Seb, a film-maker Antony knew (it was a mystery how Antony knew all these people), to move into a pavilion in the garden, and encouraged him to use Wychwood as a set. His staging of one of Ben Jonson's masques – a recreation of Inigo Jones's designs backed by psychedelic film-projection – was the first of the shows to which she was impresario. His film ran for weeks, to audiences of people who all seemed to know each other, at a grubby cinema in the Fulham Road. Flora was there every night, and every night Seb brought a dozen friends – boys trailing Indian silk scarves, garrulous older women – back to the Roses' flat on Chelsea Embankment where they smoked dope and ate quantities of kedgeree.

At Wychwood Flora kept on the staff who'd known her as a girl, but upset Underhill by insisting the silver be allowed to tarnish to the yellow sheen of a snail-shell, and that the chandeliers in the drawing room (Lil had had them wired for electricity) be furnished again with real candles, to the great detriment of the paintwork. Lil's constructivists were confined to the long gallery. Elsewhere the house was swaddled, as it had been for centuries, in velvet and brocade, and tapestry forests once more hid the walls, creating a continuity between the woodsmoke-scented rooms, and the woods which girdled the park.

*

Up for anything, impressed by nothing – that was Jamie's idea of the right approach to the diverse opportunities Oxford presented. It wasn't always easy to sustain.

Take drugs, for instance, or rather, don't take them. His first trip was disastrous. Never drop acid on your own, everyone said, but they didn't tell you how – once you and your friends were all completely out of it – you could stop the others wandering off. Finding himself alone at dawn in the covered market, which had somehow transformed itself into a labyrinthine prison peopled by vicious troglodytes, he'd tried to fight his way out, then spent what seemed like a decade explaining to the stallholders, who were trying to get some breakfast inside themselves before business began, why they really had to help him find a motorbike. Why? He'd never ridden a motorbike in his life. The café-woman knew him. She brought him egg and chips, which usually quietened down the drunks, but the Formica-topped table was rippling so alarmingly he thought he might drown in it. He was far too spaced-out for food.

The next day, with fireworks still going off spasmodically behind his eyes, he had to apologise to pretty well everyone. Mortifying. He'd made such a point of laughing along when the market people were telling stories about silly-arse students getting off their trolleys. So he wasn't up for acid. Never again. Grass was OK.

He was all right when he was working. His tutor – an old-fashioned right-wing libertarian – was as truculent as he was but much more intellectually rigorous. Arguing with him, out loud in tutorials, on paper in essays, felt strenuous and invigorating. When he wasn't nursing a hangover, Jamie studied diligently.

Social life was harder. No one he'd known at school had come to Oxford. He had to start from scratch. After spending his teens wondering how on earth you met girls, he now found they were the only people he could meet. The boys clung together in packs. Perhaps they were snooty: perhaps they were just as socially inept as he was. Girls, though, were approachable. Towards the end of his first term Spiv Jenkins singled him out – he was still amazed at the luck of it – at a party where everyone was drinking a foul liquor brewed from potatoes. The still was a bathtub. Having picked him up, Spiv put him down again pretty quickly, but they kept on seeing each other in the library – she was as ambitious as he was – and she'd take him around with her. And so he met her friends Francesca, who clearly considered him impossibly uncouth, and the quieter Nell.

Writing for *Cherwell*, he became someone. It was a sudden and absolute change. He could go into the King's Arms and instead of having to worm his way to the bar through groups of people with their backs turned – excuse me, sorry, excuse me – he was greeted, and waved over. But, apart from Manny, who had the room downstairs from him, he didn't exactly have any male friends. Nor, he noticed, did Selim, but that was different. Selim kept himself aloof. He, Jamie, thought of himself as being open-armed, open-minded and open-hearted. Though you wouldn't have guessed it from his demeanour at Wychwood. He had a way of hunching his shoulders against an uncongenial social atmosphere as though against the cold. He was doing it now.

*

Antony joined Benjie.

'Is that Helen in chain mail?'

'Yes,' said Benjie. 'She's often here. She and Hugo work together.'

'Is that . . .'

'Awkward? Only a smidgeon. You know how gracefully she backed out of my life. Now she's sidled back in again. You'll find the shocking thing about coming back to this place is not how much we've moved on, but how much has stayed the same while you've been fossicking around in Dracula country.'

'And she lives?'

'In Oxford just now. You'll be coming across her there. She's sprucing up one of the college gardens.'

'With Hugo? Are they . . . I mean.'

'No of course not. No, Helen's very liberated now, very who-needs-a-man.'

'So what do they do together?'

'They design gardens for the idle rich. He's got the eye for the big picture; she knows all about plants. The nurseries are here – the proceeds help to keep this place afloat. They're doing great stuff at Stancombe, scooping out lakes, dividing all the open spaces into secret chambers and mazes, building ruddy great stone walls. The place looks like the labyrinth. What's surprising really is not that Helen's here, but the other fellow, the third partner in their gardening outfit. Do you recognise him?'

Benjie nodded towards an etiolated young man with flaring orange hair, propped against a pilaster in the pose of Hilliard's pensive youth. Talking to him was Nell's friend Francesca.

The greatest stroke of luck that Nell had had at Oxford was that Francesca, and her equally intimidating friend Spiv, had taken her up. They kept a place for her at breakfast time in hall. She didn't know why. Perhaps they needed her as a foil. She was tongue-tied in their company, but trailed them thankfully. Spiv was half-American, wore knitted hotpants and let it be known she was not constrained by outmoded codes of sexual propriety. Boys who deduced from that that she was an easy lay were likely to be cruelly snubbed. But whether or not she was fast, in the ambiguous sense Nell's mother used the word (to mean both sluttish and dashing), Spiv was certainly fast-thinking, fast-talking and extremely hard-working. Francesca's father was a widowed diplomat; she had been playing hostess at the embassy in Rome since her early teens. The inflections of her voice were those of a much older woman. Her exquisitely conventional beauty – hair the colour of ripe wheat, lips as finely shaped and pale as the petals of an Alba Celestial rose – was rendered extra piquant by her habit of delivering, in her regal tones, syntactically perfect jokes of egregious filthiness. She and the redhead, their pearly skins a match, made a fine tableau.

'Yes, I used to know him,' said Antony. 'Quite well actually.'

'You've probably bought flowers from him. By the station. *Wildly Pretty.*'

'Yes.'

'He grew up on this place. You might remember. Car-mad. Played chauffeur for years before he got his driving licence. His father's head keeper.'

'I remember,' said Antony.

'Jack broke the old fellow's heart by turning out a poofter and now here he is, sipping champagne as though he'd never sat below the salt. Actually he wouldn't have sat at all. Under the *ancien régime* keepers and beaters ate their piece out in the stables on shooting days, while the guns had their port and stilton in here. Helen says he's the finest botanical draughtsman since the eighteenth century. But you know her. And,' said Benjie, 'the wonder is, after all that fuss, it looks as though he's straight.'

Antony, who knew otherwise, disengaged himself and was taken to the bosom of a large woman swathed in saffron-tinged embroideries from turbaned head to pointed suede toe. Across the room lovely, silver-gilt Francesca laid her hand on Jack Armstrong's green velvet sleeve and leant in to murmur. Parties, the magic they can wreak. Jamie, who had been standing with them, beast to their two beauties, turned away.

And went into the drawing room where the party swirled slowly around two still points. On one of the deep sofas sat a very famous person, ghastly pale, with dyed white hair. He had come with Seb. Everyone in the room was aware of the famous one's presence. He was one of the totems of the age, one who was said to have defined it (despite the fact that he was so very, very laconic) as well as glittering at its centre. They would talk about this, his appearance among them, for months – in some cases for decades – to come. No one quite knew, for the moment, though, what to do about it.

Seb scurried about the room, looking for people to talk to his illustrious protégé. Everyone wanted to have done so. No one much relished the prospect of the actual conversation. The famous one sat completely still, blinking frequently. He didn't turn his head towards those who bravely sat beside him. He answered their questions in a voice rather too low for audibility. How many of his famously gnomic dicta were to be lost that night, unheard beneath the thrum of party chat? A man dressed after the manner of Lewis Carroll's Mad Hatter, in stick-up collar and frock coat and extravagant whiskers, was with him now, wringing his hands as he sought for another conversational gambit.

Guy, only a few years older than Nell but precociously self-possessed, took his ex-aunt Helen by the elbow, and steered her over.

'May we join you? This is Helen. She's designed a garden based on the description of the New Jerusalem in the Book of Revelation.' This was spur-of-the-moment nonsense. The famous one, without smiling or nodding or catching either of their eyes, said, 'Piquant.'

The Mad Hatter made a dash for freedom. Guy waved Helen onto the sofa and seated himself on a tapestried stool. 'Yes, isn't it marvellous,' he said, and for the next ten minutes he coaxed Helen to hold forth about Persian gardens and Dutch gardens, about Vauxhall and the lewd goings-on there, and about the Mughal emperor who created a pleasure garden where every enclosure was a flowery prison for a beautiful girl who was forbidden to move or speak until the emperor passed by, and would then break into dance or song.

Guy leant forward and tapped the famous knee. 'Can you believe it?' he said repeatedly. 'Isn't that fantastic?' Helen smiled, and rustled the pointed floor-length sleeves of her metallic dress, and said something about three-dimensional geometry and the fourth dimension of time, about proliferation and decay. This stirred the famous person into speech. 'Obsolescence,' he said. They paused deferentially. He had nothing more to say. His eyes closed. Up came a wan young man proffering an exhibition catalogue and asking for an autograph. Guy was on his feet in a trice, graceful, backing off. 'We mustn't keep you from your admirers.'

'That poor man,' he said to Helen as they retreated towards the dining room. 'Did you see his fingernails? Positively corrugated.'

'Poor? He's got everything he wants, surely?'

'Yes yes but imagine what a bore – all the nosey-parkers and scroungers. And the people telling him how much they admire him, as though he ought to be interested in their silly opinions. At least we gave him fifteen minutes during which he didn't have to speak at all.'

'Oh Guy, no one ever has to speak when you're about.'

Guy laughed, and squeezed Helen's upper arm and drifted off towards the room's other centripetal attraction, an enormously fat, elderly black woman, a blues diva with a hoarse holler of a laugh and an iridescent Lurex dress which flowed off her like oil.

Back on the sofa the pale youth was pulling a sketchbook from his pocket. Before the night was out he would have received an invitation to America. By the end of the year he would be being stared at by scores of guests he'd never previously met, the very famous person lurking beside him, at the opening of his first New York show.

*

Nell and Selim were in the room where, over a decade ago, their host had first attempted to kiss the hostess. Selim's voice was very deep for such a slight young man. He tended to look askance as he talked, which meant Nell couldn't always hear what he was saying. She had been a forthright child, but with adolescence she had been afflicted with an anxiety to please that hobbled her. She hated the way she laughed at boys' jokes even when she didn't get the point of them.

Selim had not spoken in that week's seminar. He very seldom did. Student discussions seemed to him irritatingly jejune. When he finished his degree (history) he was destined for a place in the police department in Lahore that was likely to lead, saving upsets, to very high office. His sojourn in a damp, world-famous, half-medieval city, golden in prospect but so small and pettifogging to the near view, was to be a mere interlude in his life, a kind of trial from which he would return tempered ready for use. That, at least, was his family's intention, one that no one had ever thought to question until, just around this time, it had begun to occur to Selim that he might perhaps become something else entirely. He felt so cosmopolitan, so interestingly suspended between two cultures. With such an anomalous perspective he could, he thought, be a novelist. Or a singer-songwriter perhaps. To the latter end, he was learning to play the guitar.

'Is he dead, do you think?' asked Guy, joining them. No need to ask whom he meant. An assassination attempt had been made, not long ago, on the famous guest.

'Whether or not, it doesn't seem as though it would make much difference,' said Nell. She liked Guy. He was older than her other Oxford friends, because he'd bummed around a bit before coming up. He didn't take much notice of her, but they had Wychwood in common, which meant she knew him in a different way from the people who'd landed in her life with no back story, like aliens or angels. Funny how much easier it was to talk to men who were queer.

'Why do we all stare at him?' asked Selim.

'Well he's answered that question himself, hasn't he, in five different media,' said Guy. 'We're conformists. We stare because all the rest are staring.'

There was a sudden blare of music from the marble hall. The crowd eddied and jostled as a couple came through, silent and fierce, their joined hands extended to form a prow. They were dancing a tango, dipping and rearing in tight shiny clothes, their faces impassive. Flora had seen them cutting through the mob at Tramps and invited them before she even knew their names. Was it exploitative or generous of her to blur the line, like that, between guests and floorshow? She neither knew nor cared.

People shuffled aside. Benjie, with his back to the dancers, was gesticulating effusively as he brought to a close an anecdote about his mother (Italian, chosen model of several artists of half a century back). One of his flying hands was on course to give the oncoming female dancer a back-handed slap in the face. She swayed away from it. Her partner made a swift adjustment, and swung her round so that she seemed to fly almost horizontal, her hennaed hair sweeping the floor beneath Benjie's arm. He skipped, looked around nonplussed and, seeing the others laughing at him, waved them over and introduced them to a woman wearing an enormous veiled hat stuck with silk roses.

Guy said to Nell, 'I need some air. Let's go and howl at the moon.'

Nell didn't want to move away from Selim. She yearned towards him, as a geranium yearns towards a window. But he was talking about Palestine to the hat woman, ignoring her, so . . .

Damask curtains the silvery green of willow leaves. Shutters folded back into their embrasures. French windows chilly to the touch.

'Just a little respite from being amusing,' said Guy. 'Let's visit those sinister fish.'

In the starlight the canal glimmered. A furrow cut the jetty surface, a pallid shape beneath.

'Aren't they horrific?'

Nell had always thought so. She said, 'I didn't know you were such friends with Antony.' She had seen them hugging as they greeted each other.

Guy looked at her sideways. 'My pretend uncle,' he said, 'by which I don't mean what you might think I mean. He was kind to me in Berlin when I was doing my Wandervögel thing before Oxford.'

'What might I think?'

'Oh Uncle Ant is a man of many mysteries,' said Guy.

They were on their way back across the lawn now. Antony was visible through the glazed door. Narrow shoulders, narrow hips, his velvet jacket buttoned up, greying hair brushed straight back, a tall man without any of the loose-limbed shambliness of tall Christopher, or tall Guy for that matter. He is exact, thought Nell. He always stands exactly upright, with his weight on both feet. Hardly anyone else does that. What an effort it must take.

*

In taking up with Benjie, Flora had become a hostess. Still in her teens, while most of her girlfriends ate cooked food only when taken out to restaurants by men, she had a kitchen, and a dining table. Benjie's friends had houses in Tuscany and Provence, to which he took her. Always the youngest woman in the house-party (except the au pair), she learnt to tease men, and she discovered how good food could be. Benjie, restaurateur and gourmet, approved. He fed her baby artichokes steeped in green olive oil, and chicken livers on crostini, and slivers of real Parmesan cheese, while to most of her former flatmates Parmesan was still a granular substance which came in a cardboard cylinder and carried a whiff of vomit.

In London she cooked stews under a variety of fashionable names – daube, fricassée, blanquette, ragoût, goulash, hotpot, casserole, pot au feu, kleftiko, tagine. In the Swan Walk kitchen, listening to Dusty Springfield and Procul Harum and *Disraeli Gears*, she chopped onions until the tears ran, bashed bay leaves and coriander seeds in a stone pestle, and then, for pudding, reverted to the cooking habits of the rationing generation, crumbling digestive biscuits and topping them off with tinned condensed milk.

Come night, the flat would fill up. Her friends: boys in denim, girls in leather and broderie anglaise, all of them grateful to know someone who had a place big enough to gather in. Benjie's friends: argumentative men; women who either kept their distance from her, loyal to Helen, or patronised her as a pet. She draped the table and sofas with embroidered felt hangings. She lit dozens of candles and stuck them in Moorish lanterns or in vases of red bohemian glass. She sat on the window seat, silk robes hitched up over bare legs, and scolded Guy, her almost-nephew and indispensible *cavalier servente*, who was so much nearer to her in age than Benjie was, when he put 'In-a-Gadda-da-Vida' on the record player for the twelfth time in a night.

Benjie allowed it. Sometimes he would go tetchily and early to bed, bored by the company, annoyed if they failed to pay enough attention to him, or to notice how good his wine was. But he renamed his restaurant 'Flora's' and let her loose on it. Out went the pink damask tablecloths and gold-rimmed plates. In came pews salvaged from bombed-out churches and pine tables wavy from decades of scrubbing, unmatched ironstone dishes and pewter tankards stuffed with ox-eye daisies and foxgloves and, in winter, copper-coloured chrysanthemums, their acrid tang prickling in air already sharp with woodsmoke from the open fire. And in came men without ties, without collars even, and barefoot girls in their grandmothers' tattered lace bodices and great-grandmothers' garnets. They'd have been turned away from the place a couple of years earlier: now they were desirable customers. Some of them, barely out of their teens, were world-famous.

Benjie went into partnership with a young architect, a Polish count. There was, they discovered, good money to be made from teaching the rich how to make themselves and their houses look picturesquely rumpled. And when Wychwood became Flora's plaything, Benjie, without ever explicitly telling her he was doing so, used it as bait for business. It was he who had invited the maharajah. There were three palaces in Rajasthan waiting to be converted into hotels.

*

Jamie and Guy sat on the stairs. They'd met through *Cherwell*. Guy wrote a gossip column, 'The Ligger', that was, in Jamie's view, preposterously mannered as to style and despicable as to content but, well, it was a relief to have found someone here he knew.

Jamie wore what he always wore. Corduroy Levi's, desert boots, T-shirt, denim bomber jacket. The whole point of this outfit was its ordinariness. Now it was making him feel conspicuous, and that got him angry with everyone else present – although they probably didn't give a toss about his appearance – and angry with himself for minding about something as trivial as clothes. He didn't know how Guy fitted in at Wychwood, but it was obvious he did, somehow. He kept, even while they talked, giving little fluttery waves to people walking past. Jamie found it maddening. It also irritated him that Guy seemed not to care that they both held empty glasses. Jamie wanted to go and get a refill. Through the dining-room door he could see a kind of marble trough in which bottles were embedded in ice. He didn't dare move, though, in case Guy wandered off and he found himself spare again.

They'd both been dancing. Guy with Flora, Jamie with Nell.

Guy never joined any teams or played ball games, but he was an athlete. He won races, his long, sparse hair trailing out behind him like the lines cartoonists use to denote a whoosh of speed. He could dance expertly for hours on end, with small controlled twitches of elbow, shoulder and hip. Jamie's style was more pugnacious. He met the music with his fists up, and hurled himself at it, hardly ever glancing at his partners. When the discotheque began playing T. Rex he'd snorted and stalked off. Nell started after him, then checked when she realised he wasn't going to look back. The idea of good manners might seem antiquated, but dealing with someone who didn't have any was really hard. Benjie – watchful host – introduced her to a pair of talkative male twins in sequinned denim waistcoats who clearly had no interest in getting to know her, but at least saved her from standing around shamingly alone.

'Why Berlin?' Jamie was asking.

'Jamie dear, the question is why not? Why aren't you going? Why aren't we all there? It's just *throbbing*! The orgy capital of the *world*!'

It was never easy to tell when Guy was sending himself up.

'Where will you live?'

'Lord knows. There'll be somewhere. There are advantages to being a queen, you know.'

'And what will you do?'

Jamie meant 'How will you make money?' but he knew to ask that straight out would be uncool. His own parents (a teacher and a district nurse) had seen him through Oxford – proud to do so – but the allowance they gave him would be stopped the day the summer term ended. No way was he going to be able to wander off to a throbbing European capital to inhale the atmosphere. How on earth did everyone manage? Guy had just told him he was going to *save money* by going abroad. Had these people never heard of airfares? Jamie didn't even know how he'd get back to Glasgow. Well, he did know. He'd hitch.

Guy surprised him. 'I'm a trained lifeguard. Best thing my ridiculous school did for me. There's always shift work going at swimming pools. I can work on my beautiful body, and learn German by flirting with the boys. Wet dream!' He paused for a laugh, but didn't get it. Jamie was genuinely interested.

'I could do that,' he said. 'I swim. I've swum across Loch Lomond.'

'Well, then you could,' said Guy. 'So I'll spend my mornings being pickled in chlorine, and my nights being droned at by the Krautrockers. And perhaps I'll write a novel in the afternoons.'

People kept arriving. Lil made a late entrance, gleaming in purple and gold, and left soon thereafter. She didn't regret handing Wychwood over to Flossie – not one bit – but she didn't much like being there as a guest. She brought with her a stout man dressed, unlike anyone else there, in a neat dark suit. Nell recognised Nicholas – bald now, but suave as ever.

The dancing, in what used to be the dining room, slowed as the night faded. Francesca, in Jack Armstrong's arms, leant back so that her hair brushed the hands he had clasped behind her. She looked, as usual, like an image dreamed up by an Edwardian pornographer. Her exquisite profile lay parallel with the ceiling and her bruised-plum slither of a satin dress withdrew like the calyx of a rose, helpless to cover her bosom (alabaster pale, of course).

Flora, dancing with Antony, said, 'My goodness, that girl is a show-off. I like that, don't you? So relaxing to find someone who doesn't need reassurance.' And turned expecting a complicit smile, and saw instead that Antony was staring at the couple with the shocking vulnerability of one plagued by lust. What? Antony? Surely. Not even Francesca. Oh. No. Jack. That weird white creature.

Poor Antony. Or perhaps not so poor. Jack's eyes were closed as he swayed to Leonard Cohen's mumbling. But when he opened them they weren't clouded by the erotic swoon he seemed to be miming: they were bright as cut steel in the disco lights. Flora saw him send a wink direct at Antony, who saw Flora seeing it, made as though to ignore it, and then rallied deliberately and said, 'Actually it's her partner I'm interested in.'

Flora said, 'Good luck, then.' 'Oh no,' said Antony. 'Well. There was a time. Haven't seen him for years. But yes, anyway, thanks.'

The music changed. And soon there was Jack coming up to them. And there was Francesca looking as though she had been unpleasingly shaken awake, and Nicholas bustling over to accost her, and to tell her they'd met before in Porto Ercole.

Helen was leaving with a tall man, handsome, grey hair, Roman nose. He was gripping her upper arm as though leading her away for questioning. Perhaps she wasn't so emancipated after all. Passing the estate office in the old yard, they met Hugo on his way out. Hugo didn't come to Flora's parties any more. Chloe had said before the last one: 'Are you sure they want you there? Flora hasn't invited you, has she?' And he'd had to admit, to her and – with shock – to himself, that no, she hadn't. All the same, he often seemed to find some pressing reason for dropping into his office on party nights. Now, he was looking round to see where his dog had got to – another Wully, only just released from Armstrong's strict training regime, and inclined to be skittish. He had his back to Helen and her companion. There was a moment when they were all three having to dodge to avoid colliding. The two men looked straight at each other, visibly shocked. Neither spoke. 'Let's go,' said Helen's escort, and went on without her.

'What was that about?' said Helen.

Hugo shrugged, but as she turned to go he said, 'Roger's not . . . Well, it's none of my business. But . . . I wouldn't have too much to do with him.'

'Oh I know,' she said. 'He's a scoundrel. I rather like that sort of thing.' But as she climbed into Roger's car a memory tugged at her, a rose garden, a child butting against her legs, a story about a gun. 'So how do you know Hugo Lane?' she asked.

In the long drawing room Spiv uncrossed her fish-netted legs and rose from the sofa where she had spent much of the evening. She crossed to where Selim stood with Nell. 'That's my summer settled, then,' she said, faking nonchalance. 'He says I can slave for him. I'll be in New York with my father, so . . . A fifteen-minute chance at fame.'

There was breakfast. Underhill and Mrs Duggary saw to that. Mrs D had had her own dancing days before she got involved in church work. She knew how ravenous you could be for chips, walking back from the dance hall with the other girls. You wouldn't let a young man see you guzzling like that, but ooh the sting of the vinegar on chapped lips and the grate of salt. Nothing more delicious. There were some men who saw you home, and that was a bit of a feather in your cap of course, but you almost wished they hadn't because their breath wasn't nice and the kissing, well, let's just say you'd rather have had the chips. Perhaps if she'd smoked herself she wouldn't have minded so much, but she'd never fancied it. Loved food always. Cared about tastes more than anything. Lucky she'd ended up in a kitchen. Mrs R had been a bit difficult sometimes, but with Flora she could talk. She taught Flora how to make a soufflé, and apple snow. Flora gave her things she'd not seen before. Cardamom. Worked a treat with rice pudding. Food brings people together. In the end they all have stomachs, don't they. Even the boys with mascara and the girls, so bossy. Drugs might be the thing now (they think we don't notice, but of course we do) but you still want dinner, don't you? Even if it's at a funny time. And breakfast. Anyone who's been dancing for four hours can do with some nice hot kedgeree.

Or sausages, or kippers and scrambled eggs. On the little round tables crowding the dining room, toast, sliced thin, cooled to flabbiness in silver racks. Mauve and magenta scented stocks wilted gradually. Voices grew slurred, or subdued. No one much was dancing any more. The leaving started, and then – oh no! – the birds.

Jamie drank himself stupid, stumbled upstairs and found a bed to lie on, a four-poster. Later some of the others came looking for bags and coats, and, finding him there, draped themselves around him.

'I used to sleep in this room when I was a child,' said Nell.

'Weren't you frightened, here alone?'

'There's a bell. Do you see? That rope and tassel. If I pulled that someone would come running.'

A joint was going round. 'We wouldn't use each other's toothbrushes,' said Guy. 'And yet here we are all putting this soggy thing into our mouths.'

'It doesn't count. Like kissing,' said Spiv. 'There's nothing really wrong with spit as long as you don't think about it too much.'

Selim passed the joint on when it reached him. To him there most certainly was something wrong with sucking on other people's saliva. He looked at Spiv with the slightest possible tremor of distaste. Unfair, because although she was unusually forthright she committed no transgressions against morality or cleanliness that might not also have been committed by Nell, who seemed to Selim pure as the dewdrop at the heart of an anemone.

Jamie woke up, and took a drag. 'What is this shit? It's powerful.'

'There's just the teensiest bit of opium in the mix,' said Manny. Manny, with his hyacinthine mane, thought he looked Dionysian. Somehow, though, he failed to bring it off. The mane could have done with more frequent washing, and Manny was too calculating of eye and too paunchy of figure for a personification of pagan self-abandon. His velvet jacket, spangled with tiny printed stars, flapped open not because he was elegantly careless but because it was too tight. He got his kicks delivering crowds of protesters to demonstrate in support of the revolution – any revolution. But, as his father repeatedly and irritatingly told him, he had the mind of a capitalist entrepreneur. For now, he dealt in drugs.

'Oh no. Oh Manny, why didn't you say?' Nell was remembering a night in a strange house way up the Cowley Road, shuddering and weeping for terror at what was happening to her body and, perhaps even more, for shame. As though the word opium had been enough to trigger a repeat, she disentangled herself and set off for the nearest bathroom.

There, nearly an hour later, Jamie found her sitting on the floor, her forehead resting against the cold enamel, her hands still shaky. She was pale. Her hair was bedraggled and she'd wrapped herself in a bath-towel for warmth. Jamie, who'd never really looked at her before, was moved. Self-possessed, smartly got-up girls annoyed him, however much he might fancy them. But this piteous waif . . .

'Are you all right?' he said.

'No. How about you?'

'Manny's such a bastard. I loathe that stuff. Why do we all have to be poisoned just to keep him company?'

Nell, struggling to contain another spasm, didn't speak. Indignation might be one of Jamie's commonest moods but it didn't come naturally to her. What a stupid way to end the night.

'Has Selim left?'

'Yes. He said he knew you could stay here.'

'I suppose. What about you?'

'I don't know. Want to come outside?'

Selim's car was parked by the estate office. Jack's particoloured Triumph Herald – raspberry-pink and white – was alongside it, blocked in. Jack and Antony came walking together under the archway into the darkened yard. They stood facing each other. Antony spoke at length, his long hands clasped together at the level of his waist. Jack's eyes went everywhere. He shrugged. He shook his head. At last he leant forward as though to put a hand on the taller man's shoulder. Antony flinched, stood tensed for a long moment, then turned and walked back towards the house.

Jack watched him go, silhouetted against the lights, then reached for cigarettes. He stopped to fumble with his lighter. The tiny glow fell on a patch of holly-green metal. Jack halted. He walked around Selim's car. Saw the number plate. Squatted down in front of the car and began to run his hands over the chrome of the bumper, the headlights standing proud of the chassis, the B with its speed trail. He sat down on the ground, legs sprawled apart, and let his head drop back against the great car's body.

Selim arrived with Guy and Manny.

'Oh my goodness,' said Selim, 'I'm blocking you in. I'm so fearfully sorry.' His manners were always correct. When he was stoned they became exaggeratedly punctilious. He went on and on, piling self-blame upon contrition. Didn't know where to go.

Got out in a hurry and flurry and failed to spot the little pink car. What an ass. Please forgive. Going now. At once.

'It's all right, man,' said Jack. 'I love this car. I absolutely fucking love it.'

And now Guy remembered. 'Well I never,' he said. 'Jack, isn't it?' They'd seen each other, here, as teenagers. They'd seen each other again more recently, in the vaults beneath Charing Cross station, both bare-chested, sweating, T-shirts swaying from the waistband of tight leather trousers, eyeing each other up as they danced. 'And the car. It's like the one you used to drive here.'

'It's not just like it, man. It's the very one.'

'It's Selim's. Selim, this is Jack.'

Jack said again, 'I love this car. I think I love it more than anyone I've ever known. Where's it been?'

'I bought it from an old Austrian lady in Park Town,' said Selim. 'Her sister had just died. She knew Nell's family somehow.'

'You just don't know,' said Jack, 'how gorgeous it is.' By now it was evident to all the others that he had been crying. It was true he loved the car, and equally true that he had never known how to respond so simply and ardently to any offered human love.

'Come over tomorrow,' said Selim. 'You can drive it.'

'Can I buy it? Please say I can buy it. I'll give you whatever you paid for it, plus twenty per cent.'

'Done,' said Selim. He thought he was dealing with a madman. 'You can have it. I'm leaving the country for good in ten days' time. Then it's yours.'

Jack pulled himself to his feet, and became diffident. 'Where shall I meet you?'

As Selim turned the unwieldy car in the narrow yard – it took eleven moves to get it round – the headlights swung across Spiv, in the arms of a man of whom little could be seen but broad shoulders in a leather jacket, and a lot of curly hair. Manny leant out of the window and wolf-whistled. Without disengaging herself, Spiv waved her hand behind her back, giving him two fingers.

'I guess she doesn't want a lift then,' said Selim.

'Certainly not,' said Guy. 'Or if she did, I'd volunteer to take her place.'

'A bit old for her, isn't he?' said Manny, who had had his moment with Spiv, and still felt aggrieved that a moment was all she seemed to want of him. 'Who is he?'

'Our Spiv is a very adult young lady,' said Guy. 'Mature beyond her years.'

'He's called Mark something,' said Selim. 'He lives around here. Mr Rose introduced me. They work together. Apparently he makes beautiful furniture.'

In most circumstances dawn is a time of freshness and renewal, of city streets quiet and washed, of relief from the dreary truthfulness of night-thoughts. With the light comes absolution. Tomorrow is, generally speaking, another day. Not so the morrow of a party.

In the long drawing room at Wychwood a couple lay asleep on a Chinese Chipperfield daybed like a grounded palanquin. They had dragged a bearskin rug over themselves: the beast's stuffed muzzle rested between them, a materialised nightmare. The girl's black eye make-up was blurred across her cheeks. She snored. A vase had been overturned. Pink roses and branches of philadelphus lay higgledy-piggledy by the puddle on the stone-flagged floor. There were cigarette butts in the ash of the dead fire, stubbed out in the pots of lilies, doused in wine glasses.

Nell followed Jamie through the glass doors. The magnolia leaves, with their rust-coloured velvet undersides, clattered against the panes.

'Come and join in. These dimwits don't even know the rules.' Benjie was hailing them from the croquet lawn.

A girl in a painted organza dress had thrown down her mallet and lain on a stone bench, her skirt trailing to the ground, fan-shaped like the biscuits Mrs D always sent in with the rhubarb fool. Two young men, one apparently in tears, walked along the edge of the ha-ha, silhouetted against the wan new day. The early light made them all look ashen as ghosts.

'No thanks,' called Jamie. 'We're going swimming.' Nell felt a frisson of irritation – what right had he to speak for her?

They walked up the path through the shrubbery. They had been there together once before. In their first year, Jamie had tagged along with Spiv when Nell, hating it, had succumbed to her mother's insistence that, after only a few weeks at Oxford, she invite everyone she'd met so far out for Sunday lunch at Wood Manor. Afterwards they walked up the Grand Vista to Wychwood, conversation suddenly eased (the cider had helped). She had led her little band into the garden through the side gate. As they passed the pool Jamie had said he wanted to swim, even though it was almost winter, and startled everyone by stripping to his Y-fronts and plunging in at the deep end, his stocky shape transfigured. In flight and in the water, he was neat and competent.

Now he said, 'You remember that first time I was here?'

'You swam then, too.'

'Yes. Your mother was very nice to me that day.'

A pause. He looked at her. He had surprisingly pretty eyelashes.

'I do, I really do want to swim,' she said.

'Yes, so do I.'

Again he stripped off his clothes, again leaving his underpants on. She followed suit. Thank goodness she was wearing a bra. He dived. She jumped. He worked his way noisily up the pool, doing a strenuous crawl, his short thick arms flailing, his face turning always to one side only, sucking greedily at the air. Nell came behind, her sedate breaststroke making not a sound, not a ripple.

The nausea had left her, but she was still stoned. Light buzzed, sound glittered, she was preternaturally aware of her ribs, of bones beneath flesh. The new-risen sun sent a beam of light straight through the wrought-iron gate in the yew hedge, throwing a shadow veil of baroque lace over the Buddha who presided, in his pagoda, behind the diving board at the pool's far end.

By the time they got out it was day. They wrapped themselves in the threadbare towels which smelt faintly of the rush matting, found a tartan rug (Nell knew it belonged to Flora's dog, another Lupin, but said nothing) and huddled beneath it side by side on the swing-seat. Their arms were pimply with chill.

'I once thought I'd killed someone here,' said Nell.

'Really?'

'No, not really. I was only about eight.'

'Tell me.' Jamie half-turned away from her, lay down with knees raised and rested his head on her thigh.

'He's older, almost my parents' age,' she said. 'He was staying here. Actually he was here again tonight.'

'Last night,' said Jamie, eyes closed.

'I used to listen to the grown-ups talking, all the time. That weekend everyone was talking about spies. And I got it into my head that Antony was a spy.'

'Antony? From the Ashmolean?' Jamie had opened his eyes.

'Mmm. It was just nonsense. I can't even remember what made me think it. It was to do with Berlin. Some of the men had been there during the war. My father was too, just afterwards. Was yours? Did he fight?'

Jamie ignored the questions.

'So . . . Who did you think he was spying for?'

'The Russians, I suppose. Although I wouldn't really have known.'

Nell was wishing she hadn't named Antony, whom once she had wished dead. Just a week or two before, she had met him in St Giles's and he had taken her into the Ashmolean and down into a basement, along with a girl she was with, and shown them both a marvellous piece of Roman gold, a pin the length of a kirby grip and topped with a tiny boar's head. She was touched, and a bit awkward. It was the other girl who said afterwards, 'Do you think he's awfully lonely? I think queer men are sad, don't you.' How had she known that about Antony?

'Go on,' said Jamie. 'So what happened?'

He was attentive now. Nell found she didn't want to offer up Antony for Jamie's amusement, or for his contempt. She'd heard him speaking at the union – and indeed in the pub – about privilege and corruption, and she could see which way this was going.

'Oh well, nothing did. I just thought the pool was empty and he'd be killed diving in the dark. But it wasn't so he wasn't. It's not really much of a story.'

'But why did you think he was a spy?'

'Oh, he was in Berlin, and he speaks Russian, and he's a bit mysterious about his private life. The grown-ups were just gossiping.'

'What else? What were they saying?'

'Oh, really nothing. I got the wrong end of the stick.'

'You're protecting him, aren't you.' Jamie was on his feet now, angry. 'These people. They get away with every bloody thing.'

Nell sat still, chewing her lips. She'd seen Jamie in this mood before and it frightened her.

'You're so bloody thick with all this gang.' He was pacing, his towel dragging. 'I'll talk to . . .' he said. 'I can . . . Well . . .'

He turned and saw her, as she was seeing him. Hair wet, eye make-up smudged, she seemed even more vulnerable than she had in the bathroom. Something shifted inside him.

'Hey Nell. It's just . . . It just drives me mad. It's not your fault.'

She stood up in his path and he stepped on and they kissed, teeth clashing at first, and then, in the changing hut, on the floor among the scattered towels, hungrily, Jamie thinking, Why did I never notice her before? Nell thinking, But he doesn't even like me, and, with piercing regret, Selim!, their bodies ignoring what was going through their tired and callow minds and clinging tighter and tighter until liking or not liking had entirely ceased to be the question.

*

Dear Mr Fletcher

You probably don't remember our meeting at Wychwood, even though I was doing my best to make myself conspicuous by dressing up as a Bedouin tent. Antony Briggs was kind enough to introduce us.

I'm leaving Oxford, and I'm intending to spend the winter in Berlin, which is currently, as I'm sure you've noticed, where it's all at (I can do contemporary-colloquial, you see, as well as camp-Firbankian). My interests are – in approximately equal measure – those of an elderly spinster, and of a drug-crazed voluptuary. I like austere music – classical or electronic – and tragic histories. Nero has been grossly maligned – making music in a city on fire is just my kind of thing.

May I send you brief dispatches from whatever front line – cultural, sexual, political – I find myself upon? I'll keep carbons, in the full understanding that you will probably put them in the wastepaper basket unread. But if any of them seem to you publishable you'll make me a happy man.

Yours sincerely

Guy Waterman

PS I'm sure you're above nepotism, but it would be underhand to omit to mention that my lamented mother was sister to Benjamin Rose.

Dear Guy

Yes, you were conspicuous and yes, I do remember. Send in your stuff and we'll see if we can use it. Six hundred words is about right.

Yours faithfully
Nicholas Fletcher

Dear Nicholas Fletcher

It was great to meet you at the Roses' party, and to talk to you about the Belfast Peace Lines. Sorry if I got too het-up.

I enclose copies of some pieces I've written for *Cherwell*. I leave Oxford this summer. I've been working for my local paper in the vacations. It won't be long before I get my NUJ card.

There's a story I've got wind of. It's about espionage. I'm not saying I've found the fifth man, but there's someone getting away with treason. He's very well connected.

It would be wonderful if you could employ me in your newsroom.

Yours sincerely
James McAteer

Dear James McAteer

Ring my secretary and make an appointment to come and see me here.

Yours
Nicholas Fletcher

Dear Nick

I loved our conversation across the moribund Mr W's famous lap. I'm off to New York to work for him, in what capacity I won't know until I get there. What do you think? Would it entertain your readers to have a sort of diary of my life as the living-dead genius's errand-girl?

From Spiv

Dear Ant
Enough! No more! Three letters from young hangers-on of
yours in one week. Do they think I'm the labour exchange?
  Love N

Presumptuous little gits. I haven't given any of them permission
to use my name. Let me guess – Guy, Jamie and Spiv? All sharp
as gimlets. You could do worse.
  A x

July

Christopher Rossiter had taken to spending the greater part of the year in Scotland, no longer inviting his friends for shooting parties, no longer shooting. He wasn't angry with Lil. He hardly thought about her at all. Instead he thought about waterfalls. Standing for silent hours by the burn (he still fished) he talked to Fergus about hydraulics, and the way the power of the river's movement corrugated its surface, just as muscles surge beneath skin. Fergus was growing up now. His appearance was unchanged but his comprehension of physics kept exact pace with his father's.

It pleased Christopher that the house's grounds were separated from the moor only by a straggle of sweetbriar bushes. In Scotland there are no laws of trespass. The rare walkers who came tramping up the glen weren't lawbreakers, or any kind of breakers. If they paused beside him he'd show them things – ferns or fungi or sulphur-yellow lichen. In the evenings he dined often with an elderly couple he'd known since he was a child. They talked about the past, over and over, patinating dimly remembered facts with layers and layers of nostalgia. It was soothing. Other nights a woman who hoped to marry him would appear in time for the first whisky. He hardly minded her presence at all. He liked it when she stayed the night. But it seemed to him, as a matter not of ethics but of decorum, that marrying was something you only did once.

It rained almost ceaselessly. 'It's soft today,' his housekeeper would say, as the windows misted over with drizzle. A soft life in a hard place. Only when he woke suddenly, in the awful undefended three-in-the-morning, did the dwindling of Christopher's life to that of a near-hermit seem to him pitiful.

Lil was in London, in a red-brick house near Holland Park built for a Victorian painter. In the enormous room where women had posed for the tweed-clad bearded artist, their pseudo-classical drapery slipping down to reveal their breasts, Lil held court. Helen moved in when she and Benjie split, and made the garden her own for a while. When she moved out again, Lil took in Flora's friend Seb, and Helen's shade garden, all hydrangeas and comfrey, was allowed to run wild. Indoors, Seb kept his rooms austerely neat, and then messed them up by bringing back people. However late Lil came home of an evening, there'd be someone there to talk to. It was almost like having a son.

*

'You'd need to make that last point in the opening para,' said Nicholas. 'You can't count on anyone reading beyond the first sentence, you know.'

Jamie, at a disadvantage on an unstable S-shaped steel and Perspex chair, leant forward and pinched his upper lip between thumb and forefinger. He could see that Nicholas had scrawled remarks in the margins of his copy, but he couldn't read them. He wasn't feeling as self-righteous as he would have liked.

'I can't use it, of course,' said Nicholas.

'Because you know them all?'

'I must say that alleging one of my best friends is a traitor is an unusual way of currying favour with a person who might offer you employment.'

Jamie, who hadn't known Nicholas and Antony were more than passing acquaintances, thought: Shit!

'But, speaking professionally, it's all innuendo. You can't stand it up. No one's talked.'

'But that's the story. The closing ranks and covering up. It's everything that's wrong with this country.'

Nicholas raised his eyebrows, and laid the typewritten pages face down on his desk. Silence while he looked out of the window, his feet up on the radiator, tapping teeth with pencil. Jamie struggled not to fidget.

Nicholas picked up the telephone on his desk, pressed a button and said, 'Ask Ted to come over, would you?'

'I suppose you're about to hitch-hike to India?' he said to Jamie.

'I'm not going anywhere. I haven't got the money. I have to get a job.'

Nicholas nodded and began to read through a sheaf of paper. An enormous man came and stood in the doorway.

'Ted. Could you use an extra hand for a few weeks?'

'The diary's short-staffed.'

'Have a word with Jamie here and see if you can sort something out.'

'Right you are.'

Ted was already gone by the time Jamie stood up, not sure whether he was supposed to follow him.

'He'll take care of you,' said Nicholas. 'There'll be a per diem. This isn't a proper job, but it might turn into one.'

'That's amazing,' said Jamie, and blushed.

Nicholas handed him back his piece and said, 'You'll do all right. You've got the knack. You were out of your depth with this one, though. Don't try to sell it anywhere else, or you'll have all the libel lawyers in London after you. In fact . . .' He held out his hand. Jamie passed the sheets back. Nicholas tore them across twice and tossed them in the basket. 'Go talk to Ted.'

*

Exam results came through. All but one of Nell's lot got 2:1s. The exception was Spiv, who got a first. She rang Nell close to midnight. As she picked up the receiver Nell could hear her parents' door open upstairs. The telephone was in the corridor leading to the smoking room, where she and Dickie had been watching the Wednesday play, and then, too enervated by heat and boredom to go to bed, had stayed lolling on the sofa with the blank screen doing its buzzy thing to their eyes.

'Nell, it's Spiv.'

'Oh wow Spiv, how are you?' (The upstairs door closed quietly.) 'You clever clever thing.'

'Yeah it's great. But Nell . . .'

'Yes.'

Spiv was gulping and gasping.

Dickie walked past, dripping milk from his late-night corn-flakes onto the parquet. The green baize door thumped behind him as he went through into the kitchen passage.

'Spiv. Spivlet. What's happening?'

More gasping, the sound breaking up as Spiv's distress crossed the Atlantic.

'Oh Jesus, what's wrong? I can't hear what you're saying.'

Spiv inhaled deeply and said, 'Sorry sorry.' Spiv, so assertive and demanding. Spiv who'd always made Nell feel, by compari-son, so unsophisticated and messy.

Now she could speak, with hiccups.

'It's evening again. It's evening. How did that happen? Must be the middle of the night for you. I haven't been to bed for days. Nell, I'm a wreck. I've been a total idiot.'

'Why. Why. What's happened?'

'There was a boy. He wandered off and I don't know where he went and I'm just so worried about him. I might have killed him.'

Nell remembered when she'd last heard Spiv talking like this. That breathy voice, higher pitched than usual.

'Spiv . . . Are you tripping?'

Spiv began to laugh, a cartoonish tee hee tee hee.

'How long ago did you drop it?'

'Oh, hours and hours.'

'Are you with anyone?'

'No. Well yes, but not my lot. They let Andy and everyone into the Studio, and they've always let me in before, but for some reason the guy on the rope turned nasty and Fred said he'd talk to Steve, and just to wait and I waited and waited and I was talking to these sweet boys in the queue and I gave them each a tab.'

Who are all these people she's talking about? thought Nell. And then she thought, Here I am with my parents and my little brother, and everyone I know is having these adventures. What's happened to me? What's happened to that Oxford life? I had a life, didn't I? What am I going to do?

Spiv was sobbing again. 'I've got a first from Oxford, and now I'm just the girl who calls the cab and waits on the pavement outside the nightclub. I've torn my silver dress. Do you remember I said I'd give it to you, and now look it's all tattered and torn. All forlorn.' And then she began to giggle. 'I've got a first, haven't I, I've got a first.'

'Yes, you have,' said Nell and thought, People are even more irritating when they're tripping than they are when they're drunk.

'Where are you?'

'I'm at these boys' apartment. But the one who hasn't come back . . . Suppose he's fallen off a bridge or something. It'd be my fault.'

Nell said, 'Go to bed. Or just lie on the floor if there isn't a bed. And ring me tomorrow when you come down.'

Spiv said, 'All right, Nanny,' and hung up.

*

Germans are efficient. Germans are ruthless. German men all look like Klaus Kinski, with exactly rectangular bony faces and mad pale eyes. German women are blonde dumplings, or predatory stick insects in bias-cut black satin. Germans are philosophers, and spend long nights debating the Four Last Things. Germans tear off all their clothes as soon as the sun comes out and have sex in public, by lakes. Germans create wonderful music, all storm and war-path.

I've been in Berlin for less than a month, but already I know that all of the above simple-minded racist allegations are the absolute, indisputable, copper-bottomed truth. About this place, anyway. Walled-in West Berlin is a walled garden of earthly delights positively writhing with the serpents of temptation. It's full of fetid cellars where boys and girls as beautiful as angels drive themselves out of their minds every night, and its music scene is sublime. Take the concert from which I've just reeled away.

Picture a street in which a row of buildings faces a bank of concrete half as high as they are. Picture arc-lights and watchtowers – it's easy done, you've all seen the photos. And then picture one of those houses, its iron-gated courtyard, its rooms with their crumbling plaster mouldings and massive chandeliers from which the electric wiring hangs in loops fit to hang yourself from.

Come inside. Lots of mascara, on boys and girls alike, and henna-red ringlets and sequins. Everyone is thin, except for off-duty soldier boys with their Popeye muscles. Nothing to eat. Lots to smoke.

Go down two hellishly steep flights of steps. Scores of nearly naked people all moving in synch with the eeriest, most mind-bending music to be heard in Europe since Genghis Khan led his hordes ululating off the Mongolian steppe to rap at the doors of Christendom.

On stage, five men in silver boiler-suits. This is Sonder. And the thing that looks like a deep-freeze in the process of

shapeshifting into a grand piano is the synthesiser they have built.
These aren't art-school poseurs. They came out of Berlin's
Technoschule. They are engineers, and like the shamans, they can
induce trances, and enable flight.

A young woman, whose earrings glowed like ice-shards in the
spinning lights, said to me, 'This is Nirvana.' I say, No. Nirvana
is a happy ending. What goes on when Sonder take the stage is
not any kind of ending, but the beginning of something new in
Western music. They are unsmiling. They are philosophers. At
least one of them looks a bit like Klaus Kinski (the dead-straight,
colourless hair). And they make music that kept us swaying
together all night like fronds of seaweed in a tide-race. Trance!
Ecstasy! The orgasmic whirlwind! The severe unsmiling Paradise
of the German Enlightenment regained.

Telex
From the Editor
Thanks, Guy. We can use this, but we'll have to chop it. Keep to
length next time.
　N

*

It was nearly ten when Nicholas left the office. He never went to
El Vino's any more. Editors didn't. He threaded his way through
Covent Garden. Small wiry men lugging crates of new potatoes.
The cloying scent of melons. Piles of discarded lettuce leaves
alongside cardboard boxes stained with raspberry juice.

Francesca was waiting for him at Bianchi's. She ordered saltim-
bocca. Elena, attentive and spry, said, '*Cervello fritto* and spinach
for you, Nicholas?' He nodded. He'd been coming here, alone or
accompanied, for years. He always ate what Elena chose for him,
and she never alluded, in the presence of whichever lover or
senior minister he was dining with, to any of the others.

He told Francesca about Jamie's visit.

'How crass,' she said. 'He's a bulldozer.'

'Bulldozers are useful,' said Nicholas, 'but they have to be steered.'

That night, as on many nights that summer, Francesca went back with him to his flat, with its tobacco-brown walls hung with cartoons from the paper, and photographs of him shaking hands with despots, and rather good paintings by people he knew. Her clothes were unusually adult for a girl of her age, and so was the self-possession with which she took them off and displayed herself to him. It was she who had rung him after they met at Wychwood. He had said, 'I suppose you want a job on the paper too?' She'd said, 'No, I want to seduce you.'

*

Flora and Hugo paced along Woldingham's Walk, the path that led alongside the lakes, twisting back and forth across the dams between them. Flora had asked for a meeting. 'We've got to have a talk,' she said. 'We've just been drifting along, haven't we?' Then she'd showed up in the estate office and said, 'It's such a dreamy day. We can do this out of doors.'

Hugo hadn't been drifting along. He'd been running the estate, the way he always had done. Flora's carryings-on up at the house didn't interfere much with the business of the place. The shoot, the timber, the home farm and tenant farms, the intricate game of matching tasks to the men able to perform them, the maintenance of walls and fences, of gardens and buildings, the breeding and selling of livestock, the purchase and servicing of the massive farm machines; it all went forward under Hugo's eye. He made a mechanic's job for a tenant farmer's son who'd been up before the beak for shoplifting: the boy was doing all right now. He wangled some money from the Forestry Commission for new planting. He set a team of men to battle with the waterweed which, every summer, did its best to choke the upper lake. He and young Slatter went together to the Game Fair, weighing up the pros and cons of investing in a herd of Herefords, and went for it, and made a good fist of it. And now there was the nursery garden, and this garden-design thing with Helen. He was having a lot of fun with that.

The stud farm was empty. That was a shame, but Lil was the only one who'd really loved the whole business of it, and you can't let thoroughbred horses, each one worth a small fortune, get hairy-heeled in a field. So, when the prize mare, Lucy Glitters, had to be put down, Hugo sent the rest of them to Newmarket. Driving back after the sale he pulled into a lay-by and found Charlie the head groom there already, still in his old Humber, hugging the steering wheel and blubbing like a baby. Hugo got in beside him, and they passed cigarettes and hankies back and forth, and told each other stories about the mean bastards among the horses they'd known – one of them had given Charlie his lop-sided stagger – and talked about Firefly, the most beautiful filly ever bred at Wychwood, and the most promising as a two-year-old, and why it was that none of her foals ever came to much, and then they talked about old Basily and then they needed the hankies again, and then they split a tube of Polos because both of their wives would be on to the smell of Senior Service otherwise. Afterwards Hugo was able to ease Charlie into a job with a chap he knew with a stud farm in Norfolk, and Charlie'd just bred his first winner there. Hugo had a plan for the paddocks, bit of a funny one, but it might work. Alpacas. There was a demand for the wool apparently. Just a thought.

So no, Hugo hadn't been drifting.

'The thing is,' said Flora, 'I want to do something with this place. Open it up. Use it more. Not just for us. I mean I want it to have a point.'

Hugo waited to see what this was all about. Flora waved her arms as they walked, but her gestures weren't matched by her words. She didn't really have anything definite to say. But he felt a kind of vertigo, as though he was living through a barely perceptible earthquake. Nothing broken, but the ground on which he stood was no longer entirely to be depended upon.

*

Telex to Flora Rose, Wychwood
Flora my darling aunt, you've got to come to Berlin right now. I've got the most thrilling proposition to put to you. Can you be here by Saturday? Your adoring Guy

Benjie said no thanks, he had no desire to see leather queens juggling with chainsaws, or whatever it was Guy was getting worked up about this time. He'd got some Saudis coming for the weekend. But suit yourself, he said. So Flora went.

*

All through July Nell was waiting and praying to get the curse, and Jamie hadn't rung. And then he did, and he was coming down on Saturday to collect stuff he'd left in college, and she went into Oxford with her mother, who had shopping to do, and she met him at his friend's place and they had sex again on the sitting-room floor, and actually it felt wonderful, so wonderful Nell couldn't help making noises and the sunlight transformed the dusty air into a shower of gold, but all the time the friend was in the kitchen next door, and afterwards Jamie got dressed very quickly, and she didn't know where she could wash off the sliminess, and he said that was great thank you, as though he hardly knew her and he was thanking her politely for doing him some sort of service like cutting his hair. And then he made her tea without milk, because there wasn't any, in the kind of rough pottery mugs which always seemed to her to be saturated with other people's spit. And they sat at the kitchen table, and she could feel her knickers were bunched up and sticky, and she began talking about Guy's pop-concert idea just to seem cool to Jamie and to his friend, who obviously wasn't really much of a friend and who must have heard all the noises and thought they were ridiculous.

Then Jamie announced he'd have to go soon and said, 'I'll give you a shout,' and she didn't even know what that meant but it sounded offhand, and she went to Fullers, where her mother was eating walnut cake with the one surviving aunt, whom she still thought of as a spy, and who looked like one now, with her silver-topped walking stick perfect for concealing a sword-blade in. And as Nell sat with them the aunt reached across and touched something on her neck and laughed. Later she looked in the mirror and realised there was a red mark there. A lovebite, but it didn't have anything to do with love. Her mother didn't mention it.

And then Jamie did ring, once he had started his job in London, and wanted to know all about the concert, but never said anything particularly affectionate, or even keen. He said, 'You're great, Nell. You're so laid-back.' She got the point. She didn't know him anything like well enough to tell him that she should have got the curse over three weeks ago.

Whatever was going on around her, that thought was always present in her mind. And in her stomach dread, like the feeling you get if you swallow too much cold water too quickly.

*

Flora was in a cellar in Kreuzberg that reeked of amyl nitrate.

The man with Guy was stripped to the waist. His concave chest was completely hairless and glimmered like opal in the strobe lighting. His leather trousers were held in place by a heavy belt with its full complement of what looked like real bullets, but, if his loins were militaristic, his legs, all but disabled by stiletto-heeled green snakeskin boots, would have been useless in any kind of combat. Guy – languid even amidst the shriek and gibber of Pandemonium – effected an introduction, but the name was lost as the musicians onstage fiddled with their giant machine, unleashing sounds as of a five-storey apartment building being demolished.

The next day Guy sat typing two-fingered at the marble-topped washstand in the bathroom, the only part of his apartment that got the morning sun.

Them/Us. Arthur/Martha. Yours or Mine. This is a binary world.

Berlin is binarism made concrete. Communist/Capitalist. Ossi/Wessi. There's no emollient pussyfooting here about the mutual dependency of capital and labour. 'That's you,' says the Wall, mutely but so thunderously you can hardly hear yourself think, 'and here, on the other side, is us. In/Out. Don't think you can fudge the difference.' The armed men in the watchtowers are there to remind us all of the ultimate dichotomy – Alive/Dead.

Here politics is polarised – muralised, rather. But sexuality is as secretly insidious as the sewers which flow east-west west-east beneath the streets. In Paris the '68ers wrote 'under the paving stones, the beach'. In Berlin, beneath the walled-off sectors, there's a freeflowing subterranean ocean of polymorphous sexual possibility. I'm not saying it's all orgasmic fun down there. But it's notable how blurred sexual identity is in this city.

Walled-in/Walled-out. We pity the Ossis their imprisonment, but they call it the Anti-Fascist Protective Wall, as though on this side a horde of storm-troopers might be ravening.

Let's think of some more dualisms. Tolerance/Hostility. Curiosity/Disapproval. The sour grapes of wrath/Dubonnet on ice, very nice. Here in Berlin, where the most clunkingly literalistic metaphor of confinement ever conjured up splits a city in two, we're all doing our best to obey Groucho Marx. 'Let there be dancing in the streets, drinking in the saloons and necking in the parlour. Let joy be unconfined.'

'Try to remember,' Nicholas had written last time, 'that this thing you're writing for is called a "newspaper". News, as in current events.' Guy crumpled up the paper and tossed it in the bin and tried again.

At three o'clock in the afternoon he took Flora a cup of jasmine tea.

'What's that?'

'Smells like a dowager's bath-water, but frightfully good for you.' He lay down beside her on the mattress. 'I'm wildly over-excited about our little plan,' he said. 'We have to talk business. You'll find beneath my effete exterior there's a hard-boiled entre-preneur gagging to get out.'

*

Jamie was in a pub in an alleyway running from Fleet Street down towards the river. The ceilings were low, the noise level high. He was drinking shandy and talking to one of the 'Blabbermouth' crowd, and said, before he'd even known he was going to do so, 'I think I've got an item for your Sink of Iniquity page.' 'Spill,' said the man, whose sideboards met beneath his chin. Jamie spilled – Antony, the flower-arranging boyfriend, the Russian connection. 'Great,' said the man. 'Which will you want? A byline or thirty pieces of silver?'

'The money,' said Jamie. And so, between a semi-alcoholic drink and a blasphemous joke, Jamie blew it.

Memo
From: The Editor
To: James McAteer
Thanks for yours. Sorry, no, that job has been filled, and we won't be able to offer you any further work after the end of this week. The 'Blabbermouth' editor and I talk to each other, you know. I'm sure you'll understand.

To his horror Jamie realised he was crying. He stood up, manoeuvring to keep his back to the three other people in the bunker, surrounded by shoulder-high metal filing cabinets, which constituted the diary office, and walked as nonchalantly as he could manage across the newsroom. In the corridor he kept his eyes fixed on the scuffed cork-tile floor. Through the glass partitions on either side men in shirtsleeves glanced at him incuriously. Avoiding the lift, he went down five flights of windowless stairs, and emerged, as though from the hold into the staterooms of a pre-war ocean-going liner, into the lobby, with its brown marble and sleek art deco steel chandeliers. 'Hay fever bad, is it, sir?' asked the snarky porter. Jamie ignored him and barged into the revolving door and on out into Fleet Street. 'I've got a job in Fleet Street' – he'd been saying that a lot lately. Not any more.

*

Mrs Slatter was in the Old Dairy with Mark Brown. When her husband was still alive she used to spend hours in that place. It was cold then. Dairies had to be. When Mr R's shooting stockings got holes in them – the heather-coloured or greeny-brown ones that were knitted for him in Scotland in a pattern of ribs and knots that was for him and him alone – the indoor servants passed them on to her. She'd wear four or five pairs at once, inside her father's old sheepskin boots, and still she got chilblains, standing hours on end on those stone flags. Getting up in the dark all winter long. Her butter was famous, though. And the cream, with that yellow crust on it. No one on the estate had to worry about rationing.

The first time she wandered in and found young Brown there she was embarrassed. She wasn't dotty. Not yet. But she'd lived at Wychwood so long she'd sometimes just land up in one of her old places without having exactly planned to go there, wherever it was. There was no need for anyone else to know that. The house she and Slatter had lived in for thirty years was their son's now. His wife was a nice little thing. She'd stop her sewing machine (she made all the village's curtains) and say, 'Ready for a cup of tea then, Mother S?'

Anyway, that time, Mark Brown had looked up and said, 'I think you knew my aunty didn't you, Mrs Slatter?' just as though he'd been expecting her. He said, 'I like having someone around when I'm working.' He'd got her sitting in a chair like a throne. They'd put glass in the roof, so that the place was sunny, and when Brown got out his drill, so it was too noisy to talk, she might have had a bit of a doze. It was peaceful. The woody smells were good. She started coming often. He liked her stories. You could never tell which of the younger ones would.

Now Goodyear came in. He had the gift, like her. She'd seen it straightaway, when he was just a waddling boy with arms like little rolling pins. He was always chattering on. Babble without sense to start with. But he was standing up on a chair at harvest suppers before he was into long trousers, spouting away, and all the grown people shutting up to listen. It was in his family. There was a Goodyear with the gift from Lord Woldingham's time, and some old gent who kept a diary wrote one or two of his stories down.

'Do you know the one about the two boys in the meeting-house?' she asked Goodyear now.

'Let's hear it then,' he said and settled himself on a bench. He's getting older too, she thought. She could see the top of his head, pink through his hair.

Mark handed them mugs of tea and jam tarts. Shop-bought, and not even put out properly on a plate, but it's hard for men. Not that young Mark was short of women to do for him. She'd seen him at the party, with that girl dressed up like a stripper. Their Holly had a crush on him. Half the grown girls in the village too. But he'd be after someone more London now he was in business with Mr Rose. Not that he wasn't a sensible man. And he knew how to work.

'There's a picture,' she began, 'a picture made all of little stones.'

'The Bacchus pavement?' said Mark. 'That's in the Ashmolean now?'

She looked at him with blank eyes. You do not interrupt a storyteller with banal factual remarks.

'There's a picture,' she said again firmly, 'of two boys.

'It's very old, so old that the house it was part of had all crumbled away. It was once the floor of a great lady's room, and perhaps she had twin sons, and that's why they made her a picture like that, or perhaps she wanted a picture of two heathen gods.

'The lady was Roman. She had come from where it is so hot in summer that the dogs lie for months on end in shady rooms with their bellies pressed to cold stone floors. Being accustomed to that heat the lady must have pined in England.

'The Romans came here looking for pearls. Whether they found any, I can't tell. But they liked our rain, so they stayed, and built bridges, and taught themselves how to make gardens with rose-beds and rows of lettuces and ponds full of fish. But then came other people, who chased them out, and the fighting between those other people went on and on until all that the Romans had built had been smashed to smithereens but for a few treasures, like daggers and brooches that had been buried deep, and like my lady's floor-picture, that was hidden away under moss and bracken and mud. And the Romans were so far forgotten that people came to believe their bridges had been built by giants or fairies, because no one could imagine how mortals could raise such stones. And so a thousand years went by.'

Mrs Slatter paused and stirred her tea. Goodyear was watching her but thinking about his boy, who was sweet on her grand-daughter Holly. Holly'd only just started at the grammar school in Chippy but she was a womanly little thing already. Both of them into woodworking. They'd learnt it off Mark here. It'd be a happy thing.

'There came a time,' Mrs S went on, 'when there were two boys living at Wychwood. They were cousins. One had been poor, and had wandered through foreign lands as a beggar, but he had parents who loved him. The other was a child here at Wychwood, and never lacked for food or warm clothes, but his father was a cruel man and he lived in fear.

'There was fighting again. There was a new king in London. The poor boy – we'll call him Charles – came home with his dear father and mother. They were friends with the new King so now he was rich, and he slept on embroidered sheets beneath a canopy and he had quails to eat and silver buckles on his shoes. The other one – we'll call him Edward – ran away from his fierce father, who was full of rage now the King was come, and dangerous.

'Edward hid in the forest alone. He lived on nuts and mush-rooms and the fish from the streams. One day he was digging for worms to bait his fish-hook. It was raining, so to be sheltered from the pelting of it he went into a building he knew, and as he scratched in the earth of its floor he came upon a bright-coloured pebble, and he scratched a little more, and he uncovered more of the pebbles, and he saw they were fixed into a pattern. For near a month he would come every day, after he had fed himself, to the meeting-house, as it was called. He dug up the weeds and moved the clods and the branches that must have been placed there on purpose by someone who wanted to hide the picture.

'And at last he could see the pavement clear. There were wrig-gling lines to show the waves of the sea, and there were dolphins and mermaids and seashells arranged all around the edge so that they were like the border on a rug. And in the centre there were two children. Their hair was long, and streamed out behind them, but they were bare-naked but for their flying blue cloaks, so you could see that they were boys. Each one held onto the other's feet, so that together they made a circle.

'There was another person living in the forest, a witch called Meg.'

Goodyear had been sitting arms akimbo, hands on knees, eyes to the floor. Now he lifted his head and looked carefully at Mrs Slatter. He'd never addressed her by her Christian name, but he knew it.

'Goody Meg was no friend of the King's. She wished that all the kings could be driven from their thrones. But she had known Edward's father, and she didn't like him either. She had feared for the boy, and when she saw him one evening, by the hovel he had built himself, she was glad.

'She didn't speak to him then, but the next day, she let him come up behind her as she walked along one of the wide rides. She walked on slow and steady. He slipped off into the brush-wood. She let him go. The next day and the next she let him see her again. Once she was sitting by the lake when he came down to fish. Once she sat very still, leaning against a tree-trunk, with her head nodded down as though she was sleeping and her tangled hair hanging about her cheeks. Each time he looked at her a little longer before he dodged away. He was very quick and stealthy. She approved of that.

'Then, on a bright morning, the boy Edward came around a corner, and there across the path was stretched a great spider-web all spangled with dew, and he stopped to marvel at it. And then there was a slight movement on the other side of that jewelled net, and he saw there was an old woman there. She said, "It is only when the little waterdrops are shining on them we even know they are there."

'The boy had heard many sermons in his time and he was sick of them. He thought she would say the beauty of the web was like the beauty of humility, which hides itself away, or that webs, being everywhere, were like the holy spirit which is in all things, or some such holy twaddle, and he thought of his father and got ready to back off. But Meg laughed, and lifted her stick, and slashed through the web, and whirled its tatters around her stick, as he had seen the sweetmeat-maker twirl an apple in boiling sugar. "Remember me, Edward?" she said.

'She hunkered down, there in the middle of the path, and felt in her pouch, and brought out a loaf and a bottle and began to eat and drink. Edward stood stock still. She passed him up a morsel of cheese. It was savoury and rich. He crouched down, still a little way off from her. She put the leather bottle on the mossy ground between them and showed it to him. To pick it up he had to shuffle a little nearer. She laughed at him then, and said, "My hedgehog feeds from my hand. I hope you can be as bold as he is."

'So they became friends, the lonely boy and the witch.'

Mrs Slatter sat back in her chair and sighed a little. Mark Brown brought her another jam tart. He waited this time, before he spoke, but when he saw she was not ready to continue he said, 'I'm interested that you talk about witches.'

'Why wouldn't I?' she asked. Goodyear shook his head and gave a kind of snort. Mrs Slatter ate her tart and sipped her tea until she felt inclined to go on.

'Time passed. One day Charles, the boy who had been a wanderer but then came home, was drowned. Goody Meg came to Edward and she said to him, "Every night since that other boy died, I have dreamed of him and of you." Edward knew who she was talking about. He was often near to the great house, among the trees or down by the water.

'Meg said, "You are two sides of the same medal. You are cousins, but you are more than cousins. One out one in. One home one far away. One fed one famished. One alive one dead. You are the fortunate one now, but you must be joined to him again, so that he can be alive in you."

'Edward did not understand. He thought she was crazed. She led him down to the building where he had found the picture of the Roman twins in their blue cloaks made from precious stones which had come, Meg told him, from the highest mountains in the world. Mountains so far away that the camels died of old age on the journey, and their little calves were old, too, before they finally arrived with their bundles full of blueness at the point where the great desert that covered the eastern part of the world touched the sea the Romans knew.

'Meg had blue to wrap him in too, a fine blue coat with silver buttons, and when he saw it he was afraid, because he knew it had belonged to the other boy who was dead.

'She dressed him in it, and around the meeting-house there was a congregation gathered. And a lady who had been kind to him, and called him brother sometimes, took his hand. She was called Cecily, and Meg told him to go with her. Cecily led him down to the pond that was said to be bottomless. As they walked through all those people she was talking quietly to him. She was telling him to be brave. She said, "We will step out onto the water, and we will walk across it, as our Lord walked across the lake at Galilee."

'Edward flinched then. Meg never talked of our Lord, or of bible stories, and a horror came up in him, the horror of his father. The lady Cecily saw it, and she said, "But, Edward, this is not a godly miracle, but one of mankind's. Beneath the water, there is a hidden road."

'They walked out across the lake, and there was some kind of a tussle going on behind them but they never looked round. Edward was laughing for the sheer joyful surprise of it. He had sturdy shoes, with square toes and good wooden soles. He put them down firm and straight on the water, and something he couldn't see held him up. "Is it like this to fly, do you think?" he asked Cecily. She looked at him seriously and said, "Very like."'

Mark Brown had been sitting quite still, his awl lolling in his open hands. Mrs Slatter paused again. The evening sun was coming in the window behind her now, so that she was a black shape and the light was dazzling in Brown's eyes. Goodyear had leant back against the wall and crossed his arms and spread his legs out before him. Brown said very softly, 'I've heard of something like this. At the middle lake, after young Charles Fortescue died. It's in Norris's journal.' Nobody answered him.

Mrs Slatter ate another jam tart. There was something about shop-food. It didn't taste good, not at all, it was like chewing rubber. But she liked the thought that no one had had to spend time in a kitchen to make it. Mrs Slatter had made thousands and thousands of meals in her life.

She saw the two men, both waiting for her to go on, and she thought of the soppy way her husband's dog used to stare at them both while they were eating their tea. She felt suddenly impatient with them. She said, just to tease as much as anything, 'This won't buy the baby a new pair of shoes. I have to go and help our Holly with her knitting.'

Goodyear and Brown both got that dazed look. She remembered it well. When you had been kissing and all that, and you thought you'd better not go too far, and pulled away and started to button up the front of your dress. The young men would get that look. You'd be sorry for them. You were feeling a bit of the same, your lips all puffed up and pouty and wanting to go on with it, but in those days you had to watch out.

'The fable of the two blue boys,' said Mark. He had a thing about what he called folklore. 'I don't quite grasp its significance.'

Meg said, 'Stories aren't puzzles, you know. Solving them isn't the point.' She wanted to be off now. She said, 'I'll tell you the rest another day,' and she buttoned up her cardigan and picked up her string bag with the Thermos flask and her folding plastic rain hat in it, and she walked out to where her bicycle stood propped, and hung the bag over the handlebars and got on with small, precise, carefully calculated movements and mounted, and wobbled away.

*

In an Italian restaurant between Charing Cross and the river Nell was having lunch with Jamie. The table tops were Formica, the flowers plastic, the food heavily coated in cheese sauce (Cheddar cheese, that is). Nell was in her interview dress, bought in a second-hand shop in Oxford. Cream and navy silk, high-necked, front-buttoning, prim little sleeves, probably 1940s, a faint, quite pleasant smell of talcum powder. She had come from the office in the Admiralty to which she was summoned by letter a week ago. So she'd won the approval of the Whitehall examiners.

In the great room, wood panelled, overlooking the Mall, she had faced a row of grey-haired people of both sexes, all apparently au fait with her written answers. She'd had to lay by at once her assumption that civil servants were robotic administrators, with no imagination, no culture. One of them started talking about Satan's expulsion from Heaven. She'd proposed a bit wildly in her test paper that Milton's Paradise was a kind of penal colony. Now she had to defend her argument.

The interviewers' questions were searching. Was she in favour of open government? No, she thought free and radical discussion was only possible if the participants knew they could say whatever came into their heads without fear of public opprobrium. (This question was in the news. She had her answer prepared.) What would she do if she was ordered to implement a policy of which she disapproved? She would make the case for her point of view, but if she failed to persuade her superiors, she would do as she was told. (What, she thought, as these platitudes tripped off her tongue, could they tell about her from any of this? Surely everyone gave the same answers?) If she were to learn that a poet whose writing she admired held political views that were obnoxious to her, how would that affect her estimate of his or her work? Not at all, she said, artists should be judged by their artistry, not by their opinions or their personal morality. (She hadn't stuttered yet, but the armpits of the interview dress were wet.) In which government department would she most like to work? The Home Office. Why? Immigration, prison reform – she'd mugged up on the issues. She said, 'Prisons are communities. Pathological communities for the most part. They have hierarchies and conventions. They suit some people. Some prisoners – just a few – dread their release. Inside, those ones are dominant. We need to understand prisons better. We have to make them less violent. I'd like to work on that.'

Then. Thank you very much for coming. You'll hear from us shortly. Absurdly, childhood habit took over and she shifted one foot behind the other and her hands went down as though to lift the sides of her straight skirt and before she could stop herself she'd dropped a curtsey. Thinking of it, she was mortified all over again.

'A civil servant,' said Jamie. 'Is that what you want to be? A faceless bureaucrat.'

'They take on girls,' she said, 'and give them proper jobs. How many girls are there in your office? Not counting secretaries and receptionists.'

'Yeah. Not many. Actually, I haven't got an office. I've been thrown out.'

Nell thought, Then I can't tell him. And the dread she felt at all times nowadays intensified.

She asked the expected questions. He told her a story in which he had stood up heroically to corrupt authority, and lost his own chance of advancement. She listened and thought, He's so bogus.

Across the street, in a different kind of Italian restaurant, where the tables were covered with white damask cloths, and there were posies of sweet peas, and most of the pasta sauces included either fresh basil or pine nuts, Nicholas and Antony sat at a corner table.

They ate *vitello tonnato* and talked about the tape recorders in the White House office, and the Salvator Rosa exhibition for which Antony had written a catalogue essay.

Pause.

The zabaglione arrived.

'Remember the first time we ate this?'

'There was only one good cook in England then, and that was Mrs Duggary.'

Another pause.

'So you say that there's something I need to be worrying about?' said Antony.

Nicholas looked at him levelly. Antony saw resolution, then a momentary wavering, then a what-the-hell-let's-get-it-over-with. Nicholas embarked upon a serpentine sentence, the kind people employ when it feels dangerous to be direct. 'There's something I know about you that you don't know I know, but I expect you suspect I might know because you know that it's known to a number of people, and you know that I usually end up knowing what there is to be known.'

Antony, who sat with his back to the room, glanced around deliberately, rearranged the salt cellar and pepper pot, and said, 'Once upon a time this might have been about sex. But probably not any more.'

'No,' said Nicholas.

'Then it's the other thing.'

'Yes.'

'And you've known for a while.'

'I wondered. When you kept going back to Berlin. And all that guff about the Transylvanian painted churches.'

'It wasn't guff. They're ravishing, and no one had written about them before. That's one of the reasons I got my job.'

'Well, all right. I thought you might have been playing carrier pigeon while you were there. But anyway, someone I talk to in the Foreign Office spelt it out nine years ago.'

Antony did the arithmetic. 'When my distinguished namesake and fellow art-historian made his secret confession. He must have named me. I suppose I should thank you for not following it up.'

'I was asked not to. Asked quite firmly. And frankly, I'll never be a really great editor because I don't believe in ruining the lives of people I'm fond of.'

'So now . . . Have you changed your mind about that?'

'No, I haven't. But someone came to me recently with a spy-story. I shut him up. But it was about you.'

'Who?'

'A young chap who was at that party at Wychwood. Now he's by way of becoming a reporter.'

Antony looked down and realigned a knife.

'McAteer,' said Nicholas. 'He was one of your protégés, wasn't he? You brought him there.'

Antony said, very quietly, 'If he's said anything to the Rossiters . . .'

'Wake up, Ant. Christopher knows people. He used to refer to you as Ivan. There's no such thing as a secret.'

Antony looked out of the window. He had believed in secrets. He thought what he was engaged in was serious. Seriously dangerous for him, and undertaken because of his seriously held convictions. And probably seriously disgraceful in others' eyes. He had imagined discovery would make him a pariah. So none of those people, his friends whom he had so greatly dreaded losing, actually cared either way. He was shocked. He was also afraid.

'So now what?'

'You know better than I do. I'm just telling you to watch out. McAteer was working on the diary for a bit. I wanted to keep an eye on him. I told him to kill his spy-story but he offered it to "Blabbermouth". Luckily they had more sense than to use it, and my buddy there told me where it came from. I didn't like that – I can't have someone on the staff I can't trust. So I haven't given him a job he was hoping for and he's probably sore against the whole lot of us.'

'What am I supposed to do?'

Nicholas was taken aback to see how shaken Antony looked. Surely he must have been expecting this for years?

'I don't know, old man. I don't know where you stand with all this stuff now. And I don't want to know. But if you're not active any more I'd have thought you should sit tight until you're asked. Then if you're asked, and you might never be, say, yes, but it's long ago now, and the world has changed, so what?'

A great weariness settled on Antony. He looked askance out of the window, his eyeline skimming past Nicholas's left shoulder. He saw Nell Lane, looking dressed-up, stepping out of the greasy-spoon opposite. She was always such a funny little shrimp, he thought, and now look, she's got breasts. Behind her came Jamie. Antony suppressed an urge to flinch back.

'Speak of the devil,' he said.

Out in the street Jamie said, 'Shall we go back to the flat? They'll all be out.'

Nell was speechless. Nothing he'd said so far had been remotely romantic. Or lustful. None of this was the way having a boyfriend was supposed to be. She couldn't presume anything in relation to Jamie. They were barely friends. And yet having sex with someone, she'd discovered, did make you want to do it again. Jamie's seal-like body wasn't anything like the gangly androgynous ones she found beautiful, but it was a body she *knew*.

He said, 'But it's cool if you don't want to. I don't really know, Nell. I don't know what you want.'

She was shaking.

'Hey man, you look awful. Come.'

He took her by the arm and led her into Embankment Gardens. Leaning on him, she smelt him. At least he didn't wear aftershave. Perhaps knowing a person's smell was the most profound way of being intimate. Perhaps all those couples who seemed so harmonious were as tongue-tied and awkward when they were alone together as she felt now. Jamie was looking for a bench, but she just had to say it. She couldn't wait to get it over with. She didn't even know the words to use. It wasn't done any more to say 'curse' but she'd never said 'period', in that sense, out loud. Nobody did. So she just said, standing still in the middle of the path with strangers passing on either side, 'Jamie, I think I might be pregnant.' And as she said it she felt a huge relief.

He said, 'Oh shit. I mean . . . wow.' And he did a little happy hop and flung his arms around her as he'd never done before. 'Nell, that is amazing!' And she thought, Oh God. Oh no. He wants it. That she'd never expected. Now what was she to do?

August

The Wychwood cabinet is in session again. Present, as before, Hugo Lane, Mr Armstrong, Mr Goodyear and Mr Hutchinson. Absent, Christopher. In the role of proprietor – Flora and Lil, with Benjie, affable and unobtrusive, chair pushed slightly away from the table as though to signal that he's there only as an observer. In the role of petitioners – Guy and, rather surprised to find herself in her father's work-world, Nell.

Hugo – So what happens at a pop concert?

Lil – Hugo my darling, don't pretend to be a fogey. Dickie will tell you. He's probably played at one.

Goodyear – No need to bother him . . . Mr Armstrong here's a bit of a one for that sort of thing.

Lil – Armstrong!

Armstrong (*The twelve years since the last session we witnessed have left him reduced, both physically smaller and less domineering. It is high time he handed his job over to one of the younger keepers, but no one knows how to persuade him to retire.*) – Well it was my Dora who went. I was just her chauffeur.

Everyone looks to Goodyear for an explanation.

Goodyear (*relishing the surprise*) – It was around Easter. They had what they called a festival on that bit of heath outside of Witney. Come night there were pop groups playing, but the

230

farmer who got it up, he knew that if he was going to get the families in there'd have to be more to it than that, so in the afternoon there was a children's fancy dress, and bowling and a dog show, and I'll give you all three guesses who won that.

All – Dorabella!

Armstrong (*unbending to show his triumph*) – She did. She won it. And there were dogs come from near Cheltenham. There was one come from Northampton. Dorabella's a smart little bitch. Not quite as clever as Doris yet, but she'll get there. And if she doesn't win at the fête this year I'll buy you all a drink.

Everyone from Wychwood applauds. Guy looks blank.

Lil – Dorabella is a spaniel, my darling. Doris was her grandmother.

Guy (*He is thinking about the spaniel who licked his face with such heart-melting gentleness while he lay on the yellow grass in the Garten waiting for that horrible trip to be over. He couldn't tell whether or not the dog's warm tongue was part of his own body, but he concentrated all his crazed mental energies on its motherly lapping while the branches above his head kept re-arranging themselves in fussy repeated patterns like a piece of rubbery crochet. He was afraid of the three emaciated young rent-boys who'd brought him there, and he couldn't tell if the people with him in the Garten were them, or a trio of Eumenides. He had felt very very thin, as though he might slip down a crack in the parched earth.*) – I'm extremely fond of spaniels. King Charleses especially.

Armstrong looks suspiciously at him. The old man's ability to guess a young one's sexual orientation is considerably more acute, for family reasons, than that of most of those in the room. And he doesn't like being teased. But the skinny fellow seems to mean it. They exchange slow nods.

Lil – Darlings, we all know how brilliant Flora is at putting on a show, don't we?

Flora – And Seb. But, well, I think it's different if the public are coming. You have to have loos and stuff.

Goodyear – Young Slatter and Mr Green did a lot of the work when the point-to-point was at Leafield. They'll know all about toilets and beer tents and what have you.

Nell is bristling with irritation. She's feeling usurped. When Guy rang her up from Berlin proposing a concert at Wychwood she felt important. She would be the mediator who would make this thing happen. She had an ill-defined vision of something dark and splendid. Guy began to write her long letters, and sent her records asking, flatteringly, for her opinion. But when he came back to England to get things organised he seemed to be someone she'd never met before, brisk and practical. This is surreal, she thinks. I thought I was getting under the skin of the counterculture. And here we are talking about loos and point-to-points.

Hugo is enjoying himself. To Nell's surprise he has taken to Guy. Guy's late mother had been a keen gardener. Guy picked up enough from her to be able to say, 'I adore the way you use alchemilla. Green froth! . . . Is that rose Penelope? Oh but it's stupendous! I've never seen one that height . . . And I just love the way you've kept this upper lawn so frightfully severe. Flowers and topiary just Do Not Go, do they?'

Hugo knows the boy is taking the mickey, but is pleased all the same. He hasn't seen a fellow in dungarees since he left the army, not outside of a garage anyway, and never that tight, and certainly not that colour, but the recent comings and goings at Wychwood have left him inured to the bizarreries of male fashion. He was angry when Dickie snitched the bum-freezer jacket of his dress uniform, and he still thinks they ought to wash their hair more if they're going to grow it like that. But just so long as they're polite.

Hugo – So, Guy. Fill us in.

Guy begins. So he simply adored the music of a Berlin band, Sonder, and he'd got them to play at one of the Oxford commems last year. When he got to Berlin he turned up at the studio they

232

used and hung around. And they wanted to come to England because they were into all that Glastonbury hocus-pocus, and he'd written a long narrative song for them, and they adored it – all about Green Men and the massacre of Germanicus in the depths of the forest, and ghostly hunters, and they wanted to perform it under the greenwood tree and he'd thought of Wychwood. And they really were brilliant.

Flora – He's right, you know. He took us to this grotty little place to hear them and it was just so *thrilling*. You just *knew* this was the centre of the *universe* for that night. (*Flora has adopted some of Guy's vocal mannerisms, as well as his musical tastes.*)

Benjie (*aside, sotto voce, to Lil*) – The Jugendstil apartment buildings in the East are simply scrumptious. If private property ever makes a comeback we should be there the very next day with our chequebooks.

Lil – Concentrate, Benj!

And so they concentrate. And decide on the August bank holiday.

Armstrong shakes his head and looks beseechingly at Hugo.

Hugo – I'm sorry, old man, the pheasants aren't going to like it. But it's not up to them.

Goodyear (*smiling broadly*) – Well this is a turn-up for the books. A load of hippies traipsing into the forest after all these years of working to keep them out.

Armstrong (*rising to his feet and fumbling with the lapels of his jacket*) – Well if nobody gives a toss about the shoot I don't know what I'm doing here.

The door is just behind his chair. He is out of it, slamming it behind him, before anyone can react.

Lil and Hugo both push their chairs back. She holds up a hand – leave it to me – and follows Armstrong out. Ten minutes go by, during which Flora takes Hugo into a corner, and whispers to him, while the others doodle on the blotters before them. Lil comes back in.

Lil – He's going to talk to Mr Aubrey at Blenheim. They had one of these things there last year, and they still got a record bag on the first day.

Flora – Darling Lil. You're a genius!

Lil – Well it wasn't really for me to interfere. Sorry. *She doesn't sound in the least contrite.*

There is a moment of embarrassment.

Flora – Oh Lil. Goodness. Interfere . . .

Benjie (*cutting in smoothly*) – It's quite a business putting on a pop concert, you know. Can we do it?

Flora – There are, well, how many? I mean dozens of people working on this estate, aren't there?

Hutchinson (*speaking for the first time*) – There are forty-eight, Mrs Rose, if you count in the men on the home farm.

Nell – And it's not like we're selling tickets, or wanting publicity or anything.

Hugo – All the same, we've got less than a month, and it's going to cost a bomb. What does Christopher say about it?'

Pause.

Lil and Flora each appear to be about to speak, but fail to do so.

Hugo – You haven't asked him?

Pause.

Hugo – I really think we can't do this without him knowing.

Flora – I'll ring him.

Lil – Or . . . I'm going to Morayshire soon to do a little gadabout before the twelfth. I could go a bit early and hop off the train at Pitlochry and have a talk with him.

Around the table there is a marked non-meeting of eyes. As far as anyone knows, this will be the first time Lil and Christopher have seen each other for over a year.

*

There was a place near Victoria Station, in a street of blank walls. On one side the boundary of a school, from behind which grunts arose, and the thwack of a leather ball. On the other the low concrete building, with its horizontal windows and flat roof. Nell hadn't made an appointment. She'd felt superstitious about giving her name. So she had to wait nearly all morning. No one knew she was there.

An abortion cost nearly two hundred pounds. Her parents were always going on about how they could barely afford anything. And anyway they would be so shocked. She couldn't tell them. But she couldn't get the money from Jamie. Why not? Because he didn't have any money, for one thing, and because he had never said he loved her.

The day she told him, he had acted like he had received a kind of atavistic fillip to his male ego. I'm a father, therefore I'm a man and it's a man's man's world. They'd gone back to his flat in Gloucester Road. They'd taken a taxi, something neither of them had ever done before, and he'd kissed her all the way, working his plump hands over her breasts. When they had to separate to get out and pay the driver she felt an ache like homesickness. The flatmates were out, and they tumbled each other on top of the stripy Indian bedspread on someone's double bed. It had been sweaty and noisy and ecstatic and out of a kind of tiredness Nell had surrendered to it completely and thought yes. Perhaps he loved her. Perhaps in that case she could love him. And anyway perhaps this pleasure that he could give her was all one could really ask for. Perhaps this was what people meant by the word love. She really didn't know.

Then they slept, and woke and went to the pub hand in hand, and got a bit drunk and there was a jukebox, and they danced to Martha and the Vandellas, and went back and made love again (she was beginning to use those words in her mind), this time on the single bed in his tiny room. In the morning he went to work: he'd got a temporary job in a second-hand record shop. She was woken by the phone ringing, and a stranger, looking sheepishly round the bedroom door and saying, 'It's Jamie, for you.' She wrapped herself in another bedspread (block print, tree of life) and squatted in the hallway (the telephone was on the floor) and he said, 'Come and meet me when I finish,' and she thought, I'm not alone any more.

But when they met that evening in Notting Hill he took her out into the park and they walked beneath an avenue of lime trees – the scent was piercingly sweet – and Jamie told her, very seriously, that there was a girl he loved back in Scotland. Nell didn't know whether to believe in this girl, but she had to believe the message the illusion of the girl conveyed. And somehow, since they weren't going to be together after all, the baby that might be coming was no longer anything to do with him. Irrational, but there it was. Obviously he wouldn't want to go ahead with it now, any more than she did, and he didn't even want to think about it. Didn't want to talk about it. Seemed to think that to show an interest would make a trap snap shut on him.

She'd got a train back down to Wood Manor that night, passing through the dried-out countryside in her rumpled interview dress. She'd loved and lost, and all between one clean pair of knickers and the next.

So that's why she couldn't look to him for help.

The examination. How many exams that summer had held. Peeing into a tiny plastic cup. It felt warm as it spilt over her hand. Strange warmth because not strange, because actually the warmth of her own body.

The doctor told her to bend her knees and she misunderstood and bent them upwards rather than sideways and he said crossly, 'Do try to relax, can't you.' How could anyone here be relaxed? Why on earth didn't they get a woman doctor for this job? The coldness of the jelly as he poked his metal thing up her. It looked exactly like her curling tongs. Did some people use curling tongs as sex toys? It would be so dangerous if they were switched on by mistake.

Once she was dressed again the doctor was scrupulously polite. 'Please sit down. How are you feeling? The result is positive.' She must have looked blank. 'That means that you are.'

Nell sat very still. The narrow chair felt precarious. How embarrassing if she fell off it.

'You'll need time to think about this. Talk to your family. Talk to the father. If you decide you want a termination, come back here. We'll see to it that you're properly taken care of. Don't for goodness sake go to one of those quacks who offer terminations cheap. They're killers.'

Nell didn't need time. There was no one she could talk to. She hadn't heard a thing from Jamie. She could say right away, please get rid of it. Never for one moment in the last weeks, when she had been constantly thinking about it, had she yearningly pictured a baby. This was what ought to be called the curse. The other thing, if it ever happened again, would be a blessing. But she had no money whatsoever.

She took all the leaflets they gave her and found her way down to the river. It was a muggy day, very hot. The tide was low. On the grey concrete rampart below the railing on which she leant a very thin young man was crushing a broken bottle beneath his heel, over and over again, the glass turning to powder under his boot.

*

'So how did you get onto me?' asked Mark Brown. He and Jamie were in the Plough. Jamie had hitched out from Oxford: he was crashing on the sofa in the Banbury Road flat. So Jamie began the whole humiliating story, about how he'd walked out, and then had to walk back into the office to get his bag. He was fond of the bag (appliqué, from Gujarat via Kensington Market, with tassels). But the point was, he'd left it behind thinking if he took it with him someone would say 'Where are you off to?' and luckily he had his wallet and keys in his pocket. So he'd just thought, OK I'll get another one. But once he was out on the street he had remembered with an awful sinking feeling that there was a little bag of grass in it, plus the giveaway Rizlas. No job. And busted. That would be just the sodding end. So he'd lurked about in the alley opposite the office all afternoon until he saw the diary editor leave and then he went back in and grabbed it just as a cleaner was about to chuck it out. And then one of the reporters had said, 'Working late?' and he'd said, 'There's something I need to check,' and gone into the cuttings library to look busy, and for no particular reason pulled out the file on Christopher and Lil and read the old story about the reopening of the way through to the Cider Well.

Mark laughed. 'And saw the picture of me on the barricades? But that was years ago. There's only one right of way through Wychwood, and they let people use it half the year. Good enough for me. I'm into furniture now.'

'There's going to be a music festival at Wychwood soon,' said Jamie. 'I'm going to write a big piece about it.'

'Who for? I thought you just lost your job.'

'Anyone who'll take it.'

Mark looked sceptical. 'Well, good luck with that. Anyway, where do I fit in?'

'The festival at Wychwood isn't open to the public. The estate workers get to hear it by kind permission of their lords and masters. And so do some invited nobs who probably think Muddy Waters is something to do with fishing. They're not letting the people in.'

'Why should they?'

'A private pop concert. The idea is a travesty. A betrayal of the music.'

Mark Brown glanced over Jamie's shoulder. Brian Goodyear had come in.

'So what are you going to do about it?'

'The stage is going to be on the lake alongside the right of way. No one can stop people just walking in up the path.'

'So you're going to gatecrash. Why are you telling me?'

'Me and a whole lot of other people. It's not gatecrashing. It's a matter of principle.'

Mark looked at him. 'What's your beef with these people? Nell Lane not interested any more?'

Jamie was so angry that for a moment he couldn't speak. Only a moment, though, and then he was off on the speech he'd been rehearsing, developing arguments with the liggers who hung about the record shop all day, and with his flatmates night after night. Pop music as the first truly popular medium . . . Slavery and soul music . . . music hall . . . marching songs . . . lonesome hobos wailing out the blues. Mass production of the means of production . . . the tuppenny mouth organ, the factory-made guitar . . .

'It's a business too, though,' said Mark.

'Yeah, but think of the difference between the price of an opera ticket, and a single for six and eight.'

'Look, you're making a mistake here,' said Mark. 'I'm not on your side.'

'Even the people who live here in the village won't be let in.'

Mark raised his eyebrows. 'Really? That's not clever. I'll talk to Goodyear about that. He's a pretty remarkable chap.'

Goodyear? The name meant nothing to Jamie.

*

Helen and Jack were in the library at Wychwood. The two of them had been having lunch with Flora, and together they'd arrived at a visual scheme for the concert.

'It'll have to be pastoral,' said Flora. 'I just can't imagine how you could come up with the floral counterparts of Moog synthesisers and boiler-suits.' Now, through the library windows, she could be seen out on the lawn trying to teach the new Lupin how to stand on his hind legs. She was tempting him with tiny biscuits topped with swirls of pastel-coloured icing sugar. He sat gazing hopefully up at them (he had successfully learnt 'Sit!') but he showed no inclination to prance up.

'Here,' said Jack. He pulled a portfolio out of one of the low shelves and laid it on the big leather-topped table by the window and Helen untied the ribbon around it. Some of the binding crumbled to dust. Softly softly. Easy does it. Within were Norris's drawings. There were words, place names and instructions and comments, all in a script so meticulous and minute it seemed that he must have written, not with a quill, but with a needle.

It took them over an hour to look through the first three folders, walking round and round the table to view the maps from different angles. 'Mr Green showed them to me first,' said Jack. 'Mr Rossiter let me climb up onto the table. I was that small. I thought it was magic that you could put a real place onto a piece of paper.'

'Quite right,' said Helen. 'It is.'

The plans were exquisite. Each copse and grove was represented by a tiny tree. The forest was a wash of darkness, but veined by streams and rivulets done in a darker ink. Sinuous contour lines framed each hillock, each dip.

'He was a stickler for accuracy,' said Helen, straightening up at last. She put her hands on her hips and rolled her shoulders. 'It's a selfless art, planting trees. But at least his scheme is still visible. No one's messed with it yet.'

Flora was waving at them through the window and miming 'Cup of tea?'

'Help,' said Helen. 'We haven't even begun on the drawings.'

Jack pulled out another folder. Beneath a sheet of tissue paper were blotched and yellowed drawings, each no bigger than a postcard. They were laid out neatly, gummed to brown parcel-paper in sets of eight.

'Who the hell glued them like this?' said Helen.

She rootled in her bag and brought out a magnifying glass. She peered for a while, then handed Jack the glass. She said, 'These are absolutely amazing.'

'The handwriting is quite different,' said Jack. The drawings were each captioned. The letters were much rounder than Norris's, the lines thicker.

They had tea under the cedar tree, but all the time Helen was distracted. Suddenly she said – she was interrupting Flora – 'That bedspread that was in Norris's room. Where is it now?'

'The flowery one? Still there, I think,' said Flora. She was rocking gently in the swing-seat, ignoring Lupin, who whined to be lifted up.

'Right. I'll just . . .' Helen went.

Jack returned to the drawings. He knew their every detail. Stalks angled sharply, or leant in fluid curves. Tendrils coiled, and leaves turned back, revealing the veining on their undersides. Each plant had a ladybird perched, or a caterpillar crawling, or a moth or dragonfly passing by. Squatting by a clump of kingcups there was a tiny, gulping toad.

Helen came in, her arms full of bundled linen.

Jack said, 'It was me that glued them down like that. Sorry. I thought it would make them stronger.'

'Christ,' said Helen. 'Well, you were wrong.'

'I traced them all. The drawing I showed you when I came to see you first. It was a copy of this one.' He showed her a bee-orchid.

He was shifty, contrite, but she just laughed. 'Copying. Nothing wrong with that. It's the way to learn.' She threw the embroidered cloth over the table so that it hung down on all sides. 'Look at this.' Jack had never seen it before, but he understood at once. He found the drawing of the dog rose – *Rosa canis*, with its bronze and green leaves, tight buds, and bristling Robin's pincushion.

'It's the same,' he said. 'Exactly the same. Was it the same person, do you think?'

'I don't know,' said Helen, 'but I intend to find out. And I'm sure she's a woman, or they are. I'm going back to the Institute to work on this.'

*

'What's Jamie up to?' asked Francesca.

'I don't really know,' said Nell. 'I haven't seen him for weeks.'

'Oh? I thought you two were *liés*.'

'Well. Perhaps we were. If that means what I think it does. I thought so for about half an hour. But it turns out not.'

The two girls – young women – were lying in the secret garden's ramshackle pavilion. They had each been offered jobs, Francesca in the Foreign Office, Nell in the Home Office.

'Snubs to those arrogant boys,' said Francesca, over the telephone, the day they got their letters. 'You and I will be running the country soon.' And then she had invited herself to stay, as though their shared career prospects had somehow made them closer friends.

'So you're going to take it?' said Nell.

'You bet I am. Aren't you?'

'I don't know. There's something awful about being offered a job with a pension. When do we get to be young?'

'Oh, grow up, Nell.'

'Exactly. That's exactly what I don't want to do. I might just ask if I could put it off a year.'

'And do what?'

'Well . . . I guess it depends.'

'On what?'

The thing about Francesca was that Nell could count on her not to care very much. So she was able to say, as she couldn't have done to anyone likely to show too much concern, 'On whether I'm pregnant.'

Which wasn't quite honest. To admit that she had already known for over a week, and had done nothing about it, would be too shaming.

'Jesus, Nell. What are you saying?'

And so she told her. And Francesca, as she'd foreseen, was bossy and rational. Of course Nell must ask her parents for help: she was flesh of their flesh and this was news of the flesh. And she must talk to Jamie, but not allow him to dissuade her from whatever she wanted to do. If she wanted to have the baby, well and good. It could be done. It could especially be done if she had a good steady job in the civil service. If she didn't want it, then she must be quick, and get rid of it. 'Your parents will pay. Of course they will,' said Francesca. 'They'll be desperate to sort this out.' And as she said it Nell knew it was true. Still she dreaded the conversation. It would be with her mother. She imagined that, whatever the outcome, Hugo would never, in all the years ahead, ever talk to her about any of this.

'After the concert,' said Nell. 'I'll tell them on Monday.'

Francesca gave an irritated shrug. This conversation was taking place on a Thursday.

'Fine, but ring right now and make an appointment for next week.'

There had been a matron at school who was generally hateful and hard-mannered, barking at the whimpering homesick children that they must pull themselves together, but who, when a girl fell ill, was kind. Nell, nursed by her through chickenpox, had felt as safe as though she were being guarded by a grizzly. Francesca, competent, impatient and domineering, was as sure a refuge.

*

A giraffe's head appeared, improbably high up in the arched aperture of its elegant Regency house. Still in profile, it regarded Antony serenely and at length with its one visible eye. Judging that his presence beyond the bars was acceptable, it slowly manoeuvred the rest of its fantastic body into view. The neck. How much muscle-power must it take to hold that up? The high narrow shoulders. The front legs, so long as to make it impossible to imagine the creature sitting or lying, or making itself in any way comfortable. The steeply down-sloping back. The sway. The jagged harmonies of the coat's pattern, toffee fudge outlined in vanilla.

The head wavered vaguely from side to side, using first one eye and then the other in observing a newcomer.

'Pretty well any woman I know would kill for eyelashes like that,' said the man.

Antony didn't look round. 'The hollyhocks are particularly fine this year,' he said. The zoo had flowerbeds, but there were no hollyhocks in sight.

'I prefer Michaelmas daisies,' said the other.

Antony kept his eyes front, which is what surely anyone would have done. The giraffe's calf, teetering unsteadily on its wheat-coloured pins, had shambled out into the sun in pursuit of its mother.

'There are things I have to tell you,' said Antony.

'Yes,' agreed the other. 'There are.'

'Perhaps you won't be surprised.'

'That remains to be seen. But we have been looking forward to this conversation for quite a while now.'

'How long?'

'That doesn't matter. But it's altogether better that you came forward of your own free will.'

'Better for me too?'

'Yes, much better for you. We're not vengeful. We're pragmatic.'

'Do we talk here?'

'No. Somewhere more convenient. But I need to know, do your other friends know where you are?'

'I haven't told them. But sometimes I've been watched.'

The young giraffe had found its mother's udder and settled itself to suck, leaning its hinder parts against her shoulder. She dropped her head towards it. Their coats complemented each other – brown on cream, cream on brown. Madonna and child in biscuit-coloured crazy paving.

'From now on we'll be watching you as well. But if you're as discreet as we intend to be, you're in no particular danger. A friend you made in Munich some twenty-five years ago talks to us too and no harm has come to him.'

Antony seemed to be about to ask a question, but thought better of it.

The other smiled. 'That changes things a bit, doesn't it? We frequently make a botch of things, but we're very, very patient.'

He gave instructions, while Antony abstractedly watched a plane pass overhead. Then he walked off towards the house of the small nocturnal mammals. Furtive toothy things that hunted in the dark.

Antony sat down on a bench with wrought-iron lions' heads for armrests, brought out a sketchbook and began to draw the giraffes. A couple of hours later he climbed out of a taxi near Victoria and entered a narrow terraced house. It was past midnight by the time he went home.

Lil

It really shouldn't need saying, but I'm afraid it does. If two people want to stay married to each other, they need to spend a certain amount of time in each other's company.

There were reasons why Christopher and I were uncomfortable together for a bit, but that was years ago. All my fault, of course. And because I was in the wrong I was defiant and scratchy about it. And I honestly had no idea what was going through his head. Reticence is an admirable quality, but it makes it hard for chatterboxes like me to work out where they stand. We never talked about that sort of thing, or any sort of thing for that matter, apart from the day-to-day. So I didn't know whether our being apart for months, or, after a while, for years, was because he had got fed up with me, and left me, or whether it was just that he was politely staying out of the way while I pursued whatever silly ends I chose. And rather than make the effort to find out, and risk the most God-almighty snubbing, I just kept on pursuing.

India, and that phoney guru. The art world. That was fun – is still fun. Of course all it takes to be a collector is money, but I think I do have an eye. My riding holidays with the Ladbroke Grove gauchos. My little magazine. My drowning Bengalis. My illiterate prisoners. The house in Italy with all those sots pretending to write their books at my expense. And every project brought me another courtier or two.

I do like having handsome young people about. Not always men, but mostly. Of course I know that some of them are parasites, but as long as they put themselves out to be amusing I can tolerate that. It's not as though I can't spare the cash. And some of them are real kind friends. But the truth is that, despite what everyone naturally thinks (and naturally they've been partly right some of the time – I'm not a nun), I haven't made a complete fool of myself since that wickedness with Hugo. It was wicked. I knew it then and I don't try to deny it now. Wicked to Hugo, first and foremost, but also wicked to Christopher, to Chloe, to those children, though I don't think Nell ever really grasped it. I've talked to her about that night. Unless she's a cooler liar than I believe, she didn't see us as she passed by, stalking Antony as he went up to the pool.

That was crazy. Christopher was in the garden too, with old Grampus, who was bound to come snuffling around if he scented me. That was another part of the wickedness, just not caring much about discretion. Actually wanting to flaunt it. Flaunt – odd old word, but this was a situation from a creaky old farce – people having cross-purpose trysts in a darkened garden. *A Midsummer Night's Figaro*. I am a flaunter. Look at me, aren't I a caution! But it was Hugo who might have lost his job, and his family.

Over his shoulder, I saw Nell go by, but as far as he knew she was safe in bed. When he heard her scream he ran, dishevelled as he was. I got myself back to the house, so I was there on the terrace, all concern and sleepy puzzlement, by the time Christopher and Ant reappeared.

Of course that was the end of it. I dropped in at Wood Manor as soon as we were back from Scotland. Elevenses time. Everyone on the estate knew Hugo went home for half an hour every morning – probably still does. So I plonked myself down in the drawing room and directed everything to Chloe, telling her how I was going to be spending far more time in London that winter because of this and that, and doing some bragging about what a lot of invitations we'd been getting so that I'd scarcely be at Wychwood again until Christmas, outside of shooting days, and after that of course we'd be going abroad. Weren't we lucky to have friends in Barbados. Chatter, chatter, chatter. Chloe must have wondered why on earth I was telling her all of this. I think Hugo probably understood. I was taking myself off so that we could both calm down. I'd been afraid he'd think he had to leave. He really is a very honourable man.

But Christopher is my darling, my bonny prince. It's taken me years to arrive at the thought, but sitting in the estate office yesterday I suddenly asked myself 'Why am I leading the life of a widow when I have a perfectly good husband?' And I mean exactly that. Christopher is perfectly good. I don't know what will happen when this train stops at some godforsaken early-morning hour in the middle of a purple moor, and I step off it with the taste of toothpaste and railway cake in my mouth, but I know what I'm hoping for. Perfect forgiveness. Perfect reconciliation. Perfect love. Silly old me.

∗

Today the five musicians who call themselves Sonder arrived in this country, all the way from the black forests of Germany, and ensconced themselves in something resembling a mead-hall in England's very own deep dark wood. Wychwood, they tell me, is as far from the sea as you can get in these islands. Put it another way, it's the country's centre, a place through which the umbilical fluid of myth and wilderness throb close to the surface, the navel of England. It'll soon be pulsating to a monastic drone cut-up with the screeching of the future on its way.

Memo from the Editor
We don't publish puffery, Guy. We'll send Ray to cover your woodland knees-up but I can't use this. It'll be Ray's last column (the poor sap thinks he can make a living as a novelist) which could be a lucky break for you. Come and see me when you can detach yourself from the umbilical cord of myth. N

∗

Hugo Lane walked up the track from the top lake towards the Cider Well. His rod was over his shoulder, the index finger of his right hand was hooked through the gills of a trout. Wully sniffed at the fish repeatedly, each time backing off as though in disgust and resuming his dancing progress, describing circles through the bracken each side of the way. It was a close and humid evening with the scent of summer's end in it. The midges were out.

A spaniel the colour of dead beech leaves – the only male in Armstrong's bitch's last litter, called, inevitably, Dorian – shot out from around the bend ahead, saw the Labrador and flattened himself to the ground. Wully froze, then began to creep forward, one tiptoe at a time. 'Evening, Goodyear,' said Hugo. Sometimes it wasn't necessary to see a person to know he was there.

Goodyear had one of his under-foresters with him, and Jack Armstrong.

'That'll be the last bit of p and q you get till next week, Mr Lane,' he said. 'Glad they were rising for you.'

The four men nodded to each other. Hugo laid down his rod and catch, and they all reached for cigarette packets. The smell of leaf-mould and wild peppermint was overwhelmed for a while by those of petrol (Hugo and Goodyear both had Zippos) and then of tobacco smoke.

'We were thinking about these flares,' said Goodyear.

'There's a lot to think about,' said Jack. He'd spent all day in an argy-bargy with the German group's lighting people. How to reconcile the requirements of the techies – amplifiers the size of motorcars, a snake-pit full of electric cable, screens and lighting towers and a lorryload of generators – with Flora's Arcadian vision? It was going to take half a dozen tractorloads of ivy and old man's beard to cover up that lot.

'I'm properly excited,' said Goodyear, 'I was saying to the wife, I feel like a girl in a new dress, hoping everyone will be looking at her. You know?'

'Not sure that I do, Brian,' said the other forester. 'That a feeling you get often, is it?'

No one teased old Armstrong that way. None of the other men ever addressed the head keeper, in Hugo's presence anyway, by his Christian name. Goodyear's authority was effortless. He didn't need formality. Hugo surprised himself by thinking, He could do my job, could do it bloody well. Next time around, it'll be someone like him.

He thought of the sergeant-majors he'd been bullied by in the army. Grown-up men training children (he was eighteen!) to lord it over them. Some of them were brutes. But what it must have felt like to be told you weren't officer material, purely for reasons of class. None of the men ever talked to him about their war years.

'Just you try getting up on that stage,' Goodyear was saying. He'd be alternating with Mark Brown as master of ceremonies throughout the afternoon. There'd be half a dozen pop groups playing twenty-minute sets, most of them local lads. And some girl-singers too. Guy would take over when the sun was properly down and Sonder's lightshow began.

'Well, I need my beauty sleep,' said Hugo, stamping on his fag. 'We're going to be flat-out tomorrow.' He gave a kind of half-salute and walked off into the dusk. He hadn't gone far when the others, still smoking, saw him lay down his rod again and fumble in his pocket.

'What are those pills he's always taking?' asked the forester. There was a pause, as though neither Jack nor Goodyear wanted to answer. Then Goodyear said, 'He loves his Spangles, does Mr L. Gives them to the dog too. Astonishing they've got a tooth left between them.'

*

Jamie was in a house in North London. From the front it appeared to be built on solid ground. It rose directly from the pavement. Below – a Bengali grocer's shop with steel shutters which never quite opened properly; above – a pebbledash façade with small horizontal windows blankly gazing at the street. Once you were inside it, though, you could see out the back windows that it was perched on a railway bridge. This gimcrack instance of modern building was actually a miraculous construction, as nearly airborne as bricks and mortar – or breezeblocks and asbestos – can ever be.

Manny lived in the first-floor back room. He was wandering around fidgeting with things. A mug, the fleshy leaves of an enormous rubber plant, a dirk topped with a marmalade-coloured cairngorm, which some long-ago Highlander must have worn thrust into his sock. Manny was big, and his stiff hair, crinkling out around his head to a radius of a good three inches, added a lot to his presence. A white rat watched him from its cage, and so did Jamie, sitting cross-legged on the mattress beneath the window. Rat and human visitor alike seemed at once mesmerised and fed up.

Manny was talking, as he often did, about violence. The orgasmic release of energy triggered when the taboo against bloodshed is breached. The Dionysian frenzy of a revolutionary crowd. Sacrifice as the dark heart of all the religions of the book. Orpheus dismembered by Maenads. The True Cross, an instrument of torture, encased in gold and borne aloft into battle by crusading bishops. The seraphic tranquillity of art produced by warrior nations. The one temptation to which St Anthony succumbed so absolutely the hagiographers never even mention it as a trial of his virtue – the temptation of pain.

Jamie had heard it all before. In his first year he had lived on the same staircase in Wadham as Manny, or Emmanuel as he was now calling himself. He knew that in trying to get anything organised with him one simply had to allow him to rabbit on like this until he'd talked himself out. Dürer's *Four Horsemen* bestrode the room in outsize poster-form, the black-etched figures tinted with acid colours – green, orange, purple, silver. There was a faint, incongruously old-maidish odour, as of potpourri. Sprigs of wizened herbs were strung across the windows. Manny made his own tisanes.

For all that he abjured alcohol, though, he had a healthy appetite for food. When he seemed to be moving towards a pause in his oration, Jamie said, 'There's something I want to ask you about. Let's go to the Taj. On me.'

Manny never spoke much while he was eating. Once the poppadums were on the table the flow of his talk stilled, giving

Jamie the chance to outline his plan. Manny interjected only brief exclamations.

'Tomorrow! Christ!'

'You want two hundred? Shit!'

'Two miles from the station? There isn't a bus or something?' Manny, who'd grown up in Hampstead, had seldom seen a road without pavements.

By the time they'd reached the kulfi stage, though, his reservations had all been countered. He sat back, and raked his thick curls with long fingers.

'So I do it, driven by my disinterested passion for making mayhem. But what's your motive, exactly? I don't get it.'

This was a question Jamie had been dodging whenever it crossed his own mind. He had several answers ready, but none of them were all that creditable.

He felt guilty about Nell, and angry with her for making him feel bad. After that time in the swimming-pool hut he thought he could be in love with her. But he wanted to use the story about Antony, and that complicated things. So he just put her out of his mind. He couldn't take another person on: he wasn't secure enough himself. Finals, and he was desperate to get a job. And actually there had been a girl in Scotland – that was true. They'd met on an archaeological dig the previous summer, both of them hunched all day over a chunk of Hadrian's Wall, brushing mud off Roman-cut stones with glorified paintbrushes. They sang each other their favourite songs. Her Joan Baez impersonation was feeble, but he felt the fonder of her for that. And then at night they persuaded the people they were supposed to be sharing tents with to swap, and woke up the next morning inside a single sleeping bag, as tangled together as the hawthorn roots that drove themselves down the cracks in the ancient masonry.

But it hadn't come to much, really. Not as far as he was concerned. At the end of the final summer term he went home, and saw the girl, and quite brusquely told her he was staying down south, and no, she shouldn't look for work in London, not on his account anyway. If she was heartbroken she was too proud to show it. And then he'd seen Nell again and thought, What have I been missing? There was something about her that tugged at him. He didn't know how to respond to it. His dithering over her pregnancy was reprehensible, he knew that. He assumed she'd got rid of it by now.

That was one thing. Nicholas's dropping him was another. Guy's getting ahead faster. All of these were irritants.

That was all personal, though. There was a principle. Behind all the jingles and the posturing, popular music meant something. Something massive. Times a-changing. It moved him, the idea of it did.

He left Manny propped up on cushions, the rat nestled into the soft hairless space under his chin, telephone receiver in one hand, sweat-stained leather-bound address book in the other, rallying his band of acolytes. Tomorrow looked like being exciting.

*

In Wood Manor Nell was mussing Dickie's hair.

'You've got to let it get tousled. You look like such a twit when you smarm it back like that.'

'I know,' said Dickie. 'But I just don't know I'm doing it. It's a nervous habit.'

They both contemplated his face, reflected from different angles in the triple looking-glass Chloe had thoughtfully provided when Nell entered her teens, and which was usually folded up and propped against the wall. Nell didn't want to see herself three times over. She'd never asked for her homework table to be given a skirt (nylon net over pink) and turned into a dressing table. She wanted a desk.

Dickie looked good. Tight purple satin trousers with a chiffon scarf (harlequin patterned in jade-green and black, formerly belonged to one of the aunts) threaded through the belt loops. Leather jacket spray-painted silver. Nell thought, Why is the best-looking boy I know my baby brother?

'Don't worry,' she said. 'You'll be fine and messy once you start drumming.'

'So how do you do eyeliner?' he asked.

*

'Fabulous,' said Jack repeatedly. The broken colonnade that was the tallest remaining part of the Roman villa had become the backdrop, and the stage jutted forward over the water so that the lights would be reflected and multiplied. Green was directing two under-gardeners as they trundled young trees around the stage, planted for the purpose in wheeled wooden troughs.

Jack's father stood on the house-side bank, where in a few hours, Guy hoped, hundreds of people would be dancing, and exchanged sardonic comments with Hugo. He and the other keepers would be in charge of car-parking. Most of them had done the same job at the Game Fair a year before.

'A different kind of crowd I'm thinking, today, though,' he said. 'Not so many Land Rovers.'

Hugo laughed. 'You just don't know, do you? I wonder whether they even have cars.'

'By the end of today,' said Armstrong, 'there won't be a bird or beast for miles, what with all this racket.'

Hugo looked at him cautiously. 'I know. I know. But with the Rossiters away so much . . .'

'No one cares about the shooting, you're saying. So I'm on the scrapheap.'

'That you're not. I've got big plans for the shoot.' Hugo hesitated, then went on. 'Don't bet on it, but I think Mr Rossiter's going to be here soon. Coming today possibly.'

Armstrong's deeply wrinkled face blushed. 'That's the best news. That's the best news I've heard for weeks. What's he going to say about all this malarkey?'

'We'll see.'

Armstrong held up crossed fingers. Benjie's red MG could be seen across the lake, wending its way up the front drive. The generator began to chug, and an electric guitar gave out a screech. The caterers were setting up out in the forest, near the second lake. A tractor pulling a cart laden with gas cylinders went by in that direction. Eight men were struggling to get the beer tent up, while half a dozen more lugged straw bales out of the back of a clapped-out horsebox. 'Good morning, officer,' said Hugo to a policeman who was picking his way over the tussocky grass in shoes meant for pavements. Armstrong shrugged and strode off towards the west gate.

Antony

I really hadn't been looking forward to Guy's jamboree very much. My encounter in the zoo, and its aftermath, had left me rattled. I felt I was picking my way through an unlit chateau whose every corridor contained a loose flagstone that would give way if stepped on and tumble me into an oubliette. Everything was just as it had been – my secure and prestigious job, my severe and tranquil flat ('You know, colour isn't criminal, Ant,' said Flora, 'I like grey too, but let me at least buy you some cushions'), my tolerant friends. But frequently and without warning my frightfully civilised life would be interrupted by summonses to meet people whose names I didn't know, people who had the power to disgrace me, and perhaps do much, much worse. The exquisite manners with which those encounters were conducted made them all the more unnerving. These people didn't have to yell 'Chop off his head'. If they chose to do it (do what? my mind carefully skirted around the question) it would be done neatly, without sound or fury. Over the years I grew accustomed to the situation, but thank the Lord for Mogadon. Without it I wouldn't have had much sleep since that summer.

I should perhaps explain that my secret work was pretty trivial stuff. I'm not a double agent. I've worked only for what Mr Giraffe calls the enemy, never for the British secret services, unless these little chats I'm having now count as working. I – I who adore the creations of the unfairly gifted, I who make my living by selling treasures to aristos and plutocrats, I whose daily work is converting things rendered precious by religious devotion or by beauty into commodities to be marketed – I worked only for communism.

People I'd known at Cambridge sometimes asked me to pass on messages to contacts in Eastern Europe. I knew they were Comintern. They knew that I sympathised with them in a wishy-washy kind of way. I think they thought my sexual proclivities made me a misfit and therefore susceptible. But that's not true. I'm not disaffected. In the world where I found my friends, discreet queens like me fit right in. So why did I do it?

It's partly a matter of aesthetics. I respect socialism, as I respect Piero della Francesca and Johann Sebastian Bach. A certain purity. A certain grandeur. It doesn't surprise me one bit that a Poussin expert should have gone the same way: neoclassicism is revolutionary. And then there are lower motives. Curiosity. The lure of the undercover world – I certainly found that titillating. To begin with I was flattered. Later I was somehow tangled up in good manners and fear. It's always hard to say no to something once you're even a little way in. And beyond all that, I meant it. I still mean it. Not that any currently existing communist regime is worth supporting – I lost that faith a long time ago. But though I've lived very well under this ramshackle hodgepodge of a political system of ours, I'm still affronted by its injustice. You don't have to be hungry to deplore a famine.

So. To the point. What? Where? When? In Berlin at the end of the war, mostly, but sometimes after that. In Prague. In Poland. In Romania. I've lived abroad quite a bit off and on. My German is decent, my Russian not bad. My work gave me a pretext for poking around in parts of Eastern Europe to which British tourists couldn't apply for visas without setting alarm bells ringing in the FO and MI6. Sometimes it was a matter of spouting some encrypted gobbledygook to a stranger in a café. Sometimes there was an envelope to deliver. There. That's really about it. That what I did may have had lethal consequences is something I prefer not to think about. As I say, thank God for sleeping pills.

Anyway – back to '73, which for me was the year of the giraffe, but which for most of the Wychwood habitués was the year of the pop concert. If Guy had imagined he could recreate the atmosphere of a Berlin cellar he would have been sorely disappointed, but he knew that perfectly well. He was a very sophisticated young man. Much missed now. Krautrock and an Oxfordshire deer-park don't make an obvious pairing, but he saw the possibilities, and he was determined and manipulative enough to grab them.

I don't mean that he was cynical. I think he was a true friend to Flora. Her marriage worked fine, as far as I could tell, but somehow there was always space in it, indeed a vacancy, for another man or two. I'm not talking about sex. That Benjie came with an amusing nephew as a free extra was definitely a plus.

*

Oh the fun of giving a party! Everyone else involved in the concert would have put it differently. Jack was a designer creating an enchanted space. Guy was the impresario, the Diaghilev *de nos jours*, bringing the intoxications of new music to an astonished old world. Hugo and his henchmen were doing a job, running the show as they ran the hunter trials that, each spring, filled the park with horseboxes and loudspeakers and women with headscarves drinking leftovers soup out of Thermos flasks. The musicians, from Dickie Lane, debutant drummer with the Pale Young Gentlemen, to Sonder, phlegmatic veterans of a hundred underground all-nighters, were out to blow people's minds with the energy of their music. Jamie and Emmanuel, well, we'll see what they were aiming to do. But Flora – Flora was giving a party.

The concert was by invitation only, but that didn't mean the audience would be small. All the musicians had been urging their fans to come along. Mark Brown had had a word with Goodyear, who'd had a word with Flora, as a result of which everyone from the three villages abutting the estate was included, plus friends and relations. The last big party Lil and Christopher had given had been for her fortieth birthday – thirteen years ago now. Flora had dug out the list and invited everyone on it, with their children. The hostesses of the county were giving house-parties for the occasion, just as they did for deb dances (fewer of those nowadays), so that meant lots of Londoners. Guy had mobilised the Oxford mob. They would dance for hours and hours and hours.

Flora adored dancing. And adored the way the old anxiety about partners melted away at concerts where everyone joined the mêlée, dancing with the music, a universal partner.

Nell was with her. From her dressing room they could see all the scurrying activity down by the lake. Nell was on the bed, rumpling the beautiful cover with its boldly stitched foliage, its tiny silken rosebuds. Flora was trying on outfits in front of the cheval-glass. Clothes were heaped around her. 'You're so skinny. It's not fair,' she said. 'I'm just going to have to be earth-motherly.'

'I love that one,' said Nell. It was a gauzy orange kaftan over which Flora's hennaed and ringletted hair spread clashingly. There was a portrait by Lely, downstairs, of a plump woman in tawny satin. 'You look like Lady Woldingham in it.'

'The big mamma in the dining room? That's not Lady Woldingham, it's his mistress. The wife was pearly-pale and prim.'

'All the same. Wear your emeralds.'

'They're Lil's emeralds. And she would not want them trampled into the forest floor. Is Jamie coming?'

'I don't know.'

'Is that over then?'

'I'm not sure it ever even started.'

Flora looked at her carefully. 'Well, you could probably find someone a bit merrier?'

Nell met her eye and they both giggled. Nell thought, By this time next week, but the thought was desolating.

'Why don't you cradle-snatch Dickie's bass guitarist?' said Flora, applying kohl and loading her forearms with bangles. 'He's gorgeous. OK, then. *On y va!*'

*

'If we can get through this without starting a fire I'll be jiggered,' said one forester to another. It hadn't rained for over a month. Goodyear was right behind them. 'That's what this baby is here for,' he said, cocking his head towards a trailer loaded with milk churns. 'That's why we're doing it by the lake. Keep an eye, won't you. If anything gets started it'll be all hands to the pump.'

'Sir!' the other two said, and clicked their heels in a mock salute.

Flora, onstage, spoke into a storm of static. When she realised no one could hear her she flailed her arms, wide sleeves flying, while the German sound engineer struggled to get the amplifiers under control.

'My darling wife,' Benjie shouted in Antony's ear. 'Doesn't she look just like the Christmas angel?'

The angel in question, a stocky wooden one in Wychwood's chapel who was always, by long tradition, draped with tinsel and spangled gauze for the annual midnight mass, was nothing like as animated as Flora, but at the considerable distance from which they viewed her the likeness was close enough to make Antony smile.

'Actually I was thinking Mrs Noah in that old toy ark.'

'No, no. Definitely the angel. And if she keeps flapping her wings like that she'll soon be airborne, bless her.'

The two men stood halfway up the slope towards the house, beneath one of the ancient horse chestnuts. 'Oldies and baldies,' Benjie had announced at breakfast, as it became evident the day was going to be hot, 'get first refusal on any patch of shade that's going.' He'd chosen his spot days ago. The ice-house was just a step away, and he'd got Underhill to secrete a stash of smoked salmon and vin rosé in it. His particular guests would not be eating hot dogs. Nor would they be obliged to use the trench-latrines. Underhill had a lad standing by at the narrow garden gate near to the tennis court, to open up whenever any of the chosen ones wanted to seek refuge in the house.

Between them and the lake, the grass was now all but invisible. People lay. People stood. People waved their arms at friends found, or jumped up and down on the spot in an attempt to see where friends lost had got to.

'How did Flora find such a crowd?' asked Antony.

'Oh come, come. If she can fly, she can muster the troops. She's really very, very good at this sort of thing.'

'One could make a lot of money putting on shows like this.'

Benjie turned and tapped the side of his nose and beamed at him. 'One most certainly could,' he said.

*

Mark Brown took against Manny on sight. And the more time they spent together the more he regretted giving any time to such a nutter. Jamie McAteer was OK. He was reasonable, if a bit grouchy. But Mark knew this Emmanuel's type. There were people in the Right to Roam movement who had that same self-righteous fervour, and they never achieved anything much. Mark worked within the law, always. He didn't like martyrs and he didn't like fights.

He'd made a point of chumming up with the people who opposed him. Farmers – they were the toughest nuts to crack. Not surprising, really. Landowners, agents, keepers, foresters like his now close friend Goodyear – he was matey with them all. There was nothing to be gained, he reckoned, by getting on people's wick. Show them you're one of the good guys, and eventually they might come round to thinking you've got a point. He'd been living in the village for over a decade. The cricket team, the singsongs – he was part of the scenery. He bought his timber from the farmers over whose land he'd got the footpaths opened. He had boys – and a girl, young Holly Slatter – working for him on Saturdays, teaching them the trade. One of them was turning out nice little footstools in his dad's garden shed now, and selling them in Burford too, and the family were glad of it.

He'd had a few run-ins with Hugo Lane, but they'd been rather jolly occasions, actually. There was the time, some years back, when he was cutting the barbed wire over the stile by the Leafield gate – not for the first time, more like the fourth or fifth. Lane had come up on horseback and done his 'Can I help you?' routine that scared people so. Luckily he had Nell with him, on a nervous little pony, so Mark knew he wouldn't want to get into anything ugly. Mark carried on snipping. Lane carried on telling him it was private property and so forth, but since neither was going to change his mind, or budge, they'd ended up having a good chat, over the wire, about which imported hardwoods made the best garden furniture. Mark had been amused to see a little clump of iroko saplings in the park when he went up to Wychwood a month or so later to deliver a plans-chest for the office. They didn't thrive. He could have told Lane they wouldn't

– the soil was far too heavy. But the point was that he had things in common with the people up whose noses he was getting. Far more than he did with this self-important demagogue with his nervous fidgets and his Trotskyite specs. He couldn't exactly tell them not to walk a public footpath – he, Mark Brown, the champion of walkers' rights. But he was not at all happy about what he guessed they were going to do.

Manny hadn't delivered two hundred marchers, but he'd done pretty well. There must have been fifty or sixty of his mob climbing out of beat-up vans or straggling up the hill from the railway station. He and Jamie sat under a big oak by the narrow forest road towards Wychwood's north gate. 'Free the Music' read the placard they'd strapped to its trunk. Like the standard of a medieval warlord raised in time of famine, it drew a ragtag following. A few spaced-out voyagers on other astral planes – Wychwood's magic spring was a magnet for leyline followers and druids. Veterans of *les événements* and of Grosvenor Square, people Manny had met when he was squatting 144 Piccadilly, or just people he'd bumped into when he'd gone down to the Roundhouse the previous evening, after his telephone marathon, and walked up and down the queue of people waiting for doors to open on the Patti Smith concert, handing out photocopied fliers promising free entry to a mind-blowing concert and a chance to make an outcry against elitism and the political emasculation of music. Jamie knew a few of them – he'd marched in his time. He hadn't called up any of his Oxford friends.

*

The Pale Young Gentlemen were onstage when the big green car crossed the bridge at the end of the lake and drove up the avenue towards the house. They were performing their last number – a cover of 'Go Now' – when it reappeared, taking the steep downward curves of the lakeward track with stately deliberation. Hugo

separated for nearly half that time. They each had suitors who were disappointed by their reunion. It was common knowledge that Christopher had a woman up in Scotland. I can't say on whom Lil was turning her back. There were a lot of people in her orbit. Which of those dear dear friends were, or hoped to be, lovers, is not for the rest of us to know. Perhaps none. She was well into her fifties, after all. But certainly there were quite a few who'd squired her around.

They arrived at the concert looking regal, and took up their positions on the slope as though entering the royal box. A restoration is a disruptive thing. Benjie handles such situations with finesse (odd to think how clumsy I thought him on first meeting), but the fact is his regency looked like coming to an end in the moment the Bentley crossed the bridge. I was down by the stage and even from that distance I could see how the focal point of the party shifted. Flora in her golden dress was soon sitting up on the car bonnet with Lil. She wasn't Mrs Noah any more, steering her own ark. Next to Lil, a blade of white in tight trousers and a shiny jacket, she looked like a blousy bridesmaid.

*

Jamie and his army waited in the field across from the Leafield gate until it was dark, by which time most of them were pretty stoned. They walked into the forest so quietly that a barn owl, hunting up and down the ride in the valley, carried on with its deliberate swoops unperturbed, pale and soft in outline as a moth.

The music came to them first as a pulse, and then as a wailing coupled with a drone. They regrouped by the Cider Well. Some of them waded barefoot into the stream and baptised themselves with its water, or filled bottles with it. One man peeled off and walked back the way they'd come. He'd be selling magic water in second-hand scent bottles off a stall in Portobello Road the next five Saturdays. (And since it went so well, he carried on with water from other sources. He wasn't a cynic. He kept a reserve of Cider Wells water, and each little phial contained at least a drop of it, and as he ran his kitchen tap he intoned a spell.) Others brought out their stashes and began to roll up.

Jamie repeated his orders. 'We've got right on our side here. Stay strictly on the path. Dance if you want, but always on the footpath. If we break that rule, they win. This isn't trespassing. This isn't civil disobedience. We're just doing what we're entitled to do, travelling a public right of way.'

'They're not going to get off on that, man,' said Manny beside him. 'You're making it sound like we're the fucking Ramblers' Association.'

He stepped in front of Jamie. 'We're not the transgressors here. We've – got – the – right. We're not the rich dicks breeding birds to kill them for pleasure. We've. Got. The. Right. We're not the arseholes who want to keep the people's music locked away for their private pleasure.' When he fisted the air this time his followers were ready with the response. 'WE'VE – GOT – THE – RIGHT!'

And then he was singing.

> Oh, give me land, lots of land under starry skies above
> Don't fence me in.

Jamie, who'd heard this song – the Ella Fitzgerald version – thrumming beneath his college-room's floorboards more times than he could stand remembering, was belting out the refrain with him. The straggle collected itself into a column and set off singing down the darkened ride. There was a smell of leaf-mould and crushed sorrel. Old man's beard hung ghostly on the slopes containing them. The wall of electronic sound rose as they advanced, but they gamely threw their reedy voices at it.

Let me ride through the wide open country that I love
Don't fence me in.

*

Brian Goodyear was fond of that song too. He favoured the Bing
Crosby recording. He joined in under his breath.

Gaze at the moon till I lose my senses
Dooby dooby dooby and I can't stand fences . . .

He and Hugo looked down at the marchers from the grassy
plateau which ran right to the valley's upper rim.

'So what do we do about them?' he asked.

'Not a thing. Not a single thing, provided they stay on the
right of way.'

'And if they don't?'

'We're down on them like a ton of bricks.'

'What? Fisticuffs?'

'Arrest warrants. I asked Brown to call Mr Plod as well.'

'Brown's all right.'

'Yes,' said Hugo. 'I used to hate his guts, but he's done us a
favour tonight.'

'They'll be going right through where the food stalls are.'

'You've got some of our chaps there?'

Goodyear nodded. They set off briskly, crossing to where a
track would bring them slantwise down to the third lake, near the
semi-ruined barn known, for some forgotten reason, as the
meeting-house.

*

Guy and Flora stood together at the side of the stage. Guy was doing his usual tight-muscled dance: a twitch of each shoulder, a pelvic gyration. Flora raised her arms, gauzy sleeves falling back, and swayed. They both had their eyes shut. Nell stood with them, looking not at the stage but at the dense mass of people covering the slope beyond the water, and the house above, whose lit windows showed only as an occasional dim hallucination behind the syncopated glare of Sonder's lightshow. Her brother was suddenly beside her. It was impossible to hear anything he said.

*

Down by the meeting-house a bonfire was smouldering, and scores of potatoes wrapped in foil were baking in the embers. Mr Underhill and Mrs Duggary had taken charge of catering outdoors, as it fell under their purview in the house. Mrs Slatter's famous Scotch eggs were piled on a card table covered with a groundsheet: she hoped to make enough from selling them to buy an electric bicycle. Mrs Duggary's jam-making pans ('You could boil a missionary in that one, easy,' said Underhill, with satisfaction) had been brought out with terrible warnings as to the displeasure she would feel were they to be returned dented. The surplus peas, the waste of which, year after year, caused Mr Green such regret, formed the basis of the soup now simmering in those pans on a brick-built range, to be doled out into paper cups. Ham sandwiches, fishpaste sandwiches, hard-boiled eggs, tomatoes. And alongside the home-made stuff, lots of the kind of food Mrs Duggary referred to as 'greasy muck'. Underhill had invited all the vendors who had descended on Oxford for St Giles's Fair to set up stalls. Chips, hot dogs, hamburgers, bacon sandwiches. The smells of frying onions and brown sauce hung thick.

The beer tent, its side open, was busy. In the roofless meeting-house a bar sold everything else drinkable. Jugs of orange squash and lemon barley at one end, the hard stuff down the other and, in the centre, urns full of tea.

Most of the village families were there. They'd stood in the sun all afternoon to hear their local heroes perform, dancing on the spot and singing along with the choruses, hoisting children on shoulders, fanning themselves with hats, pushing through the crowds to the increasingly horrible latrines. When the boiler-suited Germans came on, they had started to think about supper, and getting on home. They'd trooped through the great wrought-iron gates leading from park to encircling forest, open for the first time anyone could remember, taken the downhill track and clustered around the food stalls. The music was still loud, but you could just about hear yourself think.

Mark Brown dropped down the steep slope above the clearing, half-tumbling, half-scrambling, and leapt the last four feet or so, to land close to the bonfire. Goodyear was running across to the water cart where two of his men and half a dozen of their buddies stood smoking, beer-mugs in hand. Hugo Lane found Brown.

'They've passed the Cider Well,' he said. 'They're coming the long way round down Leafield Break. Be here in twenty minutes or so. A hundred of them, not more.'

'I got the constable on the line.' Brown was panting so hard he could hardly get the words out. He'd run up through the home farm. 'He's on his way, but he'll be on his own. Fat lot of use that'll be. What do we do?'

'We clear a passage for them. If they keep going on through we won't stop them.' They both walked towards the crowds around the food stalls, shouting and waving their arms.

*

Nell and Dickie slipped through the narrow door in the park wall alongside the cascade, and were abruptly in darkness. The bracken almost met across the path. They were wading through a waist-high mass of fronds they couldn't see, and there were nettles as well. They'd been coming this way since they were little. Mrs Slatter told them once it used to be a channel full of water, but somebody got drowned and it was filled in. They called it the tunnel. As children, they'd run through it, heads low, prisoners escaping to where their mother waited by the second lake, with the old frying pan which was only used for picnics.

When they were far enough off to be able to hear each other Nell said, 'What are we doing?'

*

A couple of Manny's marchers lay by the Cider Well, flat on their backs, watching the stars. The sky kept changing colour.

'Are we falling off?' asked the girl.

'Off what?' asked the boy, and snickered idiotically.

'Off the world,' she said.

He rolled over and put an arm across her belly. 'Hold on tight,' he said. 'I've got you.'

She squirmed a bit. She knew it was her boyfriend's arm, but she also knew it was the root of a freakish plant that was trying to drag her underground.

Old Meg Slatter stepped out of the trees. She looked at the two of them without any apparent interest, and went down to the stream. She had lumpy things in a cloth bag with a drawstring. It was the one in which her granddaughter took her regulation black plimsolls to school. Now she took the things out. Pop concert or not, this was the night for digging them up. They smelt of earth. She knelt down to wash them and then, tired, stayed there on all fours – knees on the stream's muddy verge, hands on the rinsed pebbles of the stream bed.

She'd never have let anyone who counted see her looking so done in, and so ungainly. But these two – she didn't know them.

And it wasn't as though they were models of decorum either, was it?

The young woman was crooning softly. The man propped himself up on his elbows and saw Meg. He said, 'Um. Are you all right?' She sat back on her haunches, feeling the joints crunch. As she did so the bag and its contents slipped from her hands. She grabbed at it and toppled sideways. The man said, 'Oh cripes,' and ran down the bank, his wide trousers flapping against thin, thin legs. Meg's clothes, the dress covered in small flowers, the brown cardigan, were just like his mother's. He got her bag for her. It was heavy. The way she'd fallen, her skirt was rucked up. He didn't know how to help her but he squatted beside her until she said, 'I don't know who you are, but you can make yourself useful,' and her tone, the crosspatch tone that certain women of her age, for some reason, felt obliged to use with the young, normalised the eerie night scene for him and he was able to say 'Do you want to grab hold of my hand?'

By the time she was on her feet they were friends. She patted his arm and told him he was a good boy. Her skirt was sopping wet but she didn't seem concerned about that. The girl offered the striped gold-threaded scarf that was tied around her head as a towel. 'Thank you,' said Meg, 'I'm Mrs Slatter.' Then, as though impelled to offer them a privilege as recompense for their help, she said, 'This is hellebore. The root. It's poisonous. Take a bit. Plant it in your garden. It's lucky. Poisonous things tend to be.' They looked uncertainly at the black knob. They weren't at the living-together stage, not anywhere near it. Neither of them had a garden. 'It's the right time,' she said. 'You can only move stinking hellebore at full moon.'

'Far out,' said the girl. 'Like it's a witchcraft thing?'

'Yes,' said Mrs Slatter, pulling down her cardigan and thinking she'd better get back to her stall. 'Like that.'

*

271

When the confrontation came Nell and Dickie were on the other side of the lake. Two more of the Pale Young Gentlemen had come after them: Rob Goodyear and the good-looking bass player who'd just joined. The glassless windows of the meeting-house were reflected in the invisible black water. So was light in all shades of flame from hellish orange to livid. Paraffin lamps, wood-fires, torches, the headlights of half a dozen stationary Land Rovers, and the sky flushing green and pink behind them as Sonder's show played itself out. They could see people they knew – their father, Goodyear, Brown and a dozen others, marshalling the crowd into two segments, between which a broad open way led down to the water. There was jostling, and some anger, and little children haring from side to side.

'I'm going over,' said Dickie. 'Coming?'

'No,' said Nell. 'No, I'll stay here.' Something told her it was Jamie. Whatever was going on he had something to do with it. She didn't want to see him. She felt queasy. Inside her something clenched and twisted.

Dickie and the others ran lightly across the dam. Nell untied the old rowing boat from its mooring-stump and pulled it under the shelter of a willow.

Antony

There was a fracas near the old meeting-house, where the food stalls were, but it took a while before any of us, up at the house, were aware of it. The Germans were twanging and twaddling away. I really do not know why Guy was so impressed by them. But for me that evening was blissful.

I got Jack back. Not for long, as it turned out, but one thing the prolongation of life has given me plentiful opportunities to learn is that the prolongation of pleasure is futile. A moment's bliss is as transformative in the short term, and as much of a solace when recollected, as five hours, or five years of it. The whole companionship/loneliness dichotomy is different of course. For that duration matters.

At the back of the crowd a lot of people were lying in the grass. I dislike almost everything about marijuana. Under its influence the most amusing people lapse into silence. The most sophisticated start to giggle at asinine jokes, or no jokes at all. Oddly enough, though, the music was rather good. One of my most discerning clients of the next decade came to me as a result of a chance conversation during which we'd discovered how much we both liked Jefferson Airplane.

I'm beating about the bush. I've noticed that I do so when approaching a memory that carries an intimidating load of emotional freight. To the point. I found Jack among the supine concert-goers. I sat down beside him. His friends drifted off. Jack stayed. We didn't talk. The music was too loud. After a while he rolled over and smiled into my face. There was always something feral about his disordered teeth. He stood up and walked slowly to the narrow iron gate into the garden. I counted to twenty and followed him. I guessed where he had gone. In the blackness of the passage between the doubled yew hedges he came up behind and seized me.

Helen said to me once, later on, 'We're both traitors, aren't we?' I was shocked: I thought Nicholas must have told her something – I knew they were still close – but that wasn't what she meant. She went on, 'I'm a feminist with a thing for dastardly men. You're the insider who's always looking for a way out. All that slipping off to Berlin or wherever. And Jack – wasn't he your escape route?' She was wrong. He was more than that. I loved him.

By the time Guy got up on the stage and shushed the band with a flailing of his arms, I was weak and shaky and preternaturally clear-headed. We could see the stage from the gap in the yew hedge, the gap across which Jack had once walked on his hands. Guy called out, 'Fire!' The rest of what he said was lost in the static. Jack said, 'Fuck!' And leapt over the ha-ha. I'd forgotten how acrobatic he was. Seconds later he was in the great green Bentley, driving like a bat out of hell down towards the west gate.

*

The marchers walked into the clearing singing. Jamie, leading from the front, met Hugo Lane.

'Can I help you?' Hugo's famous opening line.

'No thanks. We're on a public right of way.'

'Quite right. You are. You go thataway.'

Hugo hadn't recognised him. Why would he? It was pretty dark. Jamie looked ahead. People were standing to either side of the track, paper cups or bridge rolls in hand, staring curiously at the new arrivals. An honour guard, or a gauntlet?

His followers were hungry. Two or three of them quietly split from the column and slipped into the beer tent. Manny, beside him, said, 'We've got to keep the momentum up.' Jamie marched on, singing loudly. The lights were in his eyes. It wasn't until he was right on the edge of the lake that he saw it. The marchers were pressing on behind him, not realising they needed to swing to the right. Those at the front were getting jostled into the water. There were angry shouts and splashing.

Dickie and his two friends, still in their silvery stage-clothes, came skimming towards them. A woman shrieked. A man stepped forward, his arms spread. 'Hail, astral voyagers!' he called. He ran towards the boys, without pausing, into the lake. He was some four feet wide of the dam. He floundered and went under. Manny's friend Gus had bought fifty tabs with him, and he'd sold a good lot of them that afternoon. It was a hot night. Within seconds half a dozen spaced-out walkers for the freedom of music were hurling themselves into the lake-water. There was rude laughter from those who'd gathered, nervous, to oppose them. What had been looking like a battle was turning into a mudbath.

Hugo wasn't laughing. 'For Christ's sake, man,' he said to Jamie. 'There's mud to sink into, there's water lilies to get tangled up in. Wipe that smirk off your face and get them out of there.' Goodyear was already down by the bank, hauling out girls whose long hair and skirts dripped, and who babbled with terror. A fat fellow was sinking. It took five men to drag him out of the shoes the mud wouldn't yield up. Nell rowed over. Her boat was grabbed from all sides. She poled it to the bank, and once all her lost souls were safe on land, she dropped over its side and swam back into the blackness. Dickie and his friends were on the dam, yelling at the flounderers to crawl up.

Marchers were slipping away in the dark but there was still a tight knot of thirty or so determined to get the fight they'd come for. Someone shouted, 'The filth are here,' and there was a panicky surge forward. (It was true that PC Dodd had arrived on the scene, but he wasn't making his presence felt.) A child was knocked down. A father said, 'What the hell do you think you're doing?' and got hold of a big young man and shook him by his sideburns until he howled. A girl stumbled against a trestle table, toppling it. It was dark down by the water. No one could really see what was going on. Someone picked up a branch from the bonfire and ran with it.

'Stop that idiot,' shouted Hugo.

More people were snatching up flaming branches. There was light where there shouldn't have been. And where there should have been light there was darkness, as the generator juddered to a standstill. The children's crying had a newly frantic tone to it. Women yelled at their husbands to bloody well get them out of there. Some of the marchers were singing again, a hoarse and desperate anthem.

Nell swam away, out into the centre of the lake. Things moved beneath the surface, furtively caressing her legs and sides. She knew they were the stems of water lilies, but her mind filled with images of babies' tremulous limbs, pale and malleable and purposelessly flailing. The lake-water, stirred up by the now dozens of people in it, gave off its secret smell, of life multiplying itself, fecund and silent, underwater, away from human eyes. Clean but also noisome.

Something was happening inside her. She was close now to the far bank. She could haul herself along by clinging to the stands of waterweeds. She was terrified of mud, of its warm lubricious sucking. She needed ground beneath her. A harbour, a tiny bay, barely two foot wide but floored with flat stones. Her hands reached it. She dragged herself up. A body drowns when water rushes into it. What was happening to Nell was something quite opposite. She was slumped on the bank now, hands grasping and twisting at tufts of dying grass, helpless, whimpering, legs spread, while something flowed out of her. Her child.

Lil

I've always liked rings best. When we got engaged Christopher gave me his mother's pearls, four strings, perfectly graduated, with a whopping heart-shaped sapphire in the clasp. I hope I was gracious, but I had to force myself to wear them. What's the point of a necklace? It's not as though the wearer can get any pleasure from admiring something that's worn out of her own line of vision. But rings, yes. Rings I can enjoy.

I have long fingers. No nail varnish. There's something so pleasing about the exact match between fingernails and those small pink seashells – when nature gets things right one should leave well alone. Our engagement ring was a boat-shaped diamond. When Fergus was born Christopher gave me an amethyst surrounded by pearls. I've worn both rings every day, ever since, pure light and purple light, one on each hand. And because I wore them always I never lost them – I spread my

fingers now and here they are. Whereas brooches, earrings, brace-
lets, I've scattered them abroad. God knows where they all went.
I hope the cleaning ladies got them. I'd rather that than that they
each just disappeared down some crack in the floorboards. But
the point I'm trying to make is that when you don't much care
for a thing, when you don't keep it close, it takes itself off. The
same is true of a husband. And the same, I'm beginning to realise,
is true of a life.

I thought I could just walk away from Wychwood, take a
twelve-year excursion and walk back in. But sitting on the car
bonnet I realised what a blind fool that makes me. I'm a different
person now. Wychwood is different. Too many people blowing
through it, too many people for whom it's just a house.

The concert was boring after a while. We went in. There was
supper laid out ready, but hardly anyone had come in for it. We
ate. We were quiet. Both tired, but also constrained. There's too
much that can't be talked about. We'll need to live together again
for a while before we can chatter on in the old way. We didn't
know where to plonk ourselves. Our little sitting room was full
of other people's stuff. No dogs to walk. We went up to Lady
Woldingham's room. Flora seems to have made it her bedroom. I
rather salute her temerity, but Christopher was upset. There were
clothes lying hugger-mugger on a circular bed, and heaps of cushions around the fireplace. We stood by the middle window, so
elegant. The parterre is still pretty much as John Norris planned
it. I took his hand. What a strange ambiguous frisson, the famili-
arity of flesh, of bones I know so well. That extra knuckle at the
base of the thumb. I wonder, did she ever notice that, his Scottish
concubine? Did she ever kiss it?

He let me. It is all as it was, and all quite different. Sadder. His
face is his face, but his eyes are circled with soft folds. Life is so
short one really mustn't waste a moment of it. But how to fit it
all in? How to have the rapture of being completely with one man
– and I do see that that would be rapture – without shutting off

all the other possibilities. Can't be done. People talk about giving themselves. That's not something I do. It's rather shaming to admit it, but I think that I am the only person I've ever really loved.

He stroked my head, the back of my neck. He smells as he always did, of cedarwood. His touch is so light. He passed his thumbs over my eyelids. He is so tall. He leant against the shutters and gathered me up. He has always had, even in moments of the most abandoned intimacy, perfect manners.

Guy's Germans were still wailing away and the sky was lurid above them. Then Christopher lifted his chin from the top of my head and said, 'What's that?' Way out in the forest there were flames leaping up.

*

Above its stone footings the meeting-house was timber framed. Three hundred years old or thereabouts, the wood flaky with age. That's why Hugo had insisted they'd put the drinks in there, and kept the cooking fires well away. But once people started larking about with flaming branches, things went haywire. First the bunting began to smoulder, then the flames ran along its tarred string as though the silly rags had been tied up there on purpose to make fuses. Soon the flames dispensed with the strings and leapt the gap between the two walls unaided.

Fierce heat; glaring eyeball-hurting light: but the noise was the most frightening thing. First whispers and crepitations. Then a juddering sound like the flexing of sheet metal. The fire was feeding, lapping at wood, sucking in hay, bolting down anything with resin in it, or tar, and all those nutrients were converted on an instant into power. Then came the wind, and the roaring.

There was a stampede back up the track towards the gate into the park. Children howling. Young Bill Slatter started up the hay-lorry, with its great flatbed, and drove it away loaded with the littlest ones and their bleating mothers. Goodyear's chaps were coming up with their milk churns. One way the fire would be stopped by the lake. Another it was likely to peter out among the stony rubble of the slope behind it. The danger lay on the opposite side of the ride, first a mass of dry brown bracken, and beyond it a stand of conifers. It mustn't be allowed to go that way.

Manny lifted up his voice. It was high-pitched and rasping. It carried. He'd seen fires on family holidays in Italy, he'd seen how the olive-farmers fought them with brooms and branches. Hugo waved arms at him semaphoring God knows what, but Manny was already deploying his troops across the width of the clearing. Goodyear's foresters were drenching the ground in a broad band. People seized each churn as it emptied and ran to the lake with it, refilling it and then toiling back. There was a pile of hazel boughs by the water's edge, cut for pea sticks, but never used. Manny got hold of one, wetted it and began to flail at the bracken. Wherever a flame appeared, he beat it down. Others saw, and imitated. They made a line. Someone was using an empty sack to beat the fire. Men dragged off their shirts. A young woman was using her skirt, its mirror-work patterns throwing off flakes of coloured light.

Mr Green was by Hugo, shouting something. Impossible to hear. He turned and kicked his precious motorbike into life and sputtered off up the track that led slantwise into the forest, towards the upper lake. A group of the marchers had managed to haul a great sopping mass of waterweed off the lake's surface and were dragging it up to the firebreak. One of the tractor-drivers reversed down to help them. Attached to the tractor's rear it squelched over the ground, a monstrous slug-shaped vegetable mass.

The meeting-house was falling in on itself. Walls toppled with dreamy slowness, dematerialising into ashy heaps. There was a great revving as all motor vehicles, the tractors and trailers, the Land Rovers and little three-wheeled sheep-trucks with their puttering two-stroke engines, backed away up the track, away from the danger zone.

Jamie was stomping on the bracken. He felt elated. Words ran through his mind. Conflagration. Holocaust. Inferno. Ardent. Arson. He'd write about this. He most certainly would. A short story. His first fiction. And then he'd piss off out of England, and leave all this footling stuff he'd got involved in behind. What the hell had he been up to? Allowing himself to be sidetracked by a dispute about footpaths and pop music. Manny was going to Israel, to a kibbutz. Jamie'd go too. Manny might lend him the airfare. If not, well, he could probably talk his parents into it. And then see what happens. No one here is writing about the Palestinians, Selim had said to him. The English all pretend to be Arabists, but they're not paying attention. That'd be his story. He'd kept the tape recorder the paper had given him, and no one had asked for it back yet. He'd sell his guitar and buy a camera first thing.

There was a change in the fire's ghastly caterwauling. Hugo Lane was sitting on the ground, his head down between his knees. Whenever he tried to stand the pain in his chest came again, and his eyes seemed to have stopped working. He couldn't tell where up was, or down. Like being a spaceman. Peculiarly unpleasant sensation, that. He felt perfectly lucid, but unable to command his body to do what he wanted it to do. Just sit here for a bit. Bound to be fit again soon. He was staring at the ground, trying to get over the queer up-down thing, so he was probably the first person to notice that the earth beneath him was becoming sodden. He got it at once. Clever old Green, he thought. Good man, that.

Mr Green and Jack Armstrong stood on the dam between the second and third lakes, panting. The sluicegate had seemed immovable, however much they struggled with it, until Green had had the idea of using his Triumph to drag the winch around. Nearly pulled off his handlebars, but it had worked. They'd lifted it only part-way. No need for a tidal wave. But water was seeping silently over all the ground downhill of them, shining beneath the weirdly illuminated sky like a molten lava-flow. It spread at a steady speed. 'Fire's not going to like that,' said Green. 'How did you know to come here?'

'Norris's plans,' said Jack. 'You know. It was you showed them to me when I was a kid.'

'Not as green as you're cabbage-looking, are you?' said Green. 'Reckon we've probably saved the day.'

*

They spread bracken in the back of a Land Rover and laid Hugo on it, and took him home. He got up for breakfast the next morning, but then went back to bed and stayed there while Chloe called the doctor and begged him to come out again. The doctor, who was an excellent harmonica player but not so good at inspiring confidence, said, 'Keep him in bed for a bit. And off the booze. He'll live. Louis Armstrong survived eight heart attacks before the ninth one did for him. Bet you anything your husband will die out hunting. And not for a long while yet.' Hugo was grey-faced for days.

Christopher came to see him and said, 'We don't want you back at work until the shooting starts. If then. Take Chloe away for a bit.'

Hugo said, 'I just might do that,' but they both knew he wouldn't. Afterwards he said 'dicky heart' when people asked what the matter was – 'But I've got these magic pills.' He gave up smoking. Chloe pretended to be pleased but actually that frightened her more than anything. When he thought he was alone he would come suddenly to a standstill and rub his chest. Sometimes his hands went numb, or tingled, and he'd clench and unclench them, looking at them as though they were puzzling small beasts.

*

To begin with the fire ignored the water, roaring on above it like grown-ups doggedly carrying on a conversation while children, at their knee-level, tug at their clothes and whine.

It took a while for Jamie to register it too. The ground he stood on became slippery, and then spongy. Moving his feet was more laborious. The shouting changed its timbre. People were slowing down, looking round, pulling away up the valley's sloped sides. The meeting-house's ruins began to hiss and steam. It was getting darker again. Mark Brown was shooing the firefighters back, herding them up the track towards the park entrance. Everyone out. Everyone out now. Go Now Go Now Go Now Now Now Get the Hell out of here you twerps. They went. Confused. Goodyear sent two men haring up to the dam to help Green close the sluice. By the time they'd wrestled it shut the valley was knee-deep in roiling scummy water.

Nell's brother waded past Jamie, going towards the lake. Recognised him, turned, shouted, 'She's on the other side. Nell.' Jamie went after him. They were running in slow motion. The floodwater churned as it met the lake-water. The boat, abandoned, was spinning down towards the next dam. They saw something pale and still on the far bank. The water was rising fast. Jamie was kneeling, tearing at the laces of his sodden desert boots. He said, 'You run around. I'm going across.' Dickie was off, but the dam was impassable. Jamie gave up on the laces. Tugged the boots off anyway. Dived in.

The water smelt wild but it took him gently. It was busy doing what water does, going downhill, no argument, no sweat, and it carried him inexorably with it. He fought it. He burrowed through it, diving in search of a stratum of stillness beneath the rushing surface. He tunnelled, he dodged. There were things in the water, branches and clumps of torn-away weed. He couldn't avoid them. Couldn't see them even. Just had to hope for luck. He was aiming himself against the colossal weight of liquid, pushing with all the power of his lumpen muscular shoulders.

Came up for air. Near the middle of the lake. Dived again, and found shelter. He was in the lee of a kind of underwater rampart, in an invisible corridor of calm water. He followed it, his lungs straining, until his hands touched mud. Vegetation, not slimy. Grass, not waterweed. The far bank. Breathe. Find Nell.

*

Darling Aunt

Metaphorical fire and flood I'm all in favour of, but I really hadn't intended to unleash the real thing. Truly, I am most awfully sorry to have brought such mayhem to Oxfordshire.

Not, as we all know, that it was me who brought it. We're not allowed to say a word against him, now he's been sanctified as a cross between brave Leander and young Lochinvar. And as a fellow-swimmer, I have to say (through enviously gritted teeth) that I salute him. I've got a certificate to prove I'm a life-saver, but I've never actually saved a life, and I certainly would have thought thirteen times before plunging into the lake that night. Full marks for courage and natation then. All the same, *entre nous*, Jamie is a surly, humourless, attention-seeking plonker, *nicht war*? I'm so glad he's buggered off to Israel. I gather there's a war coming up there – he'll like that. Meanwhile over to you, dear universal aunt and everyone's favourite big sister, to introduce poor Nell to someone with a little more *sprezzatura*.

On the subject of buggering off, I'm aware I left you short of moral support the day after the concert, but I thought the most helpful thing I could do was to take my dour Germanic geniuses off your hands as soon as poss. They were very pleased with themselves, and with the turnout and the setting, etc. etc. They seemed to think Wychwood forest had been blooming and growing for hundreds of thousands of years for the sole purpose of providing an appropriate *Umwelt* for their show. I don't suppose they do thank-you letters, but you never know, one day they might write you a song.

Your adoring nevvie Guy

*

Once the fire had hissed and sputtered to a soggy ending, once Nell and Jamie had been loaded into a Land Rover and dispatched to Wood Manor, Mark Brown came up and shook Manny by the hand. They were both black-faced and filthy.

'You're an effing troublemaker,' said Brown. 'But you did all right down there.'

'Thanks,' said Manny. 'Jamie talks about you. I gather you're The Man hereabouts.'

'You have to own a few thousand acres before you're big in this world,' said Mark, but he was pleased.

They walked together into the park. There was a smell of crushed hay, and spilt beer and tens of thousands of cigarette butts.

'So this concert,' said Manny. 'It was free, right?'

'Mmm,' said Mark. 'Invitation only. They don't want hoi polloi in, however much money it could make them.'

'There are other places, though, aren't there?' said Manny. Agitation was a bit of a thankless pursuit, but these concerts. They didn't just happen. Someone had to get them going. He thought he might be rather good at that.

'Want to have a drink tomorrow lunchtime?' he said. 'There's things I'd like to talk to you about.'

'Staying the night, are you?' said Mark, teasing, then relented. 'You can crash in my workroom, if you like, and then, yeah, tomorrow we'll talk.'

*

The evening after the concert, Mrs Slatter walked down to the old meeting-house. From half a mile away she could smell sodden ash and the rottenness of underwater things exposed to air. She took her time, when walking, nowadays.

The lake had shrunk back to its usual limits. Brambles and underbrush had been uprooted and carried off. The meeting-house no longer had any walls above shoulder-level. The flood had washed away all the jagged debris – burnt timber, torn branches. Where there had been rubble of all sorts, the remnant of the building was floored now only with a water-smoothed layer of lacustrine sludge.

Brian Goodyear was there before her, on his hands and knees, caked in black mud. He looked up.

'How did you know?' he asked. 'Have you seen it before?'

She paused. She wasn't being cagey. It was a difficult question to answer.

'My nan talked about it,' she said. 'Perhaps she showed it to me.'

'It was buried pretty deep,' said Brian.

'Well, you know,' she said. He kept looking at her, waiting. 'I just saw it somehow.'

'I heard that story, too, or something like it. But the way I heard it things happened another way. In a different order.'

'That happens with stories,' she said. 'You can't keep them fixed.'

He nodded and moved aside so she could see what he had been doing. A muddle of little squared-off stones. Drab colours mostly. Different shades of brown and grey and pinkish-white. Black ones laid together to make a curving line. Kneeling, and using his forearm laid flat to the ground, Brian wiped more of the silt away. It was only an inch or so deep. A shape done in the red of flower-pots or old brick. Could have been a fish of some sort. More of the pinkish-white. The muddle resolved itself into a pattern, repeating, symmetrical. A patch of straw-yellow, the colour of the big house. Then, so bright it looked like a mistake, like something brand-new dropped in amongst all those faded old stones, shiny and smooth as glass, a fragment of lapis lazuli.

Meg Slatter put her hand on Brian's shoulder – she'd known him since he was a boy after all – and lowered herself by careful degrees onto her knees beside him. Their hands – his broad and freckled, hers longer, and ribbed with greenish veins – pushed the veil of black mud aside. Wherever they moved it, it smeared and gradually seeped back, but in the spaces they cleared they could see – as one might see, through breaks in the cloud cover, angelic hosts flying high in the firmament – they could see the two blue cloaks, the two boys.

1989

September

Selim

When I went back to England I was in a blue funk. And angry. My mother was ashamed of me. My friends in Lahore couldn't protect me, and some of them thought I had disgraced myself. I thought I was being brave and high-principled, but I was just a fool.

I have a cousin in North London. Ten years older than me, she has a career as a doctor, a Scottish husband and two little boys. When I rang from the airport, waking her in the small hours, she hesitated, as though unsure which one I might be out of a number of Selims. I said 'your cousin', and she promptly invited me to stay with her, but as soon as I arrived I could tell she was afraid.

Their house is tall and narrow, with long windows and steps leading directly from the pavement up to the front door. I've lived long enough in England to know it would be considered the acme of elegance here, but Amina's parents would feel sorry for her – it is so old and inconvenient. The staircase takes up at least a quarter of the space. The rooms feel like the compartments of a display cabinet. It is a house in which you never really feel inside: you just perch behind its façade.

I noticed Amina kept moving me, as it were, to the back of the shelf. She made me sit at her desk in the hindermost part of the first-floor sitting room, or chatted to me standing up by the kitchen sink rather than settling with me at the table which is so close to the people on the pavement outside that, until the shutters are closed at night, any passer-by can count the fish fingers on the boys' plates. She showed me to a small room in the basement – at the back of course – and I saw her checking the bolts on the French window. As soon as I decently could, I asked to use the telephone, and called Nell Lane.

I wasn't particularly close to Nell at Oxford, but soon after I left she sent me what I think, despite its reticence, was a love letter. She must have thought, I'll never see him again, so I might as well. I was touched.

It is a piquant irony that imperialists, while despising the intellects and administrative competence of their subject races, habitually worship those subjected ones' looks. At Oxford I more than once turned down, or adroitly deflected, approaches from much sought-after women. Spiv, sinewy and hard-edged, was one. To me there was so little femininity in her I could barely see her as a woman. Nell, though, was dreamy and reserved. She seemed passive, not out of feebleness of will, but as though she would have considered it unseemly to disclose her own preferences and desires. All this I liked. Her letter made me, briefly, regretful. I thought it best not to reply.

After Oxford I went home to Pakistan to break it to my parents that I would not be going through with the marriage they had arranged for me, and to inform them that rather than taking up the promising opening my uncle had made for me in the police department I would be returning to England to make my way as a writer and musician. I had expected, and braced myself for, bitter arguments. Instead I was met with a baffling flexibility. Of course, of course. Just enjoy your vacation. No need to rush into anything.

We visited Sunita's family. Her hands were long and graceful, her voice had a pleasing throb to it. We were left alone together while our parents loudly discussed cricket in the next room. Preparations for the wedding resumed. England seemed very far away. I had friends, England-returned young men like me who confidently expected soon to be running their country. The people I had known at Oxford, with their exaggerated respect for novelty and style, their puerile adoption of an irresponsible counterculture, no longer seemed to me very interesting.

Years went by. I wrote to Nell from time to time and she wrote back. News about people we'd known. It was an effort to recall them. We had professional interests in common. I was putting people in jail. She was looking for ways of making their time there more salutary. I was surprised when she said she was marrying Jamie. I had quite liked him but I hadn't really thought that she did.

And so why was I in my cousin's sitting room? This is a story that all the world knows.

A celebrated novelist, an Indian living in England, wrote a book. His work has always made me uneasy. My own taste is for exact realism and pared-down prose, whereas he is a fantasist and a spinner of Rabelaisian sentences that ramble through labyrinths of subordinate clauses in pursuit of a pun or a piquant grotesquerie. But I recognise that his writing has verve. To speak personally, I have never met the man, but in our occasional dealings, always conducted via an agent, he has been gracious.

The novel reached me early. I had left the police, to my father's disappointment, and was the editor of a highbrow journal in Lahore, which made him proud. We use words like 'highbrow' without irony. The self-deprecation which is so fundamental a part of English manners is not our thing at all.

I read the book, and foresaw none of what was to follow. I obtained permission to publish a brief passage from it, evoking the experience of immigrants from the subcontinent to the British Isles. There was no response from the public. I thought no more about it for a while.

I need not describe what happened next. The angry faces on television, the histrionic book-burnings, the fatwa, the author's enforced retirement from the public scene. This was not an England I recognised.

The fuss spread to Pakistan. There were marchers in the streets and then brawls. The author's effigy was burnt. It took a week or two, then someone noticed that, three months back, we had published the extract. Our office was surrounded by angry shouters, day and night. I called a meeting at a nearby tea-shop. My staff consisted of only two people, but I summoned all our regular contributors. I was nervous. To be part of a collective is comforting. I hoped to be dissuaded from incurring any further danger.

We could apologise. It was agreed that to do so would be craven. Shameful. No way.

We could publish a statement defending our right to free speech. Yes, we would.

We could demonstrate our determination to exercise that right by publishing another extract, this one from the most contentious part of the book. That which, according to the zealots waving placards outside the windows, was blasphemous.

I didn't want to do it. There had been death threats against publishers and translators of the book, as well as against the author himself. But the suggestion was made. Had I been prompt and authoritative I could have quashed it, but I havered, and the others present got enthusiastic about the idea. It made them feel noble. I was too cowardly to risk being called a coward. So two days later our rag came out with one of the offending passages on the front page.

I was in the office when the stones began to bounce off the steel shutters. The telephone rang. It was one of my old mates from the police department.

'You're a target. It'll be very tiresome for us if this escalates. You've got relatives in London, yes? Have you got your passport with you?'

'Yes.'

'Is there a back way out of the building?'

'We can get over the roofs and down through the Excelsior Cinema.'

'Do it now. Walk straight through the cinema and there'll be a car waiting by the Jinnah Street entrance to take you to the airport. Your ticket will be ready for you at check-in. Tell the others to stay inside the cinema until the next show ends and then leave with the crowd.'

'I can't just go.'

'You can't just stay. If you're killed there'll be no end of bother. Go to England. You told me once you wanted to be a songwriter. Write those songs. Go.'

He gave me a number to call when I got to London. He hung up and the phone rang again. It was my father.

'Anwar rang already?'

'Yes. I'm leaving.'

'I'm so proud of you, you idiot.'

He was sobbing.

It dawned on me I might not ever come back. I said the things you say in those circumstances. But actually when I got to the airport he was there and we sobbed some more. He is five inches taller than me, my father, with a profile like Julius Caesar's. My disagreements with him have been many and furiously argued. I was more distressed by leaving him than I was by leaving my wife and son.

And so I got the plane. And so here I was at Amina's desk, dialling the number of Nell's flat in Shepherd's Bush. Answering machine. Her recorded voice told me to try another number. A long one, not London. I did so. Someone else answered, and went to get her. Footsteps sounding down a long corridor. Where is she?

'Selim.'

'Nell, after all these years. Nell, I'm in trouble.'

'I know,' she said. 'I saw the paper. Come here.'

'Where? I don't know where you are.'

'I'm at Wychwood. My father died two days ago.'

Upstaged. It was disgraceful, but all I felt was irritation. When you're in mortal danger you can expect a certain amount of attention. But those who might be going to die soon have to cede place to someone who has just gone and done it.

'Oh Nell, oh my golly, I can't bother you now.'

'Yes. Come. We need something to do. We're all just sitting around here. You remember Flora. There's endless cottages you can hide out in. We'll work something out. Dear Selim.'

She sounded as if she was going to cry.

I said stupidly, 'He was always jolly nice to me,' which was true. Nell's grandfather had been in the British Army in India. By a vagary of history Hugo Lane and I – the quintessentially English, huntin'-and-fishin' gent and the darkie, as he once, quite affectionately, called me in the course of a game of croquet – had been born in the same hospital in Lahore. Nell's home was filled with bits and pieces the grandparents had brought home with them. Hugo had liked showing them off to me. There were some quite good things: a fine old papier-mâché letter-case from Kashmir, a couple of silk carpets. I know how to flatter. We hit it off.

Nell ignored me. 'Go straight to Paddington,' she said. 'Can Amina drive you there? Get the four-fifteen.'

There are many irksome things about my predicament. One is the excitement it generates in others. Repeatedly I've had to suppress a snappy answer to people, whose comfortable lives have afforded them few such thrills, who begin to act in my presence as though they were extras in a James Bond story. Another is the licence people seem to think it grants them to order me around.

London is full of people who look like me. A rural estate in Oxfordshire is not. If I needed to be inconspicuous, this seemed like an idiotic plan. But I wanted to see Nell. And Amina would be thrilled to be rid of me. I said, 'Right you are, officer,' heard Nell laugh, and got going. There was so much I didn't know about the life she had been living all those years, that it was absurd of me to be as amazed as I was when I saw her on the short station platform, immensely pregnant. She was married, and sixteen years had gone by since she wrote that letter, but I'd been vain enough to imagine that this reunion would be, for her anyway, a romantic one.

'We're going to Oxford,' she said. 'I have to register my father's death.'

What a strange day for us to have come together again.

She said, 'You'll have to make allowances. You do realise, don't you, that I'm mad with grief.'

I hardly knew the part of town we went to – a part in which people other than students lived. It was drab. There were pawn-brokers, and shops with brooms and plastic buckets piled up on the pavement outside. There was a canal overhung with weeping willows, but the water was stagnant. I felt sorry for the tourists emerging from the bus station, looking eagerly around for some-thing to photograph. We drove past my old college. I saw tree-tops above the wall. For three years I'd come and gone freely there. I thought how galling it must be to live in this city, whose gardens and cloisters are reserved for transients, whose settled inhabitants are confined to the clogged streets – like servants stationed in a palace's corridor, only glimpsing the splendid rooms through doors left ajar.

Nell led me to a Victorian municipal building of a kind that was familiar from home. A woman questioned her in a patient, tactful tone, as though dealing with an invalid. While she filled in her forms at an otherwise empty desk I looked out of the window at a buddleia whose pendulous purple flower clusters were being greedily sucked at by white butterflies. I thought, No one would think of looking for me here. And, I must call that number.

'That was lovely, wasn't it, so peaceful,' said Nell, when we were walking towards the car.

Then she laughed and said, 'You see, I am mad. But I just can't tell you what a treat it was to be able to sit still and be quiet in there. Grief is very tiring.'

We drove back by a different, longer route. Nell pulled over in a narrow lane and said, 'I'll show you where it's going to be.' The lane petered out, and became a grassy track. At the end of it was an ancient church, very small, with fragments of faded wall paintings, and with wooden stalls, like pens for animals. Nell took me into one. There were narrow ledges to sit on along its wooden walls. 'Dickie and I used to bring that old Noah's ark with us,' she said, 'and line up all the animals during the sermon. We thought no one could tell. I suppose everyone in the church was listening really. There's no electricity. We brought candles in winter.'

Her father would be buried here in two days' time, she said. She cried a bit. I went out into the churchyard and paced around looking at the hoary old evergreen trees and the view across the valley. Wheatfields, meadows full of red cows, big trees laden with dark leaves, tattered white and yellow flowers. This was the rural England the people who came to my country yearned for in their homesickness. In three years at Oxford I had never been anywhere that excluded the twentieth century so successfully. I thought about exile. I wondered where I would sleep that night.

There was a row of half a dozen more or less identical tombstones, with handsomely carved scrolls and volutes. The two most recent read 'Fergus Rossiter 1951–1958' and next to it, 'Christopher Rossiter 1910–1985'. I'd never met the man, but I remembered how Flora and everyone used to talk about him on those days when we went out to Wychwood for Sunday lunch. We'd lounge around on the floor, with music playing, and the old butler bringing in coffee with cream and chunks of brown sugar that was like the jaggery at home. I remember how decadent it all seemed, how we were like tribals gorging themselves in the palace of a deposed emperor. They were all a bit afraid of Uncle Christopher, but they all said how gentle he was, how generous.

I thought, What on earth am I doing here? I lay down in the sun, and the smell of new grass was there. Had it not been for all this hullaballoo I might never have had it in my nose again. I thought about my son, the silky wetness of his mouth, the way he lies on his back and pats his tummy, asking to be tickled, the tiny plugs of snot I prise from his nostrils with the nail of my little finger – what an extraordinarily intimate action that is. I shut my eyes, and felt tears seep out of them, and then I think, forty-eight hours after leaving my country, perhaps for good, I think I went to sleep.

*

Nell my darling
Lil just rang me with the dreadful news. I am writing to your
mother of course, but I wanted to write separately to you
because one of the things I remember most fondly of Hugo is
the way you and that fat yellow dog of his would follow him
around. I wonder whether you remember how devoted you
were as a small girl, always on his tail. And he adored you. I
hope you know that. Of course he was the sort of Englishman
that might never have said. You could probably tell that he'd
have been as lost without you as vice versa. But just in case you
couldn't, I'm telling you now. He was a lovely man, and you
have been a lovely daughter to him. Take care of yourself, and of
that baby. I'll come to the funeral.
    With much love
    From your not-uncle Nicholas

Antony

It is really rather extraordinary how lucky I've been. A homosexual who was never publicly shamed. A traitor who was rumbled, but never overtly punished. A mediocre scholar who has been able to make a decent living writing about beautiful things.

I don't think it's improper to start counting your blessings when you hear of a death.

Hugo and I were never close. I think I gave him the creeps. I wonder what happened to him at Eton. I've seen photographs – he was a very fetching boy.

When I first started visiting this place he was the one who was always coming up with money-making schemes – rent out the empty cottages, let the fishing. He was an energetic man. He couldn't stand the waste of it all. Christopher would hear him out and then say, 'Let's leave it until the bailiffs are at the door, shall we?' As far as Christopher was concerned, Wychwood existed for his pleasure and that of his friends. It wasn't a commercial asset.

Flora owns Wychwood now. Christopher put the deeds in her name, keeping only a life-interest in Wood Manor for himself and Lil. 'Darlings, I really must take you to see *King Lear*,' I said. But the arrangement worked.

Flora gave me the lease of this lodge for a laughably small sum so that Jack could be near his parents while I nursed him. Lil and I came for a snoop around it, and as we stood looking at the view from the bedroom window she said, 'Fergus would have had Wood Manor once he was old enough to want a place of his own.'

I asked her, 'Did it take away the point of Wychwood for you when he wasn't here to inherit it?'

'Oh gosh, inherit,' she said. 'No one's going to inherit anything any more, haven't you noticed? That's why you lot have so much stuff to sell.' She's right. Death duties make excellent lubrication for the picture trade. She said, 'Woldingham's son drowned too, you know. Continuity – it's just a con.'

Flora has made her life into a performance, and this place, which was once so private, into a public show. Benjie busies himself, effectively selling Flora – my precious pimp, she calls him – which means that he is also in the business of selling Wychwood. For Benjie, everything is business. Has to be. I think the bailiffs are, if not at the door, at least heaving into view over the far horizon.

I remember the fuss when young Mark Brown led some harmless walkers into the forest. Now there are cars rattling over the cattle grid outside my door at all hours. The old stud farm transformed into a kind of ghetto for holiday-makers – a quadrangle of tiny dark houses where the horses used to munch and blow. Drinking troughs, that were functional when I first saw them, full of bedding plants. (How old Green would have despised them. He never allowed annuals outside the kitchen garden.) The tack room lined with washing machines. The mounting block fenced off in case some idiotic child falls off it. In the outbuildings on the home farm people doing 'craft'. Coaches en route from Oxford to Stratford stop there, and out pour trippers to buy unglazed pots and woolly shawls and garden ornaments made out of old tree-stumps. Even Green's precious walled garden is now a garden centre where people can buy potted fig trees in the fond hope that one day these little plants will sprawl like the ancient one that was hacked back to allow free passage for their shopping trolleys. They're the wrong variety, young Green told me. He couldn't get hold of examples of the proper one. They'll never thrive.

The trippers and shoppers and weekend-renters are a host of Gorgons. The thing they come to see is killed stone-dead by their gaze. Even the house's private parts (and, yes, I know that phrase is a euphemism – I'm talking about violation here) feel different when, glancing out at the park, one is likely to see a golf-buggy putter across one's eyeline, taking a group of old codgers to the clay-shooting range.

Hugo tolerated it all. We used to argue about it. He wasn't sentimental as I am. He understood that estates like this one were always sources of income whose proceeds allowed their owners to play peacock at court. But Woldingham made something precious here, something that is now, or so it feels to me, being unmade. And I'm not just talking about the gradual dispersal of his picture collection.

Museum people are all conservators of a sort. But I'm a bit taken aback to find that I am hardening into a conservative as well. Funny that. I must tell Mr Giraffe next time we meet. I can imagine the little grimace he'll reward me with. He doesn't like jokes.

*

'Anwar told me to ring you.'

'Right. We'll talk on the other line. Can you wait by the phone.'

'Yes sir.'

Click. Silence. Phone rings.

'No need for the sir. Call me Bates. So what are we going to do with you?'

'I'm hoping you'll tell me that, please.'

'Mmm. I'll come down. Can you stay where you are?'

'Yes. Yes, I think so. For now anyway.'

Selim gave the address, and the name of the railway station.

'Noon tomorrow.'

Click. Silence.

'So?' said Flora.

'Someone's coming to see me. Tomorrow.'

'You must be knackered.'

'I'll be OK.'

Flora and Benjie lived upstairs in the west wing. The great rooms on the ground floor were open to the public often enough to make it simpler just to keep them closed up between times, rugs and upholstery protected by sheets of polythene, curtains drawn. 'It breaks my heart,' said Underhill, to anyone who visited him in his lodge. But it was no longer his business.

Every Thursday the crew came down and spent the night, so as to be ready for the Friday-morning shoot. Flora's get-ups, since the series sold in America, had become ever floridor (a little pun her producer liked). Fashion had veered away from her. Other women her age wore stretchy black clothes under leather jackets. She upholstered herself in chintz or brocade. Her face was large, her long hair worn in looping swags above it, held up with combs made of tortoiseshell or mother-of-pearl. She had earrings shaped like birdcages, or like galleons or pineapples or helicopters. She made a spectacle of herself, not just in the way she dressed but in the way she swooped and fluttered. For the show she wore high-heeled shoes in jewel colours, with pompoms on the toes or laced with satin ribbon, that made her seem freakishly tall.

Benjie watched her metamorphoses.

'Have I done this to you?' he asked. 'Once upon a time I was the one in fancy dress.'

'Don't flatter yourself,' she said. 'I was in disguise. I looked like a perfectly nice ordinary girl when you met me, but there was always this weirdo waiting to get out.'

Standing by the window with Selim, though, she was perfectly nice and ordinary again. Face bloated from crying, huddled into a baggy tartan dress.

'I'm in the way,' he said. 'I feel so bad. I shouldn't have come.'

She put her hand on his arm. 'Honestly. It's good for us to be distracted. It's the oddest thing about a death. There's really not very much you can do about it. Have a bath, why don't you. Dinner in an hour. We'll make a plan for you tomorrow when this person's been.'

*

In Berlin, Jamie learnt to play chess.

He had a flat, but it was just a place to be lonely in. Jamie liked to work with noise around him. He'd carry his typewriter down the apartment building's grand stone stairs, which smelt of ammonia, and around the corner to the Turkish café where the Gastarbeiters argued loudly over their glasses of tea. The proprietors were two brothers; one tall, gentle, with beautiful down-drooping eyes, the other cleverer and troubled by a perpetually dripping nose. They let Jamie take over the table by the window. He'd told them he never drank alcohol until he'd finished work for the day. He thought shame might help him make the claim good.

There were views of Istanbul on the walls, some in evocative old photographs, some woven into rugs coloured with harsh synthetic dyes. Come suppertime he'd bolt down whatever the brothers' wives (who stayed behind the beaded curtain across the kitchen door) had cooked – spinach and aubergine and gristly meat, spiced with substances Jamie couldn't name and spooned over mounds of rice. He'd talk to himself as he ate, trying out phrases. Then tiny cups of sweet sludgy coffee while he rapped out his story. The brothers let him use their fax machine. By the time he'd sent off his piece one or other of them would be at his table, the board set out and the raki waiting. Soon the other brother would pull up a chair to watch. Every night Jamie was defeated. Every night Mustafa or Akbar would patiently explain, in their rapidly improving English, where he had gone wrong.

One night Akbar said, 'There's something happening in Prague. People climb over a wall there. They vanish from the country they are in, and *sesame sesame* they are in another country.'

'Yes,' said Jamie. 'It's magic. West Germany's embassies are turning into black holes, wormholes, white-rabbit holes.' (He was trying out phrases again.) 'It's happening in Warsaw too.'

A television played silently in the corner of the café. On the screen a man in a belted jacket stood in a refugee camp near

Budapest, gesticulating towards some coaches lurching over the track behind him.

'Your friend!' said Akbar. The man had joined Jamie's table more than once. 'Will you go there too?'

'I hope,' said Jamie. 'But my father-in-law . . . I don't know.'

Selim

In the airport I saw my face on the television – my flight was news even before I had boarded the plane. I thought I was scared and indignant. But a part of myself that I didn't want to look at was exulting. I matter! Here, though, I'm an uninvited guest, not that much of a nuisance, just beside the point.

They put me in what they call the Fortescue room. It's cold. Flora apologised for it, but said, 'We're just there, across the landing. I thought you might like to have other people around.' She showed me the bell pull. 'Not that we've got housemaids running around with oil-lamps and coal scuttles,' she said. 'But you know. Just so as you know you could raise an alarm.' It was thoughtful of her.

I fell asleep again, woke up in the dark, and thought of my boy again, and of Sunita. For fourteen years we had longed for a child. Then at last we were blessed. What had come over me, that I had just abandoned them like that? I thought about kidnapping and blackmail. I moaned and whimpered aloud. I didn't think about intellectual freedom or religious tolerance or any of the principles for the sake of which I'd just messed up my life. I thought about Hugo Lane. I thought, All that lives must die. There is nothing special about you, I said to myself. Know ye not 'tis common. Commonplace. How undignified to race from one country to another, trying to escape the inevitable.

For a while my whole body shook uncontrollably. I wrapped my arms around it, trying to restrain it, but it bucked and juddered like a panicking sheep. I looked at the bell pull, but I thought if this is death, let it come. But it was nothing of the sort. It was just fear and a deep self-disgust. When it passed I slept again, for a long time.

Next morning, when I looked out of the window, I could see a peacock strutting at the far end of the lawn and a Mughal-style pavilion at the head of an ornamental canal. There are no nations, only places. Everything mingles. Birds, gazebos, assassins. You can't keep them out.

Antony

It turned out that no one was going to do anything for Nell's friend Selim. A man from Scotland Yard came down. Quite elderly. I took against him. Brusque in a way he probably thought was authoritative, but could equally well be described as plain rude. He said, 'Hugo Lane used to be here, didn't he?'

'He died last week,' I said. I'd offered to do the station run, and as it was a drizzly day I brought him and Selim back to the lodge and left them in the kitchen with tea and biscuits. I put myself on sentry-go, dead-heading roses in the front garden, so as to be ready to deflect any nosey visitors. No one came. I got out the special sharp spade and began dividing up clumps of comfrey and transplanting feverfew. They say a witch had this house once.

Living with a garden designer doesn't mean you have a live-in gardener. I used to give Jack trowels and secateurs for birthdays. Now I use them myself. He never got his hands dirty. 'The shoe-maker's children go barefoot,' he would say. His mother, a rather annoying woman whom I have to bless for the pragmatic calm with which she accepted my role in her son's life, had a huge stock of such old saws (or oldish – I suspected her of making a good few of them up). Towards the end, of course, there was no question of his digging and delving, but I think he liked to watch me doing so. He'd lie on the bath-chair, that astonishing hair of his spreading around him, pale as a blessed damosel, and berate me for the clumsiness of my pruning technique.

Eventually Selim waved at me to come in. I felt like a parent being given the result of a child's medical examination. The man said, 'Well, we've had a good talk.' Selim gave me a beseeching look. I weighed in.

'So what can be done to protect our friend here?'

The other said, 'To call a spade a spade,' waving at the implement I'd propped by the garden door, 'we're going to be no use whatsoever to Mr Malik.'

He trotted it all out. Scotland Yard were taking care of the book's author but it was costing a bomb and there was no way they could do the same for those, as he put it, 'peripherally involved'. He was in touch with the protection team. They had given advice, which he had now passed on. Selim might be a prominent target in Pakistan, but were any nutters (his word) planning mayhem in this country they would be looking for the author, and if they couldn't find him, they would go for his publishers and agents. Bookshops. Easily identifiable and accessible targets. Selim should keep his head down. He was leaving various telephone numbers and he wished Mr Malik well. In other words, you're on your own, mate, sink or swim. It was pretty much what I would have expected, but I disliked the relish with which he refused to help. Selim was gazing at him like a drowning man watching while the lifeboat wheeled round and chugged back to shore.

As soon as we'd put the man on the London train, Selim said, 'I wonder, Antony. Could the people you're in touch with help at all? I mean I'd just love to know that someone was watching over Sunita and the boy. And my parents. I just don't want to walk out on them and not do anything.'

I kept a straight face. I said, 'Well, my only Foreign Office friends are on the cultural side – you know, negotiating the exchange of artworks, visiting ballet dancers, that sort of thing. I don't think they'd be much help.' He was still sitting in the back and I watched him in the rear-view mirror. I saw him do a sort of double take – a sort of come-off-it and then a perhaps-I shouldn't-have-said-that. I suppose Nell told him – I know they've been exchanging letters. But who told her?

I thought, I met this man years and years ago, just once or twice, and he's been living the other side of the world ever since. This is just about the first conversation I've ever had with him. Is there no one who doesn't know all about me?

*

BY FAX
Memorandum
From: The Editor
To: Jamie McAteer
You don't have to tell me how big this story is. Another five thousand *Ostdeutschen* crossed into Austria this morning. But I like to know my reporters are human beings. Anna can cover it. I salute your dedication, but now you've got to get on that plane. Go to Nell. I'll see you at the funeral.

Lil

There isn't a word for the parents of dead children. Widows and orphans – those words carry so much melancholy freight they've actually become ridiculous; a catchphrase of sentimental philanthropy; or the punchline of a cynical joke. I'm an orphan, I used to say when my parents died, trying out the word facetiously. I really didn't feel sorry for myself at all, then. Sad, yes. I was fond of them. But losing them didn't leave me depleted. Freer really, to expand into my place in the world, to throw off little Lillian and become Lil. Oh, you know Lil, people have always said, as though the name gave me an all-purpose amnesty.

Lil's up for anything. Lil can't abide bores. Lil gets away with blue murder.

But what to call myself when Fergus died. No name for it, no role prescribed. I stopped eating for a bit, and everyone seized on that as though with relief. Mrs D making tiny tomato soufflés in the gold-glazed cocotte pots – fluffy pink food for a silly sad woman. Christopher riding all the way across the forest to Leafield and coming home with pockets full of Mrs Goodyear's famous mulberries, only slightly squashed. Even Chloe, who'd just arrived at Wychwood and who – as I didn't yet realise – never, ever cooked, came over one day with pheasant pâté and crystallised fruits. The point was that getting me to eat was something at least worth trying. They couldn't stop the sadness. They couldn't do a thing about Fergus being dead. But it made them feel better to fret about how many mouthfuls of lunch I'd swallowed. I thought it was a bit much to burden me with their emotional needs. But you learn after you've been kicked about by a few bereavements that that's an essential part of the job. Mourning. It's not just a state of mind. It's a task.

Chloe is good at it. She went into full black immediately, which is so far from obligatory nowadays it's eccentric. Of course lots of women wear black all the time – but she never has, so it makes a point. She writes letters punctiliously. She holds up. No one has seen her cry. She knows all Hugo's favourite hymns. Actually everyone in the parish does – he got the vicar to go for them over and over again. He loved reading the lesson and so on. I wonder whether he believed in God. I wonder whether he ever gave the matter a moment's thought. I doubt it.

When he was dying in the hospital Chloe was there pretty well around the clock, with only Nell and Dickie and her in-laws allowed to visit, so it is as though she's been in the valley of the shadow and came back to us having left him there – Orpheus without Eurydice. *Ahimè!* She's always been withdrawn. I used to think it was a form of selfishness. Actually I still do. But it's a strength too.

So now we're both widows. For this grief there is a name. It has another meaning too. Chloe told me yesterday that printers use it to describe an annoying word at the end of a paragraph that runs on to an extra line. She goes into Oxford two days a week to dogsbody for a publisher. She knows that sort of thing. Get rid of the widows, they say, and it'll work nicely. It's the closest I've heard her get to self-pity. And then I saw her aghast at herself. It's four years since Christopher died. She once told me that when she is with other people she's never free of self-consciousness. She's always thinking, 'What will they think of me?' 'If only I could just not care about other people at all, I'd be much more friendly,' she said. And so of course she was thinking, 'Does Lil think I'm getting at her? Does she think I'm saying she's a redundant adjective? Will she hate me? Does she think I hate her for taking over Wood Manor?' How draining. No wonder she's the cat who walks by herself.

In reply to the last question, I do think she has a bit of a grievance. But it was Chloe who was set on buying the house in the village, on owning their own roof. So now I sleep in their bedroom, in their carved Indian bed that was assembled here by Hubert the carpenter and was too big ever to take away downstairs. Christopher's gone and I'm in Hugo's bed at last. Does anyone else ever think how shocking that is? When I moved in I found a pair of his old shoes, all furred with dust, in the bottom of the walk-in cupboard. There was a flowerpot stuffed full of cigarette butts in the greenhouse. Chloe wouldn't let him smoke, pretended she didn't know that's what he was doing out of doors. His garden grows up around me. He'll never see it mature.

We are both widows. And I am widow to both, to her husband and to mine.

Selim

I won't be going to the funeral. I met Hugo Lane only a handful of times: to join the mourners as though I was a close friend would seem to me presumptuous. And I don't want people seeing my foreign face and asking 'Who is that?' I was afraid that Nell might think me uncaring, but when I told her I preferred to stay away she seemed relieved.

Instead I honoured her father by telephoning my own. He talked at length about Cicero. I honestly don't see many points of comparison between my case and his, but to hear my father rolling Latin names around his mouth was comforting. Even when he got to the great orator's assassination – his severed head and hands displayed in the forum, the termagant Fulvia stabbing his dead tongue with her hairpin – the horror of what he was saying was nullified by the majestic pomposity with which he said it. My father can be up to date. He is the only person of his generation I know who has an Amstrad at home. But his mind is so lavishly furnished with classical tags and ancient instances that there is simply no place in it for strident twentieth-century opinion, or the sheer nasty brutishness of twentieth-century violence. Not that there is anything refined about a hairpin through a tongue, but it does at least have a certain symbolic precision.

What might happen to the author is unlikely to be so artistic. I have pretty well ceased to believe that anything bad is going to happen to me. But why then am I so afraid?

*

Jamie was in time for the funeral, but only just, so that Holly Slatter – Holly Goodyear now – who should have been with her family, had to pick him up from the station off the last possible train. Nell turned briefly, as he slipped into the pew behind her, and looked at him as though from a great distance.

The organ worked like a bellows. Air had to be driven into it by pedalling, to be exhaled in gasps as music. It was as though the church itself was sobbing. Mark Brown played, with his eldest daughter helping pump the pedals, and somehow he managed to lead the singing simultaneously, some sixty choked or feeble voices jostling to keep up with his boom.

> On the Ro-ock of Ages founded
> Whaaaat can shaaake thy suuure repose?

A deep intake of breath. A gathering of power for the mighty leap upscale. Bullockish head butting with the beat.

> (*fortissimo*) Wiiiith salva-a-ation's walls surrou-ounded,
> (*diminuendo*) Thou may'st smile o-on all thy-y foes.

Brian Goodyear read the passage about the new heaven and the new earth and no more weeping. Benjie read from *The Pilgrim's Progress*. Then Dickie was in the pulpit. He looked better than he sometimes did, but that wasn't saying much. These days he'd go from being fat and pasty to being gristle-thin. This was a thin stage. He was sweating. His mother and sister, and his wife, Soo Yung, all tensed, all willing him to get through this.

He said, 'People used to say I looked like my father. I used not to like it. No teenager wants to be a poor imitation of his dad. But now I'd be just so proud if I could believe it was true.

'Perhaps it once was. It isn't any more. I've messed up, as most of you know. I never properly apologised to him. I'll never get over that. My fault.

'My father and I used to fight. Or rather I fought with him. He was always pretty reasonable. He just didn't get what I was up to.'

Nell and Chloe were both remembering a Saturday afternoon when Dickie had come up the drive, his car swerving so as to cut scalloping curves in both grass verges, staggered out from behind the steering wheel and passed out on the patch of lawn in front of Wood Manor. He'd smelt sweetish, like a piece of rotting fruit. The two of them had sponged him down with water from a washing-up bowl as he lay there, and when he began to gibber they'd managed to haul him into the house. He'd snored and muttered on the sofa until after it was dark, and then insisted on getting in the car again, and driving back to Wychwood. All that time Hugo had been out in the garden, hacking and pruning. No, he didn't get what Dickie was up to then. Nor did any one of them.

He said, 'I know I'm not here to talk about myself. But the point is that I'm an awful come-down compared with him, and I'm not trying to make excuses, but I do think the Wychwood I was part of was an awful come-down compared with the one he ran.'

Chloe kept her hands folded in her lap, head down, but Nell glanced across the aisle and met Flora's stricken look. After the concert, all those years ago, Dickie refused to apply for university. He got work as a tourist guide in London, but when that petered out, and he still hadn't become a rock-star, he didn't have anything else planned. Flora took him into Wychwood and made him Ariel to her Prospero as she set about turning the place into an artsy kind of commune. There were a lot of people passing through, and most of them enjoyed making a pet of Dickie – charming Dickie, pretty Dickie, Dickie who was always at a loose end and ready for a long talk about nothing much over the meals that merged into each other through the long aimless afternoons around the dining-room table.

Sometimes Nell was there, but he'd avoid her. He had quite a few girlfriends in those years, most of them older than him. He wasn't a cynical lover. He was desperately smitten with each one. It was only later that he'd wondered about those liaisons, when Guy – of all people – said, 'You know, Dickie darling, at least rent-boys get paid. What do you get out of being available *gratis* at Chateau Wychwood?' At night he'd take charge of the record player and, increasingly, of cooking-up. His parents' home was less than two miles away, but he hardly ever went there. When he saw his father crossing the yard from the estate office he'd slip off upstairs.

When his breakdown came Flora was no help. She just sent him back, as though, as Chloe said, she'd only ever had him on approval, and decided against. He went through the Priory. He did the twelve steps. When he was out the other side of all the therapy he wasn't anyone his family knew. He certainly wasn't Ariel. Nor was he the musician he'd been set on becoming. He'd been in Never Never Land through the years when he might have been growing up, so his adult self felt a bit makeshift. Hugo had a word with someone he knew, and the someone fixed Dickie a job as an estate agent in Cheltenham. He tried to quit after a month, but by that time he'd met Soo Yung and she wasn't going to let him go under again, or indeed to let him go. She was his boss: she got him back to work, and pretty soon after that, to his parents' wonderment and relief, she married him.

Flora dropped in – the Lanes had moved down to the house in the village by then – and offered Wychwood for the wedding. She didn't seem to understand why Chloe walked out of the room, her face tight with rage, and never so much as said no thank you.

Now Dickie said, 'I can't talk about him. I honestly feel I'm not good enough even to understand what he was. I've just got some poems he liked.' He read them haltingly – Housman, Kipling, four lines of the dirge from *Cymbeline*, and then, very deliberately ('Take it slow,' Nell had said. 'Remember his rule about reading the lesson – HALF the pace that feels natural, and NO expression'), he fumbled out the last piece of paper, and read, 'He was a man. Take him for all in all, I shall not look upon his like again.'

*

When the service was over Jamie took Nell's hand and walked beside her to the grave. 'Dust thou art, and unto dust shalt thou return.' The little graveyard was packed with people. Everyone who had ever worked for Hugo had shown up. Chloe had insisted they had prior claim to places in the pews, so the crowd of those who hadn't got a seat in church included a number of bigwigs – local landowners, Hugo's old friends down from London, a Lord Lieutenant – unaccustomed to being so relegated. No one complained. A man at the back of the assembled mourners – formally dressed, black wool suit that must have been uncomfortably hot – produced a hunting horn and blew a long wailing note.

'"Gone away!"' said a familiar voice. 'These archaic instruments pierce one to the *quick*, don't they?'

'Guy!' muttered Jamie. 'I didn't expect . . .'

Guy, always thin, was dwindled to a spray of dried rushes, tied at the neck with a knitted silk scarf. His hands shook on the chased-silver knob of his walking stick.

'The Pink Pimpernel. They seek me here they seek me there. I *never* disclose my future plans. But Hugo was a duck. You remember the concert you did your best to sabotage? He was splendid over that.'

Jamie stood in son-in-law position two paces behind Nell while people he'd never laid eyes on took it in turns to reach across her immense belly to peck her cheek or enfold her in a bear-hug. There would be tea at Wychwood, but no one wanted to leave the churchyard because to do so would be to admit that Hugo's life among them was over. Eventually Lil took Chloe's arm and the two of them climbed into the immense green Bentley, and sailed off up the lane. Dickie was driving, Soo Yung in the back with their twin children, moon-faced and solemn in black romper-suits, wedged between her and Lil.

Nell turned to her husband and stared at him wordlessly.

'You look wiped out,' he said.

'Take me away,' she said.

'Don't you have to be at this do?'

'Come on. I've got the car. Let's go back to Mummy's. Just for a bit.'

Ten minutes later they were surrounded by the furniture of her childhood bedroom, but the room had a spare-room's forlornness. She took off her shoes and slumped into a wicker chair. Jamie hovered.

'I'm sorry I couldn't come yesterday.'

Nell opened her eyes. 'It didn't matter.' She closed them again. 'Let me just sit for a bit. We'll go along there soon.'

Jamie lay down on the bed.

'I wish he'd met the baby,' he said after a while.

She began to gasp, as though her breathing was obstructed. For a moment he thought it was labour, but it was only sorrow. He stood behind her and stroked her hair roughly, as though he was stroking a dog. She leant her head back into his hands.

They arrived at Wychwood simultaneously with the last guests, a contingent from the hunt who'd failed to find the church. 'We just stopped the car in this muddy track and said Our Father anyway,' said a woman with a wind-roughened face. 'A bit like missing the meet but having a jolly good day all the same.'

'He'd have liked that,' said Nell. Over and over again, that afternoon, with no conviction, she and her mother said those words.

*

A tall woman with very short white hair came and found Selim. He was sitting on a bench reached by a path between two tall black hedges. Opposite the bench there was a gap and a view over the park. She said, 'Sorry to intrude, Selim. People always seem to choose this spot when they need to be alone.'

She sat down beside him nonetheless.

He said, 'Were you hoping to be alone?'

'No, I was hoping to find you.'

He looked worried.

'I'm not an assassin. I just thought you might like some company,' she said. 'You've forgotten me. Helen. I picked your brains about Mughal gardens once.'

'Slim pickings, I expect.'

She laughed. 'True. I ended up teaching you.'

She had a long, clever face. Her clothes were in various shades of grey, and hung loosely off her. They looked homespun, but Selim could tell they were expensive. She wore several large silver rings.

'I worked with Hugo,' she said, and then he did remember. Nell's father designed gardens. This woman was his partner. She had been some sort of an academic too.

She said, 'He liked symmetry. He had a very good eye. But he knew bugger-all about botany.'

Selim detested the way English women swear.

'I used to drive him mad,' she said, 'asking for the Latin names. He thought I was a frightful pedant. But we had a lot of fun.'

Selim saw that he ought to make some comment on the dead man too, but he could think only of banalities. 'He was nice to me. Nice to all of us.'

'Anyhow,' she said, and left a pause.

When she went on, it was in quite a different manner. She talked about gardens in a way that was probably a coded comment on Selim's predicament. About enclosure and exclusion and confinement. She said, 'You know the East Germans call the Berlin Wall the "Protection Wall"? Some of them probably believe that's what it is. We think they're imprisoned, but they just think they're safe. Gardens and prison camps, they have a lot in common.' Selim thought about the dark hedges surrounding the pool garden. 'Nell's very interesting on all this stuff,' said

Helen. 'She's the only person who ever makes any sense on our committee.'

'Committee?' Selim asked vaguely.

'On prison gardens,' she said. 'Very therapeutic. And useful training too. A lot of the people I employ have been inside.' She looked at him sharply. 'I thought you and Nell were such friends. Haven't you asked her about her work?'

No. He hadn't.

Then she was there, Nell. She propped herself on the table in front of them, her belly cupped in her hands. She said, 'Everybody's being sweet but I had to get out of there.'

Helen said to her, 'My friend Roger told me an odd story about your father. He said Hugo once threatened to shoot him.'

'What's he on about? Daddy would never have done that. "Never never let your gun/Pointed be at anyone."'

'Not that sort of gun. A revolver. This was in the war. In Berlin.'

Something stirred in Nell's mind. A memory of lying on chilly green-slimed stone fenced in by women's legs. By this woman's legs.

'Was Roger at Eton, do you think?'

'What? Well, he could have been, easily. He's arrogant enough.'

'Did he tell you the rest of the story?'

'No. I asked, but he told me not to bother my pretty little head. He can be obnoxious, can Roger.' There was a kind of fondness, though, in the way Helen said it. Nell let it go. A person dies and a legion of stories dies with him. She'd never get to know her father any better now.

*

'We had a funeral here today,' said Flora. 'The agent, used to be. He ran this place for thirty years. Everyone's in floods. I really don't think we can do this week.'

'You'll find,' said her producer, 'that you can, and we will. We'll be on the usual train.'

'No, honestly. It would be too crass. I can't go flouncing about on camera as though nothing has happened. It's just not decent.'

'Flora my dear, I'm sitting across from Chris on foreign news. He's talking to a presenter who's standing on top of an office block in Beirut. I've just heard him say, "If they come up onto the roof, move so the cameraman can get them in shot. No one likes being filmed murdering a journalist." That guy is still broadcasting. For God's sake, Flora. You've got a job to do. I thought you posh girls were supposed to be so gutsy.'

'He bloody well hung up on me,' said Flora.

'Won't take no for an answer?' Benjie was flat on his back on a sofa, shoes off but funeral suit still buttoned.

Lil sat upright, black lace feathering around her knees. She said, 'Well I suppose everyone will be going back to work tomorrow.' She was in demand these days. A very expensive tour operator paid her a tremendous sum to give tea parties for their clients in the long dining room on days when the house was otherwise closed. She would put on her biggest rings, and tell stories about Princess Margaret – always the same ones so she wouldn't be tempted into any real indiscretion. There were, of course, cucumber sandwiches. 'What do you think?' she had asked Hugo once. 'Is there anything to choose between this and prostitution? Morally, I mean. Of course it's nothing like as dangerous, and only disgusting when one has to shake their clammy hands.'

Flora stared out of the window. The telephone rang again.

'Hello,' she said blankly.

'Did anyone film the funeral?'

'Of course not. Well, Heather, the Lanes' old nanny. Not in the church, but people arriving. The burial. I was furious.' Flora stopped short. 'Why?'

'Right. What we're going to do is we're going to make this week's episode a tribute to the man who died. What's his name?

You do your usual intro, but make it elegiac. Then we interview the guys who worked with him – keeper, gardeners, all those types. And Mrs Rossiter. She's great on camera. And you said he'd been there thirty years. Spirit of the place. Change and decay. All that kind of thing. Weather forecast's terrible so we can do moody darkness-closing-in lighting. And falling leaves. Very sad and respectful. It's a great human story. Great television. We've done enough history. This is our chance to do the people who are the life of the estate now. Blah blah blah. You get?'

Flora said, 'I can't begin to tell you how distasteful I find this conversation. We just came back from the funeral. I haven't even changed my clothes.'

'Fine. Fine. I'll leave you to get on. This Heather, we can reach her, can we? I'll give you a shout in the morning.'

Selim

Flora said, 'You can stay as long as you like, Selim. The Changing Hut's free from this Saturday. It'll be boring for you once Nell's gone back to London, but do make yourself at home.'

Hut? I thought it was a joke, or an insult, but The Hut, so called, would house a large family comfortably. There is another building in the walled garden called The Shed: its furnishings include a set of eighteenth-century dining chairs and a stuffed bear. They rent it out weekly for a sum approximately equivalent to a quarter of my annual salary. In this country landowners don't call their houses 'palaces'. That would be flashy. How they must laugh as they book their holidays in Rajasthan.

I actually changed here once. 'Anyone forgot their bum-bags?' Nell's father said, sixteen years ago. 'There are some spares in the hut.' And so there were, along with enormous threadbare towels, board-stiff from having been dried in the sun. Now the towels are smaller and newer, and have a sickly fake-floral detergent smell. There are bowls of dried petals – not, I would guess, from the garden but bought in a packet. Nell opened all the windows at once, and then looked at me. 'Sorry, perhaps you're cold? I can't stand potpourri, can you?'

There's a new swimming pool closer to the house – heated. Its 'hut' – the portico of a classical temple, perfect but for the fact that there isn't a temple behind it – was once an orangery. It has showers and a fridge full of beer. The pool that my windows overlook has reverted to being an ornamental pond, with water lilies. Tall black hedges enclose it. A pine tree spreads its wings over my refuge like a hen. Its needles patter on the tarred roof. I feel safe here, but not happy.

I rang Sunita again this evening, careless of what time it might be at home, and as soon as I heard her voice I began to cry. She was speechless too, but she held the boy to the receiver and his clucks and gurgles crossed the Eurasian landmass.

My mother writes to tell me that when her friends ask her about my ungodliness she doesn't know what to say. Her letters are sent to Cousin Amina who reads them to me over the telephone. Amina said this morning, 'Like sister like sister. How we distress them. My mother tells me that every time she thinks of my examining male patients she weeps for me. My degradation, she calls it.'

October

Nell and her mother lay on a rug facing each other, each propped on an elbow. Between them, bracketed by their curved bodies, lay Jemima, Nell's tiny daughter. For over an hour they had been crooning hymns to her while she fought with all her indomitable will to cling to wakefulness. Even now her narrow mauve feet twitched ceaselessly.

'She's trying to swim back up,' said Chloe.

'Did I do that?'

'I don't honestly know. Nanny Gee hardly ever let me near you.'

'Is she afraid of sleep? I think she has awful nightmares.'

'Poor little bunny. We don't think enough about how scary sleep is. How's she to know she'll ever wake up again?'

Flora stood on the edge of the ha-ha, the park her backdrop, striking poses. Her voice came to them across the lawn piecemeal, in overemphasised fragments of speech and occasional trills of laughter. She was talking about trees. She knew almost nothing about the subject, but Goodyear had coached her well.

'Quincunx . . . alchemical . . . Mr Norris . . . isn't it AMAZING to think . . . no power-tools . . . chop chop chop . . . I mean, the BLISTERS . . . and can you imagine? Must have thought NO

Peculiar Ground

ONE will EVER see it … now … balloon … perfectly
HORRID … TERRIFIED.'

'She hasn't really been up, has she?' asked Nell.

Chloe rolled very slowly over onto her back and said, 'She
jolly nearly did. By mistake. She was posing in the basket for a
photographer. Pink and white dress to match the balloon. It's
supposed to be on the front of the *Radio Times* next week. And
then there was a gust of wind.'

'Oh no!'

'Lots of shrieking – you can imagine, but they grappled her
back to earth OK.'

'She's really brilliant, isn't she?'

'I suppose so.' A pause. 'Well no. I don't. I just so disapprove
of the whole thing.'

Nell looked at her. 'I didn't know that. You're very good at not
showing it.'

'I've been the agent's wife since I was twenty-three years old.
You learn not to show what you think. Anyway I know I'm not
fair to her. I know she's not malicious. She's generous. But the
fact is she wrecked Dickie's life. Sheer bloody carelessness. You
can't expect me to forgive her.'

This had never been said between them. It's because I've had a
baby, thought Nell. I'm thirty-six years old. At work I'm quite
somebody. But it's only just now she's noticed I'm one of the
grown-ups.

Chloe said, 'But anyway, I dislike all this fakery. All this
publicity. It's so … so tarty. But we could never say anything.
That's the hard part. Daddy hated that too, you know.'

Nell took this in.

'I thought he loved his life. I've been saying that to everyone.'

'Mmmm. Well yes he did, most of it. Remember how easy it
was to find him if he was out in the garden – whistling all the
time. That was the sound of a contented man. Being a servant,
though. Having to bite your lip. It's humiliating.'

321

Very cautiously Nell stretched her arm across the sleeping baby and laid her hand on Chloe's shoulder. 'He absolutely adored you, didn't he?' she said.

Chloe's eyes were closed. She said, 'I can't imagine how there'll ever come a time when I'm not thinking about him every minute.' After a bit she went on, 'Yes I think he really did.' And then, bafflingly, 'Bad luck on Lil.'

Selim walked across the grass and squatted beside them. Nell nodded towards the baby and put a forefinger to her lips.

The crowd of technicians walked backwards ahead of Flora as she progressed slowly along the herbaceous border, her long skirt brushing against the catmint and valerian, locks of hair tumbling from her striped silk head-wrap. As she came closer her voice carried to them over the shoulder of the soundman who was holding a boom above her face. The camera trundled on silent wheels.

'Fertilisation, you see . . . insemination by ruffled taffeta . . . Absolutely ENORMOUS hooped skirts . . . could hide anything, I mean, LOVERS, chamber pots . . .'

The procession passed on into the yew passage.

'Flora is very interesting,' said Selim, forgetting the injunction to silence. 'In my part of the world people have been amusing outsiders by making themselves into imitations of themselves for centuries, but for the British I think it is a new thing.'

'Hey Selim,' said Nell. 'Aren't you supposed to be in hiding? The place is crawling with strangers today.'

'Sometimes I just think to hell with it. I think I just made up the danger.'

'If we can get Jemima into the pram without waking her we'll come up to the pool garden and keep you amused.'

'Nell, I'm not another child for you. I don't need babysitting.' He was suddenly enraged.

'Sorry. I just thought . . .'

He snapped upright, and vanished up the path.

'I don't really know what he's doing here,' said Chloe. 'It's a strain. He's been getting odder and odder. When you're not here he doesn't ever come out.'

Jemima's arms began to pump. That terrible thin wail, the aural equivalent of vinegar.

'Oh little rabbit.' The baby's head was at once infinitely vulnerable and hard as a club. She bumped it against Nell's chin and fought with arms and legs.

'I'll try the pram,' said Chloe, heaving herself up. 'Stay there and get some sleep.'

*

Jamie didn't, in his view, drink all that much. He worked long hours. He flew frequently. There were nights, when he had a report to write, that he didn't go to bed. It wasn't a healthy life, not a life of regular meals and exercise. But he got things done. All the same, there were occasions when Nell woke up to find him, still in the bulky leather jacket he always wore, snoring on the sofa, having arrived home too pissed to undress.

Before they married Nell would come to meet him in the pub, or they'd go to Lemonia and eat sardines. She'd have spent all day thinking about imprisonment: usually she didn't want to talk about it. So he'd ramble on. His narrative style was all over the place. He'd launch into an anecdote about some person she didn't know, never pausing to explain the context that would have given the story meaning. As the wine went down his coherence decreased. It was fine with her. She let her mind spin out of gear and enjoyed the food.

He was, she thought, a good man. He was altruistic. He had integrity. Surprised at herself, she found that those were the qualities she wanted in a lover. Not irony, not wit, not the things she valued in her friends, but something more fundamental. And then of course there was the sex.

His every mannerism, his doggy way of cocking his eyebrows, the compact solidity of his chest, the slurred softness of his face when he'd been drinking, all spoke to her of pleasure. It suited her that he worked late, staying night after night at the paper until the foreign-news pages were put to bed. She liked to kid herself she was self-sufficient. She liked going to parties on her own. Someone once asked her 'Why's Jamie never with you? Has he got a wife or something?' and she had a brief glimpse of their semi-detached life as abnormal, but it worked for them both. They were best together in darkness. Their minds were amiably disposed acquaintances, but their bodies embraced each other without reserve.

She was careless. Sleeping sometimes at his flat, sometimes at hers, she'd leave her pills in the wrong place and miss a day or two, and risk it. She got pregnant. She couldn't fail another child. She resigned herself to marriage. She suspected Jamie was as half-hearted about it as she was, but it was hard to tell.

She was startled by the intensity of the orgasms she was experiencing. Sometimes Spiv rang her early in the morning – midnight New York time, six a.m. in London. One dawn when Jamie wasn't there Nell said, 'You've done this twice, tell me.' 'Tell you what?' 'What was sex like when you were pregnant?' Spiv laughed, 'Aha! You're having the turbo-super-charged-washing-machine effect, aren't you?' 'Well yes, that's quite an accurate description.' 'Make the most of it,' said Spiv. 'Once it's born there's not much time for all that.' Spiv was a professor now, bringing up two children alone.

So they were going to be a family, but how to synchronise the selling of her flat, the surrender of his lease, the finding and acquisition of a place they could both be happy in? The task was repeatedly postponed. She badly wanted to complete her report on power-structures among prisoners. She'd been working on it for three years. And then Jamie got the Berlin job.

'I don't have to take it,' he said.

She couldn't be bothered even to pretend she thought he meant it. Of course he'd take it.

'Go,' she said. 'We'll manage.' It wasn't as though he was going to be any help with the baby.

A month after he went, her father had another heart attack. And then another, and then, two weeks later, the *coup de grâce*. Jamie stayed for three days after the funeral, and they discovered that, even as enormous as she had become, the washing-machine phenomenon was still operative. They juddered with pleasure, guilty voluptuaries in her widowed mother's spare room, and then Jamie, who hadn't touched a drop at the funeral, went back to his ringside seat at the decline and fall of an imperium. When Jemima was born he flew home again and wept copiously in the maternity ward, undone by joy. Once more, after only three days, he went back. What else could one expect?

Antony

Mr Giraffe summoned me, even though we had met not so very long ago.

'The situation at the moment is volatile,' he said. 'People we've been watching will be weighing up their options. We believe it's not impossible someone we're interested in might contact you. You know we expect you to keep us informed.' When delivering his messages he speaks as though he'd learnt English from a Dalek.

He gave me instructions as to what I was to do in this, that, or the other case. We were in a restaurant near Covent Garden. There were people I knew there, as he must have guessed there might be. I wonder if he was hinting that he could, if he chose, embarrass me. More than embarrass me. Ruin my life. We sat side by side, which I never like to do, on a mauve tweed banquette. It occurred to me, for the first time ever, that the hearing aid he always wears might conceivably be just that, a hearing aid, not a bug, and it was deafness that made him want to sit so close. How aged we all are. Physically decrepit and intellectually inclined towards compromise. Perhaps that's why the Cold War is staggering towards a final whimper.

The table was made of frosted glass, which didn't help the acoustics. There was so much olive oil on the mimsy-pimsy portions of cold food we ate that I could feel my scalp becoming greasy. I've never liked capers.

He saw, perhaps with satisfaction, how prickly I was getting. He soothed me.

'You realise, don't you, that there's a chance everything we've been doing may be about to become redundant?'

'"We" including me?'

'Yes, including you.'

'Suppose my other friends don't think so.'

'Then you and I will continue to meet. I'd rather like it if that's the way things turn out. I've enjoyed our talks. I don't flatter myself that you feel the same way. But however frequent or infrequent these occasions will be in the future we will keep your secrets, as we trust you to keep ours.'

By giving me lunch in about the least private place I know? I could see Helen across the room. And I recognised the man she was with. That senior policeman with a spurious air of distinction, the one who came to see Selim. She once said to me, when I questioned the company she kept, 'You know, Antony, choosing a lover is not the same thing as hiring a nanny. Kind and dependable doesn't really cut it for me.' Which made me wonder about my good friend Benjie, my good friend Nicholas. What did she see in them, that I have been spared seeing?

'Call it normalising our relationship,' Giraffe was saying. 'Remember I'm your old friend from Munich. Students together. We drifted apart as one does. Look at you in the art world, so glossy and cultured. Look at me – a dull stick of a civil servant.' His ostensible job was in Ag and Fish. He was sometimes to be heard on the wireless talking about foot and mouth disease. 'But we meet every now and then for old times' sake.' This was the story we had agreed sixteen years earlier. 'We can dispense with the St James's Park palaver now. I might even invite you to dinner. My wife is a great one for art.' He must have read in my face how little I looked forward to such an evening.

The world owes a great deal to Mr Gorbachev, but few people in my circle probably feel as grateful to him as I do. I no longer feel quite so despairing about the creed I used to adhere to. Perhaps socialism can be enlightened and humane. Perhaps I haven't been as much of a fool as I've thought in my gloomiest moments.

Back at Wychwood, though, there is Selim, a piece of jetsam from an entirely different world-historical upheaval, and, increasingly, a worry. 'He's been here over a month,' said Flora yesterday. 'Do you think he's having a breakdown sort of thing?'

Lil

Flora's producer prevailed upon me to talk to him, or rather to the camera. It is terrifying how easily I was seduced. I wore tweed. That was the first self-betrayal. Lil Rossiter, famously stylish, out shooting in her tailored coats and skirts: I used to love that role, but there's no substance to it now and to pretend otherwise was to make myself into a fake. The shooting's all taken by the syndicate. Perfectly nice young men, but it's not the same. They work in the City, mostly. One of them is a pop-singer. Very polite and gentle, and far and away the best shot among the guns. He explained, 'In my line of work you have to be good with your hands, and fit. I work out every day.' How dismal the phrase 'working out' sounds. Dancing used to be something one did for fun.

So – the tweed, and the ostentatious brooch and then the ridiculous pronunciations. I heard myself but couldn't stop. Orf and lorst. Laandry and gels and 'this house remained unchanged for yaaars and yaaars'. I sounded like a toff in a television fantasy, which is exactly what I was. Before it was over, even, I knew I'd made a fool of myself. If only Christopher had been here. He'd have known at once to say no. Only housemaids talk to newspaper people, his mother told me. Flora was impatient. 'This is the modern age,' she said. 'If we don't use television, it'll use us up.' But Guy knew what I was talking about. 'The simulacrum is a parasite on reality,' he said. 'It devours it. From now on everyone who meets you will be seeing Lil the Sim.' I hadn't really wanted him to agree so promptly. I wanted reassurance. I'm not used to feeling I've made myself cheap.

I grow old. I do it surreptitiously. People tell me frequently that I haven't aged a bit, and I'm shamefully pleased. I have young friends. I buy large pieces of metal sculpture from the Lisson Gallery. I dress like Cruella de Vil for parties, and by day like Cherubino in snazzy breeches – a wizened boy in lipstick and a jaunty hat. No need to be a bore, or dowdy, just because one's birthdate is receding into the distant past. But you can't fool your body. When I climb out of a car I'm a tin woman badly in need of an oilcan. I feel the cold. I don't recall ever, in the first half-century of my life, really caring much about wrapping up. No wonder the young are driven mad by old ladies fussing about shawls and cardigans. Now I've discovered how pleasing it is just to be comfortable – warm enough, a stool on which to put one's feet up, a cushion the right size for the small of one's back.

How considerate of nature to make us so appreciative of little pleasures when the big ones wear out. The other sort of *volupté* is over for me. But again there is a mitigating kindness. The sorrow of knowing that those astonishing sensations can no longer be summoned up by a little pressure on one or other body part – and it is a sorrow, I'm not belittling it – is matched by the immense relief of being liberated from desire. How I used to yearn and crave. How exasperated I got with men who weren't in the mood. How jealous. How humiliating the whole business could be. There is really nothing one can do to set a man who doesn't admire one in that way alight with passion. You can seduce him, at least you can if you've got the knack, and I had it. You can lure and pester and coax him into bed, but where's the fun in that? Being in love is the thing. When Christopher first touched me, he began to stammer, as he hadn't since his childhood. Once he kissed the top of my head as he passed behind my chair at a party where we'd been seated at different tables. *Extase!* I was lucky then.

On the day after Hugo's funeral I went to see Chloe, and as we sat in her kitchen we could hear Nell and her Jamie upstairs. We both pretended for a bit not to notice, and then – an upward glance, the slightest of smiles. Two widows content to let the next generation take over the generation business.

Chloe is admirable. She knows, she must, that there was a *tendresse* between me and Hugo, but I feel absolutely certain she will never mention it, let alone ask to know more. What actually did or didn't happen between us no longer seems to matter a jot. At one of Nicholas's big dinners last month I was sitting next to a man who was once my beau. Handsome, a chatterbox. All evening I was asking myself – did we go to bed? I really couldn't remember. Still can't.

*

Francesca was reading Nell's draft report aloud.

'People removed from society at large are driven to replicate its structures in miniature. They have their own hierarchies and heroes. St Benedict foresaw that monasteries could become dictatorships, and prescribed rigorous spiritual exercises for abbots, all designed to throttle the will to power. Blah di Blah's study of Tasmanian convict settlements gives us a persuasive account of the rapidity with which a group, of which each

member begins equal to all the rest, sorts itself into dominators
and dominated . . .

'Who's Blah di Blah?' asked Francesca.

'Oh I don't know yet,' said Nell. 'I'll find someone who said
something of the sort. It might not be Tasmanian convicts.
Marooned sailors, public schoolboys, those cannibal footballers.
Any group that's properly cut off will do. And that's been studied
by an anthropologist. We like an academic study in my
department.'

'Mine too.'

'Keep reading.'

'A prison is a community of a more complex nature than any of
the above groups, in that it contains two separate orders – the
inmates and the staff.'

'Inmates?'

'We don't say "prisoners" much these days.'

'So you're happy to deprive them of liberty and the pursuit of
happiness, but you protect their delicate sensibility by refraining
from telling it like it is?'

'It's not their sensibilities we're worried about. It's our own. It
doesn't feel good to be an imprisoner.'

The two women were in the pagoda again. Or rather in the
pagoda's replacement, built by Holly Goodyear from iroko-
wood and coloured in sugary shades copied from traces of the
original paint. The secret garden was now The Secret Garden
(open to Wychwood visitors, on payment of £1.50 extra, and
wheelchair-accessible by a paved walkway from the Leafield
gate). Francesca reclined on the rococo daybed, Nell's paper in
hand. Nell lay flat on her back on the floor, her hands clasped
over Jemima's bottom. Visitors, mostly retired locals at this time
of year – the coach-tour season petered out at the end of August

– peered in at them, looked affronted at finding the space occupied, and then, seeing the baby snoring between her mother's breasts, smiled and passed on.

> 'Like ancient Sparta, a prison is a two-tier community in which one group is vastly better off than the other, but in which no one is free. The relations between the two orders create a complex pattern of mutual dependency and mutual fear. The resulting tensions afford numerous opportunities for a determined individual to create a special status for himself . . .

'Who will read this?' asked Francesca.

'My boss. And if he approves it'll be circulated. If he really, really approves it might be published.'

'What's the point?'

Nell was hurt. 'This is what I do.'

'I mean – what are you hoping to achieve here?'

Nell screwed up her eyes. Francesca thought, She used to do that before she spoke in seminars. Our minds may mature, but our bodies never really change their little tricks.

'Well basically,' said Nell, 'I want to question the value of confinement. An enclosed community is toxic. It festers. It stagnates. The wrong people thrive there. The sort of people who actually like being walled in.'

Selim

Brian Goodyear comes to see me pretty well every day. He is a storyteller. He sees me as subject matter. The secular hermit, the prisoner in the palace, the madman in the changing hut. I lend myself handily to mythic stereotyping.

Now Nell's father is gone, Brian is running the estate, though no one in the big house thanks him for it, or even seems to notice he is doing it.

The British newspapers are full of indignant letters protesting at the author's treatment. Each of these letters is signed by dozens of other writers. One of the covert messages I hear in them, inscribed in invisible ink behind the mostly banal content, is the repeated refrain 'Look over here! Look at us! We matter! He matters, so we must matter too!' My 'hut' is equipped with a television, as well as a microwave and a bulky electrical contraption for making coffee that burps and dribbles all morning long. People appear on the television saying things like, 'I feel I must speak out.' Why must they? Why should we care what any of them think?

I am repelled by their pompous self-regard because it is a mirror of my own. I wish most sincerely that I had never left the police force. At least in those days I never doubted that my work was useful.

Sunita and the boy are with her parents, safe and comfortable enough. I dream of her. I dream of him. The gentleness of her hands as she dresses him. The way he likes to pull the spectacles off my nose.

November

Guy and Flora were in bed together. Over their heads the sun-god's frescoed steeds whinnied silently. Behind their backs a dozen pillows propped them up. Before them, so arranged as to block the view through the three arched windows, stood a television, the only unlovely thing in the room but the one on which their eyes were trained. Guy was immaculate in a freshly ironed kurta. He kept pulling the sleeves down. He no longer liked the look of his own arms. Flora was frowsty in one of Christopher's old paisley silk dressing gowns, her hair coming out of its plait. Each cupped hands around a mug. It was past six o'clock in the evening and neither had been up and dressed that day.

They cried out simultaneously.

Flora – 'Look! Look! Look!'

Guy – 'Well, did you ever?'

On the screen, looking older and more burly than in life, Jamie was to be seen in conversation with a young couple, identically dressed in pale blue denim, who were attempting to get on a bus. It was evident from the way their eyes slid past him, and their anxious clutching of their rucksacks' straps, that they were unhappy to be so detained.

He turned to the camera and said, 'Though the people of East Germany have been forbidden to travel to the West, there have been few restrictions on their movements behind the so-called Iron Curtain. Poland, Czechoslovakia, Hungary – all these were approved destinations. Now, though, each of these Eastern-bloc countries has sprung a leak.'

Benjie came in, and dumped his briefcase. 'Budge up,' he said, and lay on top of the quilt next to Flora, his small feet, in their polished oxblood brogues, neatly crossed. Flora didn't budge. Guy mustn't be jostled, now his frangible bones had so little flesh to swaddle them.

'Five planes took off from Prague today, carrying East Germans who had forced their way into the grounds of the West German embassy there, and demanded asylum. They are now en route for Bonn.'

The camera peered through high wrought-iron gates at a mass of nylon tents, pitched hugger-mugger on a lawn. Three women lined up and waved through the iron curlicues at the camera, their children jumping up and down on the gravel around them. 'Meanwhile thousands of East German citizens are travelling to Hungary, and thence across the recently opened border into Austria.'

'Potter says Warsaw's crawling with Huns,' said Benjie, 'and it's not exactly as though the Poles are fond of them.' Potter was Benjie's business partner. He had been christened Piotr, but gave up, early on, the attempt to teach the English how to pronounce his name.

Onscreen now was the familiar image – sheer concrete, wire, a kind of waterless moat, men in helmets, very tiny and far away, standing on wooden platforms. Cut to a city street blocked at one end by a blank barrier. Cut to an expanse of wall covered with garish purple and silver graffiti. Zoom in on an image of a skeleton whose gun spewed roses.

Another voice, not Jamie's, said, in the portentous tone people who don't much like poetry adopt when called upon to recite the stuff, '"Stone walls do not a prison make,/nor iron bars a cage."

For over twenty-eight years, though, the people of East Germany have been immured in their own country. How much longer before this wall comes tumbling down?'

'Bathtime,' said Benjie. 'I'll leave the water in, shall I?'

He turned at the door. 'Selim been about today?'

'He's never about,' said Flora. 'Not since Nell went back to work. He's as skittish as Lupin.' The pug was so inbred it was close to madness, and lived most of its life in the long corridor by the kitchen. There was no risk of it biting the trippers. It cowered. Even old Underhill, the only person who felt any affection for it, couldn't coax it out for a walk.

'Poor sod,' said Benjie.

Guy looked at him quizzically. 'You're going to have to watch your language,' he said. 'We sods are frightfully quick to take offence these days.'

'Bugger that,' said Benjie and went out singing.

*

The wall ran in an immense and gradual curve all around the park, but at one point, not far from where paired wrought-iron gates stood across Tower Light, it swerved inwards so as to leave the remains of the meeting-house outside. The fire and flood at the concert had swept away a lot of the accretions that had disfigured the building – the half-roof of corrugated iron, the bodged-together partitions made of hurdles and chicken wire. There was a fine arched window set, oddly, into the side next to the park wall. If the building was really some kind of a place of worship, this window should have been open to the east, to sunrise and resurrection. As it was, when Benjie first turned his attention to it, it looked out on a stone barrier.

Goodyear pointed out the obvious. 'The wall wasn't there when the chapel, or whatever it is, was built.'

'But how could anyone be so perverse?' asked Benjie. 'The wall could have jinked around to give it a bit of room.'

'I'll ask Meg Slatter,' said Goodyear.

Going on for ninety now, Mrs Slatter had shrunk to a wisp, but she was still formidable. Seated, mumbling, in the front window of the house on Church Street from which Holly and her husband ran their joinery business, she had become a curiosity.

The people who rented the holiday homes came to see her. They conversed with her nervously, and bought her spells. (The spells consisted of seeds and tiny bones packaged in scented handmade paper with woodchips in it. Holly bought them in bulk from an Indian supplier in Southall.) There were postcards on sale, too, showing her a few years back, standing by the Cider Well in a wide-brimmed black hat, a basket full of dried herbs on her arm. Holly sold tiny coloured bottles of Cider Well water, too.

The old woman made no objection to being faked-up and marketed. 'It's better than being ducked,' she said. The spells she used for her own family didn't take tangible form. She worked with a casual touch or a slanted look. Warts peeled away. Migraines were relieved. Her grandson, Holly's anxious small nephew, sat with her to do his homework. Once his mother found him weeping at bedtime. 'If Grammer dies,' he said, 'how will I get the magic?' 'What magic?' 'The magic that makes my head feel peaceful.' 'You don't have to believe in things exactly,' his mother said to Holly afterwards, 'to know that they work.'

Goodyear reported back to Benjie. 'The wall was put there to spite the chapel folk. They were dissenters. Lord Woldingham wanted rid of them.'

'I thought Woldingham was all for laughter and forgetting.'

'It's to do with his son, the one who drowned.'

Benjie wasn't curious enough to pursue the story. To him old buildings weren't memory-hoards. They were opportunities. Once Christopher was dead, he had a breach made in the park wall, leaving the edges a bit rough, and filled it with a panel of reinforced glass, so that after centuries of darkness the morning sun could shine into the chapel again. The shell of the old building, partially rebuilt, became a walled garden. Jack planted herbs in a wave pattern – the last of his designs he lived to see realised. There was a counter where one could buy ice-creams and cakes. It made a popular excursion. The little train that ran around the estate stopped there and discharged its elderly passengers. Children came with wet hair, after a dousing in the 'lily-pad paddling pool'. Joggers paused to swig from their water bottles, clasping their feet to their buttocks or rolling their shoulders before starting off on the three-lake circuit.

Selim didn't go there. Like the deer, he preferred to avoid the paths humans used. He had taken to wandering through the park at day's end. At home the sunsets charged the dust-haze with lurid colour for minutes only, and then the sky went dark. Here the light faded so gradually that he was repeatedly caught out by it, and blinked and peered about as though what was happening to him was not nightfall but blindness. In the avenues, where the beeches held their brown leaves all winter, there was a ceaseless soft rustling, while at the end of the long lines of trees a paleness like an open door showed that the sky was still alight.

Antony

It turned out that Mr Giraffe did have another use for me after all. Someone I'd known as Oleg was coming out. I hadn't seen him for twenty years, but no one else in this country had seen him ever.

'Go,' said Mr G. 'You have friends in Berlin, don't you? You'll have fun. It'll be the biggest street party in history. If it happens.'

I said, 'I don't dance in the streets. Never did, and I'm certainly not going to be doing so now.' I almost said, 'I don't want to leave

Jack.' Absurd. But also, absurdly, true. When he was alive and needy there were times when I longed for a pretext to be off and away. Sickrooms are exhausting. But now, oddly enough, I find that all I want to do is linger about the places we were together.

Mr G said, 'We need you to identify him.'

I said, 'Can't you just take a photograph?'

What made me so recalcitrant was what Giraffe wasn't telling me. If Oleg was coming West now he must have been working for this lot all along. By how many people, how many interests, was I duped? I loathe politics now. I don't even vote.

*

The wildlife park was Wychwood's biggest money-maker. The numbers of animals that died there, unable to acclimatise to Cotswold winters, was carefully kept from visitors, who enjoyed walking through what had once been the stud-farm's paddocks, getting up close to the yaks and alpacas, or marvelling at the destruction wrought by the rootling of wild boar in the pinewood.

Its gate had been commissioned from a local artist. Nobody liked it. Nobody could bear to admit what a mistake it had been and pull it down. Made of painted aluminium, it showed two giraffes, their long necks crisscrossed near the apex to form an arch. Flora drove through it, in a phaeton pulled by two zebras. The zebras could never be counted on, but this time they trotted far enough to give the camera crew a clear shot before skittering to a halt. Flora waited motionless, smile fixed, until she got the signal, then scrambled out. She carried a silver-topped cane and a pair of kid gloves, all found in Christopher's mother's wardrobe (still unsorted, nearly four decades after her death). Her riding habit was dashing, but uncomfortably tight.

The crew were packing up. She blew kisses to the cameraman. The director appeared just behind her left shoulder.

'It didn't really bite you, did it?'

'Yes it bloody well did. If I get rabies your insurers are going to be wishing they worked for Lloyd's.'

'Or yours will. The proprietor is liable. Anyway – it's a great shot. A live mink around the shoulders is so much more becoming than a dead one.'

'Oh, for goodness sake,' said Flora. She turned her back, took a breath, deliberately dropped her shoulders, and said, 'Thursday.' A model who used to come to the restaurant had once told her the three magic words with which to tame a camera – 'boy' for a pout, 'sex' for cheekbones, 'Thursday' for a winning smile.

Emmanuel Joseph stepped out of his car and spread his arms wide. 'Manny,' said Flora. 'Let's walk, shall we?' They went up the tarmacked front drive. When Christopher first saw it, its inorganic slickness so ugly in comparison with the hay-coloured grit it replaced, he had clenched his fists in his pockets. No point shouting when the deed was done.

'It's looking good for the third series,' said Manny.

'What? How much more can we get out of this? I'm having to share the screen with wild animals already in order to keep the excitement up.'

'I've been talking to people. The channel like the idea of a rethink.'

'Which means?'

'Getting you out and about more. Other locations.'

'But then you lose the whole point. The whole point is me in this place. Take me somewhere else and I'm just a television presenter.'

It was not lost on Emmanuel that being a television presenter, a job that most of the people he represented longed for, seemed to Flora to be infra dig. He was proud of what he'd made of her, but sometimes he found her maddening.

'So what are you now? Get real, Flora,' he said.

'Oh Lordy,' said Flora, who had heard the irritation in his voice, and resumed her public persona in self-defence. 'Whatever made you think I could do *that*? Reality is so *depressing*.'

A short pause while they both controlled their tempers.

'Well,' said Flora. 'So Selim was a friend of yours?'

'Kind of. Same year at Oxford. I thought he might like to see a familiar face. So where is he?'

'Here.'

They left the main drive to continue its pompous way to the grand portico and took the track that led past the old stable yard. A man, one of young Green's boys, stood by the Tudor archway in doublet and hose, ready to direct visitors to the knot garden. They passed on to where a yew tree, its poisonous berries fleshy as swollen lips, overhung the gate into the rhododendron grove.

'Rhodos are so gloomy, aren't they?' said Flora. No reply. It's unlikely Manny would have known what she was talking about.

A tall mesh fence, like that around a tennis court, or a prison yard. Flora unlocked the gate, tugging the bell pull beside it. A few more paces through dense shrubbery and there, in the pool garden, Selim was waiting. For the first time in his life he had put on weight and his skin was greenish. Manny pulled him into a hug which involved almost no bodily contact. 'I'll leave you to it,' said Flora. 'I need to get all this clobber off. Come down to the house for a drink later, Manny. Upstairs. Just ask anyone who's around to show you. And you, Selim. Guy was asking about you. You haven't been down all week.'

Selim

I dislike that man intensely. I know that he's made Flora his property, but he doesn't own me. When he was sitting here, stroking his own thighs and tousling his own hair as though his body was some boisterous animal that needed to be placated, I felt angry, and pleased to be angry. It was a good feeling. I indulged it.

Emmanuel he calls himself now. Manny the drug-dealer is now Emmanuel, the show-offs' agent, the impresario, the procurer. Still messing with people's minds, still peddling oblivion or ecstasy or torpor. That's how he makes his living.

He suggested that I exploit myself as a commodity. He wanted to have me interviewed. To sell me. After-dinner speaking, he said, is a growing market. Am I then to be taken to market, like a case of mangoes? He wants me posturing on TV, displaying my anxieties like the beggars at home waving their stumps. He doesn't understand me. He's not interested in me in the least. He doesn't understand any of these things either – decorum, loyalty, reticence. How I dislike that man.

Antony

We're a barren lot, we Wychwood stalwarts. Me, for obvious reasons, but Benjie and Flora, too, and Nicholas, Christopher and Lil.

I don't know about the others, but I used to enjoy our child-lessness. No one had to set a good example or say '*pas devant les enfants*' or hurry home because little so-and-so would get grouchy if he didn't get his milk and biscuits on time. Or her. But perhaps the others all grieve over it more than I've known. Nell and Dickie were the only children around in the old days, and now Nell comes here with her baby and it's as though a lack we never acknowledged has been supplied.

There've been ghosts about the place, not of dead children but of children unborn. Pink unmarked feet on the stairs at evening. Eyes that don't yet know it's rude to stare, taking us all in. Falstaffian farts and belches emanating from a creature whose skin is pearly-pure. The weight of a baby, which leaves a bright red patch on her cheek when she wakes, so heavily has her head lain. The smallness of babies is astonishing. That a person, and Jemima is unmistakably a person, with desire and will, can be so miniaturised.

Child-yearning – I bet there's a compound German word for it. I thought that we queens were immune from *Kindersucht*, or whatever it's called, but I know now that I was wrong. I wonder, was it a son I looked for in Jack? No. No. That was a completely different emotion. Although perhaps when he was dying. Caring for someone is a great provoker of love.

I remember when Fergus first went to that prep school. Hair slicked down beneath his cap. Face rigid and pale. His legs so fragile beneath grey flannel. Lil had insisted I go with her to the railway station. When the train pulled out she took my arm and said, 'Now, Ant, you've got to keep me amused *all day*.' And I tried. We had milkshakes in Fortnum's – a little-boy's treat because we were thinking all the time about a little boy. And then, feeling sick, we took a taxi to Little Venice, and paced up and down the towpaths along the canals. They were foul-smelling then, and full of abandoned prams. Not the most cheerful place to take a mother suffering from *Kindertrauer*.

He ran away three times. Each time the games master, his tormentor, tracked him down and brought him back. 'He didn't talk to me,' Fergus said to me once, 'he just picked me up like a parcel and put me in the dog-boot of his car.' He was beaten. Each time. In the dining hall the entire school sat in order of seniority. Runaways – regardless of age – had to go to the bottom of the lowest table. Relegated. Relegated. Relegated. Each time the parents were told. Each time, though they never mentioned it to me, Lil and Christopher must have talked it over. Each time they concluded he had to stay. It cost a lot, that penal colony, in money and in grief.

When he died she never called on me. There are some things beyond the reach of a Fortnum's strawberry float.

Now I am supplanted. I see how Guy has taken my place in her life. I used to find him maddening. I don't like camp, and I don't like precocious know-it-alls. Now he's got a good reason for histrionic posturing, though, he's dignified. The dandy will keep smiling, like the Spartan under the bite of the fox.

*

Once the clocks went back Brian Goodyear took to visiting old John Armstrong, not in the evenings, as he'd done at least once a week through the summer, but early. He knew the old man woke before first light, as he had all his life, and that as soon as he was awake he wanted to be up and dressed, however inflexible his joints might be. There were kindly women, daughters and granddaughters of men he'd known, and tyrannised over, and pursued as poachers in his days of power, who would come up from the village in turn to get his breakfast ready, and to ready him for breakfast. It gave him a lot of satisfaction to let them find him in his chair, fully dressed except for his shoes, with his Puffed Wheat already half-eaten. It was partly his old bloody-mindedness. He liked to put them at a disadvantage. And partly something composed equally of self-respect and terror. The day some fat young woman with too little to do had to put his trousers on for him would be the day he knew he was done for.

He didn't mind Brian Goodyear, though. He was a good chap. Brian always brought Dorothy with him, and the clever little spaniel would sniff around Armstrong's feet and then scratch herself a nest in the folded rug her grandmother and great-grandmother had slept on before her. Brian was allowed to take both Armstrong's hands and haul him upright, and then while he was in the bathroom, with its astringent smells of Vim and carbolic soap, with its pile of neatly torn squares of newspaper (no point wasting good money on something to wipe your backside with), Brian would dig out a presentable shirt for him.

While Armstrong dressed Brian would stand by the window, looking out mostly, but keeping an eye, ready to deal with the cardigan's leather buttons and finally to kneel and help with shoelaces. When one of the interfering women came later she would remove those shoes and bring the slippers. Armstrong pretended to be annoyed, but God Almighty it was a relief to take his suffering, knobby feet out of those torturing leather cases. With Brian, though, it felt good, just for a bit, to be got up like a man again, shod for outdoor work.

They talked fitfully, easily, with long ruminative pauses. Brian always knew what the bag had been the previous Saturday's shooting day.

'That pop-singer chappie out, was he?'

'He was. Wearing a boiler-suit. Quilted.'

Armstrong snorted. He liked to hear how outlandish the world had become since he withdrew from it.

'You can't fault his shooting, though. Got a right and left. And never forgets the beaters.'

Armstrong nodded with approval. It was a scandal how many people omitted to tip. Stinking rich some of them, too. Rolling in it. Perhaps that's how they got their cash together, though. They say millionaires are all stingy as a witch's tit.

There were a dozen-odd stems of chrysanthemums on the table, colours of damson and custard, stuck into an enamel jug. Their scent filled the room, intimations of luxury and winter.

'I see young Green's been visiting,' said Brian.

'Eh? Eh?' It took Armstrong a while to twig. Brian wagged his head towards the flowers.

'Oh. Oh. No. That was Mrs R brought those. Brought me the picture too.'

A photograph in a brown leather frame, gold-tooled, was propped on the ledge above the iron stove, next to one of the late Mrs Armstrong and several certificates commemorating Doris's dog-show wins and adorned with red rosettes. The photograph showed Christopher Rossiter, aged ten or thereabouts but instantly recognisable to anyone who had known him later in life, in tweed knickerbockers and belted tweed jacket, holding a dead

cock pheasant up by its feet. He wore round tortoiseshell spectacles and stood very straight. His hair looked at once mussed and
smoothed, as though the photographer had hastily oiled it down.
Behind him, much more at ease, stood an extraordinarily handsome young man, tall, legs confidently spread so that the ampli-
tude of his plus fours was displayed, gun on his arm, face turned
down at the boy but startling pale eyes glancing up at the lens so
that they met the viewers with conspiratorial amusement.

Brian whistled. 'Well, I've always known you were a looker,
but this is something else.'

Armstrong chuckled. 'It was his first pheasant. And my first
year in the job. He called us the "new bugs", the two of us. I
always picked up for him. That's my Wully there. I wasn't yet a
spaniel man back then.'

'Wully? So Mr Lane's dogs . . .'

'Were Wully the fourth and Wully the fifth. He was a splendid
boy, Master Christopher. And he was a jolly good boss too.'

Armstrong began to fumble in his trouser pocket. Brian waited.
He knew better than to offer to help. Out came the spotted handkerchief. Armstrong wept a bit, then blew his nose with a noise
like the last trump. This tended to happen. The passage of time
has an added poignancy for those who have been especially beautiful when young. Brian acted as though the whole process had
been invisible to him. When the handkerchief was stowed again
he said, 'I expect you've been following this German hoo-ha.'

Armstrong loved the television. His family was the first on the
estate to get one. Nell and Dickie used to go to the Armstrongs'
cottage to watch *Bill and Ben*, and once long ago Mr and Mrs R
had come down from the big house for *Panorama*. That they
enjoyed it enough to buy their own set before the following
Monday was, Armstrong had always felt, a compliment to his
up-to-dateness. Played ruddy havoc with their dinnertime,
though. Mrs Duggary said it'd be his fault if they got indigestion,
eating food off their laps like that when they weren't used it. Not

that anyone else had a dining room, or even – most families – enough chairs to sit down altogether.

He dragged his mind back to now, and Leipzig. He said, 'I saw young Nell's Jamie.'

'That's right,' said Brian. 'Looked a right 'nana, didn't he, trying to talk to the Krauts.' Brian had never forgiven Jamie for the burning of the chapel. And, having done his national service in the Rhineland, he, unlike Jamie, spoke German very well.

'Antony's gone out there too,' said Armstrong. 'It's going to be a bit of a turnaround for him, all this.'

'What do you mean?'

'He's a Russian spy.'

'What are you on about?'

'Jack told me. He told Jack. And I asked him lately and he said yes. It was all a long time ago, mind.'

Brian sat back, and gripped the arms of his chair, and whistled, and shook his head, and acted out astonishment. Armstrong waited with a tight smug smile. He said eventually, 'You didn't expect that, did you?'

There was a great deal about the relations between the senior John Armstrong and Antony Briggs that no one would have expected. That the latter was now effectively the former's widowed son-in-law was part of it. But perhaps more remarkable was the staunch friendship between the two. 'You think you've got an opinion on something you don't know much about,' the old man said to Antony after Jack's funeral. 'And then it crops up in your own family and you realise your opinion isn't worth diddly-squat.' They'd taken to going for walks together, slow but long. They talked about the emancipation of the working class. They surprised each other.

'I was in the army for six years,' said Armstrong to Antony. 'You meet all sorts. You think things out.'

'But you came back to gamekeeping for one of those who grind the faces of the poor.'

Armstrong didn't rise to the irony.

'Old Mr Rossiter did the right thing. Every man who'd done his bit got his job back. He was a good boss.'

'Christopher didn't fight, did he?'

'He could never see a thing. You should have seen the thickness of the lenses on those gig-lamps he wore, even when he was just a little chap. Mind you, there was a fellow in my platoon whose eyesight was every bit as bad. His people wouldn't have known how to get a fancy doctor give them a certificate, or they couldn't afford it. I'm glad he didn't go, though. I'm glad he stayed safe.'

'You'd never make a revolutionary,' said Antony, thinking, Nor would I.

'Slow and steady,' said Armstrong. 'Look at our Jack, worked alongside Mr Lane, and Brian Goodyear doing the agent job now, who started out no better off than I did. There's no need to string people up. Just keep plugging away.'

'Our' Jack, thought Antony. Our Jack. Am I one of the people allowed to say that?

'You're very good to old Armstrong,' said Lil to Antony.

'He's first-rate company,' he replied. 'As I know you know. I hear you're a regular visitor too.'

'We've got a lot in common. He's the only person I can talk to about Fergus.'

They say that the birth of children can cement a relationship. Their deaths can too.

*

'I really have to go,' said Antony. He had a habit, when he was nervous, of rearranging things that didn't require it. For the last five minutes he had been tidying the sugar lumps in the metal dish between them.

'Off you go then,' said Nell. 'We'll be fine. If he doesn't show up soon I'll just go back to the flat.'

'You're sure you know the way?'

'Of course.'

It was a relief when he finally took himself off. Nell settled herself back in her chair. Jemima, in her sling, slept and drooled between her breasts. It was peaceful. Jamie would come eventually, she supposed. When she'd told him she was thinking of coming out to Berlin with Antony he'd sounded anxious. 'I'm working non-stop,' he'd said. But then, to her surprise, because he didn't say things like this, he'd said, 'I do really really miss you both.' So she'd come.

One of the things about having a baby was how much one valued quietness. Her table was hard up against the café's window. Outside the plate-glass people kept passing, and looking in at her, or rather at Jemima. If I was in England, she thought, I'd feel obliged to respond somehow, but when you're a foreigner, you can act invisible. She shut her eyes.

Time passed. Jemima stirred and snuffled and arched her tiny body. There was a spluttering noise from her lower end and at once Nell could smell it. A woman out on the pavement was rapping at the window and shouting. The glass was thick. Nell couldn't make out what she was saying, probably wouldn't have understood anyway: her German was rotten. The woman kept banging on the window. She looked wild. A waiter made a shooing gesture. She waved both arms in the air and jumped up and down and then went on down the street dancing. Nell could see her banging on other windows, still shouting. Other people joined her. Some sort of a demo?

'Come, little mouse,' said Nell to Jemima, picked up her big bag (so much luggage for such a tiny person) and went to the *Damen*. There was a changing table – Germans really are better organised than us, she thought. She stripped Jemima to her vest, and cleaned her bottom and put the used nappy in a scented bag.

Why do I buy these bags? she thought. The smell is sickening. I actually prefer the smell of poo. She put the nappy in a bin and got out the new one and she and Jemima played the usual games of where's-it-gone and bum-up and tickle-tummy and all the time she was singing to her, or rather crooning, just little scraps of nursery rhyme, and because they were in Berlin she began to sing the rhymes that Gerti had taught her, Gerti the au pair girl who came to them after Heather left, when even Dickie was really too old to need a nanny any more but who still sometimes saw them into bed when their parents were out, and sang them the songs of her own childhood.

Hampti Dampti, ein schneeweißes Ei
fiel von der Mauer und brach entzwei.
Der König schickt Ritter mit Pferd und Lanz,
doch wer von den Herren macht ein Ei wieder ganz?

When the new nappy was on she played the All-of-Jemima game. Here are Jemima's FEET. And here are Jemima's KNEES and here is Jemima's BOTTOM and so on, always giving the part in question a gentle little shake which made the baby laugh and wriggle. And then she sang Gerti's rhyme again, and this time, because she was interested to know whether something she had memorised phonetically, as a sequence of meaningless sounds, would make sense now she understood at least a bit of the language, she translated it for Jemima.

Humpty Dumpty, a snowy-white egg –

Which gives it away. It's a riddle-rhyme. Spoils it to begin with the answer.

Fell off the . . . *Mauer* –

Mauer.

Off what did Humpty Dumpty fall?

Now she knew what the madwoman had been shouting. No wonder she looked deranged. Hampti Dampti sat on a *Mauer*.

What did Humpty fall off? The *Mauer*. *'Die Mauer ist gefallen!'* That's what she'd yelled. *'Die Mauer ist gefallen!'* No wonder she was shouting and dancing. No wonder Jamie wasn't there. Humpty Dumpty sat on a wall. The Wall *ist gefallen*.

'All fall down Wall fall down,' she told Jemima as she poppered her into a clean red suit with a panda face on the chest. 'Wall fall down,' she sang as she got her back into her sling. Jemima began to wail. This wasn't right. She'd been hoping for a bottle. They walked back out into the café just as the kitchen door swung open and a dozen people burst through it shouting. Nell could see they had the television on in there. Three of them ran straight through the café and out into the street. The others were spinning between the tables, and people were rising to their feet and hugging each other and shouting and kissing and they were all saying what that first mad-looking Cassandra had been saying. *'Die Mauer ist gefallen.'* A huge red-faced man hugged Nell and Jemima together and Jemima went quiet in astonishment and then began to cry louder and louder and Nell fought her way back to their table, and found the bottle of formula and got it into Jemima's mouth, and struggled into her own coat, and got the sling back on because the world may be changed utterly but if you're looking after a baby you still have to do these things and then at last she found the dummy that she really hardly ever used and popped it into Jemima's mouth and by this time they were almost alone in the café, but she still went up to pay, but the cashier was dragging on her own coat and said something Nell couldn't follow but which was pretty easy to understand and the three of them, cashier, baby and the serious-minded civil servant who was, at one of the great turning points of twentieth-century European history, in the ladies' loo wiping shit off her daughter's bum, went out into that stirring night.

Selim

When I was first here, if I switched the light on at night, dusty moths came and circled the bulb, casting enormous shadows onto the inside of the paper shade. Now, nearly two months later, the insects have left. I am grateful for the companionship of the dribbling of the little fountain in the centre of the pool.

'Have to turn that off soon,' said young Green. (It is only this week that I have understood that 'young' is not his name, but a descriptive adjective.) The pipes, he said, have to be drained before the first frost or they are likely to burst. He explained this carefully, as though to a small child. I didn't tell him that I lived three winters in Oxford, and that I am a skilled amateur mechanic.

My colleagues on the magazine have apologised for printing the offending extract. I was not consulted: I accept that in fleeing I forfeited my authority. Not one British newspaper has taken notice either of our original defiance, or of our subsequent grovelling surrender.

Nell has gone to Berlin. The television is full of news from Eastern Europe. There is a kind of hushed rapture in the commentators' voices. It is as though the Western world is watching the last lap of a steeplechase, and their horse is coming up on the outside and there's only one more fence before the finish and they are all rigid with hope and hardly daring to breathe for fear of missing the moment when their horse's nose goes out in front. (When I was small my father used to take me to watch his Pathan friends racing in wooden wheeled chariots down the dirt roads of the Punjab – 'Attend,' he said. 'You are seeing what the Greek Alexander saw.' Homesick in my first winter at Oxford, I'd spend as many Saturdays as I could manage at the races.)

They're watching the wrong horse. The wrong race. For people here it looks as though, all of my lifetime, the world has been cut by a slash that ran through Berlin. East/West Communist/ Capitalist Soviet/American. Now that cut is closing and everyone is getting ready to celebrate, as though once all's right with Europe, then all's right with the world.

Have they forgotten what brought me here? These ideological disputes between two sets of white Westerners can perhaps be resolved. Not so the antipathy between those who are harbouring me, and those who would have me stoned.

My father has written me a long letter. There is a great deal about Ovid in it, but less about Cicero, because he does not want to tell me, any more, that he expects me to be killed.

When I stepped out in the dark before dawn one morning, I found myself heehawing like a donkey, trying to control my breath. I think it is possible to die of fear.

*

Jamie wasn't going to the press conference. 'My wife's coming over with the baby,' he said at lunchtime in the press-club. 'I've got to stick around.'

'My wife'. 'The baby'. The words still embarrassed him. Saying them, he felt like he was acting. Not that he didn't love the two of them. He did. He really did. When Jemima reached out damp translucent fingers, and poked two of them up his nose, he fell in love absolutely and for ever. I'd die for her, he thought, pleased with himself. But though he might perhaps have died for his daughter, had circumstances required it, he wouldn't, as it turned out, miss out on a story in order to welcome her to Berlin.

His friend from Associated Press, who had four children, and was no longer either sheepish or wonderstruck about paternity, said, 'The family can wait. Something's going to happen. Don't know what. Don't know when. But if you take your eye off the ball for a second you can bet your fucking life that's when it'll all go up.' And Jamie thought, He's right, and found a telephone, and called the flat, and got no answer, but he left a message on the machine anyway and he went through the checkpoint with the

AP man and settled next to him in the uncomfortable plastic chairs in the ministry's press-room. But he'd been up since the small hours walking among the crowds keeping vigil on Potsdamer Platz, searching, as everyone there was doing, for a sign, and while Schabowski was droning on he fell asleep.

Jamie was a snorer. The AP man would elbow him when the whistling and the hog-snorting got too loud, and he'd shift in his chair and nod off again. But about three-quarters of an hour into the East German minister's statement the elbowing became brutal and he woke up angry. Something was happening. People were scribbling. 'What?' he said to the AP man. 'Travel restrictions lifted,' muttered the man and leant forward rudely so that Jamie couldn't keep pestering him for more. The big grey-faced man on the podium was shuffling through papers. Impatient. Seemed not to find what he was searching for. Looked a bit irritated. Said, without emphasis, or much conviction, '*Sofort.*' Straightaway.

And straightaway Jamie felt the kind of lurch you get in dreams when you realise you're onstage and you don't know your lines, don't even know what play you're in, and you're not even sure your trousers are on. The man from the *Telegraph* was on his feet, asking, 'Where does that leave the Berlin Wall?' and the AP man was running, and so were most of the other journos, for the corridor with its bank of phones.

*

Guy seldom got up now. Flora, Benjie and Lil took it in turns to sit with him. His room was in the old part of the house, pre-Woldingham. A four-poster bed, linen-fold panelling. Two mullioned windows just a maddening little bit off-centre for the vista of the great beech avenue. 'Norris had this room,' said Benjie. 'People say he planted the avenue mainly for his own pleasure, but if so I do think he might have got it straight.'

Lil came up every morning from Wood Manor, leaving her car by Antony's lodge and walking along the Grand Vista, taking her time. When she reached the junction of the two avenues she paused.

After Christopher died, she'd commissioned an artist whose work she'd been eyeing for decades to make an installation for that place as a memorial to him. Everyone had made a fuss at first.

'You know that's the highest point, Mrs Rossiter,' said old Armstrong. 'They'll be able to see it from church tower to church tower.' Of course she knew.

Benjie said, 'I know a chap who's been rescuing big things from Eastern-bloc countries and floating them down the Bosphorus. He's got some socking great obelisks. The Magyar nobility loved them, apparently. You'd only have to pay transport.'

'Women,' said Lil, 'do not erect obelisks.'

Antony trusted her taste. He said, 'Christopher always talked about putting something there.' It wasn't true, but Lil said, 'Yes, he did, didn't he,' and he thought, She's lying too, but we mean well.

Now the piece was installed, and it was an obelisk's antithesis. A disc of black metal laid flat on the ground and so highly polished it exactly reflected the sky. A circle of mirrored glass structures of about human height, like standing stones, positioned around it. 'The Amalienburg,' said Antony, when he saw the plans. Wet leaves floated on the black circle. The mirrors reflected and matched the negative shapes between wet black tree-trunks, sending flashes of uncanny light across the space. Some things, Lil thought, as she did every time she passed this way, I have done right.

Ensconced in the wing chair in Guy's room she reminisced inconsequentially, conjuring up her past life for him as he drifted in and out of consciousness. Normally reticent in the extreme, she talked to him as openly as though she were talking to herself.

As though it was safe to do so; as though he was already gone. In his lucid moments he brought up memories too. 'The first time I came here,' he said, 'I was with Helen and Benj, in that noisy red car. And I saw you walking across the lawn with Hugo, a long way off, and I didn't know either of you, but I was sure that you were lovers, or that you ought to be. You were both exquisite. In white.'

'We'd been playing tennis, I suppose,' Lil said, prosaic.

Guy ignored the interruption. 'Did you love him?'

Lil looked out of the window, took time answering. 'I think I thought then that he loved me, and that was intoxicating. But I don't know now whether he did. He was a very conventional person, really. He liked being married to Chloe. He loved his dog and his children. Beauty is very confusing. You see someone who looks divine and you suppose they must have remarkable interior lives as well. It's not fair on them.'

'I know,' said Guy, 'God, don't I know!' and they both thought of the dozen or so boys he'd brought out to Wychwood over the years – lovely as the day is long, but pretty annoying, some of them.

'Well I can't say I was ever dumbstruck with wonder by your choices,' said Lil and they laughed. But she thought, and perhaps he did too, Where are those men now? Marriage may be an outmoded institution but in-sickness-and-in-health isn't a bad rule. All those wild years and gaudy nights. All those myriads of men. They've all pushed off and left, and he has to come back to his family. Or sort-of family.

Guy's father had kept his distance for years, disapproving. Now he wanted to do the right thing, but Guy said, 'He's left it too late.' For all his studied levity, he could be harsh.

In the afternoons Guy slept, then Flora came up with tea and cake and they switched on the telly. They saw Schabowski's press conference and couldn't believe it and then saw it repeated over and over again – the exhausted face, the tetchy tone. Benjie rang a Berliner architect he worked with sometimes. 'No one knows,' she said. She sounded anxious. 'The crossings haven't opened. But everyone's celebrating. All this dancing in the streets. It's premature.'

'Oppression is a con,' said Guy. 'Liberation could be too. Act like it's happened, and happen it does.'

*

The hotel lobby in which Antony sat was all brown. Dark stained-wood floors. Leather chairs designed like sections of a cube. Wall lights with mottled brown glass shades. His companion – her ostensible job was in the trade department at the embassy – was in brown too, a suede coat, smudges of brown eyeshadow. Even brown lipstick. And their drinks – lager for him, rum and Coke for her. Antony was amused. Sepia, he thought. Having a highly trained eye does occasionally yield unexpected pleasures. What a good thing, he thought, I packed my brogues.

'Oleg wants his house in the Home Counties,' she was saying, 'and his golf-club membership. He's certainly earned it.'

'But why's he coming now?' asked Antony.

'He expects the transition to be bloody.'

'Do you?'

'Not really. Mr Gorbachev is a very brave and cunning man. But of course it can all go wrong. Everyone *en poste* in this part of the world keeps a bag packed.'

'But why do you need me?'

'We have to know he is the person he claims to be. And it's safer for him. Because as far as our Russian friends know, you're still one of their people. You'll be his contact from now on. If he's being followed, and he's seen with you, then he can say he's been running you all along.'

'But I haven't given them anything for decades.'

'Not as far as you knew. But you have actually. Their messages to you have been intercepted, and replied to in suitable form.'

How many people am I? thought Antony. How many 'me's have I never met?

He made as though to say something. She was watching him carefully. She said, 'We've been very lenient with you, wouldn't you agree? There was always going to be a time when you had to make yourself useful. As I think my colleague told you at your first meeting, we are very, very patient.'

'Why here?'

'It was convenient.' An upturning of her hands meaning 'enough said'. She looked at her watch. 'We'll walk through the bar now. He will be sitting in the far corner to our left, facing us. We'll go slowly. I'll walk on your left so you can look at him while appearing to talk to me. Take as long as you need. He may or may not acknowledge you. It's better if you make no response. When we are quite close I will stop and ask you something meaningless, so that you can turn towards me and get a further look. If you're already sure just take my arm and we'll walk on.'

And so they did. The man was big. The flesh of his face drooped off his skull. There were two people with him and he was listening to their conversation as though too tired to join in. It could have been the man with whom Antony had had a cryptic, pre-scripted conversation in a café in Bucharest thirty years before. It could just as easily not be. Antony had met lots of Russians who looked like that. Soulful and a bit seedy.

The woman put her hand on his arm, and said, 'By the way, Magda would like to see you. Should I ask her to join us for dinner?'

Antony said seriously, and just a little louder than was necessary, 'I'm always pleased to see the old lot.' The man in the corner allowed his pale, bulging eyes to pass over him and as they did so Antony saw clearly that the man recognised him, and he thought that he knew him as well. He took the woman's arm and they went on, uttering fake banalities, until they stepped out of the hotel's front entrance and the woman found her car and drove away and Antony walked out onto the square where the rumps of the famous bronze horses could be seen looming above the wall, and there was something happening there. Shouting and the tremendous sloshing of water cannon in use.

Selim

Tick tick tick tick tick. I woke at first light and knew at once there was someone in the hut with me. Not that it needed any extrasensory cunning on my part. There was a noise. Tick tick tick tick.

I lay for a while in the dark. The ticking stopped. Resumed. There was also a shuffling. I went into the other room and there was a woman sitting at my writing table. An old woman, very bent. She was reading my scribblings. She looked straight at me and said, 'I'd be glad of a cup of tea.'

I went to the bathroom, made myself presentable. Went to the kitchen, set out a tray. By the time I carried it in she had tidied up my papers and sat herself in the armchair. 'I'm Mrs Slatter,' she said. 'I expect you've heard about me.'

I had. Brian Goodyear had recommended I meet her. He said she was a witch. I told her so, and I said, 'They used to say that about my grandmother too.'

'Good,' she said. 'We'll get on fine then.' Her hands had a perpetual tremor. The ticking must have been her wedding ring – she wore no other jewellery – knocking on the table.

We talked. Or rather I talked. I told her everything I could remember about my grandmother. I felt more at ease than I had for a long time. I talked about coming to school in England, and Oxford, and about how I simply couldn't believe that people could eat such disgusting food.

As I spoke I experienced it all again. I smelt my grandmother's clothes, tasted the sweets she used to give me, saw again her wrinkled hands and the bangles she wore. I felt the freshness in the English air and the stuffiness in libraries where I studied. I talked about Sunita, and how we had all but resigned ourselves to childlessness. I told her my grandfather had advised me to take a second wife.

I told her about my panic. I said, 'I hadn't seen Nell for years and years, but I somehow thought she could save me.' Mrs Slatter said, 'There's her blood on the floor beneath us. Under this. They couldn't get it out of the rush matting, so Mr Underhill told Mrs R they needed lino in here.' 'Why?' I asked. 'Was she hurt?' I imagined some childish accident. Mrs Slatter laughed and said, 'No. No. Not that sort of blood. No harm done.'

When the sun was fully up I walked with her down to the big house where her granddaughter Holly was waiting with two toddling girls in the kind of dungarees that workmen used to wear. 'Stay with Grammer,' said Holly, 'and Mum will be back for you at lunchtime,' and she gave them each a squeeze before getting into her car. Mrs Slatter put her hand on my arm – it was leaf-light – and said, 'You'll be fine,' and then she led the girls off down the stone-paved corridor to the kitchen. That repellent black dog struggled up off its cushion and waddled after her. I felt ridiculously envious of the children. I wanted to whine, 'Take care of me too.'

*

Schabowski's press conference was televised live. Immediately, all over East Berlin, people dropped whatever they were doing and went to the crossing points. Some of them carried bags. Most went just as they were – to see, simply to see. When Jamie arrived at the gate there was already a crowd. He got out his notebook and his tape recorder and began to ask questions. He found a woman in pale blue pyjamas under her anorak whose voice was improbably high-pitched. 'I came like this,' she said. She was proud of having run out without dressing. 'I just couldn't wait.' All the time she was talking to him she was bouncing up and down, trying to make herself taller, trying to see over the people who stood between her and the crossing gate, trying to see over the wall.

People crowded round him. They wanted to make solemn declarations – the end of an era, the first taste of freedom, a night that changed history, the night they had waited for all their lives, the day the World War finally ended, the day Germany was reborn, a night they would never forget. Jamie didn't note the platitudes. He noted their ages, and whether they had ever been West. Did they have relatives on the other side? Weren't they afraid the guards might open fire? Weren't they afraid this might be the beginning of a new war?

Most of them quickly got bored of talking to him. Waving at a camera was fun, but some of them had had more than enough of being recorded on tape. Only the woman in the pyjamas kept pogoing beside him, and telling him in her squeaky voice about how fast she'd run to get there, how much she hoped the gate would open. She said, 'I worked in a laundry over there. If only I'd stayed with my friend that night. Twenty-eight years ago.'

Nell was only a couple of hundred feet away, on the other side. Jemima's weight dragged her shoulders down. She found a railing she could hoist the baby onto, and there she stood, watching for something that had yet to happen. People jostled her, but then stopped to apologise. It was a polite crowd. Jemima slept. When the first Ossis came through, blinking, their faces bleached by the strident brightness of the searchlights, she thought of the labour room. The same ugly light, the same predominance of hard surfaces, metal and concrete, people all dressed alike in the same sort of blue, the same straining and straining at a narrow passage and then, at last, the arrival, from a place unknown and all but inconceivable, of a stranger.

By the time Jamie came she was done in. He walked straight up to her, as though he'd known all along where she was. He reached across the bulk of Jemima to embrace her, as he had done when Jemima was still in her belly. He said, 'I'm so glad, I'm so glad, I'm so glad you saw it, you both saw it.' She could feel the excitement coming off him. 'I have to file,' he said. But he wouldn't let go of her. They were turning, dancing, clumsily joined. She said, 'I love you.' He probably didn't hear her. He said, 'Remember this. You've got to remember this.' He kept saying it. She thought, He's drunk, and then, No he's elated. And she thought, We really do get on pretty well.

Later everyone said the Ossis looked like angels, with their blond hair permed into ringlets, but perhaps they were more like Adam and Eve issuing, naked and blinking, from the enclosure where an all-knowing God forbade them knowledge. They came through on foot, those first few hours. Later they came driving their identical white cars. The Wessis cheered and sang and hugged them, but they were a little cautious, a little withdrawn. Who's to say, their stance implied, that what you have here is something for which we should reach out with yearning and that we should accept with joy?

Most of them, after a brief sortie, went back home.

Antony

In Prague, in 1972 or thereabouts, I went into a church. Gothic, black stone ribs and white distemper. I was interested in an altarpiece I thought I'd find in one of the side chapels, by a master with whom Altdorfer is said to have worked, but I didn't get to see it that day. I was on my own. I nearly always travelled alone. Perhaps that's why people whose business needed to be discreetly managed found me useful.

The church was silent when I walked in, letting the door slam behind me, but it wasn't empty. Oh no. Every pew was full. Every paving-stone was hidden by people sitting on the floor. People of all ages, in working clothes. I found a stone ledge to perch on just as the soprano rose. They were singing Mozart's *Great Mass in C Minor*. '*Et incarnatus est.*' And he was made flesh. Christian doctrine has tenets weird enough to defy the credulity of even the most devout – this is one of them – but the music etherealises it. I sat until the end, listening to the text's promise of justice and consolation and death defeated, and to the offer made, and made good, by the music of transcendence, of the tranquillity of perfect form. No one fidgeted.

I've been thinking about that experience since the wall came down. That was the culture of Eastern Europe under communism. What did the Ossis find in the West, when they broke through their wall? Bananas, pornography, bigger cars. What were they given? Money to go shopping with. Shopping! Was it for this . . .?

No one else seems to feel as I do. Jamie said, 'It's not the West they want. It's a better East. No more snooping. No more fear.'

Nell said, 'A lot of the inmates in open prisons actually have more freedom of movement than they'd have on the outside. People who work all day, who are too poor to travel – is that freedom? But they're still traumatised by imprisonment. The very idea of being shut in triggers depression.'

Nicholas said, 'So you heard some Mozart in a church. Lucky old you. They have jolly good concerts in St Martin-in-the-Fields too, and the clergy here don't endure endless harassment. You do know what's been done to Christians in the Eastern bloc, don't you?'

Benjie said, 'I've got a friend who's been buying up the Trabants as they come over. The Ossis can't believe their luck when he tells them how many Deutschmarks he's giving for them. And the Wessis adore them. A souvenir of *Mauer-gefall*, and jolly cheap on the road. You know they run on two-stroke?'

I did know, as it happened. That weekend in Berlin the area around the crossings reeked of lawnmower fuel. A whiff of summer gardens and of cosy tedium amidst all that chilly concrete, all that arc-lit overexcitement.

Guy said – Guy whose appetite had so dwindled he lived entirely on soups Flora made for him, and that Lil fed him in tiny sippets from the Meissen cocotte pots – Guy said, 'Don't underestimate bananas.' And I thought, He's right, I've never, ever been hungry, except on long drives when I forgot to stop for lunch. What do I know about the needs of the huddled masses?

Guy was a very clever young man.

*

Helen and Nicholas had lunch.

'Last time I was here I saw Antony with his spymaster,' she said, offhand. 'Poor old Ant. I hope he'll be off the hook now. So what did you have to tell me?'

'I'm getting married.'

'To Francesca?'

'Of course.'

Helen sat back and crossed her arms and stared at the ceiling. Nicholas waited.

'I'm just checking,' she said, 'but I'm not detecting any symptoms of heartbreak.'

Then she leant across the table and took both his hands and said, 'In fact I think I can truly say I'm pleased.' They smiled broadly at each other. 'So now,' she said, 'when are you going to run that piece of Nell's on prisoners' power-structures? It's really quite significant.'

*

It was weirdly hot, even in the kitchen whose stone flags, on winter days, sent shafts of icy chill up through the calves of those who stood upon them. Flora, cooking pheasants with apples in Mrs Duggary's famous missionary-boiling pot, kept pushing her hair – striped grey now – back off her increasingly ruddy face.

'Nicholas is bringing Francesca,' said Flora.

Benjie said, 'For people who refuse to commit themselves, those two have been together a hell of a long time.'

'Ant thinks they're secretly married.'

'Why the secret?'

'Who knows? He's always been cagey, hasn't he? And I think she rather likes masquerading as the superwoman who doesn't need a prop and stay.'

Mrs Duggary, dipping grapes in syrup at the other end of the long table, said, 'There's enough women have to put up with being on their own, without those as has got husbands trying to pretend they can do without.' Mrs D's arthritis made her slow now, but in the kitchen she was still dictatorial. She said to Flora, 'There's some Calvados would go nicely in that. No one drinks it since Mr R went.'

'Is Guy all right?' asked Benjie. He was opening the red wine.

'Holly's with him,' said Flora.

'I talked to the doctor on his way out. He says he really needs hospital nursing now.'

They looked at each other. Unsayable things passed between them. Guy was their other one; their family.

There was a clatter and a murmur of voices off. 'Well,' said Benjie. 'I'll go and fetch Selim, shall I?'

'Please. Take the torch.'

Benjie went out. It was a breathless night. Muggy and still and extraordinarily warm. As he walked through the gate into the pool garden he could see Selim silhouetted in the hut's window. He was leaning his forehead on the glass. His hands were over his eyes. Benjie paused, and let the gate clang shut behind him. Selim straightened up at once and sat down at the table. When Benjie knocked, and opened, calling, 'Only me,' Selim was apparently absorbed in his writing.

'Ready to come over?' said Benjie.

'Yes, of course,' said Selim. He was fat, and his face had lost its mobility. 'I'll just . . .'

He went into the bedroom and came out swaddled in a big coat and a grey scarf. 'You won't need those,' said Benjie. 'It's warm as a tart's armpit out.' Selim shrugged. He didn't speak as they walked down through the shrubbery to the house. Benjie gave him the torch, but took it back when he saw how its beam wavered. Everyone knew how it scared Selim to walk between those dark bushes.

'I was just saying to Flora,' said Benjie, light as anything, 'that if you're staying much longer you really must move over into the house now winter's here.'

Selim's little laugh would have registered as insulting, had it not come from someone so evidently distressed.

Antony

You could tell that something freakish was happening from the moment we got off the plane. The air was clammy.

The green Bentley was there waiting for us at Heathrow. To me the scent of its leather seats said 'car-sickness'. I'm supposed to be the one who treasures beautifully made things, but how glad I would have been of an efficient modern car that took us from A to B without all this history.

Nell drove. It was their rule. She had made Jamie swear he would never drive, unless she explicitly asked him to, when Jemima was in the car.

It was Flora's idea to make our return a gala night – is there nothing that woman won't use as a pretext for a party? – and invite a whole lot of the estate people to come in for a knees-up. Nothing wrong with that, but she really shouldn't have asked Manny. And when he turned up with the crew she should just have showed them the door. But she owes them, I suppose. The work of a television presenter is so different from anything we're accustomed to thinking of as a job that one has to keep reminding oneself that he is actually her boss.

Jamie had brought a chunk of wall home. The planes flying out of Berlin that month must have been carrying a lot of inordinately heavy luggage. Everyone had their bit of rubble. Mine is about the size and shape of a fig, a piece of concrete with a flash of lime-green paint on it. It fitted in my pocket. It still sits on my desk. But Jamie, who never had much of a sense of proportion, had lugged home a piece that was almost as large as his daughter. Flora had put it in the middle of the table, wreathed it with ivy and surrounded it with candles.

Everyone got quite raucous. Benjie's plumpness has turned to old-man flab, but he's still quite the twinkle-toes on the dance floor, and he still loves to get a singsong going around the piano. I went out into the hall at one point, and there above was Guy, sitting enthroned in the minstrels' gallery, Holly, watchful, leaning over the railing beside him. He fluttered a hand. He looked older than I did.

Mark Brown had come with Manny. Once the intruding outsider, Mark is now triply in – Benjie's collaborator, Flora's competitor (his how-to TV shows are popular), Lil's chosen escort around the private views. He and Francesca were giving us the 'Chorus of the Hebrew Slaves', their voices floating like smoke. All the songs that night were about exile and return, confinement and release. Benjie allowed them their dying fall and then segued straight into Joshua and Jericho and the wall coming tumbling down, and through the open door I saw Jamie dancing with his mother-in-law and Brian Goodyear gently helping old Mrs Duggary up and giving her a twirl.

When I looked up next Guy was hobbling back towards his room with his arm around Holly's shoulders. His striped djellabah (how many years had he had that?) billowed behind him like the draperies of a saint ascending into a baroque heaven. To Benjie he was a surrogate son. To me, he once offered sex. I was shocked.

He laughed, and said, 'You can but ask,' and didn't so much with-draw the offer as erase it on the instant, so that it was as though it had never been. In the drawing room Benjie was strumming lustily and singing, 'Carry us away . . . captivity.' I never saw Guy on his feet again.

The film crew were setting up in the hall and Manny was muttering to the man with the sound-boom. Nicholas touched my arm. I followed him into the library. Selim was there, blubbering.

'I don't know what's brought this on,' said Nicholas. 'He won't talk to me.'

I sat beside the poor fellow and put a hand on his knee. He jerked away as though he'd been touched by something filthy. I pretended not to notice. I said, 'Do you want to go home?'

He nodded. It occurred to me the question was ambiguous so I said, 'Back to the hut?' He nodded again and got to his feet, wiping his nose clumsily on his sleeve – he, who was so fastidi-ous. I saw the distaste with which he rejected any chair upon which snuffly old Lupin might have sat.

I said, 'We'll be OK,' and Nicholas said, 'Well done,' and went back towards the drawing room. Selim found his coat and scarf – even in despair he feared English winter weather. I took him through the hidden door in the panelling that led into the kitchen corridor, found the torch and went on out into the yard. The door was torn from my hand and slammed back against the outside wall. Two dustbins came past, hurtling over the cobbles, fetching up against a wall with the clangour of gigantic gongs. The rushing air was in spate, and filled with tornaway leaves, twigs, branches. A bicycle skidded after the dustbins, lifting and clashing as the current tossed it. A tarpaulin sailed overhead, trailing ropes like terrible tentacles, toothed with the metal pegs that should have held it down.

I said, 'Christ!' and spread my arms to prevent Selim following me out, but he was already through, and I saw the wind take him.

He staggered, was flung forward, scrabbled on all fours, was felled again, caught himself up and scrabbled forwards until he reached the archway leading out onto the great lawn. He passed through it upright, his long coat bearing him up like a kite. There was light falling from the windows but the sky was pitch-black.

Once, some years ago, alone in the mews house, I heard stealthy movements downstairs. I had always thought that should someone break in I would pretend to be asleep, avoid confrontation, but that time I surprised myself. I didn't even pause to put on a dressing gown, but went downstairs at speed, half-naked and vulnerable without my specs, and said, 'What the hell do you think you're doing.' The man ran straight out, carrying the suede jacket (new, expensive) I kept hanging on the hook by the door. (I knew who he was. He must have noted the fragility of the house's defences on the night I brought him home with me from the Coleherne. Some queens found the risks we used to run exciting: I was mortified by them.) It was only after I'd slammed the door behind him and shot the bolt that I began to shake.

Then I was braver than I'd anticipated. This time, the reverse.

It amuses me that popular culture celebrates those who work in the secret services as action heroes. I may be the most craven, but we were – are – on the whole, so far as I've ever been able to see, a shifty lot.

It was perfectly obvious what I ought to have done. You don't just turn your back while a fellow-being is blown away. If you've got a shred of decency you catch onto his coat-tails and either wrestle him back to earth or let the wind take you too. I didn't do it. What I did instead was drop to my knees. I kept my eyes tight shut against all the flying stuff, my head down, and crawled back the few feet to the doorway. It was hard to breathe. The air was racing so fast I could scarcely snatch enough to keep my lungs fed even had I not been gasping with fear. A fencing panel, heavy enough to break a man's back, somersaulted by and smashed into a window. By the time I made it indoors I was so battered I had to sit on the floor, head hanging between knees, until I was brought back to my senses by old Lupin, lapping with his obscene pink tongue at the blood trickling from my knuckles.

Mrs Duggary was there. She said, 'It was after the rushing mighty wind blew out of heaven that the disciples began to speak in tongues and all the people on earth could understand each other.' She's always referred to herself as 'a godly woman'. When I first started coming here she used to carry round the embroidered velvet pouch for collection every Sunday at evensong. (Matins, of course, she couldn't do. Sunday lunch for the house-party was the culminating act of her life's weekly drama.) I wonder whether anyone from the house goes to church now. She sat down beside me – an elaborate sequence of ungainly moves – and held a tea towel against the cut on my bald head and handed me a glass of brandy, which I really didn't want. 'I don't think it's going to work here, do you? That poor man – he speaks English like a teacher, but nobody seems to understand him, for all that.'

Selim

Blown away.

Blow-Up – Nell's favourite film, she said, and I went to the Moulin Rouge to see it – perhaps I really was more interested in her than I acknowledged even to myself – and I recoiled from its self-satisfied decadence. Blow-dry. By-blow. *Blow-Out* – another film: that one amused me. To have seen a lot of pretentious European films during your student years, said Jamie, who hadn't, was the mark of a sexually unsuccessful man. Nonsense, said Francesca, I'd never have slept with Nicholas if he hadn't been able to blather on about *400 Blows*. Blowpipe. Blowhole. A blow to the head. A blow to one's pride. A blowing-up. Blowjob – how dismal that phrase is, with its acknowledgement that for so many a sexual act is joyless work. Blow into this, says the speed-cop. Blow winds and crack your cheeks. Now blow, says the doctor, his stethoscope to your chest. Blow bonny breezes. It'll all blow over, sings the idiot optimist.

I blew it, and then I was blown away.

There they all were, with their silly brick decked out like an idol in the middle of the table. Flora blew me a kiss as I came in (she did that to everyone) and said, 'Sit here, Selim.' They were all blowing hot air. And I blew my top. How many of them really cared about Germany? Only Guy, and he was upstairs on his deathbed. How unseemly to be carousing beneath him. Some of them had fought to break Germany into pieces. To blow it up, to blow it to smithereens, to blow it to kingdom come. Benjie had anyway, and who knows what Antony has done?

I wanted to make a scene. I wanted to bang the table with my fist. I wanted to send things crashing and breaking. Once, in that same house, instead of a chunk of concrete, a feast might have been assembled around the carcass of a deer. Savage, that. Kill a beautiful wild creature, and flay it, and torture its dead flesh with fire, and then lay it out on your finest platter and garnish it with hazelnuts and damsons and wreathe it with aromatic herbs and then grow drunk while devouring its meat. Savage but meaningful. Kill – eat – thrive. The triumph of violence. There's a ghastly splendour in it. But this travesty sickened me, this ignorant honouring of a namby-pamby freedom.

I am feeble. I don't rage. I sulk.

Brian Goodyear watched me. He has eyes like a bird's. He knows how I think.

Nicholas sat next to me. I said to him, 'The story you're all so worked up about is over. The story I'm part of is the one you need to think about.'

He said, 'Go on.' He has never been in the least bit friendly to me, but he is attentive.

A man with a heavy camera hoisted on his shoulder was manoeuvring between the scattered chairs, the soundman following him close with his boom. They kept glancing back at Manny who shifted them from one group to another with small hand movements, as a shepherd directs his dogs.

Francesca leant across the table and said, 'You're right. We're hearing now from people we've never heard from before.'

She talked about the Islamic scholars and imams being given a voice in the British press. She said how startled some of her friends had been by their intransigence, but also by their gravitas, the thoughtfulness by which they have arrived at their world-view. She said, 'Not my colleagues. In the Foreign Office we all know that wherever we are stationed we're going to be the clumsy ignoramuses blundering about in societies whose mores we don't understand.'

A vision crossed my mind of British officers, scarlet-faced and scarlet-tunicked, seated on chairs because their poor legs were so stiff and inconvenient, plumed hats laid awkwardly on the tessellated floor beside them, engaged in a colloquy with an Indian potentate and his court, men with watchful faces and loose robes who lounged at ease on cushions.

Mr Armstrong, the old keeper, came in. He was wearing a three-piece suit and, unlike anyone else there, a silk tie. Christopher's bespoke finery, passed on to him by Lil. Mark Brown, who had been sitting next to Francesca, stood up to take his elbow and lead him to a seat. Jamie slipped into Mark's place and raised his glass to all of us, saying 'To glasnost'.

'We were talking about the other big story,' said Nicholas, 'the one of which, as Selim rightly reminds us, he is part.'

For a second Jamie looked blank then said, 'Oh yeah, the fatwa.'

His off-handedness annoyed me more than it ought to have. I said, 'Yes, the fatwa. Which has come as such a nasty shock to you people here because you think the only significant others in the world's affairs are other white Europeans.'

'Oh, come off it,' said Jamie.

Nicholas said, 'Our coverage of Middle Eastern affairs is generally considered to have been pretty thorough.'

Francesca said, 'I can assure you my days are absolutely jam-packed with seminars on the Iranian Question. The Iraqi Question. And of course we'd all be out of a job if it hadn't been for the Palestinian Question keeping us all running around in circles for the past half-century and more.'

Jamie interrupted. When we were all young he could be very entertaining when drink loosened his tongue. Now, though, it makes him belligerent. He leant across the table and said, as though hurling his words into my face, 'I can't stand all this self-pitying drivel. I've spent most of my evenings for the past six weeks with a pair of Turkish Muslims and they're as concerned as any other Berliner is about what's going on. The way you're talking – it's over. Antediluvian. Dividing the world up religion by religion. That's just not the way it is.'

Francesca was saying, in her talking-slowly-to-the-idiot way, 'In fact, Jamie, we all think religious affiliations are still highly significant. In the Arab world especially.'

Jamie and I were glaring at each other.

Nell came towards us, her child sleeping on her shoulder. Her hair was straight, with grey in it. Her dress was dark blue, plain, quite long. She looked exhausted. She was thinner. I thought – as I had never thought when she was a girl – that she was beautiful. She put her hand on Jamie's shoulder, and he reached up without looking round, and laid his own paw on it. She lifted the baby down and left her in Jamie's arms, smiled at me with her face but not her mind, and went to join Armstrong and Lil. Jamie barely looked at his daughter, but his arms closed gently around her, cradling her. Francesca was still talking. I watched the baby's tiny wet mouth working, sucking a dream of a nipple perhaps. Saliva pooled between lips as dainty as rose petals. My boy's lips were plump and purple. On the table between us there were grapes that had been dipped in syrup so that, cooled, each was encased in a glassy skin of sugar. Still sleeping, Jemima blew a perfect bubble, just their size, and just as magically combining the properties of translucence and formal perfection and extreme fragility.

I couldn't bear it. What blew me, blundering, from my seat, in blind search of somewhere secluded in which to break down, was nothing to do with religious affiliations or the realignment of power-blocs in the post-Cold War world. It was the simple yearning of an animal for its young, the kind of pain that makes a cow whose calf has been taken away from her bellow all night through in the stall, or sets a cat prowling up and down a house croaking out her dismay when her kittens are gone. The kind that makes men whose wives have left them, taking their children, into drunks and obsessives, addled by vindictiveness and self-pity.

My son has learnt to blow kisses. He thinks kisses are called blowies. Blowie blowie, he says, climbing my legs as I sit in my chair, climbing as doggedly as a sherpa trudging up a Himalaya. Blowie blowie. Snuffling and nuzzling at my knees as though to remind me how kissing is done. And then, when I lift him, his chortling filling my ear with damp warmth. Blowie blowie.

I was undone. I was mad, but also abruptly cured of madness. I would go back at once, the very next day. Mrs Rossiter – Lil – had come to me weeks before. She'd tapped on the door of the hut and said, 'Have you got a moment?' and we'd sat on the rattan chairs by the pool while she said, 'I don't know how you're placed, Selim. I mean for money and so on. But if there's anything you need, you know, you can ask. I don't suppose you want to be the Hermit of the Hut for ever. It'd be silly for you to be stuck here for lack of the airfare.' Then she'd changed the subject and we'd talked pleasantly enough about Kashmir. She'd been there in the '50s. She'd found the houseboats on Lake Dal ravishingly pretty, she said. Had I noticed that the fretwork decoration of my hut's eaves had been inspired by them? (I hadn't – the imitation was barely approximate.) She didn't seem to know that Srinagar was a lost paradise for my people.

I was resentful at the time. She's trying to get rid of me, I thought. She's bribing me to go away. Now I just thought, She's right.

I went into the library and Nicholas followed me. He gave me water to drink, and a monogrammed handkerchief. I couldn't speak. He said, 'Just take your time, and if there's anything I can help with, tell me.'

There wasn't. He is too smug, too much at home here.

Eventually I could control my voice sufficiently to get out, 'Where's Antony?' I don't know exactly why I wanted him. I suppose I scented a vulnerability in him that matched my own. His secret work: the pathos of the fact that it's a secret everybody knows. I thought he would understand why he shouldn't ask for explanations. He came. He led me out.

'Let's blow,' Guy used to say, when a party bored him. I blew, and then I was blown away.

*

There was no transitional stage. There was breathless calm. Then there was storm. A watcher in the park would have seen trees thrashing, bending, their leaves stripped, their branches snapping, their roots straining, while for another infinitesimally small moment others stood nearby serenely immobile, not yet seized by the onrush. The noise came first. Then the tremendous punch of invisible energy. Then the blasting torrent of air.

Some creatures had foreseen it. Worms and small rodents burrowed deep. Fish nosed into mud. Creatures made for standing flattened themselves. It didn't help them much. Things not made for flying flew and became missiles. Things not made for lying were flung down, crashing onto whatever was beneath them. Lupin, too deaf and foolish to sense the danger, waddled out the door Antony had left open and was bowled over and dashed against the wall of the kitchen yard, his back broken.

Inside the house there was a sound as of a bombardment. Goodyear took charge. All windows closed. All shutters closed. All doors shut. Fires extinguished. The smoke blown back down the chimney made the air acrid. There were enough candles lit already to save them from groping in the dark when the electricity cut out, but the flames flew horizontally sideways. 'Torches,' shouted Mark Brown. There were some in the pantry.

Benjie herded people out of the drawing room, where the long French windows creaked and vibrated, and over to the lee side of the house, to the marble hall with its massive sustaining columns. 'This was built to last,' he said. 'Should be all right here. We'll wait it out.' Antony had a knob like a cartoon character's on his forehead. He kept saying, 'What about Selim? Shouldn't we go looking for him?' 'No point,' said Goodyear. 'He knows where we are, but we'd never find him. He'll have found somewhere to lie low.'

They waited. They were excited and afraid. Time went by. And then, when nothing much was happening but more soughing and roaring and battering, they were bored. Jemima wailed, however much her parents shushed her and rocked her, and spat out the teat of the bottle they offered her.

'Where's Mrs Slatter?' asked Mark Brown.

'She didn't come,' someone said. 'She said it wasn't a night for being out in.' There was a pause. Of course no one really believed the old lady had magical powers. But still.

Holly came downstairs. 'Guy's sleeping through all this,' she said to Flora. 'Should I wake him?'

'No,' said Benjie. 'No, best leave him be. His room's on the safer side of the house.'

The wind flattened itself to the thinness of a sheet of paper and tore under the massive double doors, lifting the polar-bear-skin rug and rattling the pictures on the walls. The temperature had fallen steeply. Holly and Flora went upstairs and returned with armfuls of blankets and eiderdowns. People began to bed down on the floor, looking in the weird light of torch-beams like an army encamped.

The wind's hullaballoo erased all other sound. Afterwards they all agreed how extraordinary it was that they hadn't heard the noise the great cedar made when it tore up its own roots and toppled towards the house, its upper branches smashing half a dozen windows in the garden wing.

A quarter of Norris's beech avenue was felled by the storm, each great tree bearing another down so they lay with roots entangled in each other's fallen crowns. The furthermost trees crashed onto the wall, reducing it to a low-lying jumble of stones over which the terrified fallow deer leapt, escaping its enclosure, as their forebears had been pointlessly trying to do for over three hundred years.

*

Shortly after the almighty din gave way to an eerie quietness, a dawn with no birdsong, Guy began to move his long hands, alternately clutching and smoothing the crewelwork bedcover Flora had spread over him. An hour later he died. All that time Benjie and Flora were beside him, Benjie in a chair, with his head bent, praying, Flora lying alongside Guy on the bed. He didn't speak, but he fixed his eyes on hers as though their connected eye-beams could keep him grappled to the consciousness from which he was slipping away.

Benjie stirred. Flora glanced over at him, just for a moment. Guy's eyes wandered and dimmed. When she turned her gaze back to his she could find no purchase. The connection was gone. She knew he was dead but she waited a while before she said, very softly, 'He's stopped breathing,' and then turned on her back. The position she had held for so long had become excruciating. Benjie took Guy's hand, immobile now, and kissed it, muttering.

How strange he is, this husband of mine, she thought. We all have someone we talk to in our minds. Benjie has God, and I never even knew it. I have Guy. She wondered whether she would still address her thoughts to him. She thought she would.

Benjie was sobbing, and talking aloud to Guy now. She knew there were people who thought the two men had been lovers. She wondered whether it was true – it was a matter of indifference to her. Benjie loved sex, as she had plenty of reason to know, and no conventional sense of propriety would have held him back. But Guy – she didn't think Guy would have wanted to try anything so incestuous. He'd had liaisons with older men, it wasn't that, but he was exogamous. She suspected he was a masochist. He quested through parks and clubs and along empty shopping streets at night, exchanging glances with strangers reflected in the lit windows of clothes shops, in pursuit of difference and titillating pain. There are two kinds of promiscuous people, she thought. Those like Benjie, who just love to do it. And those like Guy, who are barely interested in pleasure, for whom sex is an adventure of the mind. None of that mattered very much. It was his voice she'd miss. His contralto laugh. His excitable body, always twisting, curving. Guy never stood up straight.

There was something unfamiliar about the light. She went to the window. And then out into the gallery, and all the way around it to the triple-arched window on the other side of the house. What she saw was so hard to comprehend she stood there for a long time, shivering. Then she went back to Benjie. He stood up. They were both still fully dressed, and in their mouths was the dirty taste of sleeplessness. He held her. They rocked on their feet. They didn't speak. Neither wanted to be the one to say futile, comforting things. She began to cry loudly, with a lot of tears and snot. She had never been a dainty girl. At last she managed to say, 'The cedar's down. So many trees down. Hundreds of years. Nell and Dickie were little children when I came here. I hadn't even met you. There were peacocks. They'd been here for hundreds of years.' Benjie crooned and rocked her. 'And fucking Manny,' she said suddenly. 'He was filming. I stole the place from Lil and Christopher and then I let him in. I made the puncture.' Benjie said over and over again, 'It's not your fault.' He didn't know what she was talking about. He said, 'Do you want to stay with him?' She looked startled. She said, 'No, no . . .' and then, 'His father. We must tell his father . . .' And then, as though she'd only just noticed, 'We never had a child.'

*

A very old woman walked along the periphery of the park. A hump had grown between her shoulders, pushing her head forward, but she held herself as upright as it permitted her to do. A mess of torn branches rose to the height of the wall on her right, driven and dumped there by the wind.

The path was repeatedly obstructed by fallen trees. When she found them she picked her way carefully around, past brambles and the great pits revealed by torn-up roots. She sang to herself as she went.

Her granddaughter ran after her, and took her arm. Holly. It was bright and still. Everything had been turned over, churned up. Clots of wet leaves had lodged themselves in the crooks of high branches. The dead bracken and grass lay flat to the ground. Branches that had fallen a century ago and lain peacefully to moss over and rot had been upended. Everything was glossy, dark and wet.

'Don't you want to sit down,' said Holly.

'No,' said Meg Slatter. 'This I must see.'

There were no birds singing, none of the usual rustlings and peckings and tiny crepitations. From the house it seemed that each fallen tree opened a gap, stripping the landscape bare piece by piece. Down here, among the fallen branches, the wreckage of the trees formed new barriers. It was hard to know where they were.

'Mrs Rossiter went out early too,' said Holly. 'Most of them are asleep still.'

By the time they reached the junction of the wall and the avenue the sun was fully up and the haws on the fallen twigs were glistening.

'There'll be birds that never come back,' said Meg.

The wind must have come straight down the avenue, so neatly had the colossal trees fallen one upon the next. The two last in line – giants both – had crushed the wall, leaving the wrought-iron gates standing. Rigid black lace, the tallest thing around.

'Guy died,' said Holly.

'I'm very sorry to hear it. Very sorry. They kept the plague out of here once. They shut the gates. Kinder times now.'

They could see two tractors in the distance, by the crossing of the avenues. The mirrors had fallen and smashed. Jagged reflections came off them, throwing shards of light back up into the pale sky.

'Brian Goodyear knows what to do,' said Mrs Slatter.

Lil Rossiter was sitting on the tumbled stones. In that wrecked and rumpled landscape she looked extraordinarily neat. She rose and came towards them. She nodded to Holly but addressed herself to old Meg.

'Your godson would have been thirty-eight,' she said.

'You never forget the day,' said Meg.

They walked together round the end of the gate, supporting each other over the unstable heaps of stone. Deer watched them uneasily from among bare and toppled trees. 'They don't know where to go now they're out, poor things,' said Holly. The older women glanced round, but didn't pause.

The forest had shrunk. Where stands of mature trees had closed off the view, now there were gaps and openings and unflattering light. Rides that had been passages through dense woodland were exposed. Groupings of trees that had grown around each other had been decimated, so that instead of accommodation and symmetry there were meaningless distortions and ugly vacancies. The lakes, always before revealing themselves gradually, as glimmerings through leaves, were now instantaneously apparent.

The meeting-house's garden was, extraordinarily, intact. Its position at the bottom of the slope had sheltered it. On the curved stone bench at its centre, slumped awkwardly sideways, sat Selim.

Holly ran back to summon one of the tractors. Meg and Lil stayed with him. He was incoherent, and one of his arms appeared to be broken. He spoke very quietly. The colour came and went in his face, from grey to dun and back again. Lil held his good hand and he talked in a whisper, of his wild night. Of how he had crawled and flown, and how he thought it would be less dangerous to run with the wind than to struggle against it, and how impossible it was to keep up with its pace. How it had knocked him down and tossed him and slammed him against hard things, and how hard things had battered him. How dark it had been, how hard to breathe, that was the worst of it. How he was so whirled about that he was like a paper bag tossed, how he came over the gap in the wall and then fell and rolled, his arm so tortured that he screamed all the way as he tumbled down the slope, but the scream was just a part of the wind and how he fetched up in a ditch against the chapel wall. The terror, after the churning and the blasting of the wind, to be returned to a situation in which he had to move himself, and found that he couldn't. The wailing all night long, and then at last the strangeness of silence when the storm passed. The bathos. As though an aggressor had fallen upon him and attacked and beaten him and forced him to draw on all the strength and courage that was in him and then, all of a sudden, had smiled and waved and gone away.

When it was light he saw where he was, and dragged himself into the little garden where he knew he could be seen.

'I must go now,' he said, his voice more feeble each time he said it. 'I must go home.'

'Yes,' said Lil. 'You will, but first we must get you patched up.'

They laid him on the trailer and heaped branches around him so that he would be less shaken as they lugged him up to the house, lurching over the grass because all the drives were blocked. Holly wrapped her coat around him, and wedged her own body against his, to try to warm him, and hold him together. The doctor had only just come for Guy – there had been so many calls that night. When he saw Selim he said, 'Let the dead bury the dead – this one I can do something for,' and strapped Selim's arm and helped him very gently into the back of his car, and said, 'I'll take him to the Radcliffe – I'm going there now. You won't get an ambulance this side of night.'

Five days later Selim went to London, where his cousin cared for him, and his nephews taught him to play mah-jong one-handed, and thence, eventually, he went home to Lahore.

Antony

It took a while for the significance of that charade in the hotel in Berlin to dawn on me. I wasn't the identifier, or not only that. I was the identified. They'd never trusted me before – I was idiotically shocked when I realised it – but that flickering eye contact between me and a near-stranger had corroborated my story. Giraffe-man told me afterwards, 'The value of your information was thereby greatly enhanced.' His diction was as robotic as ever. An advantage for them. For me, though, an enhancement of risk. Had I now to fear umbrellas?

As it turns out, or as it turns out so far anyway, no, I did not.

I was once so envious of the younger men's freedom. Now

they're dying for it. And here am I, Antony the dapper art-dealer, Antony the spy, alone in my austerely elegant house that no one will muss up again. How intimately transgressive it felt when Jack first started dropping his jeans, unfolded, onto my bedroom floor and tapping the tiny marmalade-coloured hairs from his electric razor onto the bathroom's green marble. Alone again, poor Antony, poor *old* Antony now, love and politics both having failed me, but alive, alive-O.

*

Meg Slatter and Lil Rossiter each declined a seat on the tractor. 'I'll come back for you later in the Land Rover, then,' said the man Goodyear had sent. 'Don't run away.' They sat. The mosaic pavement that had survived nearly seventy human generations muffled in damp leaf-mould, whose every tessera had been nosed by legions of worms or scuttled over by myriad centipedes and woodlice, was now preserved beneath Perspex. It looked desiccated, like the two old women's skin.

'You'd have been a grandma, now,' said Meg.

'Only if Fergus'd married. So I'd have lost him that way.'

'"Not losing a son, but gaining a daughter," that's what Brian Goodyear said when his boy married our Holly.'

Lil blew out her lips like an irritated horse. She couldn't abide cliché.

Meg laughed. 'Mr Christopher used to do that when he was just a tiny maggot of a thing.'

'He loved you before he loved me,' said Lil.

Meg didn't deny it. 'I was pretty much a child too, when I was nursery-maid,' she said. 'But he'd mind me. Yes. And wave his little arms.'

'And Fergus loved you best.'

'Holly says that too. Says her girls look up and start twittering when I open the door. It's not about loving, though. You need your parents, but you need someone else too. That's what godmothers are for.'

They sat quiet for a while. Meg's head trembled persistently.

Lil said, 'Tell me what happened to the two blue boys.'

1665

All day I have been jostled and incommoded. I hoped to sleep at Oxford, but the bridge was barricadoed and guarded by men with muskets. I left the highway and cantered on to Woodstock by hidden tracks I remembered from my previous sojourn in these parts. There, the migrants on the road being fewer, the local people had yet to harden their hearts against them. There were lodgings to be had by first-comers, but not by me. I was repeatedly turned away. I arrived at this inn on a crossroads after dark, rain-sodden, hungry and fretful. I count myself singularly fortunate to have found a bed here, albeit one I am likely to share with vermin and, if I am unlucky, with some late-arriving fellow-traveller.

There is a great hubbub below. I feared I would have to wait a tedious while for my supper. But by the time I had freed myself from my outer garments, which clung to me like waterweed to a drowning man, the servant was knocking at my door. A party had just departed in haste, he said, leaving half their repast unconsumed. He hoped I would not be too dainty to avail myself of their leftovers – the kitchen being so hurried that it might be a considerable time before any fresh meal could be prepared. I gave him a coin and declared myself to be barely acquainted with the concept of daintiness, and he accordingly left me a dish of stew, somewhat less than hot, but savoury. The rushlight is too feeble to let me know for certain what I have eaten. Some scraps of dark meat, venison perhaps, with brown onion-gravy and carrots. The fire is just sufficient to raise a steam from my coat. My fatigue is so extreme as to deny me rest. All my muscles are jumping like hares. I write now to calm myself ready for sleep, rather than in any hope of arriving at a judicious understanding of the day I have passed.

One word has set this multitude on the road. A word more potent than avaunt or abracadabra, or than all the hocus-pocus of witches and witch-hunters. Plague.

In any great cataclysm there are those who refuse to recognise good grounds for fear. These are they who loiter in their houses as the flaming magma oozes down the volcano's flank, confident that it will cool and harden before it reaches their gardens' bounds. These are they who, when the enemy pours in through the shattered gates of a city, lean genially from their upper windows, loudly declaring their faith that the newcomers will abstain like well-schooled seminarians from loot and rapine. Some of them survive to boast of their sangfroid in the face of danger: some do not. There are still many thousands of Londoners of this kind, going about their business in the city.

Many more, though, have shut up their houses and, having deputed some trusted friend to keep a watch on shop or warehouse, have gathered together their families and set out on foot. Some have relatives in the countryside with whom they hope to find a refuge. Others give no thought to where they are going, but flee, headlong, as though from a fire.

Several times today I have refused extravagant sums of money, offered me for my good Bess. She is a dependable cob, and strong enough, but two months ago I could scarcely have got the price of a saddle for her. For the past week, though, it has been impossible to come by a horse, or even a donkey, within twenty miles of London. It strikes me that for one who does not scruple to feed upon the despair of others, a calamity like the one now upon us creates fertile ground for the flourishing of a fortune.

I have come from St Albans, where I have been seeing to the beautification of Lord Verulam's meadows. The chain of lakes at Wychwood have provoked such admiration that I am kept of a bustle satisfying clients who wish to follow the vogue for pleasure-grounds interrupted by sky-reflecting expanses of water. Absorbed for two happy weeks in thoughts of drainage and sluicegates, and in visions of placid waters with great platters of water-lily leaves afloat upon them, I have heard the news from London only intermittently and as it were muffled. My Lord and Lady Verulam would talk of whether it were advisable to send servants to retrieve their fine clothes from their house on the Strand, lest, the plague augmenting in the coming weeks, it might become inconvenient to return to town. I barely listened.

Once I had passed without the walls bounding Lord Verulam's park, though, the drama unfolding itself in the unhappy city forced itself upon my attention. For the past four days I have been journeying in an arc around the northern reach of London's larder-lands. From these orchards and gardens and small farms wagons go daily, in ordinary times, to feed the great mass of urban humanity who, like drones in a beehive, occupy themselves with their curious impractical businesses, depending upon others' labour for the wherewithal to eat. Now those fields have endured a visitation as strange and grievous as the cloud of locusts that descended upon Egypt.

It was not just the roadway that was crowded. The meadows and moors have grown populous. Behind every hedge I saw encampments. It is fearful how quickly a city can dismantle itself. That which takes centuries to make can be unmade in seven nights. Prosperous merchants, accustomed to tapestried walls and painted ceilings, are now vagrants. They shelter in poor huts hastily constructed from logs and brushwood, the contrivances of unhandy citizens who never before so much as thatched a pigsty. Elsewhere a cloak, hung upon a staff, is all the lodging. Each camp was teeming with people; gaggles of children in fine clothes grown dirty, elders who sat upon the ground as though stunned to find themselves lifted by dire circumstances from their chairs at the fireside and deposited out of doors, to endure hunger, fear and rain.

Farmhouses have barred doors and boarded windows. The villages have closed in upon themselves. Carts have been pulled crosswise at the approaches to greens. Piles of brushwood obstruct the roads, until each little settlement bristles, like a hedgehog tightly rolled in self-defence. There is no knowing, these days, upon whose shoulder the angel of death may be squatting.

The country people are not unkind. In Buckinghamshire I saw how matters are contrived. The migrants send their headmen to converse, by shouting across a field, with those from a village. An arrangement is made. The travellers leave money – then withdraw to a considerable distance. The villagers, all muffled up, sally forth and leave foodstuffs, then scuttle back into their houses as though a wild beast were after them. Then at last the wanderers can approach and carry off the vegetables or pails of milk that have been left.

The wonder is that these exchanges have, to date, been conducted in so orderly a manner. I fear that it cannot last. Extremity of fear is a great undoer of civility. There will be ever fewer havens for those unhoused.

Hour upon hour I passed forlorn settlements where domesticity seeks to preserve itself without roof or walls. Cooking pots without hearths to set themselves upon, coverlets without beds, buckets without wells or pumps, groups of men discoursing, not snug in a tavern, or beneath a church porch, or upon an accustomed street corner, but in the vacancy of a field black with burnt-out stubble.

I shall be glad to get to Wychwood, to be once more in that blessed enclosure. A morning's ride will bring me there.

*

The wind smelt of human excrement. All day long Meg Leafield sat near Wychwood's iron gates. She sold nosegays with no gaiety in them, and she scanned the faces of the passers-by. At nightfall she took up the piece of sacking on which she had laid out her merchandise and walked round the outside of the park wall to a place where it curved like the belly of a serpent that has swallowed a goat. There she would lean against the stones of the wall, which being scarcely more than two years out of the quarry were still sharp-cut and clean. She mumbled and sang an hour or more.

The moon rising, she strayed through the woods, filling her sack with stalks of comfrey and feverfew and pennyroyal, and the thick stems of stinking hellebore.

*

As I breakfasted this morning the publican told me, 'I'll take no more travellers this season. You, sir, are the last.' The morning was warm, but the fire in the room was banked up, as though to fumigate it. He stood by the door and kept his head averted as he spoke.

Good weather is unwelcome. There are those who believe that the sun, heating the ground, draws infection into the air. The walkers, who fill the main road westward as the spring thaw fills a river, hamper their own progress in their attempts to protect themselves. Already faint, they wrap kerchiefs across their mouths and noses. Breath, the very essence of life, is feared as a poison.

The people of the exodus are accompanied every step of the way by a lesser horde of conjurors and wizards. All along the flanks of the slow-moving crowd, wherever a gap in ditch or hedge allows it, some charlatan has set out his stall, selling the hope of survival in the form of amulets, or flasks of murky water. There are prophets, *soi-disant*, and preachers, their voices hoarse with shouting of repentance and salvation to the shuffling vagrants. Their apprentices, snot-nosed boys with the cropped heads and starved faces of unwilling novices, make their difficult way along the verges. There are ordinary pedlars there too, risking infection for the sake of inflated profit, selling baskets full of cobnuts and plums, but these youths' wares are less wholesome. They are hawking quills of paper on which are scrawled the prayers or blessings or arcane dicta of sorcerers dead a thousand years.

Now that I am clear of that desperate crowd I am ready to concede that such chaff may at least bring comfort to troubled minds, however insubstantial the physical benefits. This morning, though, I saw only parasites sucking money from the limp purses of the wretched.

A young matron walked ahead of me. Her man was pulling a kind of handcart, laden with blankets and other stuff, a baby riding atop the heap. An old man was with them, now grasping the sides of the cart for support, now leaning on the woman, whom I took to be his daughter.

As I approached Wood Barton I found Meg Leafield. She sat alongside her wares. Muslin bags full of dried herbs. Posies of the same. Amulets made of twig and bone. A curiously shaped stone to which was attached a scrap of paper announcing that it was a piece of a thunderbolt launched from heaven. It is curious to see how the plague has driven even reformers back to the idolatry that seemed to have died out in these islands a hundred years ago and more. I do not believe Cecily would have wished to see her protégée trading in such rubbish. Recognising me, Meg scrambled to her feet and made as though to draw back into the trees.

'Don't go, Meg,' I said. 'I am glad to meet with a face known to me. Mine has been a weary ride.'

As I spoke the marching column seemed to check. The people around me paused, and as others came up behind they began to stumble over each other. There was shouting. I saw a woman hoist two infants, one beneath each arm, and lug them with remarkable dispatch through a ditch and up into the woods which pressed close upon both sides of the road. Others followed. What had been a column, albeit one whose ragged order would have shamed a military man, broadened and dispersed, as a flood spreads shallowly over water meadows when a stream's forward progress is impeded by a fallen log.

Ahead, across the road into the village, I saw a barricade made of tree-trunks and furze branches. The travellers were too listless to attempt to force their way in, even had they been so minded, but I saw some men in Lord Woldingham's livery standing before the obstruction, staves in hand. They watched silently as the travellers cast about, then passed by the village along a muddy path that circled it.

When the family in front of me arrived at the division of ways, the husband set down the handles of the cart and, leading the older man by the arm, walked steadily towards the barricade. Stopping at a discreet distance he called out loudly, 'Will no one have pity on these white hairs? My father is too feeble for more journeying. Will no one take him in?'

He then coaxed the old man, who seemed to have no will of his own left, to sit himself upon a low wall bounding a garden-plot and, leaving him there, went back to his wife and child. 'In God's name,' he called out in a great voice, 'show that you are Christians. Show that you are the sons of that God, whose quality is ever to have mercy.' His wife was weeping. He took up the cart handles again and, chivvying her on, went along the side road, looking back repeatedly as he went. The men at the barricade stood like statues. 'Have you not fathers of your own?' he shouted, as he came to the bend in the road that would take him out of sight. A girl came up from within the village, and seemed about to climb the barricade. One of its guards pushed her roughly back.

Meg was at my horse's head. She took hold of the reins and led me onto a path, much overgrown with bracken, that ran obliquely down the riverbank. I had not known there was a ford there but we splashed through, Meg's dress kilted up around her knees. The opposite bank was steep. I had to cling to the mane as my horse mounted it. Meg came up on all fours. We had arrived, as it were aslant, at Wychwood's main gate. She darted past me to rap on a small shutter in the side of the gate-lodge. The keeper came out, opened the gate barely wide enough for my horse to pass, then swung it back and replaced the bolts, his boy helping him, for they were massive.

I turned to thank Meg but she was no longer with me. The gate-keeper said, 'She stays outside.'

As I rode up the drive one part of my mind was marvelling at the luxuriance of the horse-chestnut trees I had planted on either side of it. Another part was writhing under the painfulness of the scenes I had witnessed. If, as some believe, this plague is a trial sent to find out who, amongst the living, is deserving of salvation, then I do not think I will have passed muster. Selfish, I thought. Cowardly. Weak. And unable even to say, 'I preserve myself so that I may preserve my children.' My only claim to usefulness is that I have made delightful a few patches of ground, but this, my finest creation, has flourished in my absence. I should have given up my horse.

*

Cecily Rivers's mother was dead, and Cecily lived at Wood Manor with only two servants. There Mr Goodyear visited her.

'"Him that cometh to me,"' he said, '"I will in no wise cast out." When Preacher Rivers was here we kept those words ever in mind.'

Cecily sat by a window so that the grey morning light fell on her needlework. Only a few more silken leaves to stitch. The piece, bundled on the bench beside her, was too large for convenience. From time to time she clenched her eyelids together as though her eyes pained her.

'There were five families sleeping in the barn last night,' she said, 'and more in the stables. They endanger each other. If one falls ill, all will. We set out a table for them in the yard and place food and ale there, while they keep out of sight.'

'You do what a Christian should.' Goodyear shut his mouth tight. Cecily looked up and met his eye.

'I do not have the responsibilities that puzzle others. My way is plain.'

Goodyear, standing, and turning his hat in his hands, looked out of the window and saw Edward pushing a small girl on a rope-swing slung from an apple-bough.

'You should require the children also to keep themselves apart,' he said. 'Even the prettiest infant can carry the taint.'

*

Lady Woldingham has taken control of the house. I underestimated her. She is an excellent match for her husband. This morning she summoned me to the square room at the centre of the *piano nobile* in the new wing, which she has made her own. She met me standing among her people, and led me to the window.

'This is the brightest gem in the necklace you designed, is it not, Mr Norris; the lozenge at the centre of your imaginary rug. And do you know that Lord Woldingham was content to let this room, which overlooks it, be treated as a passageway?'

She was talking about the parterre beneath.

'I hope you notice that I have caused your instructions as to colour to be obeyed precisely. Wormwood and lavender. Silver, grey-blue, sky-blue and white. I apologise for the intrusion of yellow, but one cannot persuade daisies to produce blue stamens. At dusk, when they close their eyes, the effect is purer.'

She was laughing at me, and I was glad to see her playful. She is tiny and pale still, but regal. She invited me to a seat. Her secretary laid some plans before me.

'When you last had those papers in your hands,' she said, 'they depicted an ideal. Now, a reality. The wall encircles us entirely,' she said. 'It is my wish, and my husband's, that all who work for us upon this land should find a safe refuge within it. We have space within the park for all our dependants.

'I have given directions for the construction of sleeping quarters. Barracks of a kind. Not luxurious but proof against wild weather. Those who choose to shelter there can bring their own featherbeds and such. We have venison, mutton, fowl and in the lake there are fish. We have instructed Mr Green to dig up four acres of parkland and plant them with edible roots. You can imagine how he laments at having to occupy himself with beets and potatoes when he is accustomed to fill his mind only with roses. His men, however, are glad to know there will be vegetables for their winter soup. The barns of the home farm are well stocked with grain. We have our own brewery. There is no need for anyone from this place to venture out into a world polluted by disease.

'Would I, do you think, Mr Norris, have made a competent quartermaster?'

I bowed. I was a little taken aback.

'You came to talk about ornamental waterworks, and so you shall, but we have all been obliged to postpone some of our plans. My Lord and I have enquired about your movements, Mr Norris. We know that you have been out of London for some months. We do not fear contamination from you. Once provision has been made for this present emergency, we will take pleasure in discussing with you the resumption of work on your designs. I trust you are pleasantly accommodated. I have asked them to make up your accustomed room.'

A gentleman came lollingly to us and leant over the table to see the plans. I wanted to snatch them from him. The wall is built, the avenues planted. They are there for all to see. The plans are only a representation of something now irreversibly made public, and yet I was jealous of them. I was like the dog who, having a cherished tidbit, seeks to consume it privately beneath a laurel bush. Something stirred in my memory, another dispossession. The gentleman was Sir Humphrey de Boinville, my Lady's brother.

'How droll it is,' he said. 'These drawings are so meticulous. They look as neat and pure as a young miss's hem-stitching.' He was clearly a *cognoscento* of stitching: the lace on his cuffs was some of the finest I have seen, and his stockings were ornamented with clocks. 'And yet,' he went on, 'the park is full still of thistles. You are an idealist, Mr Norris. You do not draw the real.' It is a thought I have often had myself, and yet I disliked him for it. He and my Lady were raised as papists. Sir Humphrey, Mr Rose has told me, is still fervent in that faith.

*

Oh my whirling thoughts. I have tired myself today by patrolling every hillock and covert of the park. I found the sentinels I posted over two years ago, my green young trees, all upright and faithful in their stations, and came back at dusk as pleased as a general whose captains have proved true. I thought to write, and then compose myself to rest. I laid down my pen, but take it up again to scrawl like an infatuated boy the one word that beats about my mind.

Cecily
Cecily
Cecily

I left here two years ago in a pother that was partly of my own making, partly whipped up by a drama into which I had wandered as oafishly as a performing bear straying onto a stage dressed for a court masque.

Cecily and her boy walking upon the water. That was a puzzle to which I held the key. The submerged causeway. I had discussed it at length with my employer: he declaring how much he doted on the illusion it rendered possible, how I was at all costs to preserve it; I retorting that, the water-levels changing as we dredged the lower lake, and built dams to hold back water for the upper ones, it would be more than I could do to keep the level of the water so precisely calibrated as to cover the hidden stones to barely the thickness of the peel of an orange. He saw the difficulty, but would not be deterred by it. 'Alas then, Mr Norris,' he said, 'we must recalculate our water-levels, must we not?' Then he put his arm through mine, the first time he had come so close.

We had walked out that day to view the little cedar tree, which mounted scarce to our knees but which will one day rise as high as the house, and cover a part of the garden with boughs as fragrant and umbrageous as those of which King Solomon sang. 'Ah Norris,' he said then, 'would that you and I might see that! Do you suppose that, once one has joined the heavenly host, one might occasionally be permitted to peep back down through a chink in the celestial sphere to observe how one's terrestrial ventures have prospered?'

Heresy, flawed cosmology, and mockery of me: I have learnt to hold silence and assume a peculiar expression, similar to that of a man stifling a hiccough, in response to such questions.

I remember that Mr Rose was observing us from the orangery. Lord Woldingham would manage the two of us, then, as adroitly as he manoeuvres the wooden balls when playing at pall-mall.

*

*Meg came to Wood Manor and rapped on the window by which
Cecily sat. Cecily opening, the old woman said, 'Mr Norris is
returned.' Cecily laid aside her work and the two women, arm in
arm, walked the afternoon away in the garden, going around and
around the sundial as though they were the shadow of its gnomon,
sweeping through the hours.*

*

After the fracas down by the lake that day two years ago, I made
my way back to the house, as bewildered in mind as I was bruised
in body. Mr Rose, finding his horse where we had left it, had
galloped ahead and forestalled me. As I toiled across the lawn I
saw him on the terrace talking urgently to Lord Woldingham. He
kept rising onto his tiptoes, and pushing his stumpy fingers
through his hair as though, agitated, he wished he could make
himself larger, and therefore more able to convey his agitation to
another. My Lord, sipping chocolate (the household was as yet
barely awake), his striped Turkish gown flapping open over his
mournful black, listened impassive.

When I came up he said, 'Mr Norris, you have had a puzzling
time of it here. I beg you to pardon us for having embroiled you
in our curious history.'

I said, as I would assuredly not have done had I been more
composed, 'I am owed no apologies. I would, though, be glad of
explanations.' What irked me most was that Rose was evidently
more privy to the family's affairs than I.

Lord Woldingham looked at me coolly. 'So would we all,' he
said. 'So would we all.'

A great convulsion of the state leaves its people hungry for
calm. It's a hunger that eclipses all other emotions. Had Prince
Paris been long deprived of food when he first clapped eyes on
Queen Helen, I believe he would have said to himself, 'Let
gallantry bide awhile,' and allowed her to pass from the room

399

unwooed, while he reached for a platter of meat. So might his opportunity have been lost, and myriad lives have been saved. In like manner the people of England, now, reach out and grab at tranquillity, thinking that teasing at contentious questions, doctrinal or political, is best left alone until their safety from further havoc is assured. I have come to understand that the workmen who set upon the dissenters' women down by the waterside that day were not animated by sectarian passion, but by detestation thereof. They, and all England with them, had resolved to wrap their consciences in oiled cloths, that they might live muffled but in peace. The Chapel folk were like annoying children who persist in asking, when the adults have decided on sophistry and accommodations, 'But did you not tell us God wills this? But surely you have said it is wrong to do that?' Sometimes the impulse to slap such children is not to be contained.

I will lay out the story as coherently as I can, now that enough time has passed for me to arrive at a sense of it. I do not pretend to understand it all.

Both Cecily and the boy Edward left Wychwood that day. I do not know when or whether I will see them again.

There is witchery here. This story begins in superstition, and so continues. That this is not congenial to me is of no importance. So it is, and so I must tell it.

When the wretched boy Charles died some people about the estate declared they had witnessed the consummation of an old prophecy. They said that it had been foretold that when the unrighteous returned to Wychwood the earth would gape and swallow up their offspring. It seems it was old Meg who recalled, or coined, this prophecy.

The boy Edward lived with Cecily and Lady Harriet at Wood Manor. I do not know from whence he came or whether it is true that he is the child of Cecily's body. He was a skilled musician, and he aspired to be a naturalist. He would go out foraging with Meg, returning with baskets full of roots and bark and grasses. She was teaching him, and she had inveigled her way into his mind, converting his desire for knowledge, which is like a reaching for the light, into an awe of mystery, which is its opposite.

During those sad days she told him that he was like young Charles, that they were cousins and therefore in some hazy way interchangeable, that he and he alone had the power to save the poor dead boy from an eternity of desolation. 'Would you leave him,' she asked, 'to snort on mud until doomsday?' Worked upon by her, he became fixed in the belief that only when he had disguised himself as the dead boy and cast himself into flowing water could Charles be washed clean of moral taint and permitted to enter paradise.

All of this I heard from Mr Rose. In the intervening time we have on several occasions found ourselves partnered again. My respect for him has steadily increased. I have recommended him to more than one of my patrons: I think he has done the same for me. He grew up at Wychwood, the son of a smith. The father was killed fighting for the King. As a kind of recompense my Lord Woldingham took the son with him into the Netherlands and apprenticed him to a master builder there. I mistook him for a demi-Dutchman when first I met him. There is a peculiarity about his manner of speech. I took it for the intonations of a foreigner, but it is the accent of one raised in these parts. Now he is as much the gentleman as I am, but his grandam was one of those crones whose cunning so scared the populace that they made a bonfire of her. She showed him how to draw a quincunx. He watched, and learnt geometry. In these rural educations science and sorcery are helpmeets, not rivals.

Cecily is a completely rational being, of that I feel sure. And yet she, and her mother when she lived, were tolerant of strange doctrines. I walked with her once in the secret garden I had made for Lady Woldingham in the woods. It's a quaint place, just without the park. The carts dragging implements in and tree-trunks out carved a track, but only temporarily. By now the under-growth will have thickened sufficiently so that the only access to the garden will be by a serpentine path scarce wide enough for two to walk abreast, and so curving that the walker sees a mere few feet before or behind, and comes upon the garden as upon a present hidden ready to surprise a mistress.

Cecily and I wandered there on the eve of young Charles's funeral. I do not know, because the workings of my own mind are sometimes as obscure to me as the contrivances of others', what I had hoped to gain by being so secluded with her. The round pond was collared with stone flags. A toad squatted on the marge.

I am fond of toads. The loose skin pulsating beneath their non-existent chins puts me in mind of an elderly lady who was a kind hostess to me when I was first from home. Their goggling eyes entertain me. I admire the dexterity with which they fish in the air for flies with tongues so fine and fast-moving few humans have knowingly seen them. I am mightily amused by the compla-cent manner in which they swallow down said flies, and shrug themselves back into immobility as though to say, 'Me? Fly? No, I assure you, sir, I know nothing about it.'

I am aware few people share this predilection of mine. I expected Cecily to draw back, or at best to ignore the creature. Instead she knelt beside it and tickled its back with a grass-stem. It was a big one. It would have overflowed my palm. 'You know, don't you, Mr Norris,' she said to me, as I awkwardly lowered myself down beside her, impeded by my stiff boots, 'you know how the paddock got his name?'

She then launched into a fable involving a dispute between a toad, a mouse and a raven, which ended with a false etymology. I barely listened. Her finger was now tracing the lines of the toad's back. The warty beast seemed to sink into itself, as though intent on avoiding any movement that might interrupt this unexpected caress.

She said, 'I am inclined to accept the doctrine of metempsychosis. It is not incredible to me that young Charles's soul might now be contained within this blob of a creature. At least as credible, anyway, as that he is nowhere, or in heaven.'

I was certain that we were not overheard, but habit made me afraid to be party to a heretical conversation. She saw it.

'It is very hard for the living to think about death,' she said. 'However often we may have seen it. A certain amount of speculation . . .' her voice faded. The toad swallowed elaborately.

'Meg has ideas that are still more strange,' she said. I had no interest in the ideas Meg entertained. Cecily made to rise to her feet. I held out my hand to help her. I kissed her hand. I kissed her palm. I pressed her hand to my face. By now standing, we fitted together as sweetly as the two halves of a broken piece of porcelain restored by a cunning mender. I had never before fully appreciated how lonely it is to be a human being. How, without knowing it, every part of myself, body and mind, had for all my life been enduring a lack. With only the gulping toad to witness it, with only the sunlight falling on dark green water to celebrate our epithalamium, that lack was, for that happy, happy hour, alleviated, and wholeness supplied.

The next day down by the lake I saw Cecily, the woman who had seemed ready to merge with me, separate herself incomprehensibly. I thought that there was a pact between us, though no words had sealed it, but she spoke to me strangely and then stepped away without leave-taking.

Abandoning terra firma to walk upon the water, she forsook reasonable thought and allied herself instead with magic. She also forsook me. I was a dog who chases a pheasant. The dog easily gains on the two-legged scurryer, but then is left astonished when the feathery thing, with a rattle and a whirring, takes to the air.

*

Last night I embarked upon my narrative, only to be waylaid by a love story. Today I intend to stick to my purpose. The story in which I have become embroiled is full of obscurity. I record it now so that one day, perhaps, I may understand it.

Cecily and Edward walked deliberately out onto the pond. The labourers surged past Rose, ignoring his attempts to deflect them. Their fury was the more alarming for the steadiness with which they set to their disgraceful task, of terrorising a crowd of women. I shouted unconnected words. It was for a while as though I was calling upon the wind to oblige me by dropping, or begging night not to fall. Violence filled the clearing. Then it was as though the men awoke from the nightmare which sent them sleepwalking so savagely into this peaceable assembly. The late wars have taught us that people of the female sex can be as belligerent as men, but these women defeated their attackers by passivity. There is only so long that a man, however brutal, can roughly treat a woman who offers him no resistance. Their arms fell, their cudgels were laid back upon their shoulders, their knotted ropes were coiled and reattached to belts.

Still Cecily and the boy walked on. The preacher whom I had seen before, Cecily's uncle, came to me.

'We are not much liked by the workmen whom his Lordship has introduced,' he said to me evenly. 'A story has got abroad that Charles Fortescue's death was a token that our presence at Wychwood contaminates the place.'

At the far side of the pond Cecily stepped onto the bank and turned for the first time. She must have seen the swarming masons, but she gave no sign of fear. Edward stood quite still upon the water, within arm's reach of her, his figure as trim and colourfully clad as a new toy soldier. Meg hallooed to them, a wordless call like a bird's, and Edward raised his arms, turned and stepped off the causeway and immediately was swallowed up. The water just beneath that bank is deep.

'This ritual is not our teaching,' said the preacher-uncle.

'But to seek for redemption, by whichever road, shows a good heart.'

I think Edward was gone from sight a full minute. The women began to moan and cry out. Then he was climbing up the bank, his hair, which had showed mouse-colour, blackened by wetness. In his hand was something bright. He tossed it into the air and it fell into the water – a red-gold fish as long as his hand. He pulled off his blue coat, all streaked with mud as it was, and left it lying. He ran off, barefoot, up a track which led into the beechwoods overhanging the lake on the other side and thence, at last, to a gate opening onto the Finstock road. Cecily followed.

The preacher threw his arms up skyward and hollered out 'Hallelujah', and then led his flock into the chapel. We heard their voices raised in song as we made our way back up the bank. On the track beneath us the carts were moving forward again, the carters calling out to their massive horses. Patient creatures that they are, they must have been thankful for the intermission in their morning's journey. For them, only, that strange episode was a simple relief.

*

Meg – You will welcome his return?

   Cecily – I will be civil.

   Meg – He is devoted to you.

   Cecily – If so, he has been exceedingly reticent about it.

   Meg – He fears to be thought a fool.

   Cecily (exasperated) – He is thought a fool! I think him one.

   Meg – My Lady's brother will be put out.

   Cecily – Do these people's beliefs mean so little to them? I cannot marry a papist. I cannot feel any regard for a papist who would marry me. He knows what I have been.

   Meg – Mr Norris will take no further step until he knows as much. In withholding knowledge from him you make him as nervous as a dog who barks at a familiar visitor when the man dons a hat. He cannot tell what you are.

*

Young Edward, and Cecily who was to him I knew not what, left Wychwood. Two years have since gone by. I, who had been so briefly complete, was once more a jagged shard. I begged my employer to help me understand what I had seen. He said, 'Some of those who are fond of this family have been engaged in foolish conjuring. My son's death has been the occasion for doings I cannot approve. Albeit well-meant.' On another occasion he said, 'This country has been warring upon itself for twenty years and more. We walk as through a battlefield still littered with weapons. Every step may see your foot come down upon a blade. My cousin's life has been as strange as any. People of our generation, Mr Norris, must be careful in what they expect of others whose history is unknown to them.'

I went then to Wood Manor and sat a pleasant but useless hour with Lady Harriet. Without her daughter to prompt her she spoke vaguely, her thoughts as inconsequential as the discarded short lengths of silk in her sewing basket. Meg Leafield was with her. I said, 'If I were to write Cecily a letter, could you ensure she received it?' I spoke as to the mother, but my eyes briefly met Meg's, and she gave a tiny nod.

The writing of that letter took me many hours of the night, but when it was finished it was barely four lines long. What I had to say could be contained in two sentences. It could have been said in two words. I do not know whether it reached her. I had no reply.

*

Meg – I hear the moaning every night now, there along the wall. Singing doesn't soothe them.

Cecily – Meg, watch what you say. For your own safety, remember, the dead have no tongues to speak. And for my sake too. I don't like to hear fantastic tales.

Meg – He said they would rise up again. And they will rise shouting with joy. How should they not have tongues?

Cecily – Let them be. It is the living with whom we must concern ourselves.

Meg – Today I sold near on a hundred posies. People offer me bed-sheets, pewter mugs, petticoats. A woman begged me to exchange an amulet for her baby's coral ring. I asked, did the mite not want it to mumble on, and she said she had buried him in a meadow near Henley. Her eyes were dry. There are some things one cannot allow oneself to feel, for fear of being consumed by the fury of it.

Cecily – You do good.

Meg – Rubbish. What I give them is rubbish. The herbs are good for chafed skin or an itching nose in springtime. They can't keep away the plague. I cheat them.

Cecily – Why then?

Meg – For money. And because they beg it of me.

Cecily – You risk your life.

Meg – Don't fall into that error, my dear. Don't treat people as though they were barrels of gunpowder ready to explode and kill all bystanders. How many apothecaries take sick from treating the desperate? None that I've heard of.

*

Here, those suspected of being diseased are kept without the wall. In London they are kept walled in.

Wherever a person is found to have the horrid marks upon his or her body, then the invalids, and all living with them, are boxed up in their houses and not suffered to come forth for three weeks or more after the marks of the disease have passed or the sufferer has died. Whole families are thus confined, their front doors nailed shut. Any window large enough to permit a person to pass through is barred. When one dies, the corpse is taken out at night and the door nailed close again. Passers in the street hear the whimpering of those within but none dare release them. In many, many families everybody dies. Those who survive do so only because of the kindness of those who leave a jug of milk or a loaf, or a few apples, on a window ledge which can be reached from within. Mr Rose has heard from an acquaintance in the city that Cecily was until lately one of those philanthropists. Whether Edward was still with her, he could not discover.

Lord Woldingham came upon me in the park this morning as I stood near to the old meeting-house, contemplating its roof-tree, which was all that I could see of it beyond the wall that now shuts it out. Mr Rose was with me. The slope down which we two had once hurtled so precipitately had been cleared of trees and boulders, and smoothed into a green swelling as featureless as the shoulder of a wave. Above it the wall rose, blank.

'I did this,' said Rose, 'but I do not like it. I have never otherwise known his Lordship mean-spirited.'

And there was our employer, cantering towards us.

A groom came up behind him leading a spare horse. 'Come, Mr Norris,' he said. 'I have yet to bid you welcome, but now I will immediately employ you. Ride with me.' For the next two hours we toured the park.

The ownership of land is not natural. The American savage, ranging through forests whose game and timber are the common benefits of all his kind, fails to comprehend it. The nomad travers-ing the desert does not ask to whom belong the shifting sands that extend around him as far as the horizon. The Caledonian shep-herd leads his flock to graze wherever a patch of nutritious green-ness shows amidst the heather. All of these recognise authority. They are not anarchists. They have chieftains and overlords to whom they are as romantically devoted as any European subject might be to a monarch. Nor are they communists. They do not say the land belongs to us all. Simply they do not consider it as a thing that can be parcelled out.

We are not so innocent. When humanity first understood that a man's strength could create goods to be marketed, that a woman's beauty was itself a commodity for trade, then slavery was born. So, since Adam learnt to force the earth to feed him, fertile ground has become too profitable to be left in peace.

This vital stuff that lives beneath our feet is a treasury of all times. The past: it is packed with metals and sparkling stones, riches made by the work of aeons. The future: it contains seeds and eggs: tight-packed promises which will unfurl into wonders more fantastical than ever jeweller dreamed of – the scuttling centipede, the many-branched tree whose roots, fumbling down into darkness, are as large and cunningly shaped as the boughs that toss in light. The present: it teems. At barely a spade's depth the mouldywarp travels beneath my feet: who can imagine what may live a fathom down? We cannot know for certain that the fables of serpents curving around the roots of mighty trees, or of dragons guarding golden treasure in perpetual darkness, are without factual reality.

How can any man own a thing so volatile and so rich? Yet we followers of Cain have made of our world a great carpet, whose pieces can be lopped off and traded as though it were inert as tufted wool. My Lord has a swathe of it.

'Come, Norris, I'll race you,' he said suddenly. He bent on his horse's neck and the fleet creature (it is half an Arab) knew without touch of spur what was required of it. My own mount took off after. I was fortunate to have idly knotted my fingers in its mane and so given myself secure purchase. We galloped madly up the avenue known as Tower Light. The trees I had seen planted flicked past me, the glare of the low sun, piercing my eyes, repeatedly interrupted by the shadows of the young trunks. Light dark light dark. One day this broad sweep will be as grandly walled and roofed as an abbey. Already its columns begin to rise.

My Lord pulled up at the junction of the two broad avenues, so that he stood like an equestrian statue at the focal point of my design. He wheeled his horse around. It spun like a dancer. 'See. See. See. See,' he said, pausing at each right angle to gesticulate.

Twelve o'clock – church tower. Three o'clock – the broad ride ending in the magnificent black iron gates, and beyond them a wall of forest foliage. Six o'clock – another church tower. Nine o'clock – where the lake lay beneath the angle of our eyeline, the house low before it, showed only vacancy: a patch of sky. 'We will fill that hole,' he said. He was excited. 'You have promised me a fountain, have you not, a column of water? And then, my boy dying, I lost my zest for such things. But now I see how fitting it would be. Where he sank down, something marvellous will spring up. We have worked to your plans. You are returned in time to celebrate the consummation of your design.'

We rode on. I had been awaiting an occasion when I could ask my question unobtrusively. That occasion not presenting itself, I was driven to abruptness.

'And your cousin, Miss Cecily? Is she returned?'

'Returned? Has Cecily been away?'

'I had thought she left Wychwood about the time I was last here.'

'Oh yes, I had forgot. And came back again. You will see her.'

He looked at me curiously, but he forbore to mock. My mind reeled.

'We will have a celebration for the first eruption of the fountain. We have much to do, Mr Norris. I wish it to be a show of quite shocking prodigality.'

It is a pleasure to work for Lord Woldingham. He has his freaks and he is not methodical, but his enthusiasm is a polished spur to those of us whom he charges to make his fancies real.

*

After dark the only sound to be heard along the road that ran through Wood Barton was the scuffling the dogs made as they nosed through dried leaves looking for scraps. Their search was disappointing. The villagers seldom had food to waste and, nowadays, what they could spare they kept to add to the pails full of edible stuff set out at dawn, beyond the bounds of the village, for the migrants. Meg Leafield came from the direction of the lodge, her gait made clumsy by the stiffness of her knees.

She paused by the sign of the Plough, and then slipped along an alleyway and rapped on a shutter. A voice called softly. She murmured something. A door opened.

She went into a room that smelt coldly of the earth of which its floor was made. The old man whom Norris had seen abandoned was lying on a straw bolster in a corner. There were sufficient covers to warm him, but he had cast them aside.

A woman who had been lying beside him on the floor struggled to her feet.

'Can you save him?'

Meg knelt and ran her hands swiftly under the man's arms, and along his scrawny flanks.

'No,' she said. 'Come outside.'

Outside the door the two women sat in silence, their backs against the wall of the house. Meg brought out a pipe and filled it with tobacco. They passed it back and forth, the whiteness of the clay visible when their brown fingers were not, so that it appeared to float between them. From within there came a gurgling sound, as of a drain unblocked. Meg laid aside the pipe and took the other woman's hand. They muttered words in unison.

Later they dragged a large bundle out of the house and down the village street, the dogs circling and sniffing, and went off with it into the woods. Three hours later they came out onto the road again, near to where the track led off towards Wychwood.

Meg said, 'Take what you need and go now. You can be dry and comfortable in the quarrymen's hut. Their work is done. No one will disturb you. I come each night after sundown to where the wall curves around our burial place. I will bring food. If in a month you are still sound it will be safe to come home. I will see that your little ones are cared for.'

The other woman was shaking. 'He was a gentle old man, bewildered by age,' she said, and her voice cracked.

'Let us pray he has not caused your death.'

'Or yours.'

'I don't know how it is,' said Meg, 'but these things do not touch me.'

*

Today I attended on Lady Woldingham, at her request.

'We are under siege,' she said, 'and our besieger is invisible and invulnerable.' I bowed.

She said, 'Everyone has a story to tell of a hearty fellow with no marks upon him, who sickened of a sudden, and died within hours.'

I wondered, was she thinking of me. She sat with a table in front of her, a prayer book open upon it. The chair she had indicated I should sit upon was pulled well back. I thought, Fear is corroding her spirit. Her two remaining children had not been seen out of doors for a week.

She sighed.

'My husband will have told you his plans for the fountain?'

'He has.'

'I have asked my physician to search each of the guests' bodies before I can think it safe for them to enter the house.'

My surprise must have been evident.

'Lord This, Lord That. They will all think great gentlemen like themselves should be exempt from such treatment. But when they find a bubo in groin or armpit their standing at court will help them not a jot.'

'Very true, my Lady.'

'And very banal, I know. I have become a bore.'

How was I supposed to answer her? I said, 'The plague is not an amusing topic.'

She and my Lord are both of less than average height, but she is by far the smaller. In the great room, with its ceiling crowded with winged *amori* and Apollo's rearing horses dragging the chariot of the sun across pink and golden clouds, she looked minute. Her face is pinched and lustreless, her dark eyes large, not as more showy beauties' are, but as those of a starved child. I have heard gossips wonder how a human peacock like my Lord can consort with such a pale wisp of a wife.

To me there is no mystery. I do not mean that she brought him a great fortune, and that her father is a man of influence: though both these things are true, and no doubt contribute to my Lord's happiness in his marriage. But there is more to it. These washed-out women are precisely to some men's tastes. My Lord is most scrupulously attentive to her. Her dresses are simple, but her jewels are fit for an empress. In her manner, too, she is imperious.

She said, 'I have neglected you, Mr Norris. Since Charles died, I have no fondness for waterworks.'

I said, 'I understand, though, that on the day of the festivities you will watch the fountain's first eruption?'

She shrugged. We were not met to talk about fountains. 'Mr Norris, I asked you to come to me because I believe that you have been a good friend to our cousin Cecily.'

I know that I blushed. It is an annoying tendency. I cannot master it.

'I think you are a watchful man, but you are not a proficient spy like Mr Rose. He has been observing my Lord's movements on behalf of the usurpers since he was barely more than a child.'

I had not known this, but it came as no surprise to me that Rose had covert purposes beyond those of house-improver.

'During the time of exile he sent reports back to Cromwell's minions. We used to laugh at it. We knew there must be one such in our household and we were glad to know who it was. We would commit false indiscretions, and see how he savoured the chance to betray them. I do not know for certain to whom his loyalty is now due, but he still seizes on information as the goldfish seize on their crumbs. His eye is on Cecily too. He does not confide in me, but perhaps he talks to you. I hope that she does not have dangerous friendships. You understand me?'

Only in part. I was to spy on the spy for her, and on Cecily as well. But to what end?

'Dangerous?'

'It is hard for those who lived here in the time of error to turn their back on those who were once their friends. I have hoped that Cecily might marry my brother. She is alone now that her mother is gone and it would be a good match for her.'

'A surprising one, perhaps.' I detest bigotry in others, but I admit that I have a dislike, rooted in some part of my mind beyond the reach of reason, for the Church of Rome.

I asked, 'Will Cecily, too, be required to submit to the physician's inspection before being readmitted to your society?' My tone was neutral, but my meaning was insolent.

Lady Woldingham lifted her childish face and looked at me straight. 'Our duty is to our household,' she said. 'If in protecting them we must seem discourteous towards others, then so be it. I am not afraid of opinion.' And then, more measured, 'I do not intend to lose another child.'

*

All afternoon it rained, but at dusk the sky cleared and Edward took his angle and went down to the third lake. A village-woman he recognised without knowing her name came towards him on the path. He called a greeting but she went hastily away into the undergrowth towards the quarry and he let her go.

He stood on the dam, where his hook would not catch at branches as he cast it out. All around him the dark leaves let fall drops of rainwater, and the earth smelt of stinging nettles and of life. He could see the sunken causeway. He cast into its shadow. Pike lurked there and once he had hooked one, a long ugly crea-ture with a protruding lower lip.

Meg came and sat against the wall on the other side of the lake. He had known that she would. She came every night. She mourned for the communists who were buried within the wall. Edward didn't care about them. Two years had added two hand-spans to his stature. He was a man. He was tired of memories. The meeting-house was just a building now. He wanted to go away again, and the plague was preventing him. Sometimes a calamity is also an inconvenience. He was sorry for those dying. He was not unkind, he hoped. But when ill luck penned him, then he must kick against the fence confining him.

Meg always knew what he was thinking. She walked across the dam to him, midges dancing before her. He saw for the first time how very old she was. The skin of her arms was like bark. She said, 'You will be needed one more time here, child. Then you can go.'

*

That which Mr Armstrong dreamed of has come to pass. Where once a single pair of pheasants strutted near his cottage, there are now many hundreds of the birds. My Lord intends to shoot them for his pleasure, as he believes the old emperors of China used to do. They are poor aeronauts. They scuttle on the ground. In order to persuade them to take wing, to make of themselves graceful targets for sportsmen, a little army of workmen must be recruited, to chase them into the air with banging of sticks and screeching of whistles.

Mr Armstrong and I have a good understanding. When I was first planning the park I consulted with him frequently. I thought this hunting of ungainly birds a silly fashion. Strange how the wealthy make an entertainment of something that the poor must do in order to live. They have servants to bring them any fowl they wish to eat, but it amuses them to act like those who must go out to catch food for their families. Nonetheless I am always ready to learn a new science. Tutored by Armstrong, I found that the lore of game-shooting afforded me a principle whereby to organise the spaces within my plan. Here a covert, there a valley where men might stand in line while birds flew high above them. Here a row of nutbushes behind which the sportsmen could conceal themselves, there a wide expanse of uninterrupted grass where beaters could pass noisily, putting lurking pheasants to flight.

Why do I write about things that scarcely interest me. Birds and guns. Toys for men who regret the bloody business of killing in earnest. I do so to steady myself.

I walked past Armstrong's breeding grounds today, so much is true, and I thought a little about the differences between humankind and the lesser species. Why do we so prize a woman's appearance, when for most of the natural world it is only the male who must flaunt his glossy colours? Is it because we are so wilfully blind to women's innate worth that our poor sisters must tie themselves up with ribbons and strap themselves into bodices? The peahen is a drab creature, but gets her mate regardless.

More evasion. Come, let me set down plainly how I passed this afternoon.

My Lady has devised a system whereby we in the great house communicate with those without the walls. Children take it in turn to wait outside the gate, and for small coin carry verbal messages, or letters. I wrote to Cecily Rivers. I asked her to marry me. I handed my letter through the wrought-iron tracery. I waited three hours, in a kind of stupor, for a reply. It came. It was brief but entirely satisfactory. I have been like one dead these two years. Now I live again.

*

All those who worked within the park moved into the halls Lady Woldingham had had made. Those left without the wall shunned the village and took to sleeping in shacks they'd put up in a clearing near the upper lake. Some of them believed the water from the Cider Well was salutary. To sleep near to it was a comfort to them.

The shacks formed a quadrangle. In the centre was a fire, and by it stood Goodyear, rocking on his heels. He was now master of the forest, and acknowledged guardian of all of Woldingham's people left out in it. He was halfway through a tale. His eyes were narrowed to slits. His voice was penetrating and suave, quite unlike his everyday bark.

'And the thorns of the hedge were as long as sickles, and as sharp as swords, and when the wind shook them, they made a sound like the gnashing of tremendous teeth. And the child lay sleeping in a chamber at the heart of the castle, a chamber all hung around with tapestries with just one high window. And the light of the moon shone down on the child, who sometimes smiled and sometimes whimpered, but never opened her eyes. And years went past.

'Now one day there came a knight called Sir Perceforest, riding from the south. He came to the thorny hedge and he said to

417

himself, "What can this be?" And the bird that was his companion said, "It is your fate." The knight rode all around the thorny hedge, and he saw that it was as tall as a castle keep, and its wood was as cold and hard as the iron of his mace, and he said, "No man could pass through this."

'"You can pass with ease," said the bird. "For a brave man the hedge is as flimsy as a curtain of rushes."

'"In time past," said the knight, "I have boasted of my courage, but for me the hedge is formidable."

'"You have only to raise your hand," said the bird, "and it will vanish like the mist."

'The knight raised his hand, and walked into the hedge. There was a clanging and a clanking and his armour was dented and his face was scratched and blood ran down his cheeks like tears.

'"Try again," said the bird.

'The knight tried again, and this time the twigs of the hedge were pliable like whips, and they lashed at him.

'"Try again," said the bird.

'The knight tried again, and the hedge was like ice, and his limbs shook and his gauntlets froze to his hands and his feet became numb so that he staggered and he fell back.

'"Try again," said the bird.

'The knight tried again, and this time it was as the bird had promised him. The hedge parted around him, and its leaves felt like silken scarves caressing him, and his armour dropped away from him because he had no need of it, and he passed through into the hidden domain.'

Goodyear's listeners sighed. From this point on, they knew, the story would flow easily towards its resolution. Children lay curled into their mothers' sides like puppies.

'Sir Perceforest saw a moat, all choked with bulrushes. He crossed it on a narrow bridge, and the water began to ripple and shine. He pushed a rusty iron gate that was leaning awry, and it stood erect again. He stepped into a garden. It lay before him all *veiled in weeds but as he sauntered there the thistles curled up and died, and the nettles wilted and the tangled ropes of old man's beard dropped away and Sir Perceforest saw a bower on which roses were flowering, and herbs planted like the patterns on a rug, and there was a lawn as green as emerald and, as he watched, flowers sprang up there, primroses and harebells and tiny red pimpernel and star-of-Bethlehem.*

'Sir Perceforest stood before the doors of the hidden palace. *Those doors were as tall as oak trees, and the planks of which they were made were as broad as a man's two arms outstretched, and the iron studs upon them were as large as a baby's head. They hung wide open, as though a guest was expected, and Sir Perceforest stepped right in.*'

Goodyear went on. The sleeping hens, the sleeping dogs, the King and Queen entranced upon their dusty thrones. Some of his listeners were snoring too. This story was a kind of lullaby. Goodyear brought his knight into the chamber where the slumbering princess lay, and in a voice sinking to a whisper he arrived at his climax. The kiss.

'And there was a sound like a great sigh, and another sound *like the snapping of a hundred fenceposts, and another sound like the crumpling of all the pages of a gigantic book. And the hedge fell upon its own roots, as a woman fainting sinks into her own skirts. And the light poured into the castle and flocks of birds came into that silent garden and flew about it like sparks flying up from a fire. And Sir Perceforest saw his guide, the bird, leading the flock, and he watched as it flew higher and higher and all those other birds followed it up and spread across the sky, not shadowing the ground, but filling earth and air with colour and song. And the princess gazed at him with her eyes wide, not speaking yet. And the dogs and goats and hens shook themselves awake and scampered out into the wide world, and the rabbits and deer came to meet them, and they were as old companions. And Sir Perceforest and the princess took each other's hands, and walked across the garden, their clothes catching on the new-sprung lilies, and they passed over the ruins of the hedge, and they went away. And as I've heard tell' [here Goodyear's voice slowed and deepened], 'they were never seen again in that country evermore.'*

＊

The amphitheatre is to see its first performance. I have been fortunate that the people of the estate, who would normally at this season be all engaged in bringing in the harvest, are, many of them, confined to the park. Mr Slatter has recruited vagrants to supply their place so that, beyond the walls, those who, a week since, were shunned as though pestilential vapours rose as steam from their clothes, are now made useful, and becoming familiar in the fields. Meanwhile the rangers and gardeners have all become my assistants. And Mr Rose is lending me his craftsmen, lately idle on the completion of the house's new staircase, for the contrivance of the stage. It is as yet two weeks until the appointed day.

This morning, I left the park. I was furtive. I walked in clear view down to the lake. I thought I could feel my Lady's eyes following me from the long windows of her salon, but when at last I turned, as though carelessly, to glance behind me, I saw her and her husband arm in arm, walking by the canal where the goldfish glide in long curvaceous lines back and forth, back and forth, perhaps looking for an exit while pretending, as I was doing, to move solely for the pleasure of the exercise. I walked along the lake. I paused by the cascade, my notebook in hand.

The success of our plans here is most gratifying. I have told Mr Rose that I consider the water-gate is as elegant as anything Signor Palladio could have conjured up. The little pavilions housing the machinery are an especially happy touch. The water tumbles precisely as we intended it should, a roaring mass of wild energy transformed into fluid obedient silver. There is a most profound satisfaction to be had from finding actuality conformable to theory. I feel it whenever, in travelling, I arrive at a town or river appearing, pat, just where a map has told me that it should.

A humped bridge took me over the channelled torrent. I passed into the thicket of alders on the far side. Were anybody watching, he or she might have supposed my intention was to turn to the left and so pass along this more sequestered shore of the lake. Instead I went to the right, and let myself out of the park through the narrow gate alongside the place where the water runs into it. This gate is kept locked. On either side it is approached by a narrow, slimy, stone ledge overhanging the water. It is dangerous. I have had a key since the door was made: it is probable that others have forgotten that I have it.

Cecily was waiting for me. She was pale and quiet.

She said, 'It amazed me when it seemed you had forgot the toad.'

*

Where the road came over the hill towards Wood Barton there was an expanse of heathy ground. Dry sandy soil with white pebbles in it, a bank riddled with rabbit warrens. No good for crop or cattle, but partridges flew up from it in autumn, as moths and midges did of a summer's evening. There was water in the stream at the foot of the slope, and a straggle of white-skinned birches, and enough twiggy bushes to provide fuel for fires. Some twenty of the vagrants had settled there. The bracken was springy to lie upon, but one night a woman, upon setting herself down to sleep, was stung by an adder. Her leg swelled, becoming thick and hard as a bolster stuffed with sawdust, and as hot to the touch as seething meat. She whimpered and raved a day and a night. Her man went and stood near to the village, and called out about her trouble, and later an old woman, with skin wrinkled like a dead leaf, came and left for him a pannikin of water in which herbs had been steeped, and he washed his wife's wound with it. The pain abated then, and the fever ebbed, but afterwards her fellows lay themselves down warily. There were children with them, and the little ones whined for home. For two nights and days it rained, and they could not get warm.

At first light one morning a man came from beyond the village, walking alongside a cart pulled by a donkey. There were others nodding in the cart. Two of the settlers walked up to meet him on the road and questioned him. He was one who had come, as they had, from London, to save himself and his family, but now he believed that it was time to go home.

He said, 'My brother, who was with us, is a shoemaker, and he has found work in a town to the west. He has it in mind to settle there. But I have a shop in Spitalfields. The Lord stretched out his hand to smite the wicked with boils, that they might know him and fear him. But the Lord is not vengeful. He will hear our prayers. The pestilence will pass away.' He stopped awhile to get water from the stream, but then he and the people with him went on towards London.

After they had gone two of the settlers walked aside as though to gather firewood.

One said, 'I am a merchant, not a vagabond.'

The other said, 'Patience. It is not yet safe.'

Before the next sunrise the one who called himself a merchant, who was a strong fellow travelling alone, left the encampment.

*

This morning the decoration of the great drawing room was declared complete. The plasterers and painters and gilders have finished their work. The carved wooden garlands wreathing the doorframes and mantels are done. There was but one more task to be acccomplished before it was time to dismantle the scaffold upon which the fresco-painter and his apprentices lay for so long on their backs, faces turned up to the blue heaven they were making. This scaffold, of rough posts roped together, has seemed an incongruous intrusion into the ever-augmenting refinement of the room, and yet it is upon it that so much meticulous artistry has depended. The Italians swing up and down it like acrobats.

That curious vertical bridge between floor and ceiling has been retained so long only in order that the silver chandeliers my Lord purchased in France might be carried aloft.

There are two of them, each as tall as a man; not as tall as I am, but as Lord Woldingham, for instance, or Mr Rose. They were carted up from the barn in which the furniture has been awaiting its new home. Each came in a wooden crate. My Lord fussed around them like a hen waiting for her chicks to break out of the eggshell.

The nails being drawn, the walls of the crates fell open and there within, packed around with wood-shavings, were two baize bags large enough to bundle a corpse in.

The necks of the bags were untied. The chandeliers were disrobed. They emerged blue-black. Mr Underhill was ready. Calling forward his cohort, he muttered orders (his lips are remarkably pink and soft: he never speaks above a murmur). Each chandelier was laid, with the utmost gentleness, on its side. Servants, male and female alike wearing long aprons, took its branching limbs upon their laps, and began to rub them with round puffballs of softest wool. It was wonderful to see the blackness transfer itself from metal to fibre, and the lustre appearing through the tarnish, not like something revealed, but like something absenting itself. Cleaned and bright, silver has no colour: it is light solidified.

Scarlet ropes as thick as a child's arm were suspended from brass rings affixed to the ceiling's concealed beams. The chandeliers were attached to them and lifted upright, the fluted spike which forms the nethermost part of each dancing a couple of inches above the floor. Their forms are complex but pure; globes, stems, slender curving excrescences and leafy flourishes all symmetrically arranged. Tapers of fine beeswax were fitted in their sconces, and while Underhill's men, leaning out from the scaffolding, steadied them, they were hauled with infinite care aloft.

My Lord capered beneath them as they took flight, clapping hands half-hidden by his braided velvet cuffs, and calling out, as his eye fell upon me, 'An omen, Mr Norris. A happy omen for our fountain. See how we have the knack of making shining things leap up.'

The word that comes to me when I think of Cecily is 'limpid'. Her glassy fingernails; her hair as delicately tinged and translucent as Muscat wine; her eyes. I am not a mouther of texts, but there is one I remember well. 'The soul is like a well from which flow only streams of clearest crystal, rising from the River of Life.' The phrases are nonsensical, for crystal is rock-like, not fluent. Nonetheless, they have lately been a great deal in my mind.

*

There came a time when the woman Meg met each evening, and to whom she would give bread and small beer, did not show herself. When the moon was up Meg walked alone down to the quarrymen's hut. The air within was foul. When she had seen what was there Meg went round the outside of the hut, piling up dried bracken and thin branches. She brought flint and iron out of a pocket. For a long time she fumbled with them. When the fire was set at last she withdrew across the clearing. The good smell of burning wood was mingled with one it was nauseating to have in one's nostrils. She watched until the flames, which briefly seemed to reach up towards the branches of the tall beech trees behind it, had dwindled, leaving only lumps of smouldering matter. With a

forked branch, she hooked a bone out of the ash. It was still hot.
She wrapped it in a cloth, with some herbs she had about her,
walked slowly back down to the lake and cast it in, mumbling all
the while.

At first light she went into the village. Later she came to Wood
Manor leading two children by the hand. They could barely
breathe for sobbing and the fronts of their smocks were sodden
with tears.

*

I was with Mr Rose this morning in the library, working at opposite ends of the long table, when Lord Woldingham's two children hurtled in. They were in pursuit of a goat. The creature had come into the house unnoticed, following the men carrying in firewood, and had passed a contented hour or so in the corridor behind the kitchens, browsing on a bunch of the thistles that the maids use to comb out wool, and then, growing bolder, on some hyacinth bulbs ready for planting, and a straw hat.

It was a small and dainty goat, and its nuzzlings and snufflings, and the tittuping of its pointed hoofs on the paving, went unnoticed amidst the accustomed hubbub of comings and goings. It was only when it overset a pail, in which some of Mr Green's finest carnations were standing ready to be arranged in vases, that its trespass was discovered. The children and their nurse at that moment descending the stairs, they heard the clatter of the pail on the flagstones of the hall, and the shouts of the servants, and insisted on joining in the hue and cry.

The creature was afraid and skittish. It raced around the room, its twiggy legs as wayward as those of an unpractised skater, until it found one of the long windows standing open. Goat and children at high speed, and nurse less precipitately, crossed the lawn. There is a sunken walk bounding the greensward, the ground continuing beyond it at the same level as before, so that it is like a green moat. The goatling, reaching it, ran straight ahead, and such was the momentum of its going, and so great the power in its sinewy haunches, that it sprang across the void, its legs still making a galloping motion, landed and ran on smoothly towards the orchard. The children pulled up short, tumbling to the ground on the brink of the little precipice and whooping as they did so. 'It flew! It flew! It's a flying goat.' The children's governor waddled over the lawn to reassert his authority. He is a kindly man, but corpulent.

I resumed my chair. 'Where did it come from, I wonder,' I said.

'From the infernal regions, of course,' said Rose. 'All goats are devil's kine.'

'That would explain the flying,' I said.

We returned to our papers, but I was not easy. Something in our exchange snagged on something in my mind. I laid down my pen and looked up to see Mr Rose watching me intently.

'I haven't seen Meg these four days at least,' I said.

'And you so regular a visitor at Wood Manor,' he said.

I have hoped my truancy from the imprisoning park had passed unmarked, but I wasted no time wondering how he knew my movements. I am accustomed now to his omniscience. If he could be devious, I could be direct.

'Do you know where she is?' I asked.

'I don't keep my eye upon her,' he replied. 'I expect that Mistress Rivers does.'

For no reason that I can understand dread rushed upon me. My hands felt numb. I pushed my papers together. I went straight to the stables. Once horsed, I made my way to Wood Manor. I had always before been discreet in my visits there. Now I cantered straight up the drive.

The door was bolted. I rapped on the latticed window. I could see Cecily in the hall. Her hands were wringing each other, as though without her volition. She looked at me, as a woman drowning might gaze up through the film of water at one who had come too late to rescue her. She made a curious gesture, putting up both hands with the fingers extended as though to set up bars between us. Then, coming up to the window, she slowly and deliberately undid her bodice, and pulled her smock down. I watched, deeply perturbed. She was all decorum. She had never, even in our most ardent moments together, made any movement that could be considered lewd. Yet here she was acting like a drab in a pot-house.

Through the window's little panes, all bubbled like simmering water, I could dimly see that she had got her pale shoulder free of the linen. Her skin looked damp. Her breast was exposed. I could not take pleasure in the sight. I had understood what she was about to show me. I was profoundly ashamed of my former thoughts. She raised her arm, and there, in the pit, was the terrible posy. She looked me in the eye, very serious and still, and then, pulling her clothes roughly about her, passed into the far room, where I could no longer see her. She staggered as she went.

I beat on the door a long while. I shouted for Cecily. I shouted for Meg. I tried to break the window, but there were iron bars set to reinforce the lead. I went around the house, but all the windows I could reach were shuttered. I howled out that I loved her, something that, tongue-tied idiot that I am, I had never explicitly said. I imagined her lying inside, clawed by pain, with no one to tend her.

At last Goodyear came. His cottage is beyond Wood Manor. He was on his way home. He came up very softly, and found me slumped and blubbering. He did not try to comfort me. He stood before me and waited for me to be quiet.

I asked, 'Is she alone, do you know?'

'Meg Leafield is with her, unless she has already gone to God. It was she who took ill first. She would have preferred to go away and die alone in the woods, as other creatures do, but Miss Cecily would keep her, and Meg couldn't stand. She couldn't even crawl upon the ground, though she did try to.'

'When?' I asked, as though such a triviality as time of day mattered.

'Yesterday,' said Goodyear. 'The servants deserted them. My wife met them on the path and scolded them, but they were running for their lives.' He held out his hand to me, but I was not yet sufficiently in possession of myself to rise.

A woman came from the stables, hustling two children before her. She looked uncertainly at the two of us. She was one of the fugitive Londoners. She said, 'These two are from the village. Mistress Leafield asked us to keep them with us, but now we are travelling on. Do you know them?'

Goodyear addressed the girl, 'Who is your father?'

'Dead in the wars,' said the girl.

'Your mother then?'

'She went to live in the woods so she wouldn't make us ill.'

'Who cares for you?'

'Grandfather Browning. And Grammer Meg.'

'I know the family,' said Goodyear. 'Old Browning was pig-man on the home farm.' He looked at the peaked faces of the little ones and made a gesture whose meaning could have been annoyance or could have been despair. 'They can come with me,' he told the woman.

Wallowing deep in my own troubles as I was, I thought that his taking them under his protection was a saintly act, and I thought that the lives of the saints never tell us that the holiest may be irritable or tired as they perform their good works.

He left me, the two orphans dragging behind him. For hours I haunted the place. Rain fell and ceased to fall. The Londoners who had been living in the stables – five families – gathered themselves together and set out, with but one donkey to carry all their packs. They looked at me fearfully and kept well away. At dusk Goodyear came back with a loaf and a pitcher of milk and berries tied in a cloth.

'I doubt they'll be wanting to eat,' he said, 'but they'll be glad anyway of the kindness.'

I had done nothing so useful. He told me to move off, and when I looked at him with extreme agitation and made to answer, he explained patiently that the sufferers within would not open the door to take in the victuals until they were certain none stood by. I went meekly with him then, and we saw, as we stood amongst the trees a good way off, that the door opened, and an arm reached out for the things. It came along the ground, like a snake.

'Go and rest, Mr Norris,' he said. 'Your watching here can't save them.'

I shook my head. I was watching not for their sake, but for mine. Goodyear spoke to me sternly then. He is a man of great natural authority. He said, 'Forgive me, Mr Norris. This is a time for relieving the pains of others, not for cossetting your own. You may be of use come morning. Now you are frantic, and can do no good.'

Chastened and broken-spirited, I found my horse. At the lodge-gate I dismounted, gave it a wallop over the rump, and watched it trot homeward as I turned away. What I have seen has made me a vagrant too. How I envy those who can believe that they have a kind father in heaven.

*

Once Edward was certain the two men had gone he came out of the woods, a bundle full of green stuff on his shoulder, and crossed the paddock. The garden door opened easily to his key. He went directly to the kitchen. Later he passed across the hall, carrying in one hand a basin, and in the other a lantern. He paused on the threshold of the tapestried chamber and stood waiting for his eyes to see again. When he knew where the two muffled forms lay, he set his basin down carefully, and crossed between them to open up the shutters. From the settle upon which Cecily was stretched he heard a kind of bubbling. The moonlight was wan.

Meg's eyes claimed him. He turned back the shawl, and then quickly covered her again. Her fingers, fumbling at her neck, were black to the second joint, the nails like flint. The pustules rose from within her body, but seemed alien to it, as fungus is to wood. He dipped a rag into his basin and stooped, but hardly knew where and how he could touch her. She flinched and turned her head away. When her gaze came back it was full of anger and meaning. Her mouth moved, but no sound came. He thought, as though the thought had passed from her mind to his without mediation of words, It is too late for soothing. Only stay with me now. Only let me be not alone.

He kept his eyes steadfastly on hers. He wanted to see how Cecily did, but he could not look away. The lantern light was reflected in Meg's eyes, two tiny slits of flame in the blackness of them. As he watched, the flames seemed to be smothered by a dark haze. There was a ghastly noise in the room now, a cater-wauling and then a rasping and then a knocking as of an unfastened window through which all that was warm and fragrant was seeping out into the night. Edward muttered words. He didn't see it happen, but there came a time when he saw that it had happened. His legs and arms and all his body began to buck and shiver. He had to wrap his arms around his knees to try to hold himself still. Grief was shaking him as a terrier shakes a rat.

*

It is three full weeks since I wrote in this journal. I have scoffed at my Lady's precautions. I deluded myself. It appals me to reflect upon the number of people I put at risk with my reckless comings and goings. Lovers may fool themselves, fancying that, because love ruptures the membrane which divides each lonely soul off from all others, it can therefore effect other miracles as well. It can do no such thing. Hundreds, thousands of lovers have died disgusting deaths this season. I was mad. Worse, I was frivolous. That night shook me into a better understanding.

I slept a few hours in a shelter one of the rangers had left. I believe he used to watch there by night, with the intention of apprehending poachers. It was dry enough. At dawn I went back to Wood Manor. The front door was open, but barricaded with benches and other furniture pulled roughly across.

One of the Londoners stood watching. He has a girl in the village, and has elected therefore to stay and make his home here.

'They've gone,' he said. 'Young Edward woke me, and paid me to stand and keep folk out until the infection has spent itself.'

'Who's gone?' I asked.

'Not old Meg. He dragged her to the trench where they used to store turnips, and tipped her in and covered her up. He said there'll be time for bell and book when the pestilence has passed.'

'Miss Cecily?'

'He carried her out, all muffled up, and laid her on a cart. She was mewing like a cat.'

For hours I cast about, hurrying first in one direction, then another. But there were cart-tracks on every road, and no way of telling which were those I sought to follow. Around noon, I found myself at a crossroads some miles away and thought, I cannot find them. I must return so that they can find me.

I collected myself then and went slowly – for, being accustomed to ride, I was very footsore – back into the village. It had become a sombre place. Doors were closed, windows made fast. The day was almost spent. I found an empty house and ensconced myself. An old fellow who was its caretaker came and shouted out to know what the devil I meant by it. He stood in the street and hollered at me but would not come near. I answered him civilly. I told him I was not minded to live for long in such a hovel, and that I would pay its owner a fair rent. He grumbled, but he went away.

I had paper with me. The next morning I used a half-sheet to write a note to my employers. I feared I was contaminated, I wrote, and must absent myself. I thrust it in through the bars of the great gate. After a while a servant from the house gathered it up. I knew the man, and made a sign to him. He nodded and raised his hand, as he turned back up the drive. I thought he pitied me.

*

In the encampment a man was beating his wife. No one else stirred. The evening was so still that the thwack of his hawthorn was audible from twenty yards away. So was the woman's gasp each time, and the shuddering of her breath in the intervals between blows.

Another woman sat at the mouth of a makeshift shelter, her arms spread to stop her children coming out to see what was the matter. Mucus poured from her nose and tears from her eyes, and her shoulders shook. The low sun dazzled her, so that the man with the cudgel, when he came back up from the river-bank, showed black as a troll, outlined in flame. He paused before her.

'What has my sister done wrong?' She gulped as she spoke.

He was waving something in front of her face. She noticed the dirt under his ridged fingernails, he who always kept himself so nice.

'She says this was your mother's,' he said.

She rose to take it, a string of stone beads, translucent, mottled green and black. As she held out her hand he pulled back the beads and used them to thrash her across the palm.

'Idolaters. Idolaters. Idolatry.'

She put her forearms up to protect her face. The children had not come out. He mastered himself and waited, his jaw working within his sunken cheeks. She watched him from beneath her arms, her knees bent ready to run, or to throw herself between him and her brood.

He said, 'There was a time when the chosen people lived in the great house there, and I was their comforter and guide. And now beings as useless and impure as the gilded flies have overrun it again.' A tendon in his neck vibrated. His eye-whites were yellow. He muttered to himself, his hands closed like fists on the polished stones, 'They cast me out. They cast me out.' There were flecks of spittle in the corners of his thin lips. 'And now my own woman pollutes our worship with the toys of vanity fair.'

He pulled the string tight. Her grandmother had had it from a pedlar, who said he had been to Byzantium, and had bought it from a Turk there, who had it from one who claimed to have gathered up the pebbles on the slopes of Calvary hill. 'Our saviour's bare and bleeding feet,' the pedlar had said, 'stepped on these stones.' She could hear her sister moaning still.

She understood that her brother-in-law was perplexed. There were others watching. A man may chastise his wife, and his neighbour will not prevent him, but a wife's sister, who is herself another man's wife (even if that man is abroad), with her he must guard himself, and submit to being overseen. He wound the string around both hands, as children hold yarn when they play at cat's-cradle, and yanked at it repeatedly. It was a strong cord. Her father had reinforced the silk with long hairs from the tail of his black horse.

A neighbour-woman stepped forward at last and handed him a blade, one she used for paring vegetables. 'I've no liking for prayer beads, Pastor,' she said, 'but the stones are pretty. You can have the use of this if you let me keep them.' He cut the cord, but bungled it. He dropped the beads on the ground to show how little he cared for them, the blackened metal cross falling among them.

The neighbour-woman said, when he'd walked off, 'I'll keep the silk tassel, but the stones are for you, Goody. Pastor won't come searching if he thinks I have them.'

Late that night the sisters lay facing each other on the dried bracken, their children sleeping between them.

'I have sworn to obey him,' said the one whose back throbbed and stung. 'I have sworn to love him.' She was twenty-three but her voice was like that of an old woman.

'Every night I miss my husband,' said the other, 'but I do not want him with me now. It is easier to face hardship alone.'

'Such a pother about a rosary. He is far more of an idolater than I am. He believes these beads, which are mere pease of rock, have the power to damn him.'

'I would that we could go.'

'We could go. We could go now.'

The women loaded a cart with bundles and with sleeping children. They wrapped the donkey's hooves with sacking, and trudged away from the rising sun.

*

Before my father was made steward he lived like this. He was lifted up, as many boys have been, by the purity of his voice. A child carolling to himself as he walked to the fields at sun-up; a priest overhearing; a clean face and cleanish cassock and a seat in the choir; the priest's need of a clerk and the boy's readiness with lettering; a place in the counting house of the priest's college; a gentleman in search of a secretary; a young woman with an ample dowry. So it goes for a lucky few, and my father had the knack of catching fortune's eye. And so I was raised in rooms with glass in the windows and rush matting on the floor.

How quickly the past is forgotten. My grandmother was with us a while before she died. I remember her as a mumbling ancient thing, grinding her teeth ceaselessly. But I never saw the place my father came from. Now I live in the sort of village house that was his first home, and it is as strange to me as an Indian's wigwam would be.

I exchange letters with Mr Rose, and with my Lord, and so the work necessary for the fountain goes forward. The passing of missives through the bars of a gate feels like a childish game, but it is efficient, and so I am able to follow the unfolding of events within Wychwood. In the absence of any certain news as to Cecily's whereabouts, my extreme perturbation makes me thankful I am released from the need to present a smooth face to those who know me there.

The sequestering of the family in the big house feels to those within the walls like a strange curtailment of their liberty. To those in the village it is no great novelty. For them, even before the wall's building was complete, to stray about the park, without express permission, was to risk having a leg bitten off by a mantrap. Prisoners lament their confinement. Sometimes to be at large is an equal deprivation.

I have led a peregrinating life. My rooms near Gray's Inn are neat and pleasant, but I have been content to leave them repeatedly. Only now have I understood how poignant a thing it is to feel shut out.

I have made it my habit each day to visit the migrants. I teach the children to calculate, which pleases their parents, and to draw, which pleases the little ones themselves. They have been here near on a month and in that time they have established a kind of polity. They have a forum, a level place ringed with white-skinned birch trees, where a fallen pine provides a bench for the elders. Here the able-bodied can speak generally, or walk to confer apart, as they please. They receive visitors. Since the deaths of the old man from London, and the village-woman who tended him, some – villagers and travellers alike – keep themselves ever more close, but others have grown nonchalant, and, for the sake of society, cock snooks at fear.

This morning I sat among them, discoursing with an intelligent man, an apothecary, about the possibility that a trust in divine protection might save one from the sickness, not through God's agency, but because one convinced of his own invulnerability might be fortified against the onslaught of disease. I argued that such a thing was likely, because terror thins the blood and shakes the nerves as well as fraying the spirit. He said no. Before leaving London he had seen, he said, the hearty and confident struck down as surely as the pusillanimous. 'The pestilence,' he said, 'makes as little enquiry as to a person's state of mind as it does of a person's virtue. In truth I think it is not interested in persons at all, but only in the elements of which our flesh is constituted. It feeds on us. When you eat bacon, sir, you do not stop to wonder whether the pig was of a cheerful disposition before it met the butcher.'

His fatalism I found consoling. If the pestilence strikes as indifferently as rain, then we are absolved of blame and excused all effort. What can we do but let it come down.

A gaunt-faced man was pacing back and forth along the margin of the river. He is one of their chiefs. He is deferred to not out of respect, but because he is intimidating. His clothes were brushed, and his hair smooth: he looked wild nonetheless. He had been walking by himself, with hands clenched, a good half-hour, before he joined the circle.

'I have been debating with myself,' he said, 'how to inform you all of what has befallen me. My wife and her sister have abjured my protection, and forsaken your fellowship. They have left our community here. They did not see fit to inform me of their intentions. Nor am I certain of their destination. My daughters are with them.'

Glances exchanged. A tightening of mouths. I was ready to pity the man, however unamiable he might be, but I saw no trace of sympathy for him in the lowered faces around me. One woman met my eye and seemed to laugh silently. There was nothing unseemly or overbold about her manner. I thought how, when a mass of people are set in motion, there is a rattling and a joggling which unsettles the structures of a society as surely as it causes crockery to chip and cloth to fray.

I have received a letter from Edward. He tells me that Cecily is too weak to write, but that she asked him to send me a verse, one I recognised about a 'garden walled'. He writes that she said I was to reflect upon the folly contained within it. The message puzzles me, but to know that she is alive, and thinking, and thinking of me, rejoices me beyond measure.

*

A crossroads, with an inn. On the painted sign a pair of pistols held in gloved hands so as to form an X. Catty-corner to the inn two stout posts, with a crosspiece running between them at the top, in the semblance of a doorframe. Many men had passed through that invisible door to eternity. They swung there, three or four at a time, in the months of insurrection before the coming back of the King. The posts were rotted now, their bases embraced by brambles. The only swinging thing the inn-sign, creaking on its iron bracket. Beneath it a board set on trestles, with upon it bread, and a cooking pot from which steam arose. Travellers on the road, of whom there were many, though it was not yet day, stopped and dipped bowls or spoons into the savoury mess, before turning onto the road towards the south-east, towards the gathering light, and going on their way. The woman of the inn watched them eat. Her hospitality was generous, but her eyes were as hard as hammered coins. Said one traveller to another, 'They are glad to provide for us, now that we are all but gone.'

Later came cows, plodding with distended udders through the churned mud where the roads met. And then again, when the white sun was fully visible through the flimsy clouds, they passed by the opposite way, following their leader back to the meadows along the river valley. As the last one went by, the woman of the inn gave the cowherd a heel of bread, all that remained of that morning's abundance, and he handed her a pail of milk.

'*Will they find their homes again, do you think?*' asked the man, who had never ventured more than a day's walk from that place.

'*The Lord alone knows,*' she said. '*I know only that our homes here will be the safer now they're gone.*'

*

It is many days since I wrote in this journal and night falls sooner by over an hour.

Yesterday a letter came for me. Not the one for which I yearned, but a summons from Lord Woldingham. He informed me that, the plague abating even in London, and no further person having fallen sick in the vicinity of Wychwood, the gates to the park are to be opened and intercourse between the domain within and the outside world resumed. He likes to make a ceremony of anything, from the cutting open of a pie to the first flowering of his precious tulips. For what he called, with cheerful blasphemy, his 'second coming', he aimed to lay on a show to match those the Italian papists stage when their miracle-working effigies are brought out from behind their altars and paraded through the streets.

All were invited into the park for a feast to celebrate the reopening of the gates. By the time the dew had dried off the spider-webs this morning the entire population of the village was jostling and chattering in the rounded open space before the gates.

Exactly as the sun reached its zenith my Lord and Lady appeared beneath the archway before the house, and rode out slowly, their black horses keeping pace. Behind them, in procession, came their entire household in holiday attire, and at the rear two strapping footmen returned to their boyhood calling of beating upon drums.

I thought my Lord would have expected to hear a cheer go up, but the villagers watched in an uneasy silence. If the migrants from

London had been altered by their exodus, so had their coming wrought a change in the community upon which they had descended. For near a month the Woldinghams had sealed themselves in their place of safety, leaving those without to defend themselves as well they could from calamity. Their issuing forth now that the danger was passed, as though their very presence was a blessing for which their tenants (who had managed well without them for near on two decades) should be grateful, was folly. I have often been amused by my employer's extravagance, but this time I was ashamed for him.

The gates swung open. While the procession of servitors halted within, my Lord and Lady passed through and rode around the circle, my Lord flourishing his hat, my Lady nodding to all and sundry. There were murmurs, polite enough, and many of the women curtsied. Still the crowd was quiet as an audience at a bear-baiting, when – as happens on occasion – something in the bear touches the spectators' hearts, and they are distressed to see him so ill-used. Lord Woldingham leant to murmur to his wife, perhaps having decided to cut short all further ceremony, and standing up in his stirrups he called out, 'Follow me, and welcome.' He made his horse prance a little, then cantered back through the gates and veered off down to the lakeside. On the level ground alongside the remnants of the Roman villa long boards were set with some of the great abundance of provisions my Lady had been storing, needlessly, against a long winter's siege. A second crowd awaited there, those of the estate's people who had lived all this time within the walls.

There was ale to help to dispel the awkwardness. It was, to all outward showing, a joyous day, a rustic festival. I had some pleasant conversation with Master Lane, the gentleman whom my Lord has appointed his steward. He is an active fellow, who has seen Italy, as I have not, and will show me his sketches. He is officious, and will need guidance as to whom he should respect here. I noticed him addressing Masters Armstrong and Goodyear, twin potentates of this little world, as underlings, a mistake my Lord, for all his faults, has never made in my presence.

My Lord said to me, 'We once hoped, Mr Norris, did we not, to make our watery volcano erupt on the day of the autumnal equinox? We must postpone that pleasure until the spring.' I will soon to London.

I retired early. So did my Lord and Lady. But the pipes and the singing sounded on long after the glare of the bonfires had begun to outshine the light from the sky.

*

'So who am I?' said Edward.

'You are my brother,' said Cecily. 'My mother was your mother.'

She was propped with pillows so that as he leant forward from the window seat each could look the other in the eye.

'Our mother was ashamed of the truth,' she said. 'But I do not like mystification. You were born from an act of violence, but you were reared with love.'

'Tell me about my father.'

'He was a God-fearing man who believed he was God's appointed, and wanted all others to fear God in him. He was full of rage and self-love. He was a terrible man, but he was sincere.'

'How could he believe that God condoned his crime?'

'It was not a crime in his eyes. "Go forth and multiply." He prided himself on his obedience.'

'And you? He laid hands upon you too?'

'Yes. But I was very young. Other girls about my age, three of them, conceived his children. I was not yet capable.'

Edward sat back and closed his eyes. He was almost a man and his skin, in the greenish evening light, was pimpled by the coming beard.

He said, 'My very existence is an abomination.'

Cecily made as though to take his hand, but the distance between them prevented it, and she was still too weak to move. She said, 'When I seemed to be dying, I thought, with Meg gone, there was no one from whom you could know how you came to be, and the thought shocked me. Now I have told you. It was a strange world. Our experience was singular, but everyone who has lived through these times has been tested.'

Edward turned his face to the shutter. It was as though he had swallowed a noisome meal, and must labour to digest it. At last he said, 'Where is he now?'

'I have heard he is in America. I would like to believe it.'

'Will you tell Mr Norris?'

'Perhaps, if we meet again.'

'It is damnable. And that the man should go unpunished.'

'He is your father. And for me he was something for which there is no name. Godfather, he called himself. We cannot detest him without hating ourselves.'

Cecily closed her eyes. Their lids were purplish-grey and sweat beaded her white forehead.

Their Uncle Rivers came into the room. It was to his quiet manse that Edward had brought Cecily, and all the danger she carried with her, and the preacher had taken them both in without demur. He saw how blankly Edward looked at him, and checked.

'I have told him his parentage,' said Cecily.

'And you have exhausted yourself,' said Rivers. 'Sleep now.'

He led Edward out into the garden and they walked up and down beneath the poplars down by the river until it was too dark for them to see each other's faces. The trees exuded a perfume as opulent as any the magi carried with them to Bethlehem. For a long while Edward's gestures were abrupt and hostile, but then at last he hung about his uncle's neck, the neck of the man, now three inches shorter than he was himself, whom *he had sometimes thought might be his father, and he sobbed like a lost child.*

*

On discovering they have a mortal disease men, and women too, are each as one journeying in cheerful company, who finds himself suddenly separated from his friends, a fog coming down. Figures can be dimly seen, moving among the trees, but the sound of voices is muffled, and then entirely lost.

The godly say that the gate into heaven is a strait one, and that only the virtuous may pass. For those who think as I do, that straitness carries a different meaning. The thought upon which I dwell is that the aperture through which we go from nature to eternity is wide enough only for one passenger. There is no wedlock acknowledged there, no room for the holding of hands.

'In sooty weeds again, Mr Norris?' my Lord said to me this morning. 'I insist you walk always beside me today. Your blackness makes an excellent contrast with my brilliance.' His new coat is of carnation-coloured damask, with apple-green facings, and his pearly waistcoat is embroidered all over with gillyflowers. He would not be surprised to find me filling my journal with sombre thoughts of death and loneliness. I am his gloomy jester, a stock figure from the old comedies. I provide the gloom, he the jests. He likes me for it, as I like the sagging lips of his melancholy-faced hounds.

Mr Rose writes that Lord X has purchased a goodly site abutting the River Thames at Brentford. There is work to be done there. I leave tomorrow.

*

There was no court to attend at Whitehall that winter, the King being removed. Lady Woldingham's house in the Strand remained shuttered through the dark time of the year.

In the latter part of February Wychwood's trees still looked bare, their stems slick in the perpetual drizzle, but those viewing them from afar might see a greenish veil over them.

Mr Goodyear and Mr Armstrong met close by the black pyramids of yew flanking the drive to Wood Manor. Goodyear had two children tagging behind him, not his own offspring. They followed him like hungry dogs.

Goodyear nodded at the house. A light was moving within. 'Mr Lane wants it for himself,' he said.

'I daresay he does,' said Armstrong. 'But his Lordship knows what's right.'

'He knows it, but will he do it?'

Armstrong didn't answer. He had another line of thought to pursue. 'There's not many who survived. A few years back they'd have been saying she must be a witch. They'd have been looking for marks on her. You take my meaning? Her master's mark.'

Goodyear said to the girl and boy, 'There'll be snowdrops by that tree. Grub up a clump if you can. We'll plant them for Grammer Meg.' He pulled out a dibber from the pouch at his side and handed it to the girl.

They went reluctantly. Having lost one protector, they liked to stay close to their new one. Goodyear's men were astonished by his patience with them. Needy little runts, and him with a forest covering half of Oxfordshire to manage, and all the spring clearing and planting to be done, and now, on top it all, this flimflam his Lordship had dreamed up with Mr Norris.

When the children were gone he looked levelly at Armstrong, who was his closest friend, but whom he sometimes disliked. He said, 'I tell fairy stories, but that doesn't mean I believe in them. Meg was learned, and that made folk afraid of her. It didn't save her, though. You know it. We all do. If Miss Cecily came through the sickness, it's because she's had good luck.

'If all those who died this past year were cursed and cast out, then the devils down under would be having a busy time of it now. You know it's not that way. Your brother didn't deserve a bullet. And no more did the pestilence take your sister on account of anything she'd done or neglected to do. The psalmist said that the enemies of the righteous would be as chaff before the wind, as though the good grain would fall and be saved. Lord forgive me, but I cannot agree. We are blown about, all of us, regardless of our faith and of our works. There are a multitude who have lost their trade, and their children, and their lives, this past year, and I'm thankful I'm not one of them. And there's another multitude who can no longer believe that there's one above who cares for us.'

Armstrong crossed himself. Goodyear laughed, and reached out to ruffle his hair as though he was a child. 'What's worse, a papist or a heretic? You'll not mention my opinions, I hope, and I'll not tell Parson what I just saw you do.'

The children came back, their hands full of bulbs and the white underground parts of snowdrop stalks. 'Come, we'll bury those poor striplings,' *said Goodyear. Armstrong followed them over to the spot where – the churchyard being full of bodies five deep – Meg still lay. Seeing them begin to dig, the ranger's two curs set themselves to help, throwing up a spray of chilly earth until Armstrong growled at them and they slunk behind him. Six hands – two large, four small, all grievously chapped – firmed the earth around the fragile shoots. Three noses ran with mucus. Six eyes were red and wet. Armstrong fidgeted where he stood, and then said in a strange harsh voice,* 'There's many more as would have been where she is if it hadn't been for you, George Goodyear. I spoke out of turn and I'm sorry for it.'

That night, for supper, the last apples from the store were eaten, baked, with hard cheese, in Goodyear's household. 'There's *preserved damsons still,' said his wife, 'and dried currants. But there'll be nothing more fresh until the radishes come.'*

*

There are but a few days until Whitsuntide, the date set for the celebration. I am lately returned to Wychwood and there is much to be done. Mr Rose and I are turned impresarios. Outdoors, we are conjuring up a theatre. Within, the great hall is our factory and tiring room. My Lady has given us permission to rummage through the presses in the attic, where old coverlets and hangings are stored, and has granted us dominion over a pair of maids – one handy, the other gormless – who sit all day stitching the stiff and musty stuff into drapery for the scene, and robes for the performers.

I was present, this morning, when my Lord and Lady disputed the propriety of our show.

She – Is it seemly, do you think, when so many have lately been forced out of their homes, that we should be celebrating the repossession of ours?

He (*down on his knees, examining the model auditorium Rose had set out on a low table*) – Why yes! As those poor citizens celebrate when they return to their own places.

She (*reaching out to tap his cheek with her fingertip*) – You are too glib.

He – Come, this is where you will sit.

He reached up and drew her down onto her knees as well, so that the light stuff of her morning gown lay like a pool of sulphur around her, and they peeped at each other through the miniature arches, as though they were two giants peering into a mortal's garden.

She – This is better than a play. Where, tell me, is my seat?

He – There in the centre, so that all the actors' eyes will be trained upon you, and so will the eyes of those who watch from the side-benches.

She – And you by me, I dare say. You pretend that it is the spectacle that we will watch, but the actors will gaze out at the audience, and they will see all eyes trained, not on them, but on their patron. Now I understand why you are so particular over the embroidery for your new coat.

He – And why I will cover you with Brussels lace, as the road-side is covered with a froth of flowers this Maytide.

They were flirting with each other, long-married as they are. It was the effect of the miniature palisade between them. Nothing like distance and obstruction to hurry intimacy along. I have not seen them so jocular together since the death of the heir.

I wonder how many of those who come to our performance still hold privately to the opinion that such displays are the devil's work. The theatres are busy again, but minds change more slowly than laws.

Our text is to be Joshua at the walls of Jericho. It seems to me a perverse theme for a fête to be held in a house so newly walled around, a house whose denizens were, only a few months past, self-immured within those walls. But my Lord's son was given a hunting horn for his birthday, and he has been clamouring for an opportunity to display his skill in sounding it. So Joshua it will be, and the trumpets will sound seven times seven, and the people of Israel will storm the city we are constructing. It follows there-fore that the flimsiness of the aforesaid city (all made of painted cloth) will be advantageous.

There will be singing, and much dancing, but little declama-tion. I have only a small troupe of actors to call upon. Mr Goodyear is a fine speaker, and will play Joshua. My Lady has laid claim to the part of Rahab, the treacherous whore. I am prim enough to be scandalised at her wish to assume such a character. That actresses are now allowed on the London stage is no prece-dent for one such as her. That great ladies have appeared in private entertainments as allegorical virtues, or personating the Olympian goddesses, is one thing; this is quite another. But I dissemble my thoughts. Her dress, fashioned from red damask and corded with gold, will be magnificent.

*

The lime trees were in flower again along the road to Wood Manor. Robert Rose felt the sticky gum adhering to the soles of his shoes as he walked. The scent, at twilight, was as insinuating as plaintive music. He had known it since he was a tiny child in this place, but he had not had it in his nostrils in years.

He passed by the manor-house and went to a kind of fosse that bounded its orchard. In one place the ditch had been filled, turfs spread over it. He walked up and down a while, his hands clasped behind his back. John Norris came across the paddock and found him there. Each man was startled to see the other, but they greeted civilly, and sat together upon an upturned barrow.

'Meg lies here still,' said Norris. 'A village-woman has told me that the dissenters buried their dead in a plot which is now within the circumference of the park.'

'I don't believe she would rest, wheresoever she was laid,' said Rose. 'She was a Pythagorean. She once told me that she hoped to return to this world transmigrated into the body of a hare.'

'A species full of a bounding energy set dancing by the weather. I hope that she has had her wish.'

Rose said, 'She was my teacher and friend.'

'I once saw her spit on your shoe.'

'I know it. I angered her that day.'

Norris waited a while and then said, 'I would gladly know more about her.'

Rose stood, and they walked together so that they could speak without watching each other's countenances.

'My grandmother was said to be a witch,' said Rose.

'So you have told me.'

'There is but a fine distinction to be made between philosophy and forbidden enquiry. Some of my grandmother's knowledge was dross – incantations to ferocious old gods and naughty spirits. Some of it was gold – she knew how to predict weather and how to find water with a twitching twig. Her simples were efficacious. Meg was her student. When I came back here, at the time you and I were first collaborators, Meg made herself known to me with the express purpose of passing on my grandam's lore, of which her memory was, she thought, the sole repository.

'I was curious. I listened to all she could tell me and made a record of it. But I was also contemptuous. I am impatient of those who would turn sound knowledge into misty legend. I scolded her. I was arrogant and wrongfully self-satisfied. On the day that Edward shied a ball at you she had told me her intention to turn him into some sort of a human sacrifice. I berated her. I knew the boy would come to no harm. I have seen him dive. He is at ease in the water. But the ceremony smacked to me of charlatanry. He was very much bound to her. I thought she abused the power she had over him. Cecily saw no wrong in it, but to me Meg's plan was unholy, and I told her so roundly. I hold still to my opinion, but I wish we had not quarrelled.'

'I am sorry,' said Norris, though he was not to blame, or any way involved.

'She had a most remarkable mind,' said Rose. 'Would to God it could have saved her from the pestilence.'

The two men walked back by moonlight to the great house, while owls hooted to each other unseen.

Cecily

On the day of the fountain I, Cecily Rivers, came back to Wychwood.

I was not the person I had been. I wonder whether anyone can be, who has once believed herself to be dying. I have observed it in soldiers, how absent they appear even when returned from the wars. And in young mothers. They say that a careless girl becomes a matron and a worrier, both in the same instant. I think now it is not the newborn responsibility that makes her anxious, but her own danger. The pangs of birth bestow children, but also the knowledge of how tenuous is our hold upon life.

What a close acquaintance with mortality brought me, though, was a fierce grasping. I would have my mother's house. I would have Norris, for all his diffident footling. My cousin must give me a dowry: I was sure he would do it. I would have a life such as that my Uncle Rivers enjoys. I would study, yes, but I would also roam alone in the woods, and ride, and go to London to teach and be taught. I was full of impatience and greed. Edward, who had made himself my gallant protector, said he was quite frightened to have unloosed such a virago upon the world.

We slept the night in Wood Manor, with only our horse-cloths for bedding. The servants were fled, and every stick of furniture had been burnt. In the morning I made myself a garland. Though no one else knew it, not even my chosen bridegroom, I meant that day to feel again how a lanky man's body could become pliable and luxurious against mine. I had only the snuff-coloured gown my Aunt Rivers had given me, but I tacked a fine lace collar to it. Wreathed in bindweed and forget-me-nots, I thought myself a festive apparition.

Wychwood was as merrily *en fête* as I. From first light there were people passing the foot of our driveway, and turning into the lime avenue. We broke our fast with dried apricocks – tough and wrinkled as shoe leather – and Edward trotted out to beg a loaf and a pitcher of milk from the lodge-keeper. He came back with reports of the iron gates' curlicues decked with starry-blossomed blackthorn branches and posies of wood anemones. We elected to walk by way of the Cider Well, so that we would arrive unobtrusively, slipping into the park by the little lakeside gate to join the company when they were already assembled.

I had never been inside a theatre then. Perhaps otherwise I might have judged the play, or masque, or ballet (I hardly know what to call it), more stringently. But there is an especial piquancy in seeing one's friends play-acting. They are recognisably themselves, but they are also strange. The doubleness is at once frightening and delicious, like conversing with a person standing behind one's back, while watching her face in a looking-glass.

My cousin sat majestically enthroned in the centre of the audience, shining like the pale spring sun in his silvery silks. His wife was beside him until, midway through the show, she rose, cast aside her mantle and walked onto the stage, transforming herself as she did so from great lady to adventurous libertine. The audience – both the gentry seated in tiered rows around the amphitheatre and hoi polloi (myself among them) standing behind to peer through the arches of the pergola – seemed alike to quiver with pleasant shock.

How transgressive was her metamorphosis! She, who was always so demure, became, without benefit of mask or face-paint, a loose-living woman, Rahab the whore of Jericho, she who sheltered her nation's enemies and helped them to escape.

She received the Israelite spies (two young men in long smocks, who sang a vainglorious ditty about their military exploits to the accompaniment of pipes). She supervised their entertainment by a troupe of Canaanite strumpets who danced lustily, flourishing veils made from stuff I recognised as the canopy that once draped my mother's tester bed. She connived and conspired, with much fluttering of her hands and shushing with finger on lip. And at last, to a great strumming and scraping of musical instruments, she flung a scarlet rope. Or rather Mr Armstrong's son, known for his ability to crack whips and cast fish lines, stood behind her and flung a rope on her behalf.

It seemed to fly around the stage, enclosing dancers and musicians in a loop of brightness, before an attendant caught it and fixed it to a post. The spies then hitched up their smocks and, swinging from the rope, twirled themselves out of Rahab's window, and out of the hostile city of Jericho. Or rather, they skipped off the stage. The harlots (among them young Holly Goodyear, whom my mother had taught to be a rare needle-woman) were singing and simpering and waving their braceleted arms aloft. Lady Woldingham, with a profound curtsey, withdrew from the stage to great applause.

The hosts of Israel, eight men strong, came prancing on, helmeted in painted card and flourishing wooden swords. All would have been lost for the people of Canaan had these doughty warriors set seriously to work, breaching the walls and sacking the city as was surely their duty. Instead they formed themselves into a row and performed a kind of volta, kicking their legs about with admirable energy but imperfect timing.

Mr Rose, the architect, was standing near me and had saluted me cordially. Now he leant over and said, 'It is no wonder that the Romans found the chosen people so easy to dominate. Discipline and exactitude. Those are the qualities a fighting force requires.' He is a carping man, too much inclined to make a mock of others, and I did not like his enlisting me as his accomplice in cynicism, but he meant to be friendly, so I smiled a little. He said then, 'Does John know that you are returned?'

For a moment I was puzzled. I had never used Mr Norris's given name. This other's doing so felt impertinent. I was glad to be distracted by a tremendous din from the stage. The Israelites had formed up in pairs and were spinning each other around, red-faced and heavy-footed, whooping the while. Some sort of climax was approaching. I looked about me, vaguely expecting someone or something – a monster, an army, an angel – to spring up from the crowd as my Lady had done, and I found myself meeting Mr Norris's gaze.

He was seated on the opposite side of the curving rows of seats, high up. He didn't smile, or nod, or make any sign with his hand. We stared at each other. Sometimes a cat and dog meet and become as still as statues, eye to eye, until it seems that only a merciful interruption – some horse or human clattering by – can free them from a lifetime of immobility. They are held by mutual distrust. My friend and I were held by something stronger. I was all in my eyes. He seemed to soften, his whole face gentled as wax in a warm room. Whether Mr Rose was still speaking I couldn't have known. I had awoken that morning avid and proud. Now I was entirely subdued.

A boy was tugging at Mr Norris's arm. From the stage came a rumbling of wooden wheels and a squealing of metal hinges. We had been within the city of Jericho, in the harlot's house. Now screens were being trundled about so that their backsides faced us. Where drapery had been depicted, and shelves cluttered with golden vessels and clumps of ostrich plumes, now we saw only palm trees and masonry. Fluted columns crowned with carved acanthus leaves, all executed ingeniously in *trompe l'oeil* style, and sandy-coloured stones. 'Shockingly anachronistic,' said Mr Rose, 'but skilfully done. We were fortunate to have a team of Italian muralists at our command.' Two palm trees of cut paper were wheeled on, and the Israelite army marched back on led by a bear, whose second, human, face was visible through the slit in its hide only when it reared up. The audience rose to its feet to salute it.

The bond which had held me to Mr Norris had ruptured at the moment he turned away. I looked for him again but he was gone. I glimpsed him just outside the playing floor, in earnest conversation with the trumpeters.

The ladies and gentlemen settled back into their seats, the brave colours of their clothes making a rippling beauty like that of oil in water. Lord Woldingham stood up. His wig was in every sense hyacinthine. Its luxuriant dark curls were just perceptibly tinted blue.

The Israelites and the bear, the latter beaming with one face, snarling with another, withdrew behind the palm trees. My Lord stepped onto the stage, his shoe-buckles twinkling in concert with his rings, and addressed us. He said, 'The people of Jericho congratulated themselves upon the sturdiness of the walls that encircled their city. As you will presently see, their confidence was ill-founded. It is not upon heaps of stone that our safety depends, but upon the loyalty of our friends.'

'My walls,' said Mr Rose, 'are not heaps.' His tone was still facetious, but I thought his irritation was real.

'We welcome you all here,' went on my cousin, 'because you are all friends of that loyal stamp. My wife has chosen to represent one who did God's will by offering succour and protection to strangers. Rahab had strayed from virtue's path, but there was still kindness in her. For many years we were, as it were, walled out of our own country, our own home, but there were always some, under the Canaan of the commonwealth, who were ready as Rahab was to risk their own safety to aid those who sought to reclaim this nation for legitimacy. Now, safely restored to Wychwood after the tumbling down of that commonwealth, we open our gates and invite our friends to celebrate with us our own return to this blessed spot, and the return of right government to this realm. And now I must ask you once more to pay attention as the climax of our show approaches.'

He bowed and performed a quite astonishing flourish with his hat, as though he were inscribing the design of a labyrinth upon the air with its plume, and then resumed his place where his small daughter now awaited him, having scrambled up, to the detriment of her sky-blue petticoats, into his vacated seat.

'Ingenious,' said Mr Rose. 'I had wondered how he could preach out of that text.'

Now came the moment for which all this pageant had been merely a prologue. The biblical Joshua informs us that his followers, preceded by trumpeters, carried the Ark of the Covenant around the walls of Jericho day after day for seven days. We were spared that iteration. A herald announced in a piping voice (I think he was one of the chambermaids, breeched) that when he commanded us to do so we were to shout out as loudly as our lungs would allow. We nodded and clapped in sign of assent. Then on came Joshua – Mr Goodyear resplendent in buskins and with a mane of plaited straw. His breastplate was one my Uncle Rivers had worn, before he left fighting for preaching.

Joshua spoke at length, and in rhyme. Then he spread his arms wide and called upon the trumpets to sound. On came my Lord's huntsman with his horn, followed by young Arthur with his trumpet. And behind my young cousin came five more boys, each smaller than the one in front, each furnished with a pipe or a whistle, or in the littlest one's case, a rattle with bells. The band formed up to one side of the stage. The huntsman turned towards them and fixed them with a commanding gaze. As he raised his horn to lip, they began to emit as cacophonous a sound as was ever heard on earth or beneath it. The boys' cheeks puffed out and pinkened. Their chests pumped like bellows. Their feet stamped. And then, the huntsman leading, they strutted across the stage, the army following and swinging their arms vigorously to mark time. They passed behind the paper walls and re-emerged. The herald reappeared. The horns gave a final eldritch screech. Joshua shouted, 'Let the walls of Jericho come tumbling DOWN!' The herald cupping his hands, and waving them expressively, gave us to understand we were to echo him, and so we did, lustily. 'DOWN!' we hollered. 'DOWN! DOWN!' Joshua's voice boomed out above the din. Mr Goodyear is a serious man, a man of prayer, one who played a dignified and authoritative part in the community of my youth, but he is also known for his skills as an entertainer. Under his influence a stately masque was shaking itself free of stilted artifice and becoming raucous.

Another blast fit to awaken all the devils of Pandemonium, and with a certain amount of twitching and juddering, the walls were wheeled apart, and tilted over, and while the boy-trumpeters jumped up and down on them in a merry ecstasy of destructiveness, Rahab was revealed devoutly placing a cross upon the altar of the unbelievers, her hair escaping from its gilded net in the most becoming disorder. She clasped her hands, she rolled her eyes, and then abruptly Lady Woldingham became herself again. With a disregard for theatrical convention as brazen as her employing a Christian symbol in a story which predated Christ's incarnation by several centuries, she stepped to the front of the stage, gathered up her trumpeting son and then set him down again to hold out her arms to her husband and her little girl. A flurry of blossoms and green leaves were tossed down by mechanicals clinging to the top rail of the pergola.

The audience rose to applaud. I saw Mr Norris, his responsibilities ended, circling around behind the rows of auditors looking purposefully at me. And of a sudden I was abducted by bashfulness, something that had never before weakened me. I pushed away, I dodged, I ran. Passing Edward, I dragged him with me. He came, alarmed, thinking I had had some fright, as I suppose I had. I saw my future approaching and it scared me. I despise coyness, but coy I was. We ran through the shrubbery and out into the park. I wanted just to be at peace to collect myself. I didn't know what I wanted. I looked back, but neither Norris nor anyone else was following. At once I was chilled by regret.

*

The day began inauspiciously. I woke to hear someone weeping beneath my window. It was not the snivelling of a child, but the painful gasping and snorting of a grown man. Looking out, I saw one of the gardeners on his knees on the grass. I hallooed to him, asking if he had injured himself. 'Oh Mr Norris,' he said. He started and looked aghast, as though it had not occurred to him that the rumpus he was making might have been audible to those within. He shook his head, got hastily to his feet and hurried round the side of the house. Even in his anxiety to be gone he didn't fail to obey Mr Green's most strictly enforced edict – that all those who work in the gardens must carry a besom with them and sweep the gravel behind them as they go, leaving the pathways pristine. Poor lad. I recognised him by his frizzled hair. He is the youth of whom the peacock was so enamoured.

A thousand spiders had made of the lawn an expanse of lace, night had hung the fabric with dewdrops and the new-risen sun had made it scintillate. I leant upon my sill to admire the effect, and as I loitered there I learnt the reason for the boy's lament. One of Mr Armstrong's men came by, trundling a handcart. In it lay the corpses of a pair of peafowl, the hen bedraggled, but the cock arranged with utmost care, to preserve his plumage. They will be eaten tonight.

The birds have bred. Two can be spared. Wychwood will still have its exotic guests, stalking the lawns and shrieking. But I found myself sharing in the grief of the under-gardener for his unlikely paramour. It is chastening to reflect upon how much destruction we humans wreak in pursuit of transient pleasure.

The performance went off satisfactorily. This is not the London stage. The actors were rustics, for the most part, the musicians untrained children, but no one disgraced himself, and my Lady turned out to have a histrionic gift that surprised me. I have heard of actors reserved in their own persons, who are shameless and brilliant onstage, when in the guise of another. It seems she is one of them. At the subsequent feast she was once again reticent and aloof, but as the Canaanite whore she flaunted and flirted as though come straight from Drury Lane.

To my eye, though, our proudest achievement was the stage itself. How ingeniously our arches framed the spectacle, how well the tiered rows of seats transformed the audience into a secondary spectacle, and how comfortably that audience was accommodated. In my role as manager I stood to the side of the scene, chivvying the choruses on and off, but there came a moment when I had leisure to look about for Mr Rose, meaning to meet his eye and signal to him my satisfaction with the outcome of our joint labours. Amidst that patchwork of faces I found him, and there, standing at his shoulder, I found Cecily. The change in her was ghastly.

I knew her at once. My gaze and hers seemed to fly to each other, as a swallow swerves by all distraction to find its nest. There is, I knew at that instant, a sympathy between us which transcends mere visual recognition. Because she barely looked herself at all. She was thin. Her neck had become a bundle of cords – every sinew and vein standing proud as though there was no flesh left in which they could be swaddled. I saw her hands: they were pale and dry as stubble. Her hair had been cropped, and stood upright, a sparse bristling. She had wreathed herself in wild flowers. Perhaps she thought she was the heroine of a pastoral. To me she looked crazy. Her face was lustreless as ash.

Seeing her so, and so suddenly, I was seized by a greater passion than she had ever aroused in me when she was trim and thriving. Faded and pitiful she was. And something moved within me. What a derogation of our dignity it is that we each have but one body in which to experience our most exalted and our basest feelings. There is nothing poetical about the belly, which bothers us when it is empty or bloated. And yet it was there, or thereabouts in the middle of my person, that I felt a shifting as though the organs of my corporeal self – those brown and purple things that butchers toss aside – were being obliged to make way for the flourishing of something which I suppose is what the poets call love.

I had duties to attend to. I looked away. As soon as I might I went to find her, but she was gone. Rose shrugged. I felt an unreasonable impulse to shake him.

Cecily

'Cecily, wait,' called Edward. We were by the ice-house, that quaint structure shaped like a woman's breast or a beehive, and – like both those others too – full of nutriment. Seeking, for no reason I could articulate, a hiding place, I opened the door and beckoned him in after me.

The chamber is usually hung about with dead game. I suppose all the flesh available was that day in the kitchen, undergoing a metamorphosis into pies or platters of roast meat. In place of blood-caked feathers, or the sad carcasses of flayed deer, there were laid out in the niches around the circular space a hoard of sweet edible treasure. Junkets and custards in glazed bowls. Translucent jellies, displayed in long-stemmed glasses, with mint-leaves or scraps of candied peel floating suspended within them like fish trapped in the frozen northern seas. Fantastic structures made of sugar and solidified egg-white. Pinnacled palaces, piled clouds, conical mountains – all pure white. And in adjoining niches pyramids of fruits, their rich colours showing through a veil. Each plum, each fig, each apricock, had been dipped in molten sugar which, solidifying, left them with a diaphanous rind that had kept them sweet all winter. There are stories of travellers coming across houses made all of delicate foods, and being bewitched if they are foolish enough to break off a piece to eat. This was simply the storehouse for the sweetmeats that would provide a climax to this day's feast, but all the same I slapped down Edward's hand when he reached for a candied nut.

The viands were all placed well above the ground. We stood carefully on the crisscrossing wooden slats that made up the floor. A sound of seeping water arose. Then our feet were wet, and then our ankles. A rising tide was passing through the ice-house, flow-ing in from a pipe level with the ground, and rushing on out through an aperture that faced it. We had entered a storehouse. We found ourselves in a cavern bisected by a torrent. A goldfish came flailing by, tumbled on its back as it was shot out the lower opening.

'The fountain,' said Edward, and hurried me out, slamming the heavy door to behind us. Water seeped around its edges. 'We'll watch from the bridge.'

The terrace beneath which we ran, with its bushes and lead urns laid out as neat as the pattern in a carpet, had been invaded by a torrent too. The company previously lined up neatly in the amphitheatre was now swirling over the design Mr Norris had been at such pains to regularise. Wide taffeta skirts overflowed the low box hedges. The gravel was kicked up by scores of gentlemen's high-heeled shoes. The young limes, their branches pleached and bound, crucified, to rigid poles, were brushed by undisciplined hat plumes.

I once had taunted Norris, telling him he was a man all made of straight lines and right angles. I meant to make him laugh and unbend a little but he took me seriously and led me to a portrait of a court lady masquerading as a nymph. 'See,' he said, 'how her hair, her shift, her very flesh, are all in disarray. And see how the painter has placed a column there, a four-square altar there, to prop her up and contain her drapery, and see how the placing of all that voluptuous tousling within the right angles of the frame, with its exact repetitive decoration, has saved the composition from chaos. I plant avenues with set-square and rule,' he said, 'because I know that my trees will spread waywardly within them. Vitality and order. They need each other, as man needs woman.' He looked at me then, very fleetingly, and perhaps it was the first time I knew for certain that he had noticed me as anything other than one of the gentry to whom he was obliged to be civil. Now, as we hurried down the slope, I looked back and saw the terrace crowded with onlookers, the great cuffs of the gentlemen's sleeves overhanging the stone parapet, their wigs, and the ladies' fantastical head-ornaments, breaking the skyline above it.

We left the park by the narrow gate alongside the cascade. I saw Mr Rose directing a party of labourers on the dam above us. We passed along the narrow ledge, Edward leading. The workmen were turning a great bar, the kind that wretched donkeys drag round and round upon a threshing floor. The water in the channel beneath us was strangely dimpled. I looked up again and there was Norris. He saw us. He saw me. But there was no gentleness in his gaze, no welcome. He waved at me as one might wave at a herd of bullocks. Giddy up. Go back. Get away with you. Then he turned and ran away. It grieves me that in the last seconds of Edward's life I was too taken up with that other man's odd behaviour to give my unhappily begotten brother any of my thoughts.

*

The water descended gradually from lake to lake, controlled by gated sluices. The greatest fall was that between the third lake, out in the forest, and the fourth, within the park wall. The dam between them had been fashioned according to the plan agreed by Rose and Norris, with advice from a Dutchman with whom the former corresponded. The land dropping down each side of the valley, the wall dipped with it but at a steeper angle, so that at last its crest was all but level with the higher water. For a distance of near on forty yards it was not so much a wall as the stone facing for a great bulwark of earth and rubble that held back the flow. This dam was topped with a fine parapet, and two little domed pavilions, one at each end. These latter looked like mere architectural flourishes, mere lead parasols held aloft by stone cylinders prettily pierced with arches. Within, though, they were businesslike. Shafts opened beneath them. Wheels turned the moving parts of contraptions reminiscent of the steel worm with which one may remove the cork from a bottle. By this means could be controlled the vents in the dam through which water passed to the lower lake.

Water must go down. That is the imperative that governs it, and nothing movable that gets in its way, be it tree-trunk or sheep or hapless human, can deflect it, or retain a footing against its rush.

On the day of Lord Woldingham's fête five men were stationed at the foot of each lake – four to work the winches whereby the sluicegates were opened, the fifth to signal, with sunlight flashing from a mirror, to the party on the next dam. The timing must be exact. Each lake was to be filled in turn to its fullest capacity, so that the maximum volume of water could be released at the appropriate moment, its onward momentum growing greater incrementally as its mass increased.

The upper lake was all but drained. Its contents roiled over the surface of the second lake, like a tumbled blanket drawn rapidly over a smooth sheet. The second dam being opened, the waters of the first and second lake merged to rush through it, and this time the turbulence of their passing stirred up the third lake, their host.

When the tailgates of the quarrymen's cart are opened, and the cart tipped to release a load of broken stone, the noise the falling rubble makes is tremendous; the sound of violence being done to that which is designed to lie inert. The noise the water made as it pelted towards the third dam was as awful, and as eloquent of the weight and power of insensate things, but it was an insinuating noise, not a mere crashing. It spoke of the water's mobility and its penetrative slipperiness. Falling water is to falling rock as a snake is to charging boar, cleverer and much more frightening.

Edward and Cecily, walking along the slimy flagstones paving the verge where the third lake narrowed towards the dam, were seized by the churning flood. For a moment Edward saw what was upon them. He turned. Cecily had lagged three paces behind, looking up at the men on the dam. Edward reached out his hand, but then the water clubbed his back and he flew at her, transformed from helpmate into missile.

A person in racing water can do nothing to help a companion. As they hurtled through the precipitous downward channel brother and sister were rammed together and cast apart. From where Norris stood, or from where he crouched after he had fallen, bellowing, onto his hands and knees, a head was discernible for an atom of time and then gone again. A shoe. A pinkish staining of the water where it roared through the narrow passage between stone piers.

Cecily

All I can remember are brilliant refractions of light. Shards of brightness. As though in my lungs' craving for air my mind opened itself only to those flashes and gleams travelling from the breathable element into the wet darkness in which I was rolled. I wonder now whether my eyes were really open at all.

I lost Edward on the instant of the water taking us. Perhaps our useless bodies jostled each other as we were dragged along. I cannot tell. I was being pulled and pummelled by a force such as I had never felt. When, afterwards, my child was born, I screamed not so much for the pain of it, as because the creature forcing its way out of me, with no regard for my will or any other part of my intellectual being, brought me back to the helplessness I felt as that body of water drove me hither and thither. If every birth is a near escape from drowning, then it is a mercy that we can none of us recall it.

I was swallowed down and vomited up. The noise prohibited thought. There was a moment when I fought to the surface and heard myself hauling in air with a sound as ugly and desperate as a donkey's bray. My skirts dragged at me. Then came another assault. I was tumbled until there was no up or down. I was pulled under what felt like a bombardment, pelted and punched and forced down again. And then, all of a sudden, I was released into stillness.

It was very deep there, and cold. I had no strength. All the light had gone. Inert as the pale piece of cloth that I could see a little way off, undulating aimlessly as the current lifted it, I drifted upward. The water let me go. My elbow found solidity. My hands grasped at it. My knees skidded over mud. I was holding tight to a willow root. I wormed my way into the shelter of a bank. I saw sky. Air went in and out of me. I pulled myself a little higher. I have never known or imagined anything could be as heavy as my body was then but I dragged it until there was solid ground under it all. Water ran from my mouth in spurtings and dribblings. I was just a limp thing propped against the trampled bank where the deer came down to drink. There was a smell of dung and watermint. My head lolled sideways. I thought, Edward's shirt, but my mind was incapable of pursuing the thought further.

At the other end of the lake a trunk made of light and water stood trembling. As tall as the trees behind it, it was spreading itself at the top as a tree does, and showering all around it the glittering droplets that fell back, exhausted like me, to resume their fated purpose – always to go down.

*

There is something puerile about the keeping of a journal. When it came to the point where to continue my narrative of the day's events I would have had to record the moment when I saw Cecily and the boy whirled away, I found I had no wish to do it. Let me put that more strongly: the very idea of using that event as stuff to be primped and patted into literary shape filled me with revulsion.

Cecily survived, and is now my wife. When she informed Lord Woldingham that she intended to marry me he was incredulous. He is not, I think, especially proud of his aristocracy. He has learnt how useless it was to save him from the humiliations of exile. Nonetheless he thinks of himself, and therefore of his kin, as being different from the common ruck of mankind. And members of a species set apart, on the whole, mate only with their fellows. It was as though she had told him she was betrothed to a bird.

He gave her a dowry. He has been gracious, but I find I am no longer seduced by his graces. He invites us to enjoy his park, and a grudging spirit in me says, '*Your* park? Was it not I who called it into being?'

I go about the country, as I have always done, beautifying other people's domains. My wife accompanies me. She is compiling an illustrated compendium of botanical knowledge. Her drawings are meticulous. 'I am not,' she says, 'so fine an artist with the needle as my mother was, but she taught me well, and this I can do.' Each time that she has a portfolio filled I present it, as my own work, to the gentlemen of the Royal Society. It was she who suggested the deception. She says that as I become more celebrated as a botanist, she is warmed by the glow of my fame, and that she is therefore content. I do not believe this.

We have a daughter. Her name is Meg.

The fountain was a thing of a moment. Mr Rose and I had planned it with great exactitude, but our plans were flawed. We measured the fall of the land. We made careful observations of the speed of water descending at various inclines – observations that have been praised for their punctiliousness by the gentlemen of the Society. We talked about the weight of water, and about how that weight is to be multiplied by the force generated by velocity and volume. We were scientific and mechanical and mathematical. We were mightily pleased with our own ingenuity. We built channels and we designed sluices and winches. We said to all who would attend to us that we were not really artists – no, not we – for the thing we were creating would be all made of natural elements; that water is unfailingly elegant when it tosses and falls, the lines it effortlessly composes sinuous and lovely. We were dissembling. Whatever we may have said aloud to others, to ourselves we said secretly that we were the masters of a new art. The twisting helices forming in water as it flows from a spout, the luxurious darkness of deep water, the spangles of light in water as it flies in spray; these were our materials, and we would deploy them as no others had yet even thought to do.

We were proud. We were dazzled by the imagined spectacle. But we failed to give sufficient consideration to the outflow. We would bring the contents of three lakes hurtling all at once into the basin from which it would be forced upwards, and in that we succeeded.

In moments of great fear time becomes commodious. We see and feel more. Even in my extreme distress, even as I ran along the bank, even as I plunged in and waded uselessly through the slime as though my immersion in the lake would somehow persuade it to restore Cecily to me, even in those dreadful minutes, or perhaps they were only seconds, I was – I do not know whether I should be ashamed of this – I was exulting in the knowledge that all our contrivances had been effective. A column of water was shot up in the air, a prodigy, an apparition of great beauty.

I reached her. I lifted her – she was starveling thin. Muddy water poured from her mouth as I cast her over my shoulder. I ran with her up the slope. I knew the descending waters would raise the level of the lake. What I had not anticipated was that they would break through the next dam. There was a sound like the uproar of a fire. Another sound like the collapse of a building whose rafters have been burnt through. The lake, that had briefly become a turbulent sea, was draining away, and a new river raced over the marshy ground beyond, and poured, with a gabbling, through the water-gate Mr Rose had made for it, which was momentarily transformed into a weir. Villagers have told me of the freakish wave that rushed past them, bearing with it branches and torn-up ferns. Several saw red fishes in the torrent.

*

465

After the fountain had subsided the gentry withdrew to the house. The chandeliers and sconces were lit and the light fell through the unshuttered windows, making panels of gold on the gravel beneath.

News came from the village that Edward's body had been cast up on the bend of the river where children habitually went to dip for crayfish and sticklebacks. Mr Lane conferred briefly with Lord Woldingham. Nothing was said to the assembled company, either about the boy's death, or about the inadvertent draining of the lakes.

Edward's funeral was held four days later. He was buried in the village churchyard next to his mother and his cousin Charles.

After the ceremony Pastor Rivers waited by the church gate.

Mr Goodyear walked down the path with his wife, the two orphans lagging behind. The children wore stiff new smocks of whitey-brown linen with black ribbons around their skinny arms. They had black rosettes pinned to their little caps. Their faces were clean and they no longer looked so pinched.

The pastor stepped forward and said, 'Brother.' Mr Armstrong, who stood nearby, looked round sharply and moved away.

Goodyear took the pastor by the hand, bowing his head as he had never done when addressing his employer. He gestured to his wife to go on home with the children. Goodyear and Rivers spoke for a considerable time and then they walked together to Wychwood, going up the front drive and following the beech avenue, whose trees were now a little higher than their heads, across to the great iron gates at the far side of the park and out through the narrow wicket alongside them, into the forest.

The meeting-house stood empty. Its benches had been taken out for use in the garden at the time of the fountain's inauguration, and not returned. Thus denuded, the rectangular space seemed larger, and more tranquil. The floor's wooden planks had been laid tidily, but never fixed. They rattled as the men stepped on them.

Rivers stood at the centre, facing the high east window. The morning sun used to flood through it, blessing the worshippers with its radiance, interrupted only by a tracery of tree branches that cast a lacy shadow on the assembly. Now the window looked onto a wall, lately erected so close that a man standing between with arms stretched wide could touch stone wall with the tips of the fingers of one hand, and the building's mud-plastered side with those of the other.

'It is an insult,' said Rivers, 'but perhaps it was more careless than ill-meaning.'

'His Lordship is not as much of a flibbertigibbet as he'd have you think,' said Goodyear. 'He knows what he does. Mr Rose remonstrated with him. The wall could have passed higher up here, but he would have it as it is. He knows where our graves were dug, but he would not leave them out of his enclosure.'

'The sisters and brethren go to church in the village then?'

'For the main part.'

'And for the rest?'

'I pass by here most evenings on my way home. There is sometimes a light to be seen, and singing.'

Rivers nodded.

'So,' he said. 'Let us look at it again.'

Moving neatly and efficiently in concert, they began to lift and set aside the boards from the mid-section of the floor.

'It is a very fine one,' said Rivers. He was looking down at the two flying boys with their wonderful lapis-blue drapery. 'Some of the elders preach that all such things should be destroyed, but it seems to me it is enough that they should be hidden from sight. I will not take a pickaxe to a work made with such devotion.'

There were spades set in a corner, and a hand-barrow outside. Four of Goodyear's men came, as he had appointed that they should, and until it was near dark they were busy. They lifted up all the planks. They shovelled up leaf-mould and spread it over the coloured pavement, with brushwood and small stones above, and then a layer of smoothed dirt. They laid new joists, and then set the boards back so the floor was as it had been, only raised up by two foot-spans. The building seemed lower now, and dingy.

'It is a marvellous thing, but harmful,' said Pastor Rivers.

Goodyear's ruddy face was a mask of sorrow and his small blue eyes were wet.

On Ascension Day, Lady Woldingham walked the length of the chain of lakes with her husband, their attendants following. The verges had been scythed to make a sylvan promenade. There were dragonflies over the water. She leant on his arm, but their conversation was not harmonious.

He said, 'You once played Rahab, who welcomed the strangers.'

She said, 'Jericho was afterwards laid waste. And now two boys have died.'

She left Wychwood with her brother. Returned to London, she established an oratory in the house on the Strand. She kept her children close by her until their marriages, and was little seen at court. When the Prince of Orange came to assume the government of this country, Lord Woldingham, who had known him well as a child, became a man of influence, but she chose not to share his great position, taking herself off to a religious house where she lived secluded. At the end of her life the sisters who cared for her waited on her in her room. To leave its narrow compass had come to seem to her a terrifying thing.

*

'The flaming sword,' said Mr Goodyear, 'turned this way and that. By day it was as a pillar of smoke, by night a pillar of fire.'

'And a pillar of salt at dusk, I suppose,' said Armstrong, surly. 'If you tell sacred stories, confine yourself to the scripture. I don't like to hear holy writ muddled.'

There was a shifting, but none of the other listeners spoke up.

'This is a story the book doesn't tell us,' said Goodyear smoothly. 'This is the story of the garden shut up. It was a garden made as a haven for all the creatures of the earth, and its master was to be our father Adam. But Adam and his woman Eve were disobedient, and were cast out. That's in the book. But scripture doesn't tell us what happened next. How all the birds and beasts and fishes were left there without their guardians.

'There was discord and violence. The larger beasts preyed upon the smaller beasts, and ate them. The serpent's brood multiplied, and the snakes that were as thick as a man's leg reared up and spat their venom at the blackberries so that they were poisoned, and the little worms curled themselves in the heart of the apples and apricocks so that to eat the fruit was perilous. Where Adam and his mate had made clearings, and dug up the stinging weeds, strange plants appeared, the stinking hellebore and the deadly nightshade, and others whose names we have forgotten, with berries as luscious as a harlot's mouth and hairy stems. The clear streams became thick with weed, and the darting silvery fish were eaten by long brown whiskery ones who rootled in the mud. Wild pigs trampled the corn that had grown in such profusion, and there were no flowers for the bees to sip from, and the bees' nests dried up and fell empty to the ground. The cows bellowed for days to be milked, and after that there was no more milk.

'A mouse said to a beetle, "We must leave this place. This is only one part of the world, and it has been blighted. Let us find another part where we could live."

'The beetle said, "I will come with you."

'They went together to the place where the cherubim stood. The mouse and the beetle could not see them, for their bodies were like glass and it was impossible to discover where they began and where they ended. But the little creatures could hear the cherubim's song, which was very high-pitched and pure, like the sound of a glass rubbed. And they could feel the power that emanated from them, which was like the heat that trembles in the air above

469

a heated forge. They said to each other, "These beings are fearsome. Whatever it is we wish to do, they can prevent us."

'They saw how the wall around Eden stretched away on either hand, with only the one opening, as though to guard those within from hungry hordes who might wish to come inside. And next to the cherubim they saw the flaming sword.'

Here Goodyear paused, and cocked an eyebrow at Armstrong, who shook his head and stirred the dust with his stick.

'The flaming sword turned this way, to prevent any intruder entering from the east, and that way, to prevent any intruder entering from the west. But it did not ever turn in the direction of the garden. The mouse and the beetle stood together watching it for a long time. Beyond it the country stretched away, with winding rivers and low hills and stands of trees and no moving thing in sight.

'The beetle said, "These are formidable defences. No one can enter Eden. But I do not see that there is anything to prevent us leaving."

'Said the mouse, "Since the transgressors were expelled, this place has gone to rack and ruin. No intelligent creature would wish to go into such a desolate place. There are no breadcrumbs here, and no cheese."

'And the beetle said, "There is a world elsewhere."

'And as he spoke he rubbed his forelegs together and he began to laugh.'

Author's Note

This is a work of fiction, although a few real people – all public figures – are mentioned in it.

Sometimes I have been historically accurate. The party Walter Ulbricht gave on August 13th, 1961 is documented. So is Günther Schabowski's press conference on November 9th, 1989.

Sometimes I have tampered with chronology. The hymn from which my book takes its title was written at least twenty years after Mr Norris hears it sung in the chapel in the woods. In reality George Blake was sentenced in May 1961, not in August of that year. A great storm blew through England in October 1987, not, as in this novel, in November 1989.

Wychwood resembles an estate in Oxfordshire that I once knew well. Anyone trying to fit the landscape of the novel to a real one, though, will find themselves frustrated. I have swivelled avenues, shifted houses and relocated lakes.